Gender, Race, and American Science Fiction

This book focuses on the interplay of gender, race, and their representation in American science fiction, from the nineteenth century through to the twenty-first century and across a number of forms including literature and film. Haslam explores the reasons why science fiction (SF) provides such a rich medium for both the preservation of and challenges to dominant mythologies of gender and race. Defining SF linguistically and culturally, the study argues that this mode is not only able to illuminate the cultural and social histories of gender and race, but so too can it intervene in those histories, and highlight the ruptures present within them. The volume moves between material history and the linguistic nature of SF fantasies, from the specifics of race and gender at different points in American history to larger analyses of the sociocultural functions of such identity categories. SF has already become central to discussions of humanity in the global capitalist age and is increasingly the focus of feminist and critical race studies; in combining these earlier approaches, this book goes further, to demonstrate why SF must become central to our discussions of identity writ large, of the possibilities and failings of the human—past, present, and future. Focusing on the interplay of whiteness and its various 'others' in relation to competing gender constructs, the text chapters analyse works by Nathaniel Hawthorne, Mary E. Bradley Lane, Edgar Rice Burroughs, Philip Francis Nowlan, George S. Schuyler and the Wachowskis, Frank Herbert, William Gibson, and Octavia Butler. Academics and students interested in the study of science fiction, American literature and culture, and whiteness studies, as well as those engaged in critical gender and race studies, will find this volume invaluable.

Jason Haslam is Associate Professor in the Department of English at Dalhousie University, Canada.

Routledge Interdisciplinary Perspectives on Literature

1 **Postcolonial Readings of Music in World Literature**
Turning Empire on Its Ear
Cameron Fae Bushnell

2 **Stanley Cavell, Literature, and Film: The Idea of America**
Edited by Andrew Taylor and Áine Kelly

3 **William Blake and the Digital Humanities**
Collaboration, Participation, and Social Media
Jason Whittaker and Roger Whitson

4 **American Studies, Ecocriticism, and Citizenship**
Thinking and Acting in the Local and Global Commons
Edited by Joni Adamson and Kimberly N. Ruffin

5 **International Perspectives on Feminist Ecocriticism**
Edited by Greta Gaard, Simon C. Estok, and Serpil Oppermann

6 **Feminist Theory across Disciplines**
Feminist Community and American Women's Poetry
Shira Wolosky

7 **Mobile Narratives**
Travel, Migration, and Transculturation
Edited by Eleftheria Arapoglou, Mónika Fodor, and Jopi Nyman

8 **Shipwreck in Art and Literature**
Images and Interpretations from Antiquity to the Present Day
Edited by Carl Thompson

9 **Literature, Speech Disorders, and Disability**
Talking Normal
Edited by Chris Eagle

10 **The Unnameable Monster in Literature and Film**
Maria Beville

11 **Cognition, Literature and History**
Edited by Mark J. Bruhn and Donald R. Wehrs

12 **Community and Culture in Post-Soviet Cuba**
Guillermina De Ferrari

13 **Class and the Making of American Literature**
Created Unequal
Edited by Andrew Lawson

14 **Narrative Space and Time**
Representing Impossible Topologies in Literature
Elana Gomel

15 **Trauma in Contemporary Literature**
Narrative and Representation
Edited by Marita Nadal and Mónica Calvo

16 **Contemporary Trauma Narratives**
Liminality and the Ethics of Form
Edited by Susana Onega and Jean-Michel Ganteau

17 **The Future of Testimony**
Interdisciplinary Perspectives on Witnessing
Edited by Jane Kilby and Antony Rowland

18 **Literature and the Glocal City**
Reshaping the English Canadian Imaginary
Edited by Ana María Fraile-Marcos

19 **Apocalyptic Discourse in Contemporary Culture**
Post-Millennial Perspectives of the End of the World
Edited by Monica Germanà and Aris Mousoutzanis

20 **Rethinking Empathy through Literature**
Edited by Meghan Marie Hammond and Sue J. Kim

21 **Music and Identity in Postcolonial British South-Asian Literature**
Christin Hoene

22 **Representations of War, Migration, and Refugeehood**
Interdisciplinary Perspectives
Edited by Daniel H. Rellstab and Christiane Schlote

23 **Liminality and the Short Story**
Boundary Crossings in American, Canadian, and British Writing
Edited by Jochen Achilles and Ina Bergmann

24 **Asian American Literature and the Environment**
Edited by Lorna Fitzsimmons, Youngsuk Chae, and Bella Adams

25 **Transnational Feminist Perspectives on Terror in Literature and Culture**
Basuli Deb

26 **Children's Literature, Domestication, and Social Foundation**
Narratives of Civilization and Wilderness
Layla AbdelRahim

27 **Singularity and Transnational Poetics**
Edited by Birgit Mara Kaiser

28 **National Poetry, Empires and War**
David Aberbach

29 **Technologies of the Gothic in Literature and Culture**
Technogothics
Edited by Justin D. Edwards

30 **Global Ecologies and the Environmental Humanities**
Postcolonial Approaches
Edited by Elizabeth DeLoughrey, Jill Didur, and Anthony Carrigan

31 **Theoretical Schools and Circles in the Twentieth-Century Humanities**
Literary Theory, History, Philosophy
Edited by Marina Grishakova and Silvi Salupere

32 **Gender, Race, and American Science Fiction**
Reflections on Fantastic Identities
Jason Haslam

Gender, Race, and American Science Fiction

Reflections on Fantastic Identities

Jason Haslam

LONDON AND NEW YORK

First published 2015
by Routledge

2 Park Square, Milton Park, Abingdon, Oxfordshire OX14 4RN
711 Third Avenue, New York, NY 10017

Routledge is an imprint of the Taylor & Francis Group, an informa business

First issued in paperback 2018

Library of Congress Cataloging in Publication Data

Haslam, Jason W. (Jason William), 1971-
Gender, race, and American science fiction / Jason Haslam.
pages cm. — (Routledge interdisciplinary perspectives on literature ; #43)
Includes bibliographical references and index.
1. Science fiction, American—History and criticism. 2. Gender identity in literature. 3. Race in literature. 4. Science fiction films—History and criticism. I. Title.
PS374.S35H38 2015
813'.0876209—dc 3 2014047405

ISBN: 978-1-138-82793-6 (hbk)
ISBN: 978-1-138-54777-3 (pbk)

Typeset in Sabon
by codeMantra

For Julia—for everything and beyond

Contents

Acknowledgments

In many ways, this book has been in process since I sat down with my first SF novel or in front of my first SF film or television show, and so to try to thank everyone who has had an impact on it would be an impossible task. I owe more debts than can be repaid here, but certainly some groups and individuals need to be mentioned. First, I need to thank my family, especially my mother, sister, and brother, who encouraged my habits from the time I was a child until now. There are also many colleagues who have offered support and generous comments on various aspects and stages of this project: Steven Bruhm, Karin Cope, Dennis Denisoff, Joel Faflak, Brian Greenspan, John Cullen Gruesser, Glenn Hendler, De Witt Douglas Kilgore, Victoria Lamont, Karen Macfarlane, and Peter Schwenger. I want especially to thank Janice Bogstad, who was kind enough not only to discuss Octavia Butler's work with me, but also to send me a copy of the issue of her fanzine, *Janus*, which I quote in Chapter 6 (the entire run of this wonderful, Hugo-nominated fanzine is now available online). I also thank my colleagues, graduate students, and friends at Dalhousie, all of whom have been unwavering in their support: in terms of specific conversations about this project and SF in general. At the risk of inadvertently leaving someone off, I need to thank John Barnstead, Brad Congdon, Leonard Diepeveen, Anthony Enns, Lynne Evans, Christine Handley, Kala Hirtle, Catherine Hynes, Johanne Jell, El Jones, Travis Mason, Geordie Miller, Casey Stepaniuk, Anthony Stewart, Erin Wunker, and Christine Yao. Thanks as well belong to Lyn Bennett, Trevor Ross, Marjorie Stone, and Andy Wainwright. I also need to thank my many colleagues at the Association for Canadian College and University Teachers of English, the Canadian Association for American Studies, the International Gothic Association, the Northeast MLA, the Science Fiction Research Association, and the Society for Utopian Studies: all of the chapters here went through the rigorous questioning at those and other conferences, and came out better for it.

I also need to thank all of my students at Dalhousie, especially those who have taken my various SF classes: your enthusiasm kept this project alive. Another special thank-you needs to go to Darko Suvin: I was one of his last marking assistants for a science fiction course at McGill, which introduced me to the academic study of the field and gave me the foundation for this study.

Acknowledgements are also due to those publishers who have given permission to print some of the material included here. An early version of

Chapter 3 appeared as "'The open sesame of a pork-colored skin': Whiteness and Privilege in Black No More," in *Modern Language Studies* 32, no.1 (2002): 15–31; and an early version of Chapter 4 appeared as "Coded Discourse: Romancing the (Electronic) Shadow in *The Matrix*" in *College Literature* 32, no.3 (2005): 92–115; both journals kindly granted permission to reprint here.

Permissions for quotations were also provided as follows. Quotations from "Don't Dream It, Be It (aka Fanfare/Don't Dream)," by Richard O'Brien (© 1974 Druidcrest Music [BMI] admin. By Wixen Music Publishing Inc. All Rights Reserved. Used by Permission). Thanks to Syracuse University Press for permission to quote from their edition of the nineteenth-century work, *Mizora: A Prophecy* (ed. Jean Pfaelzer, Syracuse, NY: 2000. © Syracuse University Press. Reproduced with permission from the publisher). For permission to quote from Octavia E. Butler's *Mind of My Mind* (© Octavia E. Butler 1994), I thank her Estate (and WritersHouse.com for their work). Quotations from SANTAROGA BARRIER © 2002 by Frank Herbert (Reprinted by permission of Tor Books. All Rights Reserved). Extracts from "Howl" and "America" by Allen Ginsberg (Copyright © Allen Ginsberg, used by permission of The Wylie Agency [UK] Limited); additionally, the excerpts from "America" [19 l.], "Howl" [8 l.] from COLLECTED POEMS 1947–1997 by ALLEN GINSBERG (Copyright © 2006 by the Allen Ginsberg Trust. Reprinted by permission of HarperCollins Publishers).

Finally, to Julia M. Wright, to whom this book is dedicated: this and so much more would have been lost in time and lost in space without you. One day I expect you'll even be able to explain to me the scientific nature of the whammy.

Introduction

"Kindred Mysteries": The Fantastic Identities of SF

> John Crichton: But I am not Kirk, Spock, Luke, Buck, Flash, or Arthur frelling Dent. I am Dorothy Gale from Kansas.
>
> *Farscape*, "Unrealized Reality" (Written by David Kemper)

> Whatever happened to Fay Wray?
> That delicate satin-draped frame;
> as it clung to her thigh,
> how I started to cry,
> 'cause I wanted to be dressed just the same ...
> Don't dream it, be it.
>
> Frank-N-Furter, in *The Rocky Horror Picture Show* (Written by Richard O'Brien)

The two epigraphs to this book address the ways in which fiction models reality, or, more precisely, the ways in which fictional characters can figure possibilities for personal identity in what is so easily referred to as "the real world." John Crichton and Frank-N-Furter both turn to science fiction television, cinema, and literature not only to model their behaviour, but also to identify themselves to themselves. Science fiction—and for the most part American science fiction, even as these are, in some ways, works that look toward America from elsewhere[1]—becomes a mirror for them, in which they see themselves reflected, and through which they come to understand the fantastic shapes of their own identities.

I write "fantastic" because this is a funhouse mirror more than it is M. H. Abrams' mimetic literary surface. If these quotations all suggest the modeling power of popular SF, they also enact its playfulness. These passages portray fictional characters who adopt and reject other fictional characters as personal models for behaviour, even as they, on the one hand, debate the appropriateness of having any model—especially a fictional one—for one's identity, and, on the other, perform and discuss a drag show within a drag show that takes as its subject matter popular SF itself. In another episode of *Farscape*, Crichton makes this playfulness explicit:

> JOHN CRICHTON: I don't want to be like other people. I don't want to be like you. I don't want to stoop that low. Kirk wouldn't stoop that low.

SCORPIUS: That was a television show, John, and he made Priceline commercials. But, if you insist, then look to Kirk the way he really was: savage, when he had to be!

JOHN CRICHTON: He's a fiction, Harv. I know the difference. I'm real; I have to live with what I do.[2]

These works, then, mark an ontological instability, a division between fiction and reality that is as tenuous as the identifications made possible by that division are strong. Cultural representation, to echo Fredric Jameson but to look more hopefully toward Jacques Rancière, functions here as a separate sphere from that of material reality, but the very space of play provided by that separation allows us to imagine and enact new material realities.[3] This is why Crichton realises that he's not "Kirk, Spock, Luke, Buck, Flash, or Arthur frelling Dent," but is instead "Dorothy Gale from Kansas." Where the others are fictional characters clearly demarcated as such, Dorothy bridges the Technicolor world of fantasy and the drab sepia of mundane reality, the fantasy of Hollywood plenitude and the (represented) reality of the dustbowl: one can almost picture a scene in which Dorothy turns to "Kirk, Spock, Luke, Buck, Flash, [and] Arthur frelling Dent," along with Frank and his entourage, mumbling "and you were there; and you were there, and *you* were there… ." And so these epigraphs leave us in a whirlwind that spins reality and fantasy together until the mixture twists us into a new world.

American SF provides an ideal—because unstable—ground for the analysis of identity, and in particular for the analysis of racial and gendered identities. If the epigraphs point to the slippery ontologies of human identity writ large, they also address specific notions of gender, explicitly, and race, implicitly (especially through the reference to *King Kong*, a heavily racialized film): both Crichton and Frank search for models through which to negotiate their existence as white, male heroes. The fact that both Crichton and Frank come from works with varying relations to American culture, and that both characters ultimately choose American women as icons—specifically women presented as "queer icons" (either in the text of *Rocky Horror* for Fay Wray, or in general culture for Judy Garland)—serves only to further the instability of identity play in American SF. SF's ontological and semiotic slipperiness, its ability to highlight the imbrication of fictional narratives into our reality, opens up a space for self-reflexive analysis. This book argues that SF can render questionable the realities of dominant ideologies of race and gender, even though specific works offer widely varying answers to those questions. SF does so specifically by pointing to the fantasies that paradoxically structure the mundane and vicious realities of patriarchal white dominance.

In order to explore this analysis of gender and race, however, it is necessary—as it always is in a book on SF or other "genre" fictions—to define the subject at hand; that is, to define what I mean by "SF." Depending on the critic, that term can stand as an abbreviation for any number of generic or modal categories: science fiction, speculative fiction, science fantasy, science fiction and/or fantasy, scientific fictions, or other variations.[4] In general, I use "SF" as a term because it can encompass so many of the categories listed above, all of which identify different examples of non-realist narrative: forms that do not rely for the creation of meaning primarily on a "purely" mimetic relationship between material reality and narrative fiction.

Beyond such an admittedly basic and sweeping categorisation, though, and in an effort to avoid falling down the definitional rabbit hole, this text offers a particular methodological approach to SF, one that in turn demonstrates why SF is a particularly useful field through which to analyse issues of identity. Generally, this book's approach to SF echoes Rancière's definition of "aesthetic acts" of representation as such, which, he argues, serve "as configurations of experience that create new modes of sense perception and induce novel forms of political subjectivity."[5] Such configurations in SF follow this vision, but also go beyond it, since they involve not only "the sensible," in Rancière's terms, but also the insensible, and even the inexperienceable (as the Wicked Witch of the West would say, "You'll believe in more than *that* before I'm finished with you!"). SF narratives do not rely on sharing with their reader a common understanding of "the way things are," a shared sense of the world, but instead must create and recreate worlds to share, in an endlessly unstable contract between reader and text. As science fiction writer, critic, and theorist Samuel R. Delany states, "To read an SF text, we have to indulge in a … fluid and speculative kind of game. With each sentence we have to ask what in the world of the tale would have to be different from our world for such a sentence to be uttered—and thus, as the sentences build up, we build up a world in specific dialogue, in a specific tension, with our present concept of the real."[6] This constant imperative to create new understandings rather than to recreate assumptions is what provides SF with its power to challenge and potentially to change our views of such material categories as race and gender.

Rather than simply assert that SF *can* offer such new possibilities,[7] in what follows in this introduction I outline particular approaches that both lend themselves to and arise from the linguistic and structural features of SF—as opposed to those of realist fiction (what Delany has referred to as "mundane fiction"). The introduction offers two interrelated arguments, one focusing on the linguistic nature of SF, one focusing on SF as a queering of realism, both of which develop arguments offered by Delany. Linear reading fails us here (to misquote Judith Butler), because these two methodological sections of the introduction offer mirror images of each other in ways that mimic the reflective nature of SF (a meta-analysis discussed below in a reading of two well-known SF television shows). From these theoretical bases, which allow me to treat SF in particular ways, I then turn to a discussion of gender and race, pointing to the ways in which SF provides a fertile ground and figure for the analysis of the sociocultural structures of these identity categories, specifically focusing on reinforcements of and challenges to patriarchal gender structures and the social privileging of whiteness. Following these methodological foundations, I will summarise the structure of this work, and the ways in which its pointed discussion of gender and race opens up into other categories of cultural and material life.

I. THE LANGUAGE OF FANTASTIC POSSIBILITY

This first section is composed of a modified syllogism that moves from a linguistic premise and two generic premises (moving from early structuralist theories, and Tzvetan Todorov's critical use of them, to their poststructuralist counterpoints) to argue that SF can play a destabilising role within the larger, unsteady symbolic order of which it is a part. To a point, my reading in this section may seem "old-fashioned," insofar as it redeploys a (deconstructed) structuralism to address the sociolinguistic possibilities of SF, in what might strike some readers as a revision of Robert Scholes' well-known 1975 book, *Structural Fabulation*.[8] I do think that returning to the theories that support Scholes' analysis, but with the benefit of the interceding years' healthy dose of poststructuralist skepticism and materialist attention to historical context, may offer a useful methodology for reading the interventions SF can make in discussions of identity and politics. In doing so, I venture closest to appropriating some of Delany's own varying and unstable definitions of SF, as will become clear at the end of the syllogism. But I do so with Scholes' own admonition ringing in my ears, "that generic criticism is very difficult, and there is no easy middle ground in it between defining too precisely and not precisely enough."[9] Rather than a generic definition, then, the syllogism I offer below is better seen as a methodological announcement, paving the way for the particular approaches taken here, and thus also leaving to the side certain methodological roads not taken (subgeneric definition or periodization, for example).

Following Rancière's view of aesthetics writ large, this book reads SF as what he calls a "redistribution of the sensible" where that aesthetic redistribution is necessarily separated from the material world even as it forces us to think that materiality anew.[10] Thus, rather than functioning within the undeconstructed structuralist account of an isolated and hermetic structure of language, and rather than being tied to a cognitive and thus necessarily mimetic connection to the material, I read SF as pointing to those places where the semiotic systems that structure our cognitive assessment of the material world break down. In the larger semiotic systems of culture—which include the discourses of science, literature, gender, race, sexuality, and so on—SF redistributes the (in)sensible in decidedly non-cognitive ways (i.e., in ways that disrupt the ideological myths that regulate our "rational" conception of the real); SF can thus highlight the linguistic and social fractures that constitute moments of potential change.

More concisely, SF can itself function in the symbolic order in a manner similar to that of Neo in the Matrix in the Wachowski siblings' three films:

SF is at once something that can challenge received wisdom and stimulate change, even as that change can then be subsumed by the larger order for its own purposes. More positively, SF, like Malcolm Reynolds in Joss Whedon's film *Serenity* (2005), "aim[s] to misbehave": as we will see, in terms of the structures of gender and race, such challenges may still exist even when the aim might be off.[11] The modified syllogism that follows explains why this argument can be made. While many readers will be acquainted with some or all of the theories discussed in it, I offer directed summaries in order to ground my conclusions.

Proposition 1: Language is a self-referential field that, in its dominant mode, constitutes a symbolic order.

The first proposition is the foundational structuralist claim, found in Scholes' and Delany's work, which relies on Saussure's semiology and moves from that to Lacan's notion of the symbolic order. Saussure, to briefly summarise, argues that linguistic units gain specific meaning within the context of other linguistic units. While each sign seems self-contained, it actually generates meaning only in relation to other signs. In this way, then, the whole of "*the linguistic sign is arbitrary.*"[12] But, when placed together into what Saussure calls the complex system of language, signs gain a relative value: "Language is a system of interdependent terms in which the value of each term results solely from the simultaneous presence of the others."[13] The entire system of language is thus "made up of ... differences."[14] For Saussure, language is empty of content, and words only gain meaning in the context of their distinction from each other.[15]

Jacques Lacan famously imports Saussure's linguistic structuralism into his revision of Freud's concept of the psyche. If, for Saussure, it is incorrect to view each sign as an entity unto itself, then for Lacan (as, to a point, for Freud) it is a mistake to read each individual as an isolated unit (composed of however many layers of psyche that intrinsically reflect that person's essence). Instead, we exist, as do Saussure's signs, in a series of differences, our "individuality" only and always a reflection of the "other."[16] In this view, we only come into existence as "individuals" at the moment that we direct our attention outward, first to a largely fictional vision of ourselves in a mirror, and then to the other people surrounding us. Expanding on Freud's assertion that our unconscious ideal vision of ourselves—our "ideal ego" or "Ideal-I"—is formed in part by "public opinion" and the "admonition of others,"[17] Lacan argues in his famous lecture on the mirror stage that our very sense of self, our supposition that we exist as separate, unique individuals, is in fact founded on an originary split in ourselves, in which we are at once turned inward and directed outward toward the other. A person's ego or sense of self is thus ineluctably situated "in a fictional direction" that places the person in a paradoxical "discordance with his own reality."[18] Reading Crichton's assertion as an allegory for the functioning of his unconscious,[19] we can see that because his "ideal ego" *was* so deeply influenced by "Kirk, Spock, Luke, Buck, Flash" and, likely ironically, "Arthur frelling Dent," he can then still sublimate those identifications onto "Dorothy Gale from Kansas."

To introduce terms from SF criticism to be discussed below, for Lacan, the subjects are always cognitively (and a-cognitively) estranged from their own selves and from their surroundings: a person can never achieve a fully self-aware, fully self-contained identity since the very creation of that identity was achieved by looking outward, toward others. Even "*the unconscious is structured like a language*," complete with arbitrary signs.[20] The world is only and always mediated through language; what we experience on a daily basis is not the real, but the imaginary. For Lacan, while we as individuals may assert our selves as real, we actually exist in a continuous state of unreality, rendered meaningful only through a shared "symbolic order" constituted by language and other semiotic systems. An individual is, he writes, "the subject of the signifier," rendered secondary to the language in which that person functions.[21]

Thus, despite his assertion that psychoanalysis "in no way allows us to accept some such aphorism as *life is a dream*" still, as I show below, Lacan's theories set the groundwork for a reading of the fantastic element of SF.[22] But, insofar as the symbolic order delineates our lived experience of the Real—or, more properly, is the lens through which we see it darkly—still that symbolic order narrates our lives. Delany makes this point in an interview, when discussing cyberpunk. Emphasising the role of the mirror (to which this introduction will return), Delany states that "from Lacan's emphasis on the mirror stage, the text becomes someplace where you look to see what's going on, only what you see is yourself looking at the text to see what's going on—while at the same time, the text presents a gaze that is somehow darkened, distorted, and reflected."[23] One can read fractures and spaces, the distortions, within this "order" that allow for change, precisely because of the infinitude of referentiality. The unconscious structure of the symbolic order (or, to use terms resonant of related theories, ideology, or mythology), however, makes that change difficult, because the order appears as "common sense."

Proposition 2: All non-realist modes, not just "the Fantastic," can be characterised by a "moment of hesitation" between the "real" and the "unreal."

In his foundational, likewise structuralist study, Tzvetan Todorov defines "the Fantastic" as being characterised by a moment of hesitation, in which the reader (and usually a central character) becomes unable to distinguish between what is "real" within the diegesis of the narrative at hand, and what is unreal in the same narrative: to be Fantasy, Todorov argues, "the text must oblige the reader to consider the world of the characters as a world of living persons and to hesitate between a natural and a supernatural explanation of the events described. ... [T]he reader must adopt a certain attitude with regard to the text: he will reject allegorical as well as 'poetic' interpretations."[24] While realism forms a foundation of the Fantastic, it is the reader's ability to hold reality in abeyance that constitutes the Fantastic. As for Lacan, for Todorov the real must be an endlessly deferred figure that nonetheless lends a sense of substance to the experience. Moreover, any possible resolution to the text must be ambiguous at best: perhaps more than rejecting certain interpretations, the reader must recognise that the "meaning" of the text, like that of Saussure's signs, is both arbitrary and therefore multiplicitous. Ultimately, then, for Todorov, the Fantastic constitutes a radical destabilisation of the relationship between fiction and reality.

Expanding on Todorov's analysis, the Fantastic can thus be characterised as a breakdown in the symbolic order, during which the ability of language to present a stable picture of reality or self fails precisely because the arbitrariness of that referentiality is highlighted. The non-realist logic of the Fantastic, in which cause and effect and other "realist" logics need not apply, and our willingness to engage in what Coleridge termed the "suspension of disbelief," permits us to perceive the permeability of the supposedly solid boundary between what is and is not possible, even if only for a moment.[25]

Todorov restricts this defining "moment of hesitation" to what he calls the literature of the Fantastic, denying it to certain gothic and other works, including the popular genre known as "fantasy."[26] These forms, he argues, merely employ the mechanics of the "marvellous." This analysis can, however, be expanded to all areas of non-realism, including, in addition to the Fantastic, gothic, horror, science fiction, fantasy (generically considered), and so on. The definitional debates in SF criticism are lengthy, of course, with perhaps no distinction so strenuously asserted as that between science fiction and fantasy. Even at a recent, excellent exhibit at the British Library, "Science Fiction, but Not as You Know It," the first item to greet the public was a large display topped with the famous definition, slightly misquoted, offered by Rod Serling (uttered in his role as the narrator of *The Twilight Zone*): "Fantasy is the impossible made probable. Science Fiction is the improbable made possible"—a statement that is more complex in the episode than its often decontextualized repetition would have it seem, to which I will return shortly. This simple, repeated formula, however, which imparts a level of "possibility" or "accuracy" to science fiction, with concomitant assertions of the genre's logical rigour, as opposed to fantasy's merely "mystical" and unexplained divergences from reality, has been made in many different forms by many different authors, other culture creators, and critics alike. At the least, as James Gunn writes, such arguments posit that science fiction as opposed to fantasy, must "accept[] the real world and its laws,"[27] or, as Adam Roberts writes in his introductory overview of definitions, that "changes" from reality "be made plausible within the structure of the text" by following "certain logical principles that avoid self-contradiction" (9).

The "grounding of SF" is, for these critics, found "in the material rather than the supernatural"[28] (5); taken to their extreme, these generic definitions render science fiction into what Seo-Young Chu calls "high intensity" realism,[29] wherein every non-realist (read: fantastic, or even fictional) event or object would be provided an acceptably "provable" scientific or logical explanation.

This argument lies at the heart of one of the most famous and rightfully influential definitions of science fiction, that by Darko Suvin in his *Metamorphoses of Science Fiction*, a work so influential that every discussion of SF definitions must return to it. Arguably the text that made academically acceptable the "serious" study of science fiction, Suvin's book engages, in part, in a rigorous examination of what does and does not constitute the category of "science fiction," leading to its most famous generic definition, "cognitive estrangement." Science fiction, for Suvin, creates a world that is noticeably different from ours (thus, estranging) while simultaneously, and obviously, related to ours in its formation and the way in which the world functions (cognitive). Thus, "proper" SF for Suvin—and that's a remarkably narrow category—has to be a non-realist form that is nonetheless logically extrapolated from ours, and is thus different from such other non-realist modes as fantasy or the gothic, which offer no cognitive basis for their fantastic, non-realist elements.

However, it must be said that there is always an ultimately non-realistic, fantastic (in that it is non-extant) element of any text that can be called SF. Suvin uses the term "novum" to define this element in an SF text and limits its "proper" SF uses to technological or scientific developments that, while not currently extant in the author's material reality, nonetheless can be logically extrapolated from currently extant technologies or scientific theories. Thus, transportation from one building to the next using a wand, with no explanation as to how the atoms and particles of one's physical body are moved, would be fantasy, but transportation via a sub-spatial "wormhole" from one galaxy to another, the existence of which is predicated on current developments in string theory, could be science fiction. One can add here any number of unproven scientific theories or emergent technologies that are used as technical lynchpins in SF plots—from electricity in *Frankenstein* to virtual reality in William Gibson's early novels.

But, despite the excellence of Suvin's foundational work, what lies at the heart of "cognitive estrangement" is not a simple realism combined with a perfectly logical, rational extrapolation of contemporary technologies or science. The fantastic element of the "novum" cannot be so easily ignored, rendering the generic kernel of SF, at its most basic level, into a continuous tension between an empirical and a faith-driven relation to causation and creation (a division I discuss below through the opposition of the characters Scully and Mulder in the television show *The X-Files*). As British SF author China Miéville stated in a recent interview, while Suvin (and, following him, to a degree, Frederic Jameson) offers "the notion that SF is predicated on rigor," this "model [is] constantly undermined in the actuality."[30] Other critics, including Carl Freedman and, following him, Istvan Csicsery-Ronay, Jr., offer similar critiques of cognitive estrangement, but still try to hold on to the cognitive, expanding it into what Freedman calls "the cognition effect."[31] The "cognition effect," in their readings, relies on a science that is less necessarily "factual" than in Suvin's analysis, and is instead created by the self-reflexive "in-text" coherence of the (fictional) science being offered. Freedman uses this argument to posit that even though it is not always so, still SF "is overwhelmingly … a genuinely cognitive literature."[32] There may be an element of protesting overmuch here, though, as even this critical sidestep can be said to highlight precisely the textual fantasies of SF: the "truth" of cognition becomes the "truthiness" of its effect, to echo Stephen Colbert.

Moreover, as Csicsery-Ronay points out, albeit in a different way, the "cognition effect" does not escape another problem Miéville points to. In the same piece, Miéville states that "A lot of science fiction that *pretends* it is about scientific rigor is actually predicated on a kind of a late Enlightenment model of the expertise of the scientist …, a kind of caste or class model that is, in a way, the Enlightenment's betrayal of itself, since it says: do not ask questions because we have an expert here who will understand this stuff for us (and for the bourgeoisie)." Instead, Miéville states that the "boundaries between the impossible of the fantastic and Gothic on the one hand, and the impossible of science fiction on the other, are simply too fuzzy to be systematically maintained."[33] This conclusion can be taken a step further, too, for if SF "pretends" to a cognitive rigor in the same way the figure of the scientist does, then this "fuzzy" line between SF and fantasy, and between fantasy and the Fantastic, also follows Todorov's definition of the Fantastic, wherein a "moment of hesitation" destabilises the line between fantasy and reality "itself." In other words, cognitive estrangement requires the simultaneous maintenance *and* collapse of the division between realism and fantasy, cognition and estrangement, empiricism and faith.[34]

If, then, SF is characterised by this fantastic estrangement as much as or more than it is by the "cognitive" variant, then does it hold that Todorov's "moment of hesitation" may equally apply to the Fantastic, fantasy, and science fiction—that is, to SF? Certainly many science fiction texts engage in similar blurrings of reality and fiction: the hesitation in any given work by Philip K. Dick about whether something is a drug- or technology-induced hallucination or reality is one case in point; others include the shock of (mis)recognition of humans and apes at the end of Pierre Boulle's *Planet of the Apes*, and the fuzzy divisions between mechanical and human life in Dick's *Do Androids Dream of Electric Sheep?*, Arthur C. Clarke's *2001: A Space Odyssey*, or *Star Trek: The Next Generation*, dating back to Karel Čapek's *R.U.R.* and Mary Shelley's *Frankenstein*. All of these are equally playful textual moments even as they cause doubt and questions concerning the "nature" of reality and human existence. One could even compare the affective realm of the "moment of hesitation" to the feeling of the uncanny created by the gothic, and to the "sense of wonder" created by science fiction. Indeed, as I point to above, Suvin's "novum" exists in the space of hesitation: if, as Chu argues, realism "is distinguished by the alacrity with which it can imitate certain kinds of objects,"[35] then the perhaps unquestioned way in which we accept the novum (say of FTL travel, through wormhole or other innovation) does not necessarily rely on the extrapolative science of the text, but rather on the alacrity of the reader's ability to move into the space of hesitation, the willingness to accept unreality as reality and vice versa.

Proposition 3: SF allows for an increase in semiotic possibilities.

Since, following the second proposition, I can include in this discussion not only classic fantasy or Suvin's "cognitive" fictions, but also a range of non-realist modes, it may be possible to bring another statement about a specific non-realist mode to bear. Specifically, Delany—in his equally famous and oft-cited definition of science fiction—argues that science fiction is characterised by an extension of semiotic possibilities in language: that is, he argues that words can simply mean *more* in science fiction than they can in realist fiction. Delany sees this as a function of the heightened realism of SF, and the materialisation of metaphor involved therein: he uses the phrases "Then her world exploded" and "He turned on his left side" to demonstrate this extension of meaning. In "mundane fiction," he writes, the first phrase only makes sense as "an emotionally muzzy metaphor about the inner aspects of some incident in a female character's life," while the latter would imply "some kind of masculine, insomniac tossings."[36] In SF, however, the first phrase could additionally mean that the woman's planet was just blown up, while the second could reference a cyborg "activating the circuitry on his sinistral flank" (88).[37] This expansion of signification is added to what Csicsery-Ronay, Jr. calls the "fictive neology" of SF: "Readers of sf," he writes, "expect to encounter new words and other signs that indicate worlds changed from their own."[38] In this he includes, importantly, the visual and sound effects of contemporary SF cinema.

While Delany's specific analyses of this semiotic expansion limits itself to the technological branch of SF, his other work makes related arguments within the realm of high fantasy. In his sword-and-sorcery Nevèrÿon series, he explicitly discusses the semiotic slipperiness created by narrative *per se*, and by moments of hesitation in particular. Jeffrey Allen Tucker has detailed the series' exploration of semiotics and identity. But, in "The Tale of Fog and Granite" (where those two objects function as metaphor for semiotic confusion and rigidity, respectively), the central character, a smuggler, becomes the stand-in for the reader of the interlocking narratives of the series, and by extension of SF itself. Having collected and collated in his mind the various rumours and stories of Gorgik the Liberator (and often getting in trouble for asking too many questions), the smuggler contemplates the nature of signs: "The situations that resulted in such troubles had only impressed on him, finally, that the object of his obsession was not some innocent and indifferent fable, but rather a system of hugely conflicting possibilities and immensely turbulent values."[39] Always fluctuating, always adding layers of (often contradictory) meaning, the smuggler's stories highlight the exploding linguistic possibilities of SF and the reading thereof.

Taken in conjunction with Lacan and Todorov, Delany's (and the smuggler's) conclusions and Csicsery-Ronay's "fictive neology" mean that SF does not just challenge the dominant symbolic order by forcing us to question the seeming reality of its "common sense" assertions, but also that it can in fact offer alternatives to that order or, more precisely, expose places in language and other signifying systems where such alternatives have always existed, but were unconsciously silenced or placed under erasure by ideological and hegemonic discourses. The implications for more material redefinitions of identity are directly stated in Delany's descriptions, from an "emotional" woman to the survivor of planetary apocalypse. Beyond the materialisation of metaphor that Delany discusses, the multiplicitous semantic possibilities of SF can be read as moments when the expanded realities that were hidden behind ideological constraints are made visible. In "The Mummer's Tale," the second piece in *Flight from Nevèrÿon*, the narrator, discussing the smuggler, describes the role of drama in much the same way, writing that dramatic fictions "speak always in dialogue with, in contest to, in protest of the real."[40] In a more material context, the mutual interactions between fantasy and reality—even on a day-to-day level—are explored more thoroughly in "The Tale of Plagues and Carnivals" in the same work. Here, the fantasy past of Nevèrÿon, beset by a sexually transmitted plague, and the material present of Delany's New York, in the early days of the AIDS pandemic, comment on and inform each other, fantasy exploring the deadly serious conditions of material life even as the semiautobiographical narrative explores the pleasures and dangers of allowing discourse about disease to become too metaphorical. Not dominated by the supposed referentiality of mimetic realism, SF highlights, as the authorial voice of "Tale of Plagues and Carnivals" states, that "the writer is *always* generating *meanings* (and *not* organizing references), even the most topical meanings."[41] On the one hand, the transpositions of SF language can expose and challenge a reader's or a literary tradition's social expectations, what is ideologically passed down as "the real" but is, really, anything but. On the other, such challenges are not the same as escaping history or the present—they are rather means through which one may experience the material anew.

∴ fantasy/science fiction/speculative fiction/"SF" writ large precisely allows a (linguistic and therefore conceptual) space in which the dominant order can be challenged or its limits tested, which means, in short, that SF is a dissonant space of analysis of the symbolic order, paradoxically at once part of and at an ironic distance from it: such analysis of the symbolic order is in fact, what characterizes SF per se. QED.

This concluding assertion of proof is necessarily offered somewhat ironically. It does not mean that all SF participates equally in every step of the syllogism, nor does it mean that all SF offers a radical undermining or critique of the dominant order: the challenge or threat can be silenced in any given text by a return to the (unconscious) functioning of the symbolic order (as I argue, to varying degrees, in relation to Nathaniel Hawthorne's "The Birth-mark," Mary E. Bradley Lane's *Mizora*, and the Wachowski siblings' *The Matrix*, and others in the chapters that follow); still, all of it begins with the challenge and analysis of what is accepted as the unconditional "real," gesturing to its arbitrary bases. In his earlier structural analysis, Delany defines SF as this questioning or challenging space: SF is "that gravitically neutral space (free-fall) where imagination streaks between worlds," where "one departs the old matrix, and ... chooses to enter its mirror image." But some readers, he states—and one could add some texts—"cannot get free of the gravitic orientation" or the mundane, the status quo, the pull of the world we are used to. [42] The challenge to the symbolic order is always offered in SF, from the marvellous realms of the gothic through to the technological wonders of Suvinian science fiction, but then that order can be either reaffirmed, *or* the challenge/analysis can remain ambiguous, *or* alternatives can be offered. And often, because these challenges and analyses happen at the linguistic and therefore symbolic level, all of these processes together can happen in any given text. SF can thus stand at the crux of historical debate, offering a complex analysis not of "the time," but of the complex and fragile debates that transform any given time and context into multiplicity.[43]

SF argues for the necessity of the un- or a-realist imaginative, that aesthetic space beyond the everyday that Rancière tries to reclaim and that Jameson laments as the disabling space between utopia and the material. Like Rancière, I would argue that this space is disabling only if one agrees to the "radical opposition" between "appearance/reality," or, I would add, between "thinking and doing"—oppositions that are "quite different from logical oppositions between clearly defined terms."[44] In my reading, the semiotic instability, the fantasy, of SF is enabling of change precisely because it escapes—or at least attempts to escape—the clutches of the simply mimetic, even as it challenges the symbolic order that necessarily defines what is and is not "real."[45]

SF highlights that the very function of language is to *attempt* to move beyond the hard granite of the unreflective material, to allow us to glimpse the necessarily foggy unreality that is the world beyond, and within, ourselves. This is why, in a lecture at the University of Kansas (one wonders if he saw the surrounding landscape in sepia or Technicolor), Miéville argues that the "shared estrangement" of science fiction and fantasy is defined by a "fundamental logic of otherness, of alterity." SF thus becomes a meta-tool for analysing the ways in which we can, if not transcend, then transform ideologies of identity surrounding such concepts as gender and race.[46]

A possible critique of my reading here would point out that while this argument may hold for such authors as Miéville and especially Delany, who comment directly on the same theories I am employing, surely other SF *is* determined not by anti- or a-realism, but by the cognitive elements Suvin identifies. Let's return, then, to *The Twilight Zone*. Serling's famous definition, from the third-season episode of *The Twilight Zone* titled "The Fugitive," is more detailed and complex in the original:

> It's been said that science fiction and fantasy are two different things: science fiction the improbable made possible; fantasy the impossible made probable. What would you have if you put these two different things together? Well, you'd have an old man named Ben who knows a lot of tricks most people don't know, and a little girl named Jenny who loves him, and a journey into the heart of the Twilight Zone.[47]

The Twilight Zone, then, is that space of the suspension of disbelief that characterises both fantasy and science fiction, as meditations on (im)probable (im)possibilities, in which new identities, the "heart" of human existence, can be explored. Indeed, the exploration of gender identity lies at the heart of this episode. Featuring an alien king temporarily disguised as a kindly old Earthling named Ben, the episode begins with a baseball game which quickly transforms into Ben playing a game of "spaceman" with the children (and so "spaceman," rather than baseball, becomes the contemporary version of "America's favorite pastime"). Before the spaceman game begins, however, Ben says that Jenny (the only girl on the baseball team) must "write the script" for the game. Jenny responds by trying to make herself captain of the "rocket ship," to which one of the young boys replies, "Who ever heard of a dame with a brace being captain?" and she then backs down and becomes "the beautiful stowaway." In this episode, the "impossible made probable" equally applies to Ben being an alien and to Jenny's desire to explore the stars and break though barriers imposed by biases against her gender and disability. This journey becomes real for Jenny at the end of the episode. When Ben's subjects come to take him back to his planet, he assumes Jenny's shape: being unable to tell them apart, Ben's compatriots must take them both back to his planet. This ambiguity of identity presents the "impossibility" of Jenny's power as now "possible" (though, it must be said, the episode then partially silences that ambiguity: Serling, at the end, makes it clear that Ben, though an alien, is a stereotypically square-jawed, properly coiffed football-star-looking younger man. Jenny marries him and becomes his queen). Yes, some SF texts function in the realm of the cognitive, but they can only do so by first embracing the unpredictable possibilities of the fantastic. The reality of our time is governed by the fantasy of our perception, which in turn is tied to the materiality of our various and conflicting contexts.

And so Dorothy's twister spins on.

II. "I'LL BE YOUR MIRROR": QUEERING REALISM

To speak of ambiguity in relation to identity, when combined with the overtly gendered performances at play in my epigraphs and in the example from *The Twilight Zone*, and to stage it all in a quasi-Lacanian manner is to invoke queer theory, and in particular the work of Judith Butler. Indeed, Butler's theories of gender performance and its relationship to gender performativity play a significant role in this book (and not only in relation to gender and sexuality, but also to race). But what do these issues have to do with the current, introductory discussion of SF and my approach to it?

In short, building on the syllogism in the previous section, SF can be defined precisely as that which queers realism. In a manner similar to my analysis of SF, Butler argues that the process of classification, especially in terms of gender and sexuality, is a constantly problematic one, and one that, in the end, does not fall into a stable or unidirectional exercise of power and domination, but is instead destructured, decentred, and dynamic. In her now standard description of this process, Butler writes of the supposed dominance of heterosexuality, that it "is perpetually at risk, that is, that it 'knows' its own possibility of becoming undone," and so is in a constant process of being compared to various "other" sexualities without which it would cease to be understandable as a category.[48] Modifying Lacan, "otherness" in this formulation is necessary to the "dominant," calling the entirety of the binary logic and its divisions into question: "In other words," she writes, "the entire framework of copy and origin proves radically unstable as each position inverts into the other and confounds the possibility of any stable way to locate the temporal or logical priority of either term."[49]

Butler thus argues that gender identity—like language—isn't centred on an essential core. Gender identity is only the surface, the play of identity, and heterosexuality is the sexual identity that performs itself as an origin, as the most *real*—which of course it isn't. All gender performance is, to a degree, a drag performance, a putting on of an identity not one's own, because gender and sexual identity belong to no one in an essential way. This is not to say that identity is something that "can be taken on or taken off at will," however, since "There is no volitional subject behind the mime who decides, as it were, which gender it will be today. On the contrary, the very possibility of becoming a viable subject requires that a certain gender mime be already underway."[50] Our *being* in gender can only exist if the play of gender is always already underway. To expand this beyond gender and sexuality, Butler's argument makes clear, as does Lacan's, that one's very being requires that a set of fantastic identities be already enacted and reenacted around us. This is the ontological paradox of a semiotic human existence as much as it is the central paradox of SF.

To modify the conclusion to the syllogism, then, we can say that *SF is mundane fiction in drag*: SF highlights the performativity of realism by dressing it up in reality-bending fantasies in such a way as to show that the distinction between those two categories has always been a fuzzy one:

the real is the always hidden symptom of the unreal.[51] As Wendy Gay Pearson, quoting Suvin, argues (in the more specific context of an analysis of SF and queer identities):

> The subversive potential of sf as a mode through which non-Cartesian subjectivities can be represented is a function precisely of sf's ability to create a "radically or significantly different formal framework," of its very estrangement from the mimetic attempt of naturalistic—or mundane—fiction to reiterate faithfully a teleological understanding of humanity's being-in-the-world, to represent the subject as the cause rather than the effect of the system.[52]

Beyond this substantial conclusion, I argue that SF, in putting realism itself in drag, becomes an ontologically unstable form, a space for the radical questioning of all forms of identity. And this is the case even—sometimes especially—when it tries to shore them up: Tarzan's loincloth doesn't make him a man so much as it makes him a drag king extraordinaire, as *Rocky Horror* might suggest.[53]

None of this is to say that the present work simply ignores the scientific or cognitive elements of the "science fiction" arm of SF—in fact, Part I of the book is largely dedicated to early representations of modern scientific research. Instead, when I do engage these elements, it is to show the ways in which SF explores the complexities and contradictions of science as a cultural discourse, particularly through the representations of gender and race. Likewise, when examining the more fantastic arm of SF, I point to the ways in which that fantasy has origins in and effects on the material realm. The swirling reflections of science and fiction, the fantastic and the real, are recognised in SF as being too complex to separate.

Combining these linguistic and queer arguments allows us to see that SF plays the role of the mirror: not the mimetic mirror of realism, but the Lacanian mirror of the enabling and challenging fantasy. This fantasy presents us at once with an "ideal"—or, to use loaded language, utopian—vision of ourselves, even as we must acknowledge that we are not in control of that image nor of the cultural baggage—the "public opinion"—that goes into forming it. As Delany has written, it may even be possible "to read [Jane] Austen as if her novels were science fiction. ... The discourse of science fiction gives us a way to construct worlds in clear and consistent dialogue with *the world* that *is*, alas, the case. ... And in a world where an 'alas' has to be inserted into such a description of it, the dialectical freedom of science fiction has to be privileged."[54] For Delany, what distinguishes the real from the fantastic and vice versa is the action of reading itself, and the act of placing that world in a relationship with the "world that," alas, "is." As Nico and the Velvet Underground would say, SF will "be your mirror" not to repeat the mundane, but to question it.[55] As I discuss in more detail in Chapter 5, this is the mirror of Foucault's notion of "heterotopia": not necessarily the endlessly contingent, aspiringly hopeful queer utopian feeling as envisioned by José Esteban Muñoz (to which the Afterword returns), and not a "utopia of difference" (a multicultural dream that the word "heterotopia" has been reduced to on occasion), the heterotopia is a potentially destabilising re-vision of the world that is, a vision "at once absolutely real, connected with all the space that surrounds it, and absolutely unreal."[56] Characterised by the mirror as well as the graveyard, the heterotopia resists our easy acceptance of ("alas"), even as it exists within, "the world that is."

This moveable, readerly relationship, this queering of the long-analysed triangulation of reader, text, and world, however, makes any generic categorisation or sociocritical analysis of narrative at best unstable. Frederic Jameson, despite Miéville's critique, does expand on this instability, writing that it is "the very distance of culture from its social context which allows [culture] to function as a critique and indictment of" that context. But, Jameson continues, this distance "also dooms [culture's] interventions to ineffectuality and relegates art and culture to a frivolous, trivialised space in which such intersections are neutralized in advance" (xv). Placed in the context of his discussion of utopias and other SF, the distance between SF and the reality it analyses both enables and disables that analysis to begin with. Jameson's materialist skepticism can be looked at through a more hopeful, if not rose-coloured, lens, however: SF's aesthetic redistributions permit a (dis)abling distance that allows us to see the material world other-wise (which is quite different from seeing SF as disconnected from "historical specificity" which Sherryl Vint quite rightly warns against).[57] This form of redistribution occurs, for example, in Delany's imbrication of sword-and-sorcery fantasy and representation of the beginning of the AIDS pandemic in "The Tale of Plagues and Carnivals," discussed above.

Such an imbrication of the supposedly separate realms of realism and fantasy is a consistent feature of SF: to take one clear example, the television show *The X-Files* is constituted of an ongoing, largely static debate between Scully and Mulder, representing, respectively, empiricism and faith in the unseen (a division signaled best in the episode "Pusher," when Scully requests of Mulder: "Please explain to me the scientific nature of the 'whammy'"). Likewise, two episodes—"Gethsemane" and "Redux"—are framed by, and contain numerous clips from, at least two *actual* governmental panels on the supposed *fantastic* aspects of the series, specifically the existence of aliens and the practice of human cloning. The episodes contain clips from, first and most interestingly, the NASA Symposium held at Boston University on November 20, 1972, an edited version of which was turned into the 1975 film, *Life Beyond Earth and the Mind of Man*.[58] This symposium included statements by and debates between several people: an "anthropologist and social biologist," Ashley Montagu; a priest and theologian (and then Dean of Harvard's School of Divinity), Krister Stendahl; the inimitable Carl Sagan; MIT physicist Philip Morrison (who had published on the possibilities of communicating with extraterrestrial life); and

Nobel-Prize-winning biologist George Wald (who is misidentified by some *X-Files* fan web sites as Isaac Asimov). Here, the line between science and science fiction disappears, and the line between political reality and SF commentary gets likewise blurry.

This collapsing division is perhaps figured best through a device that makes a common appearance not only in SF, but in criticism, theory, and psychoanalysis as well: the mirror, and the related device, the *mise en abyme* (the latter of which generally, in cinematic examples, takes the form of series of television cameras, lenses, and screens shown in sequence, creating a tunnel-like effect). These images figure the enabling and disabling mediational distance of SF from reality, of culture from society. The mirror and related devices are readily apparent in visual media, from art to television and film: these media can allow for a direct use of the function of the mirror in and as SF, conclusions that can then be applied to literary and other forms of SF. The role of the mirror is perhaps best summed up at the NASA/Boston University symposium by the physicist, Philip Morrison, who appears in the clips on *The X-Files* episode, although the following telling statement is not included. Morrison says:

> I suppose if you were to ask what instrument would be the image of the announced topic, you would surely say ... a telescope. But in fact, at least most of the speakers have really spoken on the topic [of] what they see in the mirror. Now, that's not in any way wrong. Perhaps the most valuable part of this extraordinary enterprise is going to be the mirror with which we confront ourselves obliquely ..., as we try to ask the question of what the future is like ... of how we are going to get over ourselves to reach that future, and so on. ... But as a somewhat matter-of-fact discussant ... I am somewhat inclined to direct some attention to what I think it really will be like, and not to these mirror-like discussions.[59]

Morrison then goes on to say that the material distance between us and any possible extraterrestrial civilisation would render impossible any effect that such communication would have on "the problems of the day," a statement that Scully echoes in the pilot episode of the series. These statements are fascinating for the hard and fast line they draw between narrative speculation and fact, given that he says as a "matter-of-fact" person, he will direct attention to what "[he] think[s] it really will be like." The tension between the factual, "really," and the speculative, "I think it ... will," goes unnoticed here. Morrison is using a scientific ethos (that "caste or class model" of the "scientific expert" that Miéville discusses) to condemn any level of speculation even as he speculates.

In other words, someone should have told Dr. Morrison that telescopes often use mirrors. *The X-Files*—like many other SF works, from Edward Bellamy's nineteenth-century short story "The Blindman's World" (which actually focuses on a telescope) through to *Stargate: SG1*—uses mirrors and lenses precisely to emphasise the tension between narration and fact, past and future, and to point out that that tension is constituted by interpretation.[60] Such queer reflections highlight that any statement of fact is always in tension with speculation, that "whatever will be" may be, but the future isn't ours to see, but simply to reflect upon. Broderick cleverly sees the abbreviation SF as best being defined as "Signs Fiction"[61]; but, given that the Latin word for mirror, *speculum*, shares a root with speculative, perhaps the most accurate expansion of SF falls between these two: "specular fictions."

III. FANTASTIC REFLECTIONS OF GENDER AND RACE

This general paradigm is offered as a theoretical ground for the specific focus and readings of the rest of this book, which analyses in detail the issues of gender, race, and their representation in American SF. For, while the "cognitive" element of SF may not hold in all or even most cases, still SF, as a specular mode, reminds us that its fantasies are in a mutually complicating relationship with material reality. The categories of gender and race, their mutable histories, and the meta-history of the theoretical discussions of them run a course parallel to the theory of SF I've laid out above, making SF a perfect tool for reflecting on these identity categories, and vice versa. Gender and race have been considered "cognitive" categories, insofar as both have been viewed through an essentialist lens that posits them as easily defined and as determinative of individuals' behaviours and of their very beings; both have been considered fantasies—sets of cultural creations that do not find their origin in material reality, but are in fact fictions, scientific and otherwise; and both have been considered "readerly" processes, in that, while they may be fictions, they still have pervasive effects on material reality insofar as people use them for definition purposes, both for self and other, to build and to destroy communities. In his foundational study, John Rieder offers a useful overview of the similarities in the theoretical modeling of the categories of gender and race: "Both gender and racial identity turn on the crucial pivot that articulates biological determination and cultural construction. Both involve the expression of identity in anatomy, on the one hand, and the performance of identity according to culturally and historically variable scripts, on the other."[62] In other words, both gender and race can highlight the cultural fantasies that underwrite supposed scientific fact, even as those fantasies, in turn, allow for material transformations, the very ontological movement that SF itself narrativizes. SF, therefore, is not only able to illuminate the cultural and social histories of these categories, as with any cultural form that has a significantly long history, but, as meta-culture or culture-in-drag, so too can it intervene in those histories and highlight the fractures and ruptures present within them. If, as Miéville argues, SF is defined by a "fundamental logic of otherness, of alterity," a logic that implicates it directly in discussions of ideology, then clearly its treatment of these ideological categories of human "otherness" should be central to any discussion of the field, and vice versa. Semiotics and material history here intersect, as they always must.

My use of *The X-Files* for a generic discussion can be—pardon the pun—mirrored in this analysis of SF, gender, and race, by looking to the popular SF franchise, *Star Trek*, and in particular the episode "Far Beyond the Stars" from the series *Deep Space Nine*. In this episode, Benjamin Sisko, the African American captain of the titular deep space outpost is split (seemingly by the god-like aliens who live in the wormhole the station guards) into two figures: his original self and a 1950s science fiction writer, Benny Russell. Working as a staff writer for a small science fiction magazine, Benny Russell writes the story of Captain Sisko and *Deep Space Nine*, only to have his editor reject the story because the fictional captain is black. Eventually the story is published (once Russell frames his SF story as the *dream* of a disenfranchised black man), but the magazine's publisher pulps the story.

In some ways, this episode retells the actual events surrounding Samuel Delany's attempt to publish *Nova* in *Analog*, edited by John W. Campbell. As Delany writes:

> I submitted *Nova* for serialization to the famous sf editor of *Analog* Magazine, John W. Campbell, Jr. Campbell rejected it, with a note and phone call to my agent explaining that he didn't feel his readership would be able to relate to a black main character. That was one of my first direct encounters, as a professional writer, with the slippery and always commercialized form of liberal American prejudice: Campbell had nothing against my being black, you understand. (There reputedly exists a letter from him to horror writer Dean Koontz, from only a year or two later, in which Campbell argues in all seriousness that a technologically advanced black civilization is a social and a biological impossibility. …) No, perish the thought! Surely there was not a prejudiced bone in his body! It's just that I had, by pure happenstance, chosen to write about someone whose mother was from Senegal (and whose father was from Norway), and it was the poor benighted readers, out there in America's heartland, who, in 1967, would be too upset.[63]

While specific details vary, the relationship between Delany's experience and Benny Russell's story is clearly close. The episode, functioning as a form of *roman à clef*, offers other characters that can be read as rewritings of Isaac Asimov, Henry Kuttner, and C. L. Moore, the last of whom is represented as likewise dealing with sexism in the SF publishing field. By simply telling these stories, then, *Deep Space Nine* makes the same argument as William Gibson's "Gernsback Continuum" when the latter refers to the visions of early SF pulp magazines as having "all the sinister fruitiness of Hitler Youth propaganda":[64] "Far Beyond the Stars" points out that science fiction, far from offering new social logics, can in fact reproduce some material biases (perhaps even as it thinks its fighting them).

In many ways, this reproduction of social biases is part and parcel of the cognitive branch of SF's reliance on scientific authority, even when it is critical of such. The scientific cultural logic that SF engages in (although is not simply delimited by) is one governed by a teleology that is grounded or supported on a supposedly "rational," "factual," unbiased scientific base. But, as several critics, theorists, and scientific and cultural historians have shown, this base is *not* an unbiased one that somehow transcends and thus escapes its surrounding culture. As Haraway writes, scientific narratives "are *stories* with a particular aesthetic, realism, and a particular politics, commitment to progress."[65] Despite the centrality to Enlightenment thought of individual rights and equality, these narratives are "bound by an underlying ontology," in Michael Heim's words,[66] an ontology paradoxically based on a hierarchical system of othering and silencing that denies the value or legitimacy of entire groups of people. Analyses of this othering, many of them developed in feminist criticism, therefore rely on critiques of the ontological underpinnings of the Enlightenment project, which itself forms the foundations of modern scientific thought. For example, detailing the difficulties of the Enlightenment construction of the "individual" and the subsequent claim to the "universal" nature of this identity construct, Sidonie Smith writes that this subject, this Enlightenment identity, is characterised by disembodiment and rationality and therefore contains an

> implicit ... hierarchy wherein what is and is not appropriate, at any given juncture, to the universal subject gets staked out. Founded on exclusionary practices, this democratic self positions on its border all that is termed the "colorful," that is, that which becomes identified culturally as other, exotic, unruly, irrational, uncivilized, regional, or paradoxically unnatural.[67]

This definition of the Enlightenment subject as less a universalising concept of "human nature" and more an othering practice that serves to delimit who is and who is not considered human is one that will be returned to throughout this work. As the passage by Pearson, above, makes clear, SF as a queering of realism allows for a direct challenge to this Cartesian self.

But, the episode of *Deep Space Nine* goes far beyond simply pointing out biases. By again returning to visual and intellectual processes of reflection, the episode longs for a means to transform such practices; again, to *see* other-wise. Not merely a guise of inclusivity serving as an alibi for "enlightened" othering, these reflections serve both to highlight the material practices of that othering and imagine different ways of narrating the relationships between past and present, self and other, and even, to repeat Rancière, between appearance and reality. Throughout the episode, both Sisko and Benny Russell catch glimpses of each other and the world the other lives in, generally when looking through a window. Functioning as both a reflective surface and a transparency through which the character can glance outward, the window allows a vision of future and past. For Sisko, the images of Russell remind him of the history of racism and the necessity of re-membering it, in Toni Morrison's sense, such that it not be forgotten nor allowed to repeat. For Russell, the images of Sisko remind him of the power of the SF imagination, to offer new possibilities through its slippery signification, even while material change seems out of reach behind the looking glass (though for the viewer, watching a television show with an African American lead, some change, at least, seems to have come). Again, directly calling reality and mimesis into question (at the end, Sisko wonders who is really the dreamer and who the dreamed), this episode takes *The X-Files*' meditation on SF's reflections and uses them to re-member race and gender and directly challenge material racist and sexist social functions. Popular multimedia Afrofuturists, from Parliament-Funkadelic to Janelle Monáe, have arguably recognised these possibilities better than most.[68]

As critics from Smith, to bell hooks, to Toni Morrison and many others have shown, the histories of constructions of gender and race, of sexist and racist oppression, and of resistance to them are all central to the formation of American cultures and their ideological production of "reality." Given that fact, SF's non-realist challenges to such received notions should be central to our studies of identity. And so it is on these particular SF reflections of gender and race that the following chapters focus. While I clearly build on the solid foundations of current SF gender and race studies,[69] the present work treats race and gender in American SF as "kindred mysteries," to borrow Hawthorne's words (which lend themselves to the title of this introduction). I argue that many of the works studied here present gender and race as inseparably intertwined categories, gesturing to the ways in which such social and cultural categories can function in hegemonic ways to reinforce the biased status quo. Just as importantly, however, I also discuss the ways in which these categories can each be deployed to critique the biases inherent in dominant representations of the other. They are not alone in this process: in several places I bring in their interactions with the others of what Sedgwick calls the "coarse axes" of identity analysis—class and sexuality—as well as the "nonce taxonomy" of identity she rightly sees as equally important.[70] Still, gender and race play particular roles in relation to each other in the history and culture of the United States. Often these connections do play out in relation to, say, class and sexuality: one can think here of the "myth of the black rapist," so grotesquely constructed in *Birth of a Nation*, used to represent the brutalities of classed and racial stereotyping and material bigotries in *Native Son*, and then exposed as myth, twisted and turned about in Delany's *Dhalgren*. But, using gender and race as my stereoscopic lenses through which to analyse American SF allows a sharper focus on many of these discussions. I argue that studying these identity categories together rather than separately can add a richer understanding of the social and cultural mechanisms involved in both.

But Delany's anecdote about Campbell raises a particular material issue relating to SF and identity, which this book also attempts to address: the pernicious relation of SF and whiteness. During an interview with Delany for the S&M magazine *Black Leather in Color*, the following exchange takes place:

> BLIC: When you started writing science fiction, it was still basically a white, male heterosexual preserve. ... Why does it still seem to be a community of white guys?
>
> SAMUEL R. DELANY: Of course, there *are* no "heterosexual" male preserves. There are social groups where gay or bisexual men feel safe acknowledging themselves—first to one another, then to pretty much everyone. And there are other social groups where they don't. By heterosexual preserve, you simply indicate the latter. The gay and bisexual men are there. But the homophobia in the group is high enough to make them wary of acknowledging their presence—sometimes even to themselves. ... Why is SF still so overwhelmingly white? I wish I knew.[71]

While indicating both the material and discursive queerness that can exist within the (often cracked open) closets of social institutions, Delany admits to finding himself at a loss concerning the whiteness that haunts SF. While more writers of colour are now active in the field than at the time of this interview, and while other SF traditions beyond the American pulp history have also complicated this history,[72] the answer to his final question is still as potentially unsatisfying as it is troubling. Although not directly in the sense that Delany and interviewer Thomas Deja are using the word, as a protected and isolated space, science fiction as a literary institution *has* tended to "preserve"—keep, maintain, pickle—some of the discursive foundations of the privileging of white, straight men. As Delany goes on to note, despite a wide and far-ranging readership and a diverse group of authors, science fiction—or at least its reputation—*has* remained a largely white and, I would add, an often patriarchal, fairly straight genre. However, this discursive tendency of science fiction, the very preserved nature of dominant SF bigotries, has enabled a variety of SF resistances that, upon reflection, can serve activists in the larger social arena.[73] In other words, much SF discourse may serve the overt purpose of preserving traditional dominant social categories[74] but, as with any ideologically informed discourse, as Foucault writes, it also gives rise to a present and future "plurality of resistances, each of them a special case."[75] This text therefore situates whiteness and challenges to it as central concerns, highlighting how SF can shore up and resist, preserve and spoil, even some of its own entrenched material and discursive practices.

While other works have offered subtle analyses of SF and gender or race, many of them treat "science fiction" primarily in the Suvinian manner and so focus on technology and gender or race, a focus which often necessitates a narrowly materialist approach. Similar works approach SF through technology studies, setting aside much genre and formal discussion.[76] My study, in its more "hybrid" view of SF, moves between materialist, literary historical, philosophical, and other theoretical models in its attempt to understand the modal and historical identity dynamics at work.[77] In addition, while I have chosen many iconic works to study (*Tarzan of the Apes* and *The Matrix*, for example), I have also chosen some less critically represented works, albeit occasionally by well-known authors (William Gibson's nanotech series and Octavia Butler's *Patternist* series, for example): my aim here is to address central figures while also bringing new lines of insight and new textual resources to the larger field. For this reason, while Delany clearly informs my approach to this field (hence his centrality to this introduction), I have chosen not to analyse his works at length here. While this may seem to be a significant gap, it is one that is already filled in, not only because his work has been thoroughly explored on many of these terms, but also because my approach, as laid out in this introduction, is indebted to the conclusions he traces in both his fiction and his critical works: to analyse his SF at length here would be to engage in another form of mirrored reflection.[78]

Finally, other works that focus on these areas take an overarching view of the field, and so deal with a large number of texts, whereas I read only a few texts per chapter: while this may make my work seem somewhat more limited in breadth than these others, I hope it lends further detail to those excellent studies while also permitting me to examine the sometimes more specific and intricate elements of the works that those necessarily wide surveys may not. There are exceptions to this last point. Importantly, DeGraw analyses a small set of authors: Burroughs (focusing on his Mars series) and Schuyler, both of whom I also study, alongside Delany. DeGraw's focus is, however, much more narrowly on race; particularly, she offers a well-grounded polemic on ways to disrupt "the Anglo male triangle of protagonist/audience/author" of twentieth-century SF.[79] Thus, DeGraw's work posits a progressive, linear narrative from Burroughs through Schuyler to Delany, stating that there is an "increasing number of science fiction authors utilizing race/ethnicity in their texts," a fact that "will promote critical growth and an expanded readership."[80] While this progressive narrative holds true in many ways, my argument is instead that, since at least the nineteenth century, SF authors have both bluntly employed, and carefully interrogated, race in combination with gender (and class, sexuality, nationality, and other identity categories); that, in fact, race and gender are two of the primary focal points of SF, even—perhaps especially—as it moves into its hegemonic pulp phase characterised by a (constantly failing) desire to rigidly map the white, patriarchal triangle DeGraw sketches. By turning explicitly to gender *and* race, and specifically analysing some of SF's relationships to whiteness, my argument troubles both SF's progressive and regressive narratives, even as it shows how the latter still open themselves to questioning.

My study is split into three parts, "Race/Gender/Science/Fiction," "Virtual Whiteness," and "Muting Utopia." While these parts move roughly chronologically from the mid-nineteenth century through to the end of the twentieth (with the majority of the book focusing on the twentieth century), they do not necessarily offer a genealogy of SF depictions of race and gender, but instead examine these topics thematically, offering both diachronic and synchronic dialogues on the ways in which SF engages gender and race.

Part I begins in the mid-nineteenth century and moves through to the opening decades of the twentieth, examining particular hegemonic representations of race and gender that twentieth-century SF continually returns to, if often to critique (as does the wider culture). Chapter 1 analyses Nathaniel Hawthorne's 1846 mad-scientist tale, "The Birth-mark," and Mary E. Bradley Lane's 1880–1881 utopia, *Mizora: A Prophecy*. Both of these works incorporate dominant epistemologies of gender and race in paradoxical movements of reinforcement and critique, exposing both categories as performative structures that are, in the very process of having their definitional boundaries policed, always transgressing those borders, undermining their own ramparts at the same time as they shore up disciplinary support. Attempting to reinforce the boundaries of whiteness, they open possibilities for a critique of white supremacy. Introducing my larger analysis to the reader, this chapter tackles the issues of the book by exploring the binaries of identity presented in dominant portrayals of race and gender in the nineteenth century, exploring the interplay of whiteness and blackness, femininity and masculinity.

Chapter 2 then specifies these hegemonic discussions by focusing in particular on the development of modern white masculinity in the early twentieth century, analysing Edgar Rice Burroughs' *Tarzan of the Apes* (first published in *All-Story Magazine* in 1912 and slightly expanded and edited as a book in 1914) and Philip Francis Nowlan's 1928 novella, *Armageddon—2419 A.D.* and its sequel, 1929's *The Airlords of Han* (both published in Hugo Gernsback's seminal SF pulp, *Amazing Stories*). These latter works introduce the character Anthony Rogers, who would go on to reach fame in a variety of media throughout the twentieth century as "Buck" Rogers. Pointing on the one hand to a nostalgic past of "proper" white masculinity, and on the other to the development of a "proper" white masculine future, these pulp icons attempt to present a path for a revivified patriarchal and white supremacist America in the new century.

Part I addresses the development and fracture lines of the hegemonic functions of whiteness in relation to gender identities in the modern United States; Part II develops this focus on whiteness into an analysis of the performative aspects of race, gender, and their connections in works from either end of the twentieth century. Chapter 3 analyses George S. Schuyler's 1931 SF satire, *Black No More*, while Chapter 4 leaps ahead to the end of the twentieth century and the beginning of the twenty-first, with the Wachowski siblings' *Matrix* films. Incorporating a discussion of class, my analysis of Schuyler's work demonstrates the ways in which he ironically depicts the class system and racism as engaged in what I call a Möbius strip of performative creation, endlessly reinscribing each other even as they are shown to have no foundation outside of their own semiotic invocations. Tying this to his depiction of a white, female "race traitor" in his "Black Internationale" and "Black Empire" stories, I demonstrate that Schuyler satirically highlights the entrenched nature of performative identity categories, and the difficulty of altering them, in keeping with Schuyler's own assimilationist views. Chapter 4 then moves to the developments and transformations of cyberpunk in its most iconic film, *The Matrix* (and its somewhat less iconic sequels and offshoots). The film presents the stereotypical white male romantic hero in a new, electronic frontier, saving not only the "damsel in distress," but also the often racially othered subordinate classes of society. While seemingly challenging the hegemonic racism presented by such works as *Tarzan of the Apes* and the Buck Rogers stories, the film—like, as I show, the siblings' later production of *Cloud Atlas*—may ultimately be unable to escape the narrative mythologies it purports to analyse. Both central works in Part II thus demonstrate the impossible paradoxes of mounting challenges to such dominant narratives from within the ideological and material matrix that perpetuates them.

Part III moves from the specific analyses of whiteness and the difficulty of resistance to examine postmodern transformations of the utopian narrative. This section studies works that construct specific places (or no-places) of resistance within the United States (all of which are set in California, the contradictory symbol of frontier freedom and the origin of America's mass imprisonment; of countercultural resistance, Silicon Valley, and Hollywood). Unlike Mary E. Bradley Lane's utopia, but more like *The Matrix*, the works in Part III present these resistant spaces as, on the one hand, necessary responses to the hegemonic silencing of the underclasses—a spatially constructed return of the repressed—and, on the other, as their own hierarchically defined societies that could well reproduce rather than challenge the biases around them. The book thus comes full circle not just to utopia, but also to the interrelated linguistic and queer arguments of this introduction, highlighting the problems of the simple inversion of binaries without the complete dismantling of the larger identificatory processes that those binaries represent. Chapter 5 looks to lesser-known works by authors made famous for others: William Gibson's nanotech trilogy (1993–1999) and Frank Herbert's *The Santaroga Barrier* (1968). Gibson's trilogy, interconnected both by the possibilities of nanotechnology and by specific characters, includes a community known as "The Bridge." Developing the identically named space in Delany's Nevèrÿon series, Gibson's Bridge is a community composed of a multiracial underclass that both stands opposed to and is interpenetrating with the dominant society that surrounds it. While one central character, Rydell, fulfills a function much like that of Neo in *The Matrix*, challenging but perhaps also enabling the biased culture that surrounds him, other characters, including the almost totally silent Silencio, demonstrate the new possibilities for identity afforded in the cracks of late capitalist society. Herbert's novel, conversely, draws a more negative map of such spaces. Largely written as an analysis of behaviourist and related psychologies, and more specifically as a critique of B. F. Skinner's *Walden 2*, *The Santaroga Barrier* traces a community's evolution from an isolationist and collectivist utopia into an imperial figure, deploying antiblack racism and housing policies as a means through which to understand this transformation. In this novel, the silenced, zombie-like workers in this utopian compound serving as a reminder of what happens to those on the edges or who are left out of utopia. Both novels present these "edges" as heterotopian spaces—in Foucault's sense—that dislocate and refract the hegemonic structures of the societies that surround them, offering a recursive vision of SF itself as just such a heterotopia.

Chapter 6 picks up directly on Herbert's connection of race relations, utopian politics, and pseudo-imperialism, as well as on the silent figures of Silencio and the zombie-like workers in Santaroga by examining Octavia Butler's *Patternist* series, specifically focusing on the one novel set in the same time period as its composition, *Mind of My Mind*. Coming back to the theoretical model laid out in this introduction, this chapter shows the ways in which *Mind of My Mind* specifically addresses the role of the African American community within the nation in terms that respond precisely to the infamous 1965 Moynihan Report and its gendered and race assumptions concerning the normative American family. This final chapter demonstrates that even a complex understanding of the networked dynamics of power is shown to be vulnerable to utopian politics, demonstrating how even such mobile theoretical models can be forced back into traditional hierarchical patterns, with the postmodern heterotopia transforming into the glaring void of the "city upon a hill."

Moving between material history and SF fantasies, from the specificities of race and gender at different points in American history to larger analyses of the function of such identity categories, these readings gesture not only to the importance of SF representations of gender, race, and related issues, but also to the necessity of the careful reading thereof. SF has already become central to discussions of humanity in the global capitalist age and is increasingly the focus of feminist and critical race studies; in combining these earlier approaches, this book goes further, to demonstrate why SF must become central to our discussions of identity writ large, of the possibilities and failings of the human—past, present, and future. The Afterword to this book therefore offers its own set of alternate reflections on my previous conclusions. Highlighting the fact that the book begins with the promise of the discovery of fantastic identities but ends with critiques of utopia, the Afterword looks to define a new radical alterity that can shatter the mimetic mirror into its multiplicitous fabulous fragments. Turning to Lee Edelman's construction of the queer death drive and the figure of the robot, the Afterword tries to twist the book into new perspectives. While it may not give us a yellow brick road to follow unerringly to a better world, SF provides us with the theoretical flights of fancy needed not only to "dream it," but also to "be it," whatever we can imagine that "it" to be.

NOTES

1. *Rocky Horror* is not American, and nationally locating *Farscape* is a complex question. *Farscape* was an American-Australian co-production, while *Rocky Horror* was a British production based on a British stage show. However, the two *Farscape* passages quoted here are from episodes written by American writer, David Kemper, and *Rocky Horror* focuses its plot and allusions primarily on American culture. More importantly, both can be considered to be interrogations of American popular culture and identity, as I trace out here. In the conclusion, I analyze another work that looks to America from the outside, *Metropolis*, pointing to the ways in which the nation is defined as a particularly SF location in the global imagination.
2. "Revenging Angel," *Farscape*, written by David Kemper (2001. A&E Entertainment, 2011), Blu-ray. (*Farscape*, "Revenging Angel").
3. As I discuss below, Jameson, relying on Marcuse, makes a similar argument regarding the relation between utopian fiction (as a subset of SF) and political action (*Archaeologies of the Future: The Desire Called Utopia and Other Science Fictions* [London: Verso, 2005], xv *passim*). While running parallel to Jameson to a point, my claim for the necessity of acknowledging the separation between culture and material life—even as that separation allows for culture's impact on the material world through people's engagement and translation of that culture—relies more specifically on the work of Jacques Rancière, and his more enabling argument concerning culture's "redistribution of the sensible" (*The Politics of Aesthetics: The Distribution of the Sensible*, translated by Gabriel Rockhill [New York: Continuum, 2004], 45). In addition to *Politics of Aesthetics*, see *Emancipated Spectator*, translated by Gregory Elliott (London: Verso, 2009).
4. Recently, John Rieder has noted this definitional turn as a defining characteristic of SF studies ("On Defining SF, or Not," *Science Fiction Studies* 37, no.2: 191–209). For an excellent, recent overview of the various definitions (and meta-discussions of definitions), see the introductory chapter of Adam Roberts' *The History of Science Fiction* (New York: Palgrave, 2006). My analysis echoes Roberts', insofar as he develops a philosophical approach to science fiction that sees it as a "version of *fantastic* (rather than *realist*) literature" (3). Our definitional disagreements are thus more of degree than kind: Roberts positions science fiction as a particularly technological and rational pole on a spectrum that sees its other end in the realm of the magical, while I, though agreeing to a point, simply add more emphasis to the communication between those poles (an inverted reflection, perhaps, of Roberts placing "under the sign of erasure" the distinction between "realist" and "science fictional" [15]). In what follows, I take Rieder's lead in seeing SF not as static category, but as a form of shifting praxis.
5. Jacques Rancière, *Politics*, 9.
6. Samuel R. Delany, "Science Fiction and 'Literature'–or, The Conscience of the King," in *Starboard Wine: More Notes on the Language of Science Fiction*, rev. ed. (Middletown, CT: Wesleyan University Press, 2012), 69.
7. For other critics who assert this point, see, for example, Sharon DeGraw's *The Subject of Race in American Science Fiction* (New York: Routledge, 2007); DeGraw writes that because SF "emphasizes invention, exploration, and speculation, authors can utilize this genre to question traditional boundaries, social

conventions, and hierarchies" (12). James Gunn goes further, stating that the defining element of SF is "change. Some significant element of the situation is different from the world with which we are familiar, and the characters cannot respond to it in customary ways, that is, without recognizing that a changed situation requires analysis and a different response" ("Toward a Definition of Science Fiction," in *Speculations on Speculation*, edited by James Gunn and Matthew Candelaria [Lanham, MD: Scarecrow Press, 2005], 7).

8. A brief aside to the history of SF criticism and this work's relation to it will help to situate this argument. By invoking both structuralism generally, and Scholes and Todorov more specifically, I may be seen to be orbiting the region of a now forty-year-old debate, known commonly as the "Lem Affair," which took place in the pages of *Science Fiction Studies*. While this debate has several different threads, during it Stanislaw Lem was seen to critique SF as a field and was eventually ousted from his honourary membership in the Science Fiction Writers Association. One early moment in the Lem Affair was an article Lem wrote that was critical of Todorov and structuralism generally. These events and articles led to several responses, both thoughtful and polemical. Scholes himself responded in the July 1975 issue to defend Todorov's approach (even as Scholes' argument was taken to task in the same journal).

   The last thing I would want to do is reopen a fight which already by 1977 was being bemoaned as an event that "should be allowed to die a natural death" (James Gunn, "On the Lem Affair" *Science Fiction Studies* 4, no.3 [1977]: 324). I am also not following Scholes' structuralist attempt to define the entire field—in fact, the analysis in the remaining chapter would say that is impossible. Scholes sees SF from a similar point of view as Darko Suvin, within which SF functions in a cognitive, extrapolative way that allows it, like science, "to have predictive power," but my approach follows a less rigid model (Scholes, *Structural Fabulation: An Essay on Fiction of the Future* [Notre Dame: University of Notre Dame Press, 1975], 18).
9. Robert Scholes, "Lem's Fantastic Attack on Todorov," *Science Fiction Studies* 2, no.2 (1975): 167.
10. Rancière, *Politics*, 45.
11. *Serenity*, written and directed by Joss Whedon (Universal, 2005), Blu-ray.
12. Ferdinand de Saussure, *Course in General Linguistics*, intro. Jonathan Culler, edited by Charles Bally and Albert Sechehaye in collaboration with Albert Reidlinger, translated by Wade Baskin (Glasgow: Collins, 1974), 67; emphasis in original.
13. Saussure, 114.
14. Saussure, 122.
15. Carl Freedman traces these aspects of Saussure's structuralism, and Derrida's analysis of it, in relation to SF in a close reading of Delany's *Stars in My Pocket Like Grains of Sand*. Freedman's analysis is a specific one of Delany's text, but insofar as it focuses on Delany's construction of a "politics of difference" it does run a parallel track to my more general thoughts here (Freedman, *Critical Theory and Science Fiction* [Hanover: Wesleyan University Press and University Press of New England, 2000], 157). Indeed, a reading that expands on Freedman's brief mention of Delany's explicit invocation of Freudian theory (164), through the Lacanian revision of Saussure I go on to discuss, could add to his already excellent discussion.

16. I should note here that while critics have related Lacan to discussions of SF and identity before, it is almost always through allegorical reading, in which the "alien"—widely defined—is equated to Lacan's "other": for some of the best examples of such readings, see Freedman's excellent discussion of Stanislaw Lem and Lacan (Freedman, 107–11) and Slavoj Žižek's "The Thing from Inner Space" (*Angelaki: Journal of the Theoretical Humanities*, 4 no.3 [1999]: 221–31).

    In my reading, SF itself becomes the "other" of a structure of meaning (language) and being (identity), in a meta-representational relationship both to other cultural forms, such as realism, and to material reality. Delany, as I discuss below, sets the stage for this particular analysis. For a parallel argument, see Mark Bould, who, using Lacanian theories of paranoia and critiquing Todorov's vision, argues that what sets fantasy apart from much mimetic art is a frankly self-referential consciousness (an embedded, textual self-consciousness, whatever the consciousness of the particular author or reader) of the impossibility of 'real life', or Real life. It is, paradoxically, the very fantasy of fantasy as a mode that, at least potentially, gives it space for a hard-headed critical consciousness of capitalist subjectivity ("The Dreadful Credibility of Absurd Things: A Tendency in Fantasy Theory," *Historical Materialism* 10, no.4 [2002]: 83; also qtd. in part in Rieder, *Colonialism and the Emergence of Science Fiction* [Middletown, CT: Wesleyan University Press, 2008], 62).

    Damien Broderick's *Transrealist Fiction* also briefly introduces a similar argument, noting that what "Derrida and Lacan would have us believe is the case with *all* textuality," that "signifiers ... point only to other signifiers ... in an endless paper chase" is "*emphatically* the case with science fiction" which, he writes, "is indeed a kind of Signs Fiction" (*Transrealist Fiction: Writing in the Slipstream of Science* [Westport, CT: Greenwood, 2000], 27). I wish to go beyond this hermetic structuralism, though, to show how this "paper chase," because it offers new discursive possibilities connected to the larger ideological world, therefore offers new possibilities for identity—or at least cogent critiques of current identity formation—in the material world.
17. Sigmund Freud, "On Narcissism: An Introduction," in *On the History of the Psycho-Analytic Movement Papers on Metapsychology and Other Works*, Standard Edition of the Complete Psychological Works of Sigmund Freud 14, translated and edited by James Strachey, in collaboration with Anna Freud, assisted by Alix Strachey and Alan Tyson (London: Hogarth, 1957), 96; 94.
18. Jacques Lacan, *Écrits: The First Complete Edition in English*, translated by Bruce Fink (New York: Norton, 2006), 75.
19. In the episode, the conversation takes place in an interstitial realm between wormholes, where Crichton is given visions of alternate universes, and told that his "wanderings" through wormholes can alter those "unrealized realities." Allegorically, Crichton's unskilled attempts to undo trauma end up replicating them *ad infinitum*. While the scene—and others in the series involving John's internal discussions with a programmed alien "conscience"—functions as such an allegory, important to recall for both Freud's and Lacan's models is that this process would be a (largely) unconscious one, in which the ego functions as a mediator between the id's desires and the Ideal-I's demands.
20. Jacques Lacan, *The Four Fundamental Concepts of Psycho-analysis*, edited by Jacques-Alain Miller, translated by Alan Sheridan (London: Vintage, 1977), 20; emphasis in original.

21. Lacan, *Écrits*, 430.
22. Lacan, *Four*, 53. For Lacan, psychoanalysis is the science of the real: the process of analysis is precisely to trace trauma back to its origin in the real: "The place of the real ... stretches from the trauma to the phantasy—insofar as the phantasy is never quite primary, something determinant in the function of repetition" (*Four* 60), but the real is inaccessible in its totality, and only psychoanalysis, for Lacan, can "designate[] it for us" (60).
23. Samuel R. Delany, "Some *Real* Mothers ...: The *SF Eye* Interview," in *Silent Interviews: On Language, Race, Sex, Science Fiction, and Some Comics* (Hanover: Wesleyan University Press, 1994), 172.
24. Tzvetan Todorov, *The Fantastic: A Structural Approach to a Literary Genre*, translated by Richard Howard, forward by Robert Scholes (Ithaca: Cornell University Press, 1975), 33.
25. Samuel Coleridge, *Biographia Literaria*, edited by James Engell and W. Jackson Bate, the Collected Works 8 (Princeton: Princeton University Press, 1983), 6. It should be noted that Coleridge's creation of this now famous phrase occurs in the context of discussing his role in writing the "persons and characters supernatural, or at least romantic" in *Lyrical Ballads* (that title itself being an attempt to impossibly meld two separate genres, each with their own strained relation to what would become realism). He writes that these figures would be created in such a way "as to transfer from our inward nature a human interest and a semblance of truth to procure for these shadows of the imagination that willing suspension of disbelief for the moment, which constitutes poetic faith" (6). At the heart of literary creation itself, then, lies the ontological meeting of the material world of "human interest" and the "shadows of the imagination," or the fantastic.
26. Delany makes a similar distinction, albeit emphasizing the importance of the other side of the binary, when he distinguishes the paraliterary forms of SF from the more literary forms. In "The Tale of Plagues and Carnivals" from *Flight from Néverÿon*, the authorial narrative voice distinguishes "fantasy" from "SF" from "the literary genre Todorov called 'the Fantastic'" (*Flight from Nevèrÿon* [1985, Hanover: Wesleyan University Press, 1994], 210).
27. James Gunn, "Toward," 9.
28. Adam Roberts, *Science Fiction* (London: Routledge, 2000), 5; 9.
29. Seo-Young Chu, *Do Metaphors Dream of Literal Sheep: A Science-Fictional Theory of Representation* (Cambridge, MA: Harvard University Press, 2010), 7.
30. China Miéville, "Gothic Politics: A Discussion with China Miéville," *Gothic Studies* 10, no.1 (2008): 63.
31. Carl Freedman, 18–19; Istvan Csicsery-Ronay, Jr., *The Seven Beauties of Science Fiction* (Middletown, CT: Wesleyan University Press, 2008), 138–44.
32. Freedman, 19.
33. Miéville, "Gothic," 63–64. For an excellent, and parallel, discussion of Miéville and Suvin, see Andrew Millner (*Locating Science Fiction* [Liverpool: Liverpool University Press, 2012], 101–5). As he writes, though, he is less interested in Miéville's "intervention," than with creating a critical generic model of SF.
34. This critique of Suvin's argument can be expanded to show that SF, as with every speculative mode, is necessarily multiplicitous in its generic function: SF, even in the guise of what is traditionally called "science fiction" does, after all, often combine multiple genres into one work: many—if not most—episodes of

long-running SF television, be it *Stargate: SG1* or *Doctor Who*, for example, follow a "creature-feature" format heavily influenced by the gothic and horror; these and many other examples, including a significant portion of William Gibson's cyberpunk and later writings, explicitly build on the detective novel and film. SF is thus perhaps best seen as a mode characterized by the incorporation of unreal elements into multi-generic narrative forms. (Seo-Young Chu has made an argument for SF as a lyric mode; indeed, one of the more famous and oft-used definitions of SF is that it invokes a "sense of wonder" through its novum, in a manner similar to the sublime. But, the constant calling into question of the "real" that SF involves does, for me, invite a narrative response from its audience, in any event, even of the basic form, "Now, *what* is *going on*, here, I wonder?")

35. Chu, 7.
36. Delany, "Science Fiction," 88.
37. Delany also uses these examples in an appendix to his novel, *Trouble on Triton*, blurring the line between the "real" author and his fantastic creations.
38. Csicsery-Ronay, 5.
39. Delany, *Flight*, 22.
40. Delany, *Flight*, 178.
41. Delany, *Flight*, 281–2. Kevin Floyd also analyses the complexities of modelling and mediation in "The Tale of Plagues and Carnivals," but does so in terms of the relations between queer and Marxist theories (Kevin Floyd, "How to Subsume Difference, or World Reduction in Delany," in *Literary Materialisms*, edited by Mathias Nilges and Emilio Sauri [New York: Palgrave Macmillan, 2013], 113–24).
42. Samuel R. Delany, *The American Shore: Meditations of a Tale of Science Fiction by Thomas M. Disch—"Angouleme,"* (1978; reprint Middletown, CT: Wesleyan University Press, 2014), 160.
43. I am here differing not only from Suvin, but also from Chu's recent "inversion" of Suvin, even as I earlier echoed her language. She argues against definitions of SF that emphasize its non-mimetic or fantastic qualities, instead stating that "what most people call 'science fiction' is actually a high-intensity variety of realism, one that requires astronomical levels of energy to accomplish its representational task insofar as its referents (e.g., cyberspace) elaborately defy straightforward representation" (Chu, 7). Chu and I offer, in some ways, mirrored arguments, especially when read through her assertion of SF as a lyric mode: likewise citing both Delany and Todorov, she moves toward a definition of SF that allows it to "transcend[] ordinary temporality" and to "evoke heightened and eccentric states of consciousness" (Chu, 14). I arrive at the same general conclusion, seeing, in the figuration of gender and race, attempts to move beyond the limits of the "flat description" of ideologically reproducing the status quo. Where we differ is in the desire, and lack thereof, to yoke this "transcendence" to a "high intensity realism." While such a move would seem to side step the problem of Kantian transcendence and its concomitant (always ideological) universalizing claims, it risks undermining its own proposition in the process. In my conclusion, I return to this argument, discussing the possibility of a truly radical alterity, one that Chu, in her conclusion, denies.
44. Jacques Rancière, *Emancipated*, 12. For a longer discussion of Rancière, Kant, and aesthetic transcendence, see my "Inglourious Criticism, Basterd Fantasies:

Rancière, Tarantino, and the Intellectual Spectacle of Hope" (*The Public Intellectual and the Culture of Hope*, edited by Joel Faflak and Jason Haslam [Toronto: University of Toronto Press, 2013], 178–201).

45. A similar argument to mine has been made in fiction: Miéville's 2011 novel, *Embassytown* (New York: Del Rey, 2011), engages Saussurean and Lacanian theory in its construction of the alien species, the Ariekei. In the novel, ironically, the humans represent an SF world view, capable of metaphor and cognitive leaps, while the aliens represent realism, a mode incapable of moving beyond simile. They are extraterrestrial aliens who are beyond science fiction. Miéville even frames this situation in terms that echo discussions of the difference between SF and realism: "They've no what-ifs," one character says, echoing a common definition of SF's foundational question (Miéville, *Embassytown*, 56). But when the Ariekei finally discover "SF" in the form of a pair of humans who can both speak the Ariekei Language and yet present opposing world views, the Ariekei become addicted—fanatical even. The aliens, discovering the wonderful lies of human science fiction, become *fans*. Science fiction here works precisely because it is non-cognitive, because it is a fantastic drug that divorces one's mind from the real. (Given that the Ariekei are described as having hooves and "galloping," it seems clear that Miéville's aliens are at least an allusion to, or even rewritings of, Swift's Houyhnhnms, who similarly see language as purely referential insofar as they cannot lie.)
46. Miéville's lecture, delivered in 2009, is available on YouTube in six parts, under the title "China Mieville talk at KU"; the quotation comes from the fifth part, between 8:10 and 9:08 (China Miéville, "China Miéville Talk at KU, pt. 5," presented 24 Sept. 2009, *YouTube*, last modified 1 Nov. 2011, http://www.youtube.com/watch?v=EPABFo9cg2U/). Earlier, American SF novels make a similar linguistic argument about the transformative potentials of language, albeit relying on other linguistic theories than Saussure's (especially the so-called Sapir Whorf theory of linguistic relativity): I think especially of Samuel Delany's *Babel-17* (1966, reprinted in *Babel-17* and *Empire Star*, New York: Vintage, 2001) and Suzette Haden Elgin's *Native Tongue* (1984, New York: Feminist Press at CUNY, 2000).
47. Unless otherwise noted, all quotations from television and film are my own transcriptions.
48. Judith Butler, "Imitation and Gender Insubordination," in *Inside/Out*, edited by Diana Fuss (New York: Routledge, 1991), 23.
49. Judith Butler, 22.
50. Judith Butler, 23–24.
51. For another discussion of the queerness of SF as a category, see Wendy Gay Pearson, Veronica Hollinger, and Joan Gordon's introduction to *Queer Universes: Sexualities in Science Fiction* (Liverpool: Liverpool University Press, 2008).
52. Wendy Pearson, "Alien Cryptographies: The View from Queer," *Science Fiction Studies* 26, no.1 (1999): n.p. http://www.depauw.edu/sfs/backissues/77/pearson77.htm/, accessed 17 January 2015.
53. Indeed, following Lacan, and at the risk of delving into an SF fan's diatribe, one could argue that "realism" should only ever be used as a pejorative term to describe a particularly childish attachment to specific fantasies. "Childish" rather than "childlike" insofar as "realism" can only ever be defined in terms of

a particular sense of the world, and so presents a self*ish* fantasy that in large part can only reproduce specific personal biases rather than challenge one to look anew at the world. "Realism" could thus be seen as merely a fictionalization of a symptom of a pathological refusal to move beyond infantile narcissism—Henry James, realist *par excellence*, especially in his gothic work, knew this better than anyone.

54. Delany, "Science Fiction," 81; emphasis added.
55. Lou Reed, "I'll Be Your Mirror," *The Velvet Underground & Nico*, Disc Two of *Peel Slowly and See* Box Set, 1967, Polygram, 1995, CD.
56. Michel Foucault, "Of Other Spaces," *Diacritics* 16, no.1 (1986): 24.
57. Sherryl Vint, "Coding of Race in Science Fiction: What's Wrong with the Obvious?" in *Worlds of Wonder: Readings in Canadian Science Fiction and Fantasy Literature*, edited by Jean-François Leroux and Camille R. LaBossière (Ottawa: University of Ottawa Press, 2004), 129.
58. The second was a government hearing on human cloning, at which Ted Kennedy asked several questions, which appears as a significant plot point in the later episodes (this is possibly the hearing of the Senate Subcommittee on Public Health and Safety on "Scientific Discoveries in Cloning: Challenges for Public Policy," held on March 12, 1997, the spring before the episode aired).
59. *Life Beyond Earth and the Mind of Man*, prod. National Aeronautics and Space Administration, 1975, *Internet Archive*, accessed 11 October 2014, https://archive.org/details/LifeBeyondEarth.
60. Another scene from "Gethsemane" highlights the intrusion of narrative and interpretation using a brief *mise en abyme*, but also through intertextuality and allusion, in such a way as to undermine any notion of scientific truth: the scene involves several people using home-video equipment—through which we, the actual viewers, briefly look, framed by our own screen—as they film the autopsy of an extraterrestrial being. The emphasis on the camera, and the brief frame-within-a-frame shot of the autopsy is explained diegetically as Mulder and his co-conspirators trying to retain visual proof of alien life. And yet, the scene does the exact opposite. Repeating directly the famous 1995 alien autopsy hoax, also aired on Fox, *The X-Files*' network, this scene's emphasis on the camera lens calls televisual veracity *per se* into question. This is especially the case given that *The X-Files* had already shown another fake-alien autopsy in the earlier episode, *Nisei*, and had also earlier spoofed the 1995 footage in the Darin Morgan penned episode "Jose Chung's *From Outer Space*," an episode that emphasises the slipperiness and constant disconnect between narration and fact, as an author, Jose Chung, who wants to create a new genre he calls "non-fiction science fiction," collects tales of a particular alien abduction from the standpoint of those involved and the people investigating it ("Jose Chung's *From Outer Space*," *The X-Files: The Complete Third Season*, aired April 12, 1996, written by Darin Morgan, Directed by Rob Bowman [Twentieth Century Fox, 2005], DVD).
61. Broderick, 27.
62. Rieder, *Colonialism*, 99.
63. Samuel R. Delany, "Racism and Science Fiction," *New York Review of Science Fiction* 120 (1998), rpt. *nyrsf.com*: n.d., n.p, accessed 19 January 2014.
64. William Gibson, "The Gernsback Continuum," in *Burning Chrome* (New York: Ace, 1987), 33.

65. Donna Haraway, *Primate Visions: Gender, Race, and Nature in the World of Modern Science* (New York: Routledge, 1989), 4; my emphasis.
66. Michael Heim, "The Cyberspace Dialectic," in *The Digital Dialectic: New Essays on New Media*, edited by Peter Lunenfeld (Cambridge: MIT Press, 1999), 26.
67. Sidonie Smith, *Subjectivity, Identity, and the Body: Women's Autobiographical Practices in the Twentieth Century* (Bloomington: Indiana University Press, 1993), 9–10.
68. The notion of semiotic shifting could be readily applied to any number of Afrofuturist artists, as they challenge the Eurocentric assumptions that linger in some techno-utopian visions. On Janelle Monáe in relation to Afrofuturism in particular, see John Calvert, "Janelle Monáe: A New Pioneer of Afrofuturism," *The Quietus*, September 2, 2010, http://thequietus.com/articles/04889-janelle-mon-e-the-archandroid-afrofuturism/, accessed 17 January 2015.
69. There is a growing body of work on the representation of gender and race in SF, although the latter is still the more neglected field. The feminist study of SF has an especially strong history: from Marlene Barr's work in *Alien to Femininity: Speculative Fiction and Feminist Theory* (New York: Greenwood, 1987) and Sarah Lefanu's *Feminism and Science Fiction* (Bloomington: Indiana University Press,1988), to Barr's own subsequent studies, Robin Roberts' *A New Species: Gender and Science in SF* (Urbana: University of Illinois Press, 1993) and Brian Attebery's *Decoding Gender in Science Fiction* (New York: Routledge, 2002), to Donna Haraway's use of the cyborg as an ironic socialist feminist myth (*Simians, Cyborgs, and Women: The Reinvention of Nature* [New York: Routledge, 1991]), to developments in queer theory and SF by such luminaries as Nicola Griffiths, Veronica Hollinger, and Wendy Gay Pearson, and an innumerable number of other monographs, essays, and collections, there is a rich and complex field of feminist and gender studies in SF. The field is smaller but growing in terms of the study of race in SF: Isiah Lavender III's recent *Race in American Science Fiction* (Bloomington: Indiana University Press, 2011) gives an excellent overview of the field (and its gaps), noting that "The relationship between race and sf has been largely overlooked by scholars," with the exception of studies by and about Samuel Delany and Octavia Butler, both prominent African American SF authors (10). As Lavender goes on to discuss, this lacunae in the critical study of SF is being filled in by such excellent works as DeWitt Douglas Kilgore's *Astrofuturism: Science, Race, and Visions of Utopia in Space* (Philadelphia: University of Pennsylvania Press, 2003), Adilifu Nama's *Black Space: Imagining Race in Science Fiction Film* (Austin: University of Texas Press, 2008), to which we can add Lavender's own work, Sharon DeGraw's *The Subject of Race in American Science Fiction* (2007), and Barr's edited collection, *Afro-future Females: Black Writers Chart Science Fiction's Newest New-Wave Trajectory* (Columbus: Ohio State University Press, 2008), as well as the authors of several articles and chapters in a variety of academic journals, essay collections, fanzines, blogs, and so on.
70. Eve Kosofsky Sedgwick, *Epistemology of the Closet*, updated with a new preface (Berkeley: University of California Press, 2008; 1990), 22; 23.
71. Samuel R. Delany, "The *Black Leather in Color* Interview," in *Shorter Views: Queer Thoughts and the Politics of the Paraliterary* (Hanover: Wesleyan University Press, 1999), 115–16.
72. Focusing alone on the important form of the SF anthology, one could list, for example, the *Dark Matter* anthologies edited by Sheree R. Thomas (*Dark Matter:*

A Century of Speculative Fiction from the African Diaspora [New York: Warner, 2000]; *Dark Matter: Reading the Bones* [New York: Warner, 2004]); Elisabeth Anne Leonard's critical anthology *Into Darkness Peering: Race and Color in the Fantastic* (Westport, CT: Greenwood, 1997); Nalo Hopkinson and Uppinder Mehan anthology of postcolonial SF, *So Long Been Dreaming*; Hopkinson's *Whispers from the Cotton Tree Root: Caribbean Fabulist Fiction* collection (Vancouver: Arsenal Pulp, 2004); and Grace L. Dillon's *Walking the Clouds: An Anthology of Indigenous Science Fiction* (Tucson: University of Arizona Press, 2012), among others.

73. In addition to the feminist interventions and critical works noted earlier, particular material incidents come to mind here—all from *Star Trek* lore. The first is the scene in the fan film *Trekkies*, in which one man—in a Starfleet uniform—discusses how *Star Trek* empowered his identification with the gay community, an identification radically expanded in recent years into wider popular and political culture by George Takei. The second is the now infamous meeting between Nichelle Nichols (Lt. Uhura) and Martin Luther King, Jr.: King urged Nichols to remain on the show—despite her dissatisfaction with the unequal treatment she was receiving—because she could serve as a role model, and point of resistance, for the black community. Nichols describes the situation in her autobiography, *Beyond Uhura: Star Trek and Other Memories* ([New York: Boulevard Books, 1995], 159–65).
74. For a discussion of the conservative social aspects of some dominant science fiction forms, see, for example, Nicola Nixon ("Cyberpunk: Preparing the Ground for Revolution or Keeping the Boys Satisfied?" *Science Fiction Studies* 19, no.2 [1992]: 219–35) and Sharon Stockton ("'The Self-Regained': Cyberpunk's Retreat to the Imperium," *Contemporary Literature* 36, no.4 [1995]: 588–612).
75. Michel Foucault, *History of Sexuality*, vol. 1, translated by Robert Hurley (New York: Vintage, 1990), 96.
76. I think here especially of Lisa Yaszek's excellent *The Self Wired: Technology and Subjectivity in Contemporary Narrative* (London: Routledge, 2002), or even Donna Haraway's magnificent *Primate Visions: Gender, Race, and Nature in the World of Modern Science* (New York: Routledge, 1989), both of which do analyse the interplay of race, gender, and SF (though the former more so), but do so through a solely materialist lens.
77. In this, I echo Elisabeth Anne Leonard, who writes in the introduction to her edited essay collection:

> Joanna Russ once wrote to Samuel Delany, "Worrying about the purity of the genres is like worrying about the purity of the races," a particularly apt simile here. I have practiced editorial inclusiveness even if it results in occasionally strange pairings.
>
> (Leonard, 3)

Leonard's quotation comes from Delany's article "The Gestation of Genres: Literature, Fiction, Romance, Science Fiction, Fantasy …" in *Intersections: Fantasy and Science Fiction*, edited by George E. Slusser and Eric S. Rabkin (Carbondale: Southern Illinois University Press, 1987).

78. I have written on Delany in other contexts (see Haslam, "Memory's Guilted Cage: Delany's *Dhalgren* and Gibson's *Pattern Recognition*" (*English Studies in Canada* 32.1 [2006]: 77–104).
79. DeGraw, 52.
80. DeGraw, 184.

REFERENCES

Attebery, Brian. *Decoding Gender in Science Fiction*. New York: Routledge, 2002.

Barr, Marlene S. *Alien to Femininity: Speculative Fiction and Feminist Theory*. New York: Greenwood, 1987.

Barr, Marleen S., ed. *Afro-Future Females: Black Writers Chart Science Fiction's Newest New-Wave Trajectory*. Columbus: Ohio State University Press, 2008.

Bould, Mark. "The Dreadful Credibility of Absurd Things: A Tendency in Fantasy Theory." *Historical Materialism* 10, no.4 (2002): 51–88.

Broderick, Damien. *Transrealist Fiction: Writing in the Slipstream of Science*. Westport, CT: Greenwood, 2000.

Butler, Judith. "Imitation and Gender Insubordination." In *Inside/Out*. Edited by Diana Fuss, 13–31. New York: Routledge, 1991.

Calvert, John. "Janelle Monáe: A New Pioneer of Afrofuturism." *The Quietus*. September 2 2010. http://thequietus.com/articles/04889-janelle-mon-e-the-archandroid-afrofuturism/, accessed 17 January 2015.

Chu, Seo-Young. *Do Metaphors Dream of Literal Sheep: A Science-Fictional Theory of Representation*. Cambridge, MA: Harvard University Press, 2010.

Coleridge, Samuel. *Biographia Literaria*. Edited by James Engell and W. Jackson Bate. The Collected Works 8. Princeton: Princeton University Press, 1983.

Csicsery-Ronay, Istvan, Jr. *The Seven Beauties of Science Fiction*. Middletown, CT: Wesleyan University Press, 2008.

DeGraw, Sharon. *The Subject of Race in American Science Fiction*. New York: Routledge, 2007.

Delany, Samuel R. *The American Shore: Meditations of a Tale of Science Fiction by Thomas M. Disch—"Angouleme."* 1978. Intro. Matthew Cheney. Middletown, CT: Wesleyan University Press, 2014.

———. *Babel-17* and *Empire Star*. 1966. New York: Vintage, 2001.

———. "The *Black Leather in Color* Interview." In *Shorter Views: Queer Thoughts and the Politics of the Paraliterary*, 115–22. Hanover: Wesleyan University Press, 1999.

———. *Flight from Nevèrÿon*. 1985. Hanover: Wesleyan University Press, 1994.

———. "Racism and Science Fiction." *New York Review of Science Fiction* 120 (1998). Rpt. *nyrsf.com*: n.d. N.p. Web. 19 Jan. 2014.

———. "Science Fiction and 'Literature'–or, The Conscience of the King." In *Starboard Wine: More Notes on the Language of Science Fiction*, 61–81. Revised edition; Middletown, CT: Wesleyan University Press, 2012.

———. "Some *Real* Mothers …: The *SF Eye* Interview." In *Silent Interviews: On Language, Race, Sex, Science Fiction, and Some Comics*, 164–85. Hanover: Wesleyan University Press, 1994.

Dillon, Grace L., ed. *Walking the Clouds: An Anthology of Indigenous Science Fiction*. Tucson: University of Arizona Press, 2012.

Elgin, Suzette Haden. *Native Tongue*. 1984. New York: Feminist Press at CUNY, 2000.

"Far Beyond the Stars." *Star Trek: Deep Space Nine*. Aired 11 February 1998. Directed by Avery Brooks. *Star Trek: Deep Space Nine: Season 6*. Paramount, 2003. DVD.

Floyd, Kevin. "How to Subsume Difference, or World Reduction in Delany." In *Literary Materialisms*. Edited by Mathias Nilges and Emilio Sauri, 113–24. New York: Palgrave Macmillan, 2013.

Foucault, Michel. *History of Sexuality*, vol. 1: An Introduction. Translated by Robert Hurley. 1978. New York: Vintage, 1990.

———. "Of Other Spaces." *Diacritics* 16, no.1 (1986): 22–27.

Freedman, Carl. *Critical Theory and Science Fiction*. Hanover: Wesleyan University Press-University Press of New England, 2000.

Freud, Sigmund. "On Narcissism: An Introduction." In *On the History of the Psycho-Analytic Movement Papers on Metapsychology and Other Works.* Standard Edition of the Complete Psychological Works of Sigmund Freud 14, 73–102. Translated and edited by James Strachey, in collaboration with Anna Freud, assisted by Alix Strachey and Alan Tyson. London: Hogarth, 1957.

"The Fugitive." *The Twilight Zone*. Aired 9 March 1962. *Twilight Zone: The Complete* Series. Image Entertainment, 2013. DVD.

"Gethsemane." *The X-Files*. Aired 18 May 1997. Written by Chris Carter. Directed by R. W. Goodwin. *The X-Files: The Complete Fourth Season*. Twentieth Century Fox, 2005. DVD.

Gibson, William. "The Gernsback Continuum." In *Burning Chrome*, 23–35. New York: Ace, 1987.

Gunn, James. "On the Lem Affair." *Science Fiction Studies* 4, no.3 (1977): 314–16.

———. "Toward a Definition of Science Fiction." *Speculations on Speculation*, edited by James Gunn and Matthew Candelaria, 5–12. Lanham, MD: Scarecrow Press, 2005.

Haraway, Donna. *Primate Visions: Gender, Race, and Nature in the World of Modern Science*. New York: Routledge, 1989.

———. *Simians, Cyborgs, and Women: The Reinvention of Nature*. New York: Routledge, 1991.

Haslam, Jason. "Inglourious Criticism, Basterd Fantasies: Rancière, Tarantino, and the Intellectual Spectacle of Hope." In *The Public Intellectual and the Culture of Hope*. Edited by Joel Faflak and Jason Haslam, 178–201. Toronto: University of Toronto Press, 2013.

———. "Memory's Guilted Cage: Delany's *Dhalgren* and Gibson's *Pattern Recognition*." *English Studies in Canada* 32, no.1 (2006): 77–104.

Heim, Michael. "The Cyberspace Dialectic." *The Digital Dialectic: New Essays on New Media*. Edited by Peter Lunenfeld, 24–45. Cambridge: MIT Press, 1999.

Hopkinson, Nalo, ed. *Whispers from the Cotton Tree Root: Caribbean Fabulist Fiction*. Montpelier, VT: Invisible Cities, 2000.

Hopkinson, Nalo and Uppinder Mehan, eds. *So Long Been Dreaming: Postcolonial Science Fiction and Fantasy*. Vancouver: Arsenal Pulp, 2004.

Jameson, Fredric. *Archaeologies of the Future: The Desire Called Utopia and Other Science Fictions*. London: Verso, 2005.

"Jose Chung's *From Outer Space*." *The X-Files: The Complete Third Season*. Aired 12 April 1996. Written by Darin Morgan. Directed by Rob Bowman. Twentieth Century Fox, 2005. DVD.

Kilgore, De Witt Douglas. *Astrofuturism: Science, Race, and Visions of Utopia in Space*. Philadelphia: University of Pennsylvania Press, 2003.

Lacan, Jacques. *Écrits: The First Complete Edition in English*. Translated by Bruce Fink. New York: Norton, 2006.

———. *The Four Fundamental Concepts of Psycho-analysis*. Edited by Jacques-Alain Miller. Translated by Alan Sheridan. London: Vintage, 1977.

Lavender, Isiah III. *Race in American Science Fiction*. Bloomington: Indiana University Press, 2011.

Lefanu, Sarah. *Feminism and Science Fiction*. Bloomington: Indiana University Press, 1989.

Leonard, Elisabeth Anne, ed. *Into Darkness Peering: Race and Color in the Fantastic*. Westport, CT: Greenwood, 1997.

Life Beyond Earth and the Mind of Man. Prod. National Aeronautics and Space Administration. 1975. *Internet Archive*. Accessed October 11 2014. https://archive.org/details/LifeBeyondEarth.

Miéville, China. "China Miéville Talk at KU, pt. 5." Presented 24 Sept. 2009. *YouTube*. Last modified 1 Nov. 2011. http://www.youtube.com/watch?v=EPABFo9cg2U/, accessed 17 January 2015.

———. *Embassytown*. New York: Del Rey, 2011.

———. "Gothic Politics: A Discussion with China Miéville." *Gothic Studies* 10, no.1 (2008): 61–70.

Millner, Andrew. *Locating Science Fiction*. Liverpool: Liverpool University Press, 2012.

Muñoz, José Esteban. *Cruising Utopia: The Then and There of Queer Futurity*. New York: New York University Press, 2009.

Nama, Adilifu. *Black Space: Imagining Race in Science Fiction Film*. Austin: University of Texas Press, 2008.

Nichols, Nichelle. *Beyond Uhura: Star Trek and Other Memories*. New York: Boulevard Books, 1995.

Nixon, Nicola. "Cyberpunk: Preparing the Ground for Revolution or Keeping the Boys Satisfied?" *Science Fiction Studies* 19, no.2 (1992): 219–35.

Pearson, Wendy. "Alien Cryptographies: The View from Queer." *Science Fiction Studies* 26, no.1 (1999): n.p. http://www.depauw.edu/sfs/backissues/77/pearson77.htm/, accessed 17 January 2015.

Pearson, Wendy Gay, Veronica Hollinger, and Joan Gordon. *Queer Universes: Sexualities in Science Fiction*. Liverpool: Liverpool University Press, 2008.

"Pusher." *The X-Files*. Written by Vince Gilligan. Aired 23 Feb. 1996. *The X-Files: The Complete Third Season*. Twentieth Century Fox, 2005. DVD.

Rancière, Jacques. *The Emancipated Spectator*. Translated by Gregory Elliott. London: Verso, 2009.

———. *The Politics of Aesthetics: The Distribution of the Sensible*. Translated by Gabriel Rockhill. New York: Continuum, 2004.

"Redux." *The X-Files*. Aired 2 and 9 Nov. 1997. Written by Chris Carter. Directed by R. W. Goodwin (Part 1) and Kim Manners (Part 2). *The X-Files: The Complete Fifth Season*. Twentieth Century Fox, 2005. DVD.

Reed, Lou. "I'll Be Your Mirror," *The Velvet Underground & Nico*, Disc Two of *Peel Slowly and See* Box Set. 1967, Polygram, 1995. CD.

"Revenging Angel." *Farscape*. Written by David Kemper. 2001. A&E Entertainment, 2011. Blu-ray.

Rieder, John. *Colonialism and the Emergence of Science Fiction*. Middletown, CT: Wesleyan University Press, 2008.

Roberts, Adam. *The History of Science Fiction*: New York: Palgrave, 2006.

———. *Science Fiction*. London: Routledge, 2000.

Roberts, Robin. *A New Species: Gender and Science in Science Fiction*. Urbana: University of Illinois Press, 1993.

Rocky Horror Picture Show. Written by Richard O'Brien. Directed by Jim Sharman. 1975. Twentieth Century Fox, 2010. Blu-ray.

de Saussure, Ferdinand. *Course in General Linguistics*. Intro. Jonathan Culler. Edited by Charles Bally and Albert Sechehaye in collaboration with Albert Reidlinger. Translated by Wade Baskin. Glasgow: Collins, 1974.

Scholes, Robert. "Lem's Fantastic Attack on Todorov." *Science Fiction Studies* 2, no.2 (1975): 166–67.

———. *Structural Fabulation: An Essay on Fiction of the Future*. Notre Dame: University of Notre Dame Press, 1975.

Sedgwick, Eve Kosofsky. *Epistemology of the Closet*. Updated with a New Preface. 1990. Berkeley: University of California Press, 2008.

Serenity. Written and directed by Joss Whedon. 2005. Universal, 2008. Blu-ray.

Smith, Sidonie. *Subjectivity, Identity, and the Body: Women's Autobiographical Practices in the Twentieth Century*. Bloomington: Indiana University Press, 1993.

Stockton, Sharon. "'The Self-Regained': Cyberpunk's Retreat to the Imperium." *Contemporary Literature* 36, no.4 (1995): 588–612.

Suvin, Darko. *Metamorphoses of Science Fiction*. New Haven: Yale University Press, 1979.

Thomas, Sheree R. ed. *Dark Matter: A Century of Speculative Fiction from the African Diaspora*. New York: Warner, 2000.

———. ed. *Dark Matter: Reading the Bones*. New York: Warner, 2004.

Todorov, Tzvetan. *The Fantastic: A Structural Approach to a Literary Genre*. Translated by Richard Howard. 1973. Forward by Robert Scholes. Ithaca: Cornell University Press, 1975.

Trekkies. Directed by Roger Nygard. Paramount, 1997. DVD.

Tucker, Jeffrey Allen. *A Sense of Wonder: Samuel R. Delany, Race, Identity, and Difference*. Middletown, CT: Wesleyan University Press, 2004.

"Unrealized Reality." Written by David Kemper. *Farscape*. Aired 23 Aug. 2002. A&E Entertainment, 2011. Blu-ray.

Vint, Sherryl. "Coding of Race in Science Fiction: What's Wrong with the Obvious?" In *Worlds of Wonder: Readings in Canadian Science Fiction and Fantasy Literature*. Edited by Jean-François Leroux and Camille R. LaBossière, 119–30. Ottawa: University of Ottawa Press, 2004.

Yaszek, Lisa. *The Self Wired: Technology and Subjectivity in Contemporary Narrative*. London: Routledge, 2002.

Žižek, Slavoj. "The Thing from Inner Space," *Angelaki: Journal of the Theoretical Humanities*, 4, no.3 (1999): 221–31.

Part I

Race/Gender/Science/Fiction

1 "The races of mankind"

The Race of Gender in "The Birth-mark" and *Mizora*

In nineteenth-century thought, projects relating to the definition and exploration of human identity ranged from the theological, to the philosophical and literary, to what could be called "identity science," which eventually led to the development of social scientific explorations of human identities in, for example, what we now call sociology and anthropology. Much of the focus in these early developments had to do with what was called the "sex question," and we can, of course, trace current concerns with sex/gender identity back to these nineteenth-century formulations, as Michel Foucault, Eve Kosofsky Sedgwick, and others have.[1] Likewise, much nineteenth-century proto-anthropological work concerned itself with the constitution of and relations between the so-called "races of man," up to and including those studies influenced by Darwin's *Descent of Man*, but notably also including earlier scientific work, such as the Romantic-era studies of race undertaken by J. F. Blumenbach, discussed in more detail below. These scientific projects were often used as "depth models" to provide a seemingly factual basis on which to ground social and cultural policy—in the United States, combinations of sex/gender and racial identity studies were used by different groups on either side of the abolitionist debate, just as they were regarding the transatlantic slave trade, and as they would be later with regard to enfranchisement and civil rights arguments from the Civil War forward.

Such uses of these racial and sexual studies, however, often expose a cultural—and indeed, semiotic—insecurity that then translates onto other suspicions about the boundaries between those categories, providing us with an especially rich area through which to study the fracture lines of conceptions of the American self. This chapter examines two particular literary incarnations of the science of race and sex/gender: Nathaniel Hawthorne's short story "The Birth-mark" (1846) and Mary E. Bradley Lane's utopia, *Mizora, a Prophecy* (1880–1881). I analyse these works' use of and participation in such discourses not to develop a larger material history of nineteenth-century science or other disciplines, but to examine some of the (unstable) semiotic foundations of ideas of race and sex/gender and their conjoined cultural deployment in this gestational phase of American SF.

Both of these works incorporate dominant epistemologies of gender and race in paradoxical movements of reinforcement and critique, exposing both categories as structures that are, in the very process of having their definitional boundaries policed, always transgressing those borders, undermining their own ramparts at the same time as they shore up disciplinary support. Beginning with the more subterranean attention paid to race and gender in "The Birth-mark," and then moving on to the overt analysis of these issues by Lane, this chapter argues that the specific sciences and more general discourses of race and gender are complexly interrelated in ways that can support but often undermine each other and the particular political projects they are put in service of, be it the conservative message inherent in Hawthorne's tale or the explicitly feminist and racist project of Lane's work.

I. MARKS OF BIRTH: GENDER, RACE, AND SCIENCE IN HAWTHORNE

Barbara Johnson concludes her influential essay on the construction of gender in Hawthorne's "The Birth-mark" by noting that the character Aminadab could be read as a racialized figure of the working class. After noting Aminadab's possible racial identification, Johnson asks, "Could some of these figures be discerned through a reading of another birthmark, the birthmark imprinted on the face of Toni Morrison's Sula?"[2] This question could be rephrased, pointing not toward that other birthmark, but to another reading of Hawthorne's "The Birth-mark," in which Johnson's argument about gender is doubled by racialized figures in the story itself. In the tale, an alchemical scientist named Aylmer, with the help of his servant Aminadab, attempts to remove a birthmark from the cheek of his wife, Georgiana. Aylmer, and eventually Georgiana herself, come to despise the hand-shaped birthmark, seeing it as, in Aylmer's words, "the visible mark of earthly imperfection" on Georgiana's body, which, excepting the mark, "came ... nearly perfect from the hand of Nature."[3] In the process of removing the mark, however, Aylmer comes to understand that "this Crimson Hand, superficial as it seems, has clutched its grasp into [Georgiana's] being" (51). Because of this grasp, Aylmer's final success in removing the mark results in his wife's death. Within this narrative of a murderous husband, as Johnson and others have argued, dominant constructions of masculinity and femininity are played out in a variety of ways, all of which centre on the figure of the mark itself. These gender constructions run parallel to similar depictions of race, and the two identity formations both support and are supported by each other. In the end, however, the combination of bigoted representations of gendered and raced "others" in the story makes possible a reading of a counter-narrative of miscegenist desire that, to a degree, undercuts the allegorical representation of white, patriarchal dominance.

As Jules Zanger has noted, critics have tended to focus on the "allegorical interpretation ... that regards the mark on [Georgiana's] cheek as the external sign of her human, imperfect condition and understands Aylmer's attempt to remove it as the expression of either scientific, rational, reformist presumption, or of too aspiring an idealism."[4] Other readings, however, have focused on the explicitly gendered aspects of this allegory, highlighting one of the political dimensions of Hawthorne's story. These readings rely on feminist critiques of the individualist underpinnings of the Enlightenment project, which form the troubled foundations of nineteenth-century transcendental thought. Detailing the difficulties of the Enlightenment construction of the "individual" and the subsequent claim to the "universal" nature of this construct, Sidonie Smith writes that this subject "positions on its border ... that which becomes identified culturally as other, exotic, unruly, irrational, uncivilized, regional, or paradoxically unnatural," as discussed in this book's introduction.[5] The borders between "what is and is not appropriate" to the universal individual, to use Smith's words, are especially seen in the relationship between (white and/or masculine) disembodiment and (racially "othered" and/or feminine) embodiment.[6]

These discussions are reinforced by recent analyses of early racial and gender science. Recalling China Miéville's comments, quoted in this book's introduction, that scientist figures in SF often serve primarily to reinforce socioeconomic hierarchies, many critics and scientific and cultural historians have shown that science as a disciplinary form of knowledge does not function as an unbiased epistemology that somehow transcends and thus escapes its surrounding culture.[7] In the eighteenth and nineteenth centuries, the European sciences of gender and race in many cases clearly echo the larger cultural bigotries inherent in contemporary definitions of the nature of "man," often relying, explicitly or implicitly, on religious justifications for those same biases. The scientific understanding of human sexual differentiation, with its denial to women of the rational, teleological, even utopian dialectic of history, was redoubled in discussions of race: the "other" of the dominant class was not just feminine, but also non-white.[8]

Indeed, sex and race were very much intertwined in eighteenth- and nineteenth-century scientific and social study.[9] Londa Schiebinger writes that, while there are problems with any overly generalised comparison, "scientists of that period saw sex and race as two aspects of the same problem."[10] Johann Friedrich Blumenbach is a case in point. Often seen as the "father" of modern anthropology, Blumenbach is also the originator of the contemporary taxonomy of race, and is often cited as popularising the term "Caucasian" to describe one of the "varieties of mankind."[11] His specific scientific theories of race, however, indicate the complex imbrication of sexual and racial identity. His massively influential *On the Natural Varieties of Mankind* (the first edition of which was published in 1775) begins with a discussion of "The part which each sex takes in the generation of the fœtus, and which of the two has the greatest influence," citing others' conclusions that the embryo "would lie forever buried as it were in eternal slumber, were it not aroused by the access and stimulus of the fertilizing seed of the male." Once again, woman is relegated to the body, while man is endowed with the ability to create life and, presumably, spirit. This conclusion, proven—somehow—"by direct demonstration," is then used as the ground on which

Blumenbach's racial theories are developed, making the scientific connection of race and sex complete.[12]

That Hawthorne's "The Birth-mark" engages in this ontological and scientific project is apparent throughout the story. Aylmer's rationality and its connection to a spiritual form of disembodiment, and implicitly Georgiana's converse physicality, form the narrator's introductory description of the scientist, which sets the story at the end of the eighteenth century, when Blumenbach and others were writing:

> In those days, when the comparatively recent discovery of electricity, and other kindred mysteries of nature, seemed to open new paths into the region of miracle, it was not unusual for the love of science to rival the love of woman, in its depth and absorbing energy. The higher intellect, the imagination, the spirit, and even the heart, might all find their congenial aliment in pursuits which ... would ascend from one step of powerful intelligence to another. ... We know not whether Aylmer possessed this degree of faith in man's ultimate control over nature. He had devoted himself, however, too unreservedly to scientific studies, ever to be weaned from them by any second passion. His love for his young wife might prove the stronger of the two; but it could only be by intertwining itself with his love of science, and uniting the strength of the latter to its own. (36–37)

Aylmer, as an "eminent proficient" of science, is pictured as one who places the "intellect, the imagination, [and] the spirit" above all things, and even subordinates his "heart," the physical metaphor for his passions, to his scientific and intellectual pursuits. Further, Aylmer's marriage is described as a distraction from his lab work—the love of his wife "*might* prove the stronger," but only if it paradoxically gives up its independent existence for one "united" with science. The general thrust of the passage is toward the imbrication of science with all other facets of human and natural existence: the "kindred mysteries of nature" may *include* spirit and affect (with love pointing toward both), but they can only "open paths into the region of miracle" through scientific endeavour. If love is treated, then, following the neo-Platonism of the transcendentalists, as the drive that can lead one toward the sublime, then subordinating that sense to a more directly intellectual appreciation (and control) of the sublime moves science out of the realm of physical nature altogether. Aylmer's characterisation thus falls neatly into what Robyn Wiegman calls the "white male citizen of Enlightenment thought [who] draws his particular suit of rights and privileges from ... rhetorical disembodiment."[13]

Meanwhile, Georgiana remains as yet unnamed, and is described in the opening paragraph only in terms of her physical beauty. Georgiana's embodiment is most often associated with the small birthmark on her left cheek, which "glimmer[s] to-and-fro with every pulse of emotion" (38).

To Aylmer, the mark "expressed the ineludible gripe, in which mortality clutches the highest and purest of earthly mould, degrading them into kindred with the lowest, and even with the very brutes" (39). The mark thus becomes a "symbol" (39) of humanity's inescapable embodiment. Within contemporary feminist readings of the text, that Georgiana's body becomes this symbol points to the fact that, in Johnson's words, the birthmark "is the mark of femininity itself."[14] The birthmark highlights the essentialised embodiment of women within patriarchal discourse, making the mark an ultimate signifier of (feminine) difference. This difference, then, can create a potential for "unruly," and "irrational" disruptions, leading Johnson to note "what Aylmer wishes to do in erasing the mark is to erase the difference—to erase sexual difference."[15] Aylmer's attempt to supercede what is, in the larger patriarchal imagination of the narrative, an immutable, natural structure of gender difference thus leads to Georgiana's narratively inevitable death.

There is yet another way in which critics have noted that the "Crimson Hand" on Georgiana's cheek becomes a signifier of femininity. The mark is actually a constantly multiple signifier; that is, its meaning changes depending on situation. In the first description of the birthmark, the narrator explains that various people "read" the mark in various ways: some saw it as a "token of ... magic endowments," while others, "exclusively of her own sex—affirmed that the Bloody Hand ... quite destroyed the effect of Georgiana's beauty" (38). The narrator sums up this variety in interpretation by noting that people's readings of the mark "varied exceedingly, according to the difference of temperament in the beholders" (38). The shifting of the mark's meaning looks forward to Smith's definition of the "other" of patriarchal ontology as the "unruly" and "irrational" subject.[16]

But nineteenth-century American discourse about gender did not exist in a vacuum. It was produced alongside of and in relation to racial discourse, raising the possibility that one can add to these feminist readings of Hawthorne's story a discussion of his deployment of contemporary racial categories. Expanding on her statement that "scientists of that period saw sex and race as two aspects of the same problem," Schiebinger argues that "women stood at the center of a debate concerning race at a time when the exclusion of both women and peoples of color from science was being formalized."[17] There has traditionally been a reticence to read Hawthorne's stories in terms of race, since Hawthorne's major works seem explicitly to avoid the discussions of slavery and race that so dominated his time (though he does discuss them in some of his letters, where he makes his anti-abolitionist stance quite clear). More recent critics have recently shown, however, that these issues do appear in Hawthorne's tales, albeit, in most cases, obliquely.[18] In readings such as these, a subtext of race and racial anxiety is seen to permeate the larger narrative, but is masked behind Hawthorne's supposedly unraced, "universal" allegories and the traditional interpretations thereof. Robert K. Martin notes, for example, that Hawthorne's creation of specifically gothic allegories is one entrance point into a reading of these racial "counternarratives," due to what H. L. Malchow, for one, sees as the parallels between gothic and racial language. Malchow writes that "Both the Gothic novel and racist discourse manipulate deeply buried anxieties, both dwell on the chaos beyond natural and rational boundaries, and massage a deep, often unconscious and sexual, fear of contamination, and both present the threatened destruction of the simple and the pure by the poisonously exotic."[19]

While this—admittedly general—comparison resonates more strongly with "Rappaccini's Daughter," in which a sexualised poisoning literally takes place, there are a series of intersections between "The Birth-mark" and racial discourse. These connections range from the "colouring" of characters and Aylmer's obsession, to the story's alchemical aspects, to its use of other scientific and religious discourses. In the following pages, these convergences are detailed in order to lay the groundwork for an analysis of the tale's troubled representation of white dominance and desire.

Consider Aylmer's connection to whiteness and the birthmark's connection to non-whiteness, specifically. Aylmer is described as a "pale philosopher" (42) who "could not restrain a strong convulsive shudder" when he saw the "intense glow of the birth-mark upon the whiteness of [Georgiana's] cheek" (43). Earlier, the birthmark is said to stand out "like a bas-relief of ruby on the whitest marble" (39). The "purity" of Georgiana's whiteness is threatened by the "exotic," non-white mark, causing Aylmer to react with horror, in keeping with Malchow's conclusions. Aylmer is obsessed with the creation of an absolute whiteness, untainted by any, in his eyes, extraneous pigmentation.

The story's scientific elements also contribute to a racialized reading. Aylmer's scientific pursuits are explicitly tied to alchemy, as other critics have detailed, and the science of alchemy is itself associated with the "purification" of base metals and "the perfection of the spirit," thus once again emphasising the movement toward disembodiment in Aylmer's scientific pursuits (Burns 148). Indeed, alchemy itself is, in particular readings, associated with the opposition between whiteness and blackness. In his well-known—if perhaps idiosyncratic—psychoanalytic reading of alchemy, Carl Jung includes a discussion of the importance of colours to alchemy, summarising the alchemical concepts of "*melanosis* (blackening), *leukosis* (whitening)," and "*nigredo* or blackness."[20] The transformation from blackness to whiteness in the alchemical process is framed as one of improvement. Connecting this general congruence specifically to skin tone again, one of Aylmer's creations is a cosmetic with which "freckles may be washed away as easily as the hands are cleansed. A stronger infusion would take the blood out of the cheek, and leave the rosiest beauty a pale ghost" (47).

Further connecting the emphasis on Aylmer's fascination with the paleness of skin to the story's scientific appropriations, other images in the story lend themselves to a racialized reading, specifically images of blood.

Cathy Boeckmann discusses the importance of blood in racial discourse, writing that:

> According to scientific understandings of racial difference, when white blood mingled with that of other races the resulting offspring were inferior to the white parent. If this happened on a larger scale, the race as a whole would be degraded. As William Benjamin Smith declared, the South—in its insistence on the strict social segregation of the color line—"stands for *blood*, for the '*continuous germ plasma' of the Caucasian race*."[21]

John Cullen Gruesser has similarly discussed Aylmer's obsession with whiteness and, while not dealing with the discourses of racial science, does note that Georgiana's birthmark "relates directly to [her] blood and all of the significance attached to that word, especially during the antebellum period."[22] Combining this statement with Boeckmann's argument, I would suggest that we could read Georgiana's mark racially: even if it's not clear that her "continuous germ plasma" is "literally" (in the scientific logic of the day) interrupted, still the mark is figured as a "bloody" disorder.

In this vein, there is another congruence between Hawthorne's story and the history of racial science that deserves noting. Blumenbach—the "racial scientist" discussed earlier who popularised the term "Caucasian" to describe whites—used a woman's skull as his image of ideal Caucasian beauty and, in his *On the Natural Varieties of Mankind*, he "named" the skull "Femina Georgianæ," in connection to the skull's supposed place of origin, in the Georgian region of the Caucasus.[23] While it has proven difficult to determine whether Hawthorne knew specifically of Blumenbach's "Caucasian" skull, certainly the relationship between the "white race" and this area of the world was fairly widespread by the mid-nineteenth century. As Bruce Baum points out, in addition to Blumenbach and before him Christoph Meiners, Oliver Goldsmith also associated the "European" "variety of the human species" specifically with the "Georgians" and the Caucasus more generally.[24] Hawthorne definitely knew Goldsmith's works,[25] and the possibility that he likewise knew of Blumenbach's discussion of skulls also exists, since Hawthorne's patron at the customs house, George Bancroft, had studied under Blumenbach, and Hawthorne does reference the scientist at least once (as Jennifer Mason has noted).[26] Even the fact that Georgiana's mark is seen by Aylmer as marring her beauty could be read racially, as the hierarchical structuring of race, following Blumenbach's explicitly Romantic version of scientific taxonomy, was often framed in terms of beauty. Such a connection, in any event, adds to a raced reading of the story, in which the otherwise "ideal" feminine beauty is supposedly marred by a small piece of non-white pigmentation.

Moving to more religiously inflected pseudoscientific racial epistemologies, that Georgiana's "fatal flaw" is described as a *mark* is not an innocent depiction in nineteenth-century America—especially not in the work of a writer as focused on religion as Hawthorne.[27] One of the central religious justifications of African slavery was the widely cited claim that black people were descended from Noah's son Ham and from Cain, who was popularly represented as having been given a mark by God to signify his displeasure. This widespread belief is perhaps nowhere better signaled than by efforts to discount it in the *Southern Presbyterian Review* in January 1850. The authors of the article "The Mark of Cain and Curse of Ham" write that "men of high distinction are found to satisfy themselves with saying that God has put the mark of Cain and the curse of Ham upon the Ethiopian race, and therefore doomed them to perpetual degradation."[28] A passage from Hawthorne's tale quoted earlier closely echoes these words: Aylmer sees the mark as an image of "the ineludible gripe" that "degrad[es]" "the highest and purest of earthly mould ... into kindred with the lowest, and even with the very brutes" (39). Degradation symbolised by a pigmentary problem, and a transformation from the "pure" to the animalistic, clearly connects Hawthorne's story to the racist discourse of his day.

This religious framing also finds its way into the "science" of race. Aylmer's description of the mark, here, as well as the narrator's association of the mark with the natural order of "human imperfection" (56) both recall the hierarchical nature of the Great Chain of Being, which was consistently used in eighteenth- and nineteenth-century philosophical and scientific studies, in Schiebinger's words, "to stem the leveling tide of democracy and abolitionism"[29] by forming, as William Smellie wrote in 1790, "the human species into castes and ranks" specifically along racial lines.[30] Anna C. Brickhouse notes that Hawthorne was aware of such scientific racism, writing that "In a brief 1839 notebook entry ... Hawthorne quotes from Sir Thomas Browne's *Pseudodoxia Epidemica*," in which the seventeenth-century author theorises "racial difference and its relation to reproduction."[31] Religious justifications of slavery and the scientific hierarchizing of race become mutually informing institutionalised apparatuses for the maintenance of racial hegemony.

Indeed, in "The Birth-mark," the character Aminadab is described in terms that strongly mimic the racist hierarchies of this science, which placed non-whites closer to the animal kingdom than whites on the Chain of Being. Aminadab's first physical appearance in the story is described as follows:

> there issued from an inner apartment a man of low stature, but bulky frame, with shaggy hair hanging about his visage, which was grimed with the vapors of the furnace. This personage had been Aylmer's under-worker during his whole scientific career, and was admirably fitted for that office by his great mechanical readiness, and the skill with which, while incapable of comprehending a single principle, he executed all the practical details of his master's experiments. With his vast strength, his shaggy hair, his smoky aspect, and the indescribable earthiness that incrusted him, he seemed to represent man's physical

> nature; while Aylmer's slender figure, and pale, intellectual face, were no less apt a type of the spiritual element. (43)

The allegorical language here closely parallels racist scientific discourse in creating a direct relationship between skin tone and mental capabilities on the one hand, and embodiment and spirituality on the other, while placing both pairs in a hierarchical relationship. "Smokiness" and incrusted "earthiness" relate to being "incapable of comprehending a single principle"; "paleness" and a lack of physical strength relate to being "intellectual" and "spiritual." Importantly, the implicit racing of Aminadab also helps to clarify the racial signification of Georgiana's birthmark, because, early in the story, Aminadab looks at her and says, in his most extended verbal expression, "If she were my wife, I'd never part with that birth-mark" (43). In other words, one character who is coded as non-white does not see anything "wrong" in the image of non-whiteness attached to another character.[32]

II. MARK OF DESIRE: MISCEGENATION AND THE LOSS OF SELF

I do not want to be so reductive, though, as to determine the races of the characters in any literal fashion, turning the story into a kind of racial *roman à clef*, in which Georgiana's mark becomes the image of an extant version of the mythical "one drop" of non-white blood that defined race for some. Given the shifting symbolic nature of the mark, such a reductive reading would be doomed to failure.[33] The story's continuous use of the scientific and other discourses that inform racist and sexist assumptions can, however, point to the ways in which the imbrication of identity categories can lead to a slippery taxonomic coding, in which the supposedly clear lines between categories begin to fade. In Part II of this book, I will expand on this categorical problem by tying it to psychoanalytic theories of the performative nature of identity, as specifically framed by Judith Butler in her deconstruction of hierarchically ordered binaries of identity. Hawthorne's story sets the stage for that argument by subtextually indicating the fragile nature of Aylmer's scientific surety and, by extension, the equal fragility of the categories of identity based on that science. In this case, Hawthorne's story explicitly undercuts the notion of the self-contained and fully self-aware Enlightenment individual, but in so doing also undermines the implicit biases in the social construction of that individual and its relation to those it "positions on its border," to use Sidonie Smith's words again.[34]

Specifically, in Hawthorne's story, Aylmer's "spiritual," "intellectual," and "pale" dominance is *constantly* failing. He may aspire "towards the infinite," but "his most splendid successes were almost invariably failures" (49). Aylmer cannot achieve his aspirations, his will is not strong enough, and so he cannot be the *completely* self-contained, transcendental individual. This fact is further emphasised by his reliance on both Aminadab and Georgiana, as figures of "otherness," for his experiments. His (white) intellectual nature cannot find expression except through the (non-white) physical labour of Aminadab. And, more importantly, Aylmer's success (the triumph of his dominance) in removing Georgiana's mark (the visible representation of her chaotic difference) is pictured as his *ultimate* failure. Aylmer exclaims to Georgiana,

> "My peerless bride, it is successful! You are perfect!"
>
> "My poor Aylmer!" [Georgiana] repeated, with a more than human tenderness. "You have aimed loftily!—you have done nobly! Do not repent, that, with so high and pure a feeling, you have rejected the best that earth could offer. Aylmer—dearest Aylmer—I am dying!" (55)

Aylmer's loftiness and nobility, his "most favored" position in the world, are emptied out at precisely the moment that they erase the mark of otherness and inferiority.

Paralleling the surface Romantic allegory that damns the overly-rational, the racialized subtext, which implies the unstable nature of identity categories, perhaps makes it closest to the surface in a scene that occurs just before the mark is removed. While studying his scientific texts, Aylmer "failed not to gaze often at the fatal Hand, and not without a shudder. Yet once, by a strange and unaccountable impulse, he pressed it with his lips" (54). Aylmer's desire to erase the mark of difference coexists with an inverse desire *for* the same mark—his desire for Georgiana is paradoxically tied to both her racialized embodiment *and* to the moment of racial transcendence as the "ideal" Caucasian beauty.

Gruesser reads this moment as an indication that "the mark comes to assume the character of a fetish" for Aylmer.[35] Expanding this suggestion, one could read Hawthorne's description here as echoing, at least, the discourse surrounding what came to be known as miscegenation.[36] Aylmer manifests the double motion of a stereotypically presented miscegenist desire originating from the position of power in a racial hierarchy: he simultaneously expresses a longing for connection with someone who is differently identified, while also expressing "a fatal desire to pull apart one body from another," as Shirley Samuels describes the representation of miscegenation in Civil War America.[37] Enacting Butler's theoretical formation that dominance, in effect, presupposes for its own self-definition the very otherness that it would try to stamp out, Aylmer cannot consciously understand or put into words the reasons for his "strange and unaccountable" sexual desire for the mark itself. This difficulty is signaled even in the language of the above passage, with its quadruple negative structure of "failing not to … and not without." Aylmer fails to understand or communicate this desire precisely because, were he to do so, his own "most favored" position would be exposed as being contingent on the very mark he consciously despises. What I would call Aylmer's miscegenist desire here thus points to the tentative nature of the boundaries of his "lofty" position.

I want to emphasise that I am not saying we can or should look at this story as an overt allegory of the deconstruction of the dialectical structure of race categories and relations in the nineteenth-century United States, nor can it be read as an allegory of a victory by the oppressed, since even the frustrated, non-transcendent moment described above figures the racial and gendered "other" as the passive object of white male desire, and because Aylmer's failure is, on the surface of the story, related to what the narrator sees as Aylmer's overly proud attempt to alter Georgiana's place on the Chain of Being.[38] The implicit critique of the racial and gender aspects of Aylmer's science thus coexists with the racist and sexist aspects of the larger narrative's own teleology. If one recognizes that Hawthorne's allegory of dominance can *also* imply its own failure—much like Aylmer's narrative of his own experiments—then one can also see the ingrained contradictions lying within the scientific discourses of identity that, in turn, inform later SF interrogations of those categories. The multiplicitous signification of Georgiana's birthmark could, in this reading, symbolise the semiotic slipperiness surrounding gender and race in this SF tale: a slipperiness that forces the narrative to reflect back on itself.

III. DEGEN(D)ERATION: *MIZORA* AND THE SEXING OF RACIAL SCIENCE

If "The Birth-mark" can create these subterranean contradictions, then Mary E. Bradley Lane's utopian novel, *Mizora: A Prophecy*, explicitly delves into this textual underworld. Originally serialised in the *Cincinnati Commercial* from 1880–1881, and republished in book form in 1890, *Mizora* has recently been reexamined for its importance in the history of women's utopian writing, having been described as "the first portrait of an all-female, self-sufficient society."[39] In the novel, the Russian narrator, Vera Zarovitch, escapes after being exiled to Siberia by the Russian government for supporting the Polish Insurrection of 1863. However, she ends up being adrift in the ocean, passes through a misty barrier, and ends up in the subterranean land of Mizora, a land inhabited only by women.[40] Lane's novel has been read as a "possible influence" on Charlotte Perkins Gilman's *Herland* since, as Duangrudi Suksang writes, these "utopias both depict homogeneously Caucasian separatist feminist societies, which have emerged as a result of women's revolt against men's oppression."[41] While *Mizora*'s place within the specifically feminist aspects of the utopian literary tradition has been recently reasserted, what Suksang remains rightfully uncomfortable with is the phrase "Caucasian separatist." Few critics have done extended readings of Lane's text, but those who have generally tend either to ignore the violently racist eugenicist and genocidal elements of Lane's text, to dismiss those elements as a product of her times, or, as Suksang does, to see this racism as tainting Lane's "otherwise radical feminist stance."[42] This has begun to change with the publication of Jean Pfaelzer's excellent edition of the work, and with scholarship by Katherine Broad and Christine Mahady, among others, though the text's direct equation between feminism and racism still makes critics uncomfortable.[43] Broad makes a convincing case, similar to Suksang's but also pointing toward mine, that "Labeling a fantasy of white motherhood 'feminist' and treating whiteness as incidental but not foundational to that femininity overlooks how constructions of whiteness shape reproductive possibilities and service women's bodies in the name of racial purity."[44] Still, as noted in the abstract to her article, she argues that "Lane's conceptualization of race in imagining the ideal matriarchy compromises what have been celebrated as *Mizora*'s radical and feminist promises."[45] In other words, as Pfaelzer writes in the introduction to the text, "*Mizora* binds the era's racial anxiety and sexual anxiety together."[46] Like Georgiana and her birthmark, the racism of the "world" of Mizora and its radical assertion of women's superiority cannot be simply divorced; building on Pfaelzer's reading, and running somewhat counter to Broad's and others', I would argue that they are in fact inextricable from each other. Moving from this point, however, I turn to the ways in which the logically flawed relationship between the text's feminism and its racism do appear as ruptures in the narrative. *Mizora*—on the surface—does equate its proto-feminist politics with a racist and eugenic agenda and to grasp the text more fully one must analyse the ways in which feminism and racism do coincide within the text. But still there are moments in the text, as in the "The Birth-mark," that run counter to this narrative—not in ways that can "rescue" the politics of the text, but that can point to the political contradictions these conjoined discourses contained even in the nineteenth century.[47]

Mizora relies precisely on those biological paradigms that "saw sex and race as two aspects of the same problem."[48] While Lane specifically uses this science as the foundation of her gender critique, this connection leads to difficulties surrounding race and eugenics, difficulties that, I argue, *are* discussed *as* difficulties—albeit occasionally—on the surface of the text. Rather than simply see its gender politics as radical, and its racism as an "unfortunate product of its time," as the phrase goes, I want to point to the ways in which both function within the larger discursive paradigms of race and gender that Lane is exploiting. Lane's text becomes important, then, not for any "prophetic" power, and not in pieces, where its feminism can be lauded and its racism ignored; instead, the text is important because the problems it tries to dance through are central in the recent history of feminist and anti-racist criticism and action. If *Mizora* does serve as prophecy, then, it is not for a future feminist utopia, but for the difficulty, raised perhaps inadvertently by Hawthorne and discussed by Audre Lorde nearly exactly a hundred years later, of using "*the master's tools*" to "*dismantle the master's house*."[49]

In *Mizora*, contemporary connections between sex and race are taken to an extreme and, in fact, to a point of equivalence. This connection begins to be formed in the early part of the narrative only by association: whenever the narrator mentions the skin colour of the Mizorans, she immediately makes a comment about their sex. The narrator writes that, just after she arrives in Mizora, she "frequented a vast gallery filled with paintings and statues of women, noble looking, beautiful women, but still—nothing but women. The fact that they were all blondes, singular as it might appear, did not so much impress me. Strangers came and went, but among the multitude of faces I met, I never saw a man's" (20). She describes Mizora as "a nation of *fair, exceedingly fair* women doing without" men (21–22; my emphasis). These early descriptions hint that there is a connection between the women's skin tone and the fact that there are no men, but it is only relatively late in the work that this connection is defined purely as a racial one; that is, sex and race are treated as equivalent scientific and identificatory categories. Describing the non-Mizoran "real" world to the Preceptress (Mizora's leader), Vera, the narrator, says, "we are not all of one race." The Preceptress' response immediately on hearing this is to "quietly ask[]: '*Are there men in your country?*'" (89). Then, when Vera asks the Preceptress of Mizora the question that haunts three quarters of the text—"Where are the men of this country?"—the Preceptress answers, "*There are none. ... The race became extinct three thousand years ago*" (93). The equivalences made between sex and race in eighteenth- and nineteenth-century science are here rehearsed explicitly.

But, as Kristine J. Anderson has briefly noted, this is not an unreflexive or purposeless use of sex as a racial category.[50] In fact, as Broad argues, "In *Mizora*, assertions about gender are articulated through racial differences, determining gendered identities through racial boundaries just as, in [contemporary] medical studies, racial boundaries were policed through gender differentiation."[51] In other words, it is only through the explicitly scientific interrelations of the sex and race that Lane can make her critique of the patriarchy. If maleness is a racial category, then it can be subject to the findings of contemporary racial science, specifically the notions of degeneracy and extinction. As pointed to in the discussion of Hawthorne, much nineteenth-century racial science, implicitly relying on the spatial metaphors of the Great Chain of Being, proposed that, first, several grades of humanity existed along a chain of evolution, with black Africans usually placed at the lowest grade, and white Northern Europeans at the highest, and, second, that these gradations were mirrored in differing degrees of intelligence, enlightenment, and, most importantly, civilisation. To cite one influential example, Sir Francis Galton—Charles Darwin's cousin and the man who coined the term "eugenics," and who was himself an author of a utopia—wrote in 1869 that "the average intellectual standard of the negro race is some two grades below" the standard for whites. He further argued that the average white traveller was intellectually superior to even the highest grade of "negroes in their native country." "The result is familiar enough," Galton writes, "It is seldom that we hear of a white traveller meeting with a black chief whom he feels to be the better man."[52]

Because of this supposedly innate racial gradation, when a "lower" race comes into contact with a higher civilisation, the former, because of the processes of natural selection, would either evolve, or—and this second form was generally perceived as much more likely—would begin to fail and even become extinct (and this certainly informs the popular nineteenth-century assumption that Native North Americans were a "Vanishing Race"). As Galton argued:

> Civilization is a new condition imposed upon man by the course of events, just as in the history of geological changes new conditions have continually been imposed on different races of animals. They have had the effect either of modifying the nature of the races through the process of natural selection, whenever the changes were sufficiently slow and the race sufficiently pliant, or of destroying them altogether, when the changes were too abrupt or the race unyielding. The number of the races of mankind that have been entirely destroyed under the pressure of the requirements of an incoming civilization, reads us a terrible lesson.[53]

The "terrible lesson" that Galton points to was seen, in fact, as a direct threat, because of the circular nature of evolutionary theory as it was applied to the "races of mankind" and to their civilisations. While the biological evolution of the white race was reflected in European civilisation, that civilisation was also the support that kept the race from degenerating into a lower form. As Boeckmann has argued, when it comes to the relationship between biological and cultural development, "it is hard to point to the prior cause in an evolutionary series."[54] In any event, in a time when the terms "race" and "nation" were often interchangeable, evolutionary theory was seen as being as applicable to civilisation as it was to biology; however, most early anthropologists saw it as much more likely for a higher race and civilisation to degenerate into a lower form than for a lower race to evolve to a higher state, leading to what David Theo Goldberg has called "the panics over moral and physical degeneration."[55]

Mizora explicitly relies on the theories of racial degeneration, as Pfaelzer notes (xxxii), and builds on Galton's pseudoscience of eugenics, as Broad details.[56] While Pfaelzer, however, sees Lane's use of these theories as in large simply reflecting a fear of the "national peril" of racial degeneration, pointing both to "America's obsession with race" (xxxi) and to the perceived need for a revivified domestic foundation to society, I would follow Broad in suggesting that, because of the slippery connections between race and sex discussed earlier, Lane is more specifically—and more problematically—transforming these racist scientific conclusions into a very particular critique of the patriarchy. In telling the story of Mizora's development as a "nation of women," the Preceptress says, "Many ages ago this country was peopled by two races—male and female. The male race were rulers in public and domestic life. … Woman was a beast of burden. She was regarded as inferior to man, mentally as well as physically" (95). Moving from the prehistoric to the modern period, the Preceptress traces a history that is obviously modeled on the history of America, complete with references to a Revolution, the formation of the republic, chattel slavery, and wars that clearly parallel the War with Mexico and the Civil War. From here, though, the Preceptress' history verges into the audience's future, when women rise up against what is seen as a violent, self-defeating, and primitive male government. These times, the Preceptress says, have "a depressing effect upon me," because of "the degradation of the human race that they force me to recall" (92). The patriarchy, composed of the degenerate, low race of men, thus becomes "extinct" when women bring a radical change to society. Relying on the scientific conjoining of sex and race, Lane is able to critique a male-ordered civilisation as a low form of humanity.

But Lane goes further than this in her deployment of racial and sexual science. Her critique is inextricably tied to the figuring of a matriarchal society as an evolution of civilisation beyond Lane's own nineteenth-century America. If men are a degenerative race, then women must be seen as the generative race. Such a formulation also derives from, and lends itself to, the specifics of sexual difference in terms of reproduction, a fact Lane returns to at this point in the work. Going beyond the generic boundaries of the utopian fiction as travelogue, Lane explicitly rewrites science as a female pursuit—female in that it is performed best and performed only by women and female in that the scientific principles of nature itself are seen within a matriarchal epistemology, as opposed to the patriarchal understandings proposed by Enlightenment and post-Enlightenment scientific thinkers. While Blumenbach posited all generative power in the "fertilizing seed of the male," Mizoran scientists, when they discover the true "secret of life," disprove his theory. After the Preceptress states that the male race had gone extinct, she leads the narrator to a microscope, which displays "An exquisitely minute cell in violent motion." The Preceptress explains this sight to Vera:

> "Daughter," she said, solemnly, "you are now looking upon the germ of *all* Life; be it animal or vegetable, a flower or a human being, it has that one common beginning. We have advanced far enough in Science to control its development. Know that the MOTHER is the only important part of all life. In the lowest organisms no other sex is apparent." I sat down and looked at my companion in a frame of mind not easily described. (103)[57]

Vera's shock at this revelation would be the shock of someone raised on the cultural paradigms informed by the patriarchal science of such people as Blumenbach. So, Lane's novel uses a complex negotiation of scientific discourse: it moves sexual science to racial science through the slippery taxonomical link between them, and then it moves back to an explicitly sexual science, and in so doing posits the patriarchy as racially degenerate, and the matriarchy as biologically and socially generative; the "MOTHER" becomes the essence of evolutionary progress and generation itself.

Despite this apparently progressive use of science to point to an empowering of women—the trajectory that Anderson briefly outlines—it needs to be recognised that Lane's text still participates in racism as it has come to be seen, and indeed as some thinkers in Lane's time saw it. The racist aspect of Lane's text can also be explained through the conclusions reached by Galton on evolution and eugenics. Quoting from Galton's *Hereditary Genius*, A. S. Weber states that "Galton recommends explicitly ... that weak races should be encouraged to marry late and reduce their offspring and that 'it would be quite practicable to produce a highly-gifted race of men by judicious marriages during several consecutive generations.'"[58] Indeed, in the preface to the 1892 edition of *Hereditary Genius*, Galton frames this project in terms that resonate strongly with *Mizora*, writing:

> It is earnestly to be hoped that inquiries will be increasingly directed into historical facts, with the view of estimating the possible effects of reasonable political action in the future, in gradually raising the present miserably low standard of the human race to one in which the Utopias in the dreamland of philanthropists may become practical possibilities.[59]

The Mizorans follow precisely this chilling "reasonable political action" in order to produce, to misquote Galton, "a highly gifted race of women."

For the Mizorans to maintain the quality of their society, they must also eliminate any impure or degenerative being that may arise in their midst. Picking up on Lamarckian evolutionary theory, the Mizorans attest that a race or civilisation, unless kept pure from adulteration by lower forms and by "low" activities, would degenerate over time, just as, for Lamarck, generally speaking, offspring inherited both their parents' innate characteristics and the effects of the parents' actions, or the results of their "habits."[60] The Preceptress argues to Vera that "It is the duty of every generation to prepare the way for a higher development of the next," and therefore Mizorans "devote the most careful attention to the Mothers of our race. No retarding mental or moral influences are ever permitted to reach her" (104). This logic, of course, meant no contact with men, as a degraded race; additionally, however, as the Preceptress earlier states, non-white races had to go, too.[61] So, when looking through the hall that contains portraits of the original male leaders of thousands of years past, Vera notes:

> I had observed that dark hair and eyes were as indiscriminately mingled in these portraits as I had been accustomed to find them in the living people of my own and other countries. I drew the Preceptress' attention to it.
>
> "We believe that the highest excellence of moral and mental character is alone attainable by a fair race. The elements of evil belong to the dark race."...
>
> "And what became of the dark complexions?"
>
> "We eliminated them." (92)

Unlike the men, who seem to have become extinct passively, the Mizorans commit an active genocide on those racialized others who don't fit into their white supremacist logic: the same scientific logic that leads to the radical critique of the patriarchy envisioned by Lane, shown here in its everyday, non-fantastic garb of racist eugenics. Rather than work against her feminist project, then, as some of today's critics would and do see, the violent genocidal racism of this text is part and parcel of the sciences she uses to form that "progressive" project. Just as Donna Haraway defines cyborg science and politics, so too are Mizora's science and politics "both a feminist practice" and an oppressive "strategy," albeit Mizora's science is predicated on discovering the Earth Mother origin myth that Haraway's cyborg denies.[62] So, within the scientific logic of the text, the land of Mizora can be a functioning feminist matriarchy *only* because it is a functioning genocidal regime, and *vice versa*.

IV. CRITIQUING UTOPIAN WHITENESS, OR REFLECTION ON "PERFECTION"

The question can still be asked: does the coterminous nature of the novel's feminism and its racism make Lane's novel itself racist, as Suksang asserts? Does it become a utopian proposal for the benefits of racial eugenics? A simple "yes" can clearly apply, especially since the narrator, in her introductory statements, describes Mizora as "that ideal life that is possible for our remote posterity" (7). I would argue, though, that we can also see at certain points in the work recognition of the political problems of this embedded racism. Just after the Preceptress' chilling statement about eliminating the "dark complexions," we see one of the few moments when Vera critiques the Mizorans, even though she withholds the comment—a silence that is perhaps due to the fact that she herself has dark hair and is worried that she may become a victim of Mizora's "eliminations." Vera contemplates the issue:

> In candidly expressing herself about the dark complexions, my companion had no intention or thought of wounding my feelings. So rigidly do they adhere to the truth in Mizora that it is of all other things pre-eminent, and is never supposed to give offense. The Preceptress but gave expression to the belief inculcated by centuries of the teachings and practices of her ancestors. I was not offended. It was her conviction. Besides, I had the consolation of secretly disagreeing with her. I am still of the opinion that their admirable system of government, social and political, and their encouragement and provision for universal culture of so high an order, had more to do with the formation of superlative character than the elimination of the dark complexion. (92–93)

Vera here engages in the same form of apology for the Mizorans that some may be tempted to engage in with Lane herself—that the racism is simply a product of the context and can therefore be ignored. Additionally, though, there is a tension in this passage between the assertion of the "pre-eminence" of truth in Mizora, and Vera's denial of that assertion, between Vera's claims for Mizora as an ideal, and her condemnation of the means through which they achieved it.

Symbolically, as well, the unadulterated whiteness of Mizora is subtly associated with stagnancy and death. Vera describes "an event … of so singular and unexpected a character for that country that it requires particular description … the death of a young girl." The funeral is described in detail:

> The procession was very long and headed by the mother, dressed and veiled in black. Behind her were the sisters carrying the body. It rested upon a litter composed entirely of white rosebuds. The sisters wore white, their faces concealed by white veils. Each wore a white rosebud pinned upon her bosom. They were followed by a long procession of young girls, schoolmates and friends of the dead. They were all dressed in white, but were not veiled. Each one carried a white rosebud. (126)

After she textually records the dirge that the funeral procession chants (which includes the line "The grave is not for the roses of youth"), Vera continues:

> the mother first and then each sister took from her bosom the white rosebud and dropped it into the grave. Then followed her schoolmates and companions who each dropped in the bud she carried. A carpet of white rosebuds was thus formed, on which the body, still reclining upon its pillow of flowers, was gently lowered.
>
> The body was dressed in white, and over all fell a veil of fine white tulle. A more beautiful sight I can never see than that young, lovely girl in her last sleep with the emblems of youth, purity and swift decay forming her pillow, and winding-sheet. … The remainder of the procession of young girls then came forward and dropped their rosebuds upon it, completely hiding from view the young and beautiful dead. (127)

The whiteness of the Mizorans is here staged, over the course of several pages, until it almost seems—to echo Joyce—that "white roses were general all over Mizora." The superficial reading is, of course, that the whiteness symbolises the "purity" of the dead girl and that the heavy symbolism is used to spite death, but even Vera's analysis is slightly more complicated, noting that, in addition to "youth" and "purity," the roses symbolise "swift decay." Moreover, the whiteness of the roses is echoed not only in the staging of the body, but also of all of the other young girls, to the point that the entire scene is rendered flat, with each part indistinguishable from the other, the landscape blurring into the people, and the dead mirroring the living. Only the mother, framed in black, offsets this scene. But even this contrast has disappeared by the end of the scene, leaving an indistinguishable whiteness symbolising the unending sameness, and inescapable lack of distinguishing individuality and life, that characterises Mizora. This nearly complete whiteness, offset by one image of blackness, and indeed the whiteness and geographical structure of Mizora itself, maps neatly onto Toni Morrison's analysis of the figure of whiteness in nineteenth-century American literature: it is an image of "impenetrable whiteness," the "white form that rises from the mists at the end of the journey," the "white curtain and the 'shrouded human figure' with skin 'the perfect whiteness of the snow,'" all offset by the single figure in black.[63] For Morrison, whiteness in these figurations is "mute, meaningless, unfathomable, pointless, frozen, veiled, curtained, dreaded, senseless, implacable."[64] The veiled, hidden, concealed, decaying, and beautifully dead Mizorans seem not so out of place in this description. The whiteness of Mizora's inhabitants, symbolically rendered, again points to an underlying tension in the presentation of Mizora, in which the whiteness that characterises its perfection also characterises its ultimate stagnation.

This tension also informs the ending of the text. Vera goes back to the "real world," taking along her closest Mizoran companion, Wauna. They travel through North America in their insulated and warm Mizoran vehicle, seeing, along the way, some "Esquimaux," whom Wauna "presumed were animals" (143). After reaching Europe and then America, Wauna's Mizoran nature succumbs to the degeneracy that surrounds her, and she grows ill. Vera tries to take her home, but they cannot find their vehicle, which had been left with the "Esquimaux" for safe keeping. Vera then states, "Our progress, therefore, depended entirely upon the Esquimaux. ... Like all low natures, the Esquimaux are intensely selfish. ... In a miserable Esquimaux hut, on a pile of furs, I saw the flame of a beautiful and grandly noble life die out" (146). Broad asserts that "Wauna's death do[es] not suggest that the Mizoran ethic of purity is recognized as untenable or undesirable."[65] Certainly, her death is figured as being largely the fault of the racially degraded "Esquimaux," and so can be read in this fashion, as a racist assertion of Vera's final recognition of the rightness of Mizora's eugenicist practices; however, I would point out that Wauna is emphatically the weak figure in this final section of the text. She comes to embody all of the characteristics of nineteenth-century feminine debility, as Pfaelzer briefly notes, but this debility is figured as a failing specifically of her race. As with Aylmer and Georgiana, Wauna's death is presented as the result, in part, of the white race's movement past physicality as such.

This reading can be expanded to gesture to a disruption of the text's superficial eugenics. Contrary to Broad's conclusion, Wauna's weakness is explicitly tied to her inability to survive cold temperatures, which we are told early in the narrative is a common failing of Mizorans as a race. In other words, the Mizorans lack an ability that, in the text and in nineteenth-century logic, is the defining characteristic of the "Esquimaux" (as Blumenbach gestures to in the 1795 edition of his text).[66] The racism that Wauna spouts—and that forms the basis of Mizoran society—is aimed at a group who possess a strength Wauna and Mizora lack. Lane's text, then, can be read as what Haraway refers to as the "weaving" that "oppositional cyborgs" exercise between the poles of resistance and oppression.[67] Lane appropriates the patriarchal science of her time in order to turn it against the patriarchy itself, while also upholding and simultaneously critiquing the racism of that same science. She needs to assert the legitimacy of racial science in order to authenticate her use of it for a critique of the patriarchy—and, one could add, a critique of heteronormativity[68]—but at the same time the legitimacy of racial science is placed under erasure, as it were, both by the reasons for Wuana's death and by Vera "secretly disagreeing" with the Preceptress' opinion of "dark complexions." In addition, this double movement could be read as an inverted critique of the separatist politics that would arise out of the abolitionist movement and the racialized nationalisms of modernity.

V. THE LAST LAUGH

These inverted countertextual critiques in both *Mizora* and "The Birth-mark" are perhaps signaled best at the end of Hawthorne's story. The tale ends with Aminadab's "hoarse, chuckling laugh" (56), which seems aimed at no one in particular, implying the "under-worker's" understanding of the specific failures of the "mastery" exercised over him. The conclusion of that tale with Aminadab and his mocking voice points to a realisation that the borders of dominance are not completely static, but are formed in terms of an "other," be it through race, gender, sexuality, or any of a variety of ideological identity categories. Aminadab's vocalised narrative closure can be read to show that while the ideological construction of whiteness and blackness as opposing forces does serve to support racism, scientific or otherwise, it also creates a simultaneous affirmation and cancellation of any claims to the originality or self-containment of (racialized/gendered) identity. The nineteenth century and the beginnings of modernity, locked within the specific scientific cultural logic arising from the Enlightenment, thus find their origins in attempts to categorise, identify, and label—taxonomies that can be both silencing and enabling, but which, in any event, always leave the undefined lingering and threatening in the background, waiting for the "last laugh." The instability of semiotic identification is thus brought to the surface at these moments, if only to be denied by the authoritative narrative voice.

This chaotic laughter will haunt the remaining chapters of this book, in which the tattered edges of the taxonomies of race and gender are explored more thoroughly in works that bring to the fore the psychologically performative, semiotic play of identity, and its radical undermining of the very notions that Hawthorne and Lane, to varying degrees, unsuccessfully attempt to maintain. Before turning to those edges, however, the next chapter will expand on the fears found in the works of Hawthorne and Lane, fears surrounding the necessary disembodiment of a "pure" and rational whiteness. If, in "The Birth-mark," disembodiment leads to the death of earthly (im)perfection, and in *Mizora* to a weakness that cannot survive the real world, then the figures of Tarzan of the Apes and Anthony "Buck" Rogers attempt to recoup and perfect a physical white masculinity in the face of the scientific and social revolutions of the twentieth century.

NOTES

1. I use the awkward phrase "sex/gender" here because while it is often important to distinguish the two for feminist political interventions (as we have learned from Simone de Beauvoir forward), it is much more difficult to talk about them as being separate in the nineteenth-century imagination—and their conceptual and material intersection are still at play today. I do invoke the usual use of the division (sex-biology; gender-culture) elsewhere.
2. Barbara Johnson, "Is Female to Male as Ground Is to Figure?" in *Feminism and Psychoanalysis*, edited by Richard Feldstein and Judith Roof (Ithaca: Cornell University Press, 1989), 268.
3. Nathaniel Hawthorne, "The Birth-mark," in *Mosses from an Old Manse*, The Centenary Edition of the Works of Nathaniel Hawthorne 10 (Columbus: Ohio State University Press, 1974), 37. Unless otherwise noted, subsequent quotations are from this edition and cited parenthetically.
4. Jules Zanger, "Speaking the Unspeakable: Hawthorne's 'The Birthmark,'" *Modern Philology* 80, no.4 (1983): 364.
5. Sidonie Smith, *Subjectivity, Identity, and the Body: Women's Autobiographical Practices in the Twentieth Century* (Bloomington: Indiana University Press, 1993), 9–10.
6. For example, see Robyn Wiegman's essay comparing Hawthorne's "The Birthmark" to Ralph Ellison's identically titled story, "The Anatomy of Lynching," *Journal of the History of Sexuality* 3, no.3 (1993): 445–67. Wiegman explains that "in nineteenth-century scientific discourses on the feminine, ... cultural anxieties about (white) women's place in the emergent public sphere are mediated by returning her to the body and its ascribed inferiorities" (448–49). This feminine embodiment is placed in direct opposition to "masculine *disembodiment* ... where the rationality of the mind surpasses ... the physical limitations of the body" (449). Wiegman updates this article in her book, *American Anatomies: Theorizing Race and Gender* (Durham: Duke University Press, 1995). I use the earlier version here for stylistic reasons.
7. Miéville, China. "Gothic Politics: A Discussion with China Miéville." *Gothic Studies* 10, no.1 (2008): 61–70.
8. Haraway makes the cultural connection between racial and sexual constructions explicit, writing that "The *body* in western political theory is not capable of citizenship (rational speech and action); the body is merely particular, not general, not mindful, not light. It is sex (woman) to mind (man); dark (colored) to light (white)" (*Primate Visions: Gender, Race, and Nature in the World of Modern Science* [New York: Routledge, 1989], 154). For a brief overview of

race in Enlightenment thought, see Henry Louis Gates, Jr. ("Writing 'Race' and the Difference It Makes," in *"Race," Writing, and Difference*, edited by Henry Louis Gates, Jr. [Chicago: University of Chicago Press, 1986], 1–20); for a more extended discussion, see David Theo Goldberg, *The Racial State* (Oxford: Blackwell, 2002).

9. The relationship between gender especially and contemporary science has also been discussed. See, for example, Angela N. H. Creager, Elizabeth Lunbeck, and Londa Schiebinger, eds., *Feminism in Twentieth-Century Science, Technology, and Medicine* (Chicago: University of Chicago Press, 2001).
10. Londa Schiebinger, *Nature's Body: Gender in the Making of Modern Science* (Boston: Beacon, 1993), 158.
11. The term "Caucasian" was also used by Christoph Meiners, in *Grundriß der Geschichte der Menscheit (Outline of the History of Mankind)*, published in 1785, while Blumenbach only used the term in the 1795 edition of his work. Meiners' work, in its hierarchizing of "races" of humanity and defence of the enslavement of Africans, is much more unambiguously racist than Blumenbach's. On Meiners, and for a selection of his writing, see Christoph Meiners, "Of the Varieties and Deviate Forms of Negroes," in *Kant and the Concept of Race: Late Eighteenth-Century Writings*, translated and edited by Jon M. Mikkelsen (Albany: State University of New York Press, 2013), 195–207.
12. Johann Friedrich Blumenbach, *The Anthropological Treatises of Johann Friedrich Blumenbach*, translated and edited by Thomas Bendyshe (1865, Boston: Milford House, 1973), 69–70.
13. Wiegman, 455.
14. Johnson, 262.
15. Johnson, 259.
16. The bloody-hand birthmark, as an indication of a character's "true" identity, makes its appearance elsewhere in nineteenth-century fiction, of course—perhaps most popularly in E. D. E. N. Southworth's *The Hidden Hand or, Capitola the Madcap* (1888; edited by Joanne Dobson [New Brunswick, NJ: Rutgers University Press], 1988). Sari Edelstein briefly notes that Southworth's birthmark could also be seen as a "kind of racial marking" ("Metamorphosis of the Newsboy": E. D. E. N. Southworth's *The Hidden Hand* and the Antebellum Story-Paper, *Studies in American Fiction* 37, no.1 [2010]: 52, n. 75).
17. Schiebinger, 158, 142.
18. In her excellent reading of Hawthorne's references in his journals to slavery and race, Jean Fagan Yellin writes that Hawthorne's knowledge of these issues "fails to show itself in the great romances, where it might naturally be expected to illustrate their major theme of bondage" (76). However, Anna C. Brickhouse reads "Rappaccini's Daughter" as "a tale that covertly plays out [Hawthorne's] obsession with whiteness and purity" ("'I Do Abhor an Indian Story': Hawthorne and the Allegorization of Racial 'Commixture,'" *ESQ* 42, no.4 [1996]: 235). Robert K. Martin similarly reads *The House of the Seven Gables*, arguing that its gothic elements work "against [Hawthorne's] dominant text to recall the anxiety over race and gender in midcentury America, writing a countertext of guilt and endless expiation in the midst of a narrative of redemption" ("Haunted by Jim Crow: Gothic Fictions by Hawthorne and Faulkner," in *American Gothic: New Interventions in a National Narrative*, edited by Robert K. Martin and Eric Savoy [Iowa City: University of Iowa Press, 1998], 130).

19. H. L. Malchow, "The Half-breed as Gothic Unnatural," in *The Victorians and Race*, edited by Shearer West (Aldershot: Scolar, 1996), 102.
20. C. G. Jung, *Psychology and Alchemy*, 2nd ed., translated by R. F. C. Hull, The Collected Works of C. G. Jung, vol. 12, edited by William McGuire et al. (1968, Princeton: Princeton University Press, 1980), 229–30. For discussions of alchemy in "The Birth-mark" and other works by Hawthorne, see Randall A. Clack (*The Marriage of Heaven and Earth: Alchemical Regeneration in the Works of Taylor, Poe, Hawthorne, and Fuller* [Westport: Greenwood, 2000]); John Gatta, Jr. ("Aylmer's Alchemy in 'The Birthmark,'" *Philological Quarterly* 57.3 [1978]: 399–413); Luther H. Martin (Hawthorne's *The Scarlet Letter*: A is for Alchemy?" *American Transcendental Quarterly* 58 [1985]: 31–42); Jeffrey L. Meikle ("Hawthorne's Alembic: Alchemical Images in *The House of the Seven Gables*," *ESQ* 26.4 [1980]: 173–83); Klaus P. Stich ("Hawthorne's Intimations of Alchemy," *American Transcendental Quarterly* ns 5.1 [1991]: 15–30); Charles Swann ("Alchemy and Hawthorne's *Elixir of Life Manuscripts*," *Journal of American Studies* 22.3 [1988]: 371–87); and David M. Van Leer ("Aylmer's Library: Transcendental Alchemy in Hawthorne's 'The Birthmark,'" *ESQ* 22.4 [1976]: 211–20). Jung's psychoanalytic analysis also offers a general summary of the processes of alchemy (Jung 227–41). Stich elucidates some of the other aspects of Jungian "alchemy" in relation to Hawthorne. Shannon Burns also touches on these terms in relation to the alchemical themes of Hawthorne's story ("Alchemy and The Birth-mark," *American Transcendental Quarterly* 42 [1979]: 147–58).
21. Cathy Boeckmann, *A Question of Character: Scientific Racism and the Genres of American Fiction, 1892–1912* (Tuscaloosa: University of Alabama Press, 2000), 14; emphasis in original.
22. John Cullen Gruesser, *Confluences: Postcolonialism, African American Literary Studies, and the Black Atlantic* (Athens, GA: University of Georgia Press, 2005), 89.
23. See Blumenbach, plate 3, fig. 2, plate 4, fig. 3, and Schiebinger 153, fig. 5.2. I should note here that while Blumenbach's racial theories easily lent themselves to being used by others to further the racism of imperialist projects, still his own approach to race was paradoxical and divided: Blumenbach created what amounts to a racial hierarchy even as he insisted on the general unity of the human species, denying an inherent social hierarchy. He was also an abolitionist. Still, his racial division does posit the Caucasian as the normative, "beautiful" race.
24. Oliver Goldsmith, *History of the Earth, and Animated Nature*, qtd. in Bruce Baum, *The Rise and Fall of the Caucasian Race: A Political History of Racial Identity* (New York: New York University Press, 2006), 83. Baum also provides a full account of both Blumenbach's and Meiners' use of "Caucasian" and their similar yet differing opinions on race and slavery.
25. On Hawthorne and Goldsmith, see Laura B. Kenelly, "Hawthorne and Goldsmith? British History in 'Young Goodman Brown' and 'Biographical Stories,'" *Journal of American Studies* 23, no. 2 (1989), 295–97; and Frank Durham, "Hawthorne and Goldsmith: A Note," *Journal of American Studies* 4, no. 1 (1970), 103–05.
26. Jennifer Mason, *Civilized Creatures: Urban Animals, Sentimental Culture, and American Literature, 1850–1900* (Baltimore: Johns Hopkins University Press,

2005), 72. Lillian Handlin briefly discusses Bancroft's education at the Georgia Augusta University of Göttingen, where he took courses with "Blumenbach on natural history" (*George Bancroft: The Intellect as Democrat* [New York: Harper and Row, 1984], 61). Edgar Hutchinson Johnson III, citing Fred L. Burwick, writes further that "three of [Bancroft's] professors at the University of Göttingen—Heeren, Eichhorn, and Johann Blumenbach— ... helped shape Bancroft's concept of humanity. ... According to Burwick, Bancroft learned from the three German professors 'seminal ideas on national and moral character, the sympathetic unity of the collective mind, and the natural progression of humanity'" (*George Bancroft, Slavery, and the American Union* [Dissertation, Auburn U, 1983; Ann Arbor: UMI, 1993], 57).

27. Indeed, as Toni Morrison argues, such coded references to race occur more often than not in nineteenth-century American literature. She states that "It would have been an *isolato* indeed who was unaware of the most explosive issue in the nation. How could one speak of ... almost anything a country concerns itself with ... without having as a referent, at the heart of the discourse, at the heart of the definition, the presence of Africans and their descendants? It was not possible. And it did not happen" (*Playing in the Dark: Whiteness and the Literary Imagination* [New York: Vintage, 1990], 50).
28. "The Mark of Cain and the Curse of Ham," *Southern Presbyterian Review* 3, no.3 (1850): 417.
29. Schiebinger, 145.
30. William Smellie, *Philosophy of Natural History* (1790); qtd. in Schiebinger, 145.
31. Brickhouse, 243.
32. For other discussions of Aminadab and his role in the tale, see, for example, Robert Micklus ("Hawthorne's Jekyll and Hyde: The Aminadab in Aylmer," *Literature and Psychology* 29.4 [1979]: 148–59); Thomas Pribek ("Hawthorne's Aminadab: Sources and Significance," in *Studies in the American Renaissance*, edited by Joel Myerson [Charlottesville: University Press of Virginia, 1987]); John O. Rees ("Aminadab in 'The Birth-mark': The Name Again," *Names* 28.3 [1980]: 171–82); and Edward S. Van Winkle ("Aminadab, the Unwitting 'Bad Anima,'" *American Notes and Queries* 8 [1970]: 131–33). The last three authors study the character specifically through analyses of the name "Aminadab" and its possible meanings and sources.
33. Despite the necessary lack of precision in the mark as a racial signifier, some aspects of the story do coincide with specific nineteenth-century discursive constructions of African Americans. Specifically, Georgiana, since she *willingly* drinks what she seems to recognize as a poison, could fit into traditional, sentimental constructions of the "tragic mulatta," who, in Heather Hathaway's words, rejects her "ambiguous relationship to family and race through suicide" ("'Maybe Freedom Lies in Hating': Miscegenation and the Oedipal Conflict," in *Refiguring the Father: New Feminist Readings of the Patriarchy*, edited by Patricia Yaeger and Beth Kowaleski-Wallace [Carbondale: Southern Illinois University Press, 1989], 155). Gruesser makes a similar disclaimer to mine even as both of us recognize the problem with readings that "minimize the relevance of race" in the study of Hawthorne's works (156). Like Gruesser, I would also suggest that it is problematic, at best, to deny the explicit similarities between Hawthorne's choice of language and figures and those present in the racial discourse of his time. While recent studies have recognized the role that Hawthorne's works can play in discussions of race in the antebellum United States, still there

is some reticence. For overviews of the state of race in Hawthorne studies, see Bresky ("The Recuperative Trend in Hawthorne Studies: New or Improved?" *Canadian Review of American Studies* 41.2 [2011]: 263–74) and Goddu, the latter of whose call for more extended analyses of the subject, though from a few years back, still rings true ("Integrating Hawthorne," *Poe Studies/Dark Romanticism: History, Theory, Interpretation* 37 [2004]: 36–38).

34. Smith, 9.
35. Gruesser, 91.
36. I use the word "miscegenist" because, given the turbulent and often violent social history of interracial relationships in America, it connotes the contested nature of racial and other social divisions and the political nature of any crossing of such divisions. The term is, however, anachronistic when used to describe Aylmer's desire, since "miscegenation" was coined in 1864 in the pamphlet, "Miscegenation: The Theory of the Blending of the Races Applied to the American White Man and Negro" (New York: H. Dexter, Hamilton, & Co., 1864).
37. Shirley Samuels, "Miscegenated America: The Civil War," *American Literary History* 9.3 (1997): 483.
38. Indeed, the aspects of miscegenation in the story that challenge Aylmer's dominant position can also be seen, from a different angle, to reinforce that position, because Georgiana's death fits into Samuels' figuration of miscegenist representations wherein "bodies are refused or killed at the point of their insertion" into a dominant space (483).
39. Joan Saberhagen, Introduction to *Mizora: A World of Women*, rpt. of *Mizora, a Prophecy* by Mary E. Bradley Lane (Lincoln: University of Nebraska Press, 1999), vi. The book version of *Mizora* was originally published by G. W. Dillingham as *Mizora: A Prophecy. A MSS. found among the private papers of the Princess Vera Zarovitch; Being a true and faithful account of her Journey to the Interior of the Earth, with a careful description of the Country and its Inhabitants, their Customs, Manners and Government. Written by Herself* (New York: G. W. Dillingham, 1890). Mary E. Bradley Lane's copyright is asserted in the page following the title page. The preface, written by Murat Halstead (editor of the *Cincinnati Commercial*) is worth reprinting, if only as an indication of why people have found it difficult to find information on Lane herself:

> The narrative of Vera Garovitch [*sic*], published in the *Cincinnati Commercial* in 1880 and 1881, attracted a great deal of attention. It commanded a wide circle of readers, and there was much more said about it than is usual when works of fiction run through a newspaper in weekly installments. Quite a number of persons who are unaccustomed to bestowing consideration upon works of fiction spoke of it, and grew greatly interested in it.
>
> I received many messages about it, and letters of inquiry, and some ladies and gentlemen desired to know the particulars about the production of the story in book form; and were inquisitive about it and the author who kept herself in concealment so closely, that even her husband did not know that she was the writer who was making this stir in our limited literary world.
>
> I myself was so much interested in it that it occurred to me to make the suggestion that the story ought to have an extensive sale in book form, and to write to a publisher; but the lady who wrote the work seemed herself a shade indifferent on the subject, and it passed out of my hands and out of my mind.

It is safe to say that it made an impression that was remarkable, and with a larger audience I do not doubt that it would make its mark as an original production wrought out with thoughtful care and literary skill, and take high rank. (v-vi)

40. Annegret J. Wiemer has outlined *Mizora*'s debt to Nikolai Chernyshevsky's *What Is to Be Done?*, an 1863 Russian utopia that includes a story of a non-gender-biased future. Wiemer largely ignores the racism of *Mizora*, but does include some valuable comparisons of the portrayal of science in each work ("Corpus ex Machina: Nikolai Chernychevsky's *What Is to Be Done?* [1863] and Mary Bradley Lane's *Mizora* [1880/81]," *Neophilologus* 79, no.2 [1995]: 187–96). I would argue that the American Lane appropriates the Russian context largely in an attempt to provide an unbiased narrator who can laud the benefits of the U.S. Republic. On the hollow world tradition of which Lane's narrative is a part, see Peter Fitting's critical anthology, *Subterranean Worlds: A Critical Anthology* (Middletown, CT: Wesleyan University Press, 2004).
41. Duangrudi Suksang, "A World of Their Own: The Separatist Utopian Vision of Mary E. Bradley Lane's *Mizora*," in *Redefining the Political Novel: American Women Writers, 1797–1901*, edited by Sharon M. Harris (Knoxville: University of Tennessee Press, 1995), 132.
42. Suksang, 146.
43. Katherine Broad, "Race, Reproduction, and the Failures of Feminism in Mary Bradley Lane's *Mizora*," *Tulsa Studies in Women's Literature* 28, no.2 (2009): 247–66; Christine Mahady, "No World of Difference: Examining the Significance of Women's Relationships to Nature in Mary Bradley Lane's *Mizora*," *Utopian Studies* 15, no.2 (2004): 93–115.
44. Broad, 263.
45. Broad, 246.
46. Mary E. Bradley Lane, *Mizora: A Prophecy*, edited by and intro. Jean Pfaelzer (New York: Syracuse University Press, 2000), xxxi. Unless otherwise noted, subsequent references to *Mizora* and to Pfaelzer's introduction will be from this edition and will be cited parenthetically.
47. I suspect Broad would agree with my reading to a point, and we approach the problem with similar goals in mind, but from different directions. For instance, I fully agree with and support her political conclusion, which echoes Lorde, who I rely on heavily here: "It is only by recognizing the complex racialized history of feminism and (proto-) feminist writings contemporary feminists can better understand and conceptualize alternatives to reproductive discourses and practices that reflect the mutual constitution of race and gender in producing white citizens and the ideal nations they populate" (263).
48. Schiebinger, 158. Pfaelzer makes a similar point, writing that "'race' in the nineteenth century was frequently used interchangeably with 'sex'" (xxv). Following Schiebinger, this may be stretching the relationship, but it is certainly the case in *Mizora*—though as I argue here, it is even more complex.
49. Audre Lorde, *Sister Outsider* (Berkeley: Crossing Press, 1984), 112; emphasis in original.
50. Kristine J. Anderson, "The Great Divorce: Fictions of Feminist Desire," in *Feminism, Utopia, and Narrative*, edited by Libby Falk Jones and Sarah Webster Goodwin (Knoxville: University of Tennessee Press, 1990), 85–99.
51. Broad, 254–55.

52. Francis Galton, *Hereditary Genius: An Inquiry into Its Laws and Consequences* (London: Macmillan, 1869), 338–39. Galton was himself the author of a utopia: unpublished in his lifetime, fragments of it have been published as "The Eugenic College of Kantsaywhere," edited by Lyman Tower Sargent in *Utopian Studies*. For a discussion of eugenics and the utopian tradition, see Parrinder.
53. Galton, 344.
54. Boeckmann, 28.
55. Goldberg, 163.
56. Mahady ties Mizoran eugenics to Herbert Spencer's social Darwinism as well (101–02).
57. Broad also analyzes this passage (250), but in terms of the importance of parthenogenesis to early feminist utopias which, while critiquing the patriarchy, are still invested in contemporary gender roles and expectations.
58. A. S. Weber, edited by, *Nineteenth Century Science* (Peterborough: Broadview Press, 2000), 346.
59. Francis Galton, *Hereditary Genius: An Inquiry Into Its Laws and Consequences*, 2nd ed. (London: MacMillan, 1892), xxvii.
60. Jean Baptiste Pierre Antoine de Monet de Lamarck, *Zoological Philosophy: An Exposition with Regard to the Natural History of Animals*, translated by Hugh Elliott (Chicago: University of Chicago Press, 1984); see especially 113–27.
61. Specifically, all non-Anglo Saxon races had to be eliminated, as all of the Mizorans are tall and blonde—none even has dark hair–which was the ideal form of the Nordic branch of whiteness for nineteenth- and twentieth-century scientific racism, something George S. Schuyler explores in *Black No More*, as discussed in the third chapter of this book.
62. Donna Haraway, *Simians, Cyborgs, and Women: The Reinvention of Nature* (New York: Routledge, 1991), 170.
63. Morrison, 32–33.
64. Morrison, 59.
65. Broad, 260.
66. Blumenbach, 265–66.
67. Haraway, *Simians*, 170.
68. See Pfaelzer for a discussion of the complex relationships Vera, as a character, and *Mizora* as a whole have to same-sex desire.

REFERENCES

Anderson, Kristine J. "The Great Divorce: Fictions of Feminist Desire." In *Feminism, Utopia, and Narrative*, edited by Libby Falk Jones and Sarah Webster Goodwin, 85–99. Knoxville: University of Tennessee Press, 1990.

Baum, Bruce. *The Rise and Fall of the Caucasian Race: A Political History of Racial Identity* New York: New York University Press, 2006.

Blumenbach, Johann Friedrich. *The Anthropological Treatises of Johann Friedrich Blumenbach*. Translated and edited by Thomas Bendyshe. 1865. Boston: Milford House, 1973.

Boeckmann, Cathy. *A Question of Character: Scientific Racism and the Genres of American Fiction, 1892–1912*. Tuscaloosa: University of Alabama Press, 2000.

Bresky, Luke. "The Recuperative Trend in Hawthorne Studies: New or Improved?" *Canadian Review of American Studies* 41, no.2 (2011): 263–74.

Brickhouse, Anna C. "'I Do Abhor an Indian Story': Hawthorne and the Allegorization of Racial 'Commixture.'" *ESQ* 42, no.4 (1996): 233–53.

Broad, Katherine. "Race, Reproduction, and the Failures of Feminism in Mary Bradley Lane's *Mizora*." *Tulsa Studies in Women's Literature* 28, no.2 (2009): 247–66.

Burns, Shannon. "Alchemy and 'The Birth-mark.'" *American Transcendental Quarterly* 42 (1979): 147–58.

Butler, Judith. "Imitation and Gender Insubordination." *Inside / Out*, edited by Diana Fuss, 13–31. New York: Routledge, 1991.

Clack, Randall A. *The Marriage of Heaven and Earth: Alchemical Regeneration in the Works of Taylor, Poe, Hawthorne, and Fuller*. Westport: Greenwood, 2000.

Creager, Angela N. H., Elizabeth Lunbeck, and Londa Schiebinger, eds. *Feminism in Twentieth-Century Science, Technology, and Medicine*. Chicago: University of Chicago Press, 2001.

Durham, Frank. "Hawthorne and Goldsmith: A Note." *Journal of American Studies* 4, no.1 (1970): 103–05.

Edelstein, Sari. "'Metamorphosis of the Newsboy': E. D. E. N. Southworth's *The Hidden Hand* and the Antebellum Story-Paper." *Studies in American Fiction* 37, no.1 (2010): 29–53.

Fitting, Peter. *Subterranean Worlds: A Critical Anthology*. Middletown, CT: Wesleyan University Press, 2004.

Foucault, Michel. *History of Sexuality*, vol. 1: An Introduction. Translated by Robert Hurley. 1978. New York: Vintage, 1990.

Galton, Francis. "The Eugenic College of Kantsaywhere." Edited by Lyman Tower Sargent. *Utopian Studies* 12, no.2 (2001): 191–209.

———. *Hereditary Genius: An Inquiry into Its Laws and Consequences*. London: Macmillan, 1869.

———. *Hereditary Genius: An Inquiry into Its Laws and Consequences*, 2nd ed. London: MacMillan, 1892.

Gates, Henry Louis, Jr. "Writing 'Race' and the Difference It Makes." In *"Race," Writing, and Difference*, edited by Henry Louis Gates, Jr., 1–20. Chicago: University of Chicago Press, 1986.

Gatta, John Jr. "Aylmer's Alchemy in 'The Birthmark.'" *Philological Quarterly* 57, no.3 (1978): 399–413.

Goddu, Teresa. "Integrating Hawthorne." *Poe Studies/Dark Romanticism: History, Theory, Interpretation* 37 (2004): 36–38.

Goldberg, David Theo. *The Racial State*. Oxford: Blackwell, 2002.

Gruesser, John Cullen. *Confluences: Postcolonialism, African American Literary Studies, and the Black Atlantic*. Athens, GA: University of Georgia Press, 2005.

Handlin, Lillian. *George Bancroft: The Intellect as Democrat*. New York: Harper and Row, 1984.

Haraway, Donna. *Primate Visions: Gender, Race, and Nature in the World of Modern Science*. New York: Routledge, 1989.

———. *Simians, Cyborgs, and Women: The Reinvention of Nature*. New York: Routledge, 1991.

Hathaway, Heather. "'Maybe Freedom Lies in Hating': Miscegenation and the Oedipal Conflict." In *Refiguring the Father: New Feminist Readings of the Patriarchy*, edited by Patricia Yaeger and Beth Kowaleski-Wallace, 153–67. Carbondale: Southern Illinois University Press, 1989.

Hawthorne, Nathaniel. "The Birth-mark." In *Mosses from an Old Manse*, 36–56. The Centenary Edition of the Works of Nathaniel Hawthorne 10. Columbus: Ohio State University Press, 1974.

Johnson, Barbara. "Is Female to Male as Ground Is to Figure?" In *Feminism and Psychoanalysis*, edited by Richard Feldstein and Judith Roof, 255–68. Ithaca: Cornell University Press, 1989.

Johnson, Edgar Hutchinson III. *George Bancroft, Slavery, and the American Union.* Diss. Auburn U, 1983. Ann Arbor: UMI, 1993.

Jung, C. G. *Psychology and Alchemy*. 2nd ed. Edited by William McGuire et al. Translated by R. F. C. Hull. The Collected Works of C. G. Jung 12. 1968. Princeton: Princeton University Press, 1980.

Kenelly, Laura B. "Hawthorne and Goldsmith? British History in 'Young Goodman Brown' and 'Biographical Stories.'" *Journal of American Studies* 23, no.2 (1989): 295–97.

Lamarck, Jean Baptiste Pierre Antoine de Monet de. *Zoological Philosophy: An Exposition with Regard to the Natural History of Animals.* Translated by Hugh Elliott. Chicago: University of Chicago Press, 1984.

Lane, Mary E. Bradley. *Mizora: A Prophecy.* Edited by and intro. Jean Pfaelzer. New York: Syracuse University Press, 2000.

———. *Mizora: A Prophecy. A MSS. found among the private papers of the Princess Vera Zarovitch; Being a true and faithful account of her Journey to the Interior of the Earth, with a careful description of the Country and its Inhabitants, their Customs, Manners and Government. Written by Herself.* New York: G. W. Dillingham, 1890.

Lorde, Audre. *Sister Outsider*. Berkeley: Crossing Press, 1984.

Mahady, Christine. "No World of Difference: Examining the Significance of Women's Relationships to Nature in Mary Bradley Lane's *Mizora.*" *Utopian Studies* 15, no.2 (2004): 93–115.

Malchow, H. L. "The Half-breed as Gothic Unnatural." *The Victorians and Race*, edited by Shearer West, 101–11. Aldershot: Scolar, 1996.

"The Mark of Cain and the Curse of Ham." *Southern Presbyterian Review* 3, no.3 (1850): 415–26.

Martin, Luther H. "Hawthorne's *The Scarlet Letter*: A is for Alchemy?" *American Transcendental Quarterly* 58 (1985): 31–42.

Martin, Robert K. "Haunted by Jim Crow: Gothic Fictions by Hawthorne and Faulkner." In *American Gothic: New Interventions in a National Narrative*, edited by Robert K. Martin and Eric Savoy, 129–42. Iowa City: University of Iowa Press, 1998.

Mason, Jennifer. *Civilized Creatures: Urban Animals, Sentimental Culture, and American Literature, 1850–1900.* Baltimore: Johns Hopkins University Press, 2005.

Meikle, Jeffrey L. "Hawthorne's Alembic: Alchemical Images in *The House of the Seven Gables.*" *ESQ* 26, no.4 (1980): 173–83.

Meiners, Christoph. "Of the Varieties and Deviate Forms of Negroes." In *Kant and the Concept of Race: Late Eighteenth-Century Writings*, translated and edited by Jon M. Mikkelsen, 195–207. Albany: State University of New York Press, 2013.

Micklus, Robert. "Hawthorne's Jekyll and Hyde: The Aminadab in Aylmer." *Literature and Psychology* 29, no.4 (1979): 148–59.

Miéville, China. "Gothic Politics: A Discussion with China Miéville." *Gothic Studies* 10, no.1 (2008): 61–70.

"Miscegenation: The Theory of the Blending of the Races Applied to the American White Man and Negro." New York: H. Dexter, Hamilton, & Co., 1864.

Morrison, Toni. *Playing in the Dark: Whiteness and the Literary Imagination*. New York: Vintage, 1990.

Parrinder, Patrick. "Eugenics and Utopia: Sexual Selection from Galton to Morris." *Utopian Studies* 8, no.2 (1997): 1–12.

Pribek, Thomas. "Hawthorne's Aminadab: Sources and Significance." *Studies in the American Renaissance*, edited by Joel Myerson, 177–86. Charlottesville: University Press of Virginia, 1987.

Rees, John O. "Aminadab in 'The Birth-mark': The Name Again." *Names* 28, no.3 (1980): 171–82.

Saberhagen, Joan. Introduction. *Mizora: A World of Women* (Reprint of *Mizora, a Prophecy* by Mary E. Bradley Lane). Lincoln: University of Nebraska Press, 1999.

Samuels, Shirley. "Miscegenated America: The Civil War." *American Literary History* 9, no.3 (1997): 482–501.

Schiebinger, Londa. *Nature's Body: Gender in the Making of Modern Science*. Boston: Beacon, 1993.

Schuyler, George. *Black No More: Being an Account of the Strange and Wonderful Workings of Science in the Land of the Free, A. D. 1933–1940*. 1931. Boston: Northeastern University Press, 1989.

Sedgwick, Eve Kosofsky. *Epistemology of the Closet*. Updated with a New Preface. 1990. Berkeley: University of California Press, 2008.

Smith, Sidonie. *Subjectivity, Identity, and the Body: Women's Autobiographical Practices in the Twentieth Century*. Bloomington: Indiana University Press, 1993.

Southworth, E. D. E. N. *The Hidden Hand, or, Capitola the Madcap*. 1888. Edited by Joanne Dobson, New Brunswick, NJ: Rutgers University Press, 1988.

Stich, Klaus P. "Hawthorne's Intimations of Alchemy." *American Transcendental Quarterly* ns 5, no.1 (1991): 15–30.

Suksang, Duangrudi. "A World of Their Own: The Separatist Utopian Vision of Mary E. Bradley Lane's *Mizora*." In *Redefining the Political Novel: American Women Writers, 1797–1901*, edited by Sharon M. Harris, 128–48. Knoxville : University of Tennessee Press, 1995.

Swann, Charles. "Alchemy and Hawthorne's *Elixir of Life Manuscripts*." *Journal of American Studies* 22, no.3 (1988): 371–87.

Van Leer, David M. "Aylmer's Library: Transcendental Alchemy in Hawthorne's 'The Birthmark.'" *ESQ* 22, no.4 (1976): 211–20.

Van Winkle, Edward S. "Aminadab, the Unwitting 'Bad Anima.'" *American Notes and Queries* 8 (1970): 131–33.

Weber, A. S., ed. *Nineteenth Century Science*. Peterborough: Broadview Press, 2000.

Wiegman, Robyn. "The Anatomy of Lynching." *Journal of the History of Sexuality* 3, no.3 (1993): 445–67.

Wiemer, Annegret J. "Corpus ex Machina: Nikolai Chernychevsky's *What Is to Be Done?* (1863) and Mary Bradley Lane's *Mizora* (1880/81)." *Neophilologus* 79, no.2 (1995): 187–96.

Yellin, Jean Fagan. "Hawthorne and the American National Sin." In *The Green American Tradition: Essays and Poems for Sherman Paul*, edited by H. Daniel Peck, 75–97. Baton Rouge: Louisiana State University Press, 1989.

Zanger, Jules. "Speaking the Unspeakable: Hawthorne's 'The Birthmark.'" *Modern Philology* 80, no.4 (1983): 364–71.

2 The Whiteness of Manly Pulp From Tarzan's Jungle to Buck Rogers' Phalectrocentrism

This chapter begins with an often told tale: Michel Foucault famously argues that contemporary Western discourses of sexuality are characterised by an always reinforced but actually false sense of repression, wherein people continually tell themselves that they can't talk to each other about sex; they continually repeat that their sexual lives are never mentioned; and they constantly roll over muttering that "tomorrow, sex will be good again."[1] In the dominant form of this narrative, the modern Western subject is said to be repressed sexually because of a Victorian heritage, a repression that needs to be overcome. In Foucault's version, sexual discourse, far from being characterised by repression, is actually characterised by the increase and codification of sexual identities, a process which is enabled by the very mechanisms of this so-called repression. Other theorists have made similar claims regarding gender, arguing that while seemingly bound by a restrictive binary, the number of and relations between genders have always been in flux, following the semiotic and SF model of identity outlined in the introduction. For J. Jack Halberstam, however, the very multiplicity of gender identifications leads to the ability of a generalised, and hierarchized, binary system of gender to take hold across the social spectrum, as a hegemonic form,[2] an underlying tension discussed in relation to both gender and race in the previous chapter.

Building on these studies and on the intersections of racial and gendered discourses explored in Hawthorne's and Lane's texts, this chapter discusses the codifications of masculinity, whiteness, and their others in two prime examples of early twentieth-century American pulp SF (where SF is defined following the methodological framework offered in the introduction): Edgar Rice Burroughs' *Tarzan of the Apes* and Philip Francis Nowlan's Anthony "Buck" Rogers novellas and comics. As I argue, these works attempt to solidify the supremacy of white, heterosexual men, by both proposing a set of social challenges to that supremacy (so that those threats may be overcome), and by showing that the supposedly fixed identity of white masculinity is in fact simultaneously flexible. In the nostalgic vision offered by these and other masculinist pulp texts, men were never so perfect as they were yesterday or only a moment ago; in the dominant form of this discourse, masculinity is always on the wane, whereas the man of a moment ago was always fully waxed. But, this past perfection is always on the verge of reasserting itself, or reclaiming the future. Relying on a revised vision of American Romanticism's construction of "man's" relation to nature, these works call for a reinvigoration of white manhood and its relation to science, technology, and civilisation writ large. Their reliance on the fantastic semiotic structures of SF in this project, however, offers its own challenges that the works must necessarily and continually (fail to) suppress.

I. MANLY PULP

In these and other early twentieth-century texts, there was a fascination with the perceived need to recapture the so-called "real man," a figure who was not only white and heterosexual, but whose masculinity was unassailable. Characterised both physically and in terms of particular character traits, the "real man" is represented as serving to rescue the average man from the supposed threats of the new century: first from the encroachment of women, and second from that of other—specifically "othered"—men. The first threat is generally rendered as relatively easy to silence, because women may threaten men, but, so "the story goes" (to appropriate Foucault again), women also always desire men, and so the mere appearance of a "real man" removes that threat, at least superficially—witness Aminadab's desire for and easy acceptance of Georgiana's birthmark. The second threat, that of a generally racialized other of white masculinity, is often pictured as more profound: the white, heterosexual man is always supposedly threatened by other masculinities, which take the usual form of "othered" men. Certainly in the plethora of these "other men," one can find an ever-expanding discourse of other kinds of masculinity with which one can identify (a strategy Ed Cohen identifies in terms of male sexuality following the Wilde trials in Victorian England)[3], but the real man also changes as the threatening other changes. In other words, the essential man of a moment ago, who seems so unchanging in the dominant story of white, heterosexual masculinity, is in fact a moveable feast of masculinities in himself.

Important to note, however, is that this "moveable feast" is still being served at a private club and to a restricted membership. As both Bryce Traister and Christopher Breu have correctly noted, the discussion of the "threats" posed to white heterosexual masculinity have long characterised the field of masculinity studies, to the point that the field has "produce[d] an understanding of masculinity (which in this context functions as synonymous with white, straight, male identity) as inherently insecure and continuously under siege," an argument which "seem[s] designed to evade fully confronting the materiality of male power and privilege."[4] I agree with this statement absolutely and would expand "the 'crisis theory' of American masculinity"[5] to some sections of the field of whiteness studies, which is dealt with in more detail in the next chapter. It is a fact, however, that one of the discursive means that has been employed in the United States and elsewhere in order to maintain the material power of what R. W. Connell refers to as "hegemonic masculinity" is the portrayal of that masculinity as a victim of attack, and as such as being in need of constant support. And this is true across several decades and across any number of specific configurations of hegemonic masculinity. In other words, in this chapter the notion of the "threat" posed to the masculine identity (as the character inherent in the "natural" order of heterosexist patriarchy) should not be read as a statement of fact on my behalf, but rather as a discursive ploy put forth in these texts to reinforce an already firmly entrenched hegemonic structure. The portrayal of "The Crisis of American Masculinity" (the title of a 1958 *Esquire* article by Arthur Schlesinger, Jr.)[6] clearly serves not to describe an actual "crisis," but to pathologise any social system not defined by a white, male, heterosexual hegemony.[7] Robyn Wiegman has said of whiteness that it is not its supposed "invisibility" as a racial category that shores up its power, but instead its ability to invest itself with any number of conflicting and altering "particularities";[8] so too can the multiplicities of masculinities within "hegemonic masculinity" aid in propping up the patriarchy. But still, as I will return to, the necessity of multiplicity in relation to the ideological work of dominant gender and racial paradigms *does* open up fissures for anti-hegemonic work to be done. Or, to put it another way, within the category of the "real man" are any number of unreal men waiting to get out (just ask Foucault, with his discussion of the continual existence of a "plurality of resistances, each of them a special case,"[9] or, better yet, Frank-N-Furter: "I Can Make You a Man," he promises in one song title, but in so doing he manages to offer his audience a new position to take on Charles Atlas).[10]

Any attempt to provide a popular genealogy of the "real man" would have to take account of the ways in which this figure was popularised in the so-called genre fictions of the pulp publishing period in the United States. As several critics—notably Breu, Erin Smith, and Bill Osgerby[11]—have shown, from heroic adventurers, to hard-boiled detectives, to space cowboys, the pulp industry clearly helped to create and cement the image of the real man in the popular imagination. Like their high-modernist contemporaries, the characters in many of these works are concerned about the anaesthetising effect of modern society on the individual, and especially the male individual. Most work on the pulps and masculinity has, however, focused primarily on realist fiction, often coming closest to SF in the "adventure" form of which *Tarzan of the Apes* is clearly a progenitor. Against this trend, in this chapter I reread *Tarzan* in its semiotically slippery SF guise and move from there to Buck Rogers and his manly gadgets.

Starting in the pulps, these two characters went on to dominate the new multimedia popular culture of the twentieth century. Originally published in the October 1912 issue of the popular fiction magazine, *The All-Story*, and as a book in 1914, *Tarzan of the Apes* introduces the character who would become the focus of twenty-five more books by Burroughs and several novels by other authors (both authorised and not). As I have mentioned in my introduction to the Oxford edition of the novel, the significance of the figure of Tarzan cannot be overestimated, certainly in relation to American culture, but arguably to global culture as well, given that the Tarzan novels have been reportedly translated into over fifty languages. Just as importantly, Tarzan entered popular culture at a time when the centrality of print media was giving way to radio, television, and film.[12] Estimates vary, but it is safe to say that there are over fifty Tarzan movies, spanning nearly every decade of the twentieth century since the novel's publication. Between the late 1920s and the 1960s, Tarzan was on the silver screen almost every year. Tarzan has also swung through almost all of the other branches of popular and so-called "high" culture, from comics, radio, and stage—even song. It would not be an exaggeration to suggest that the history of Tarzan and that of U.S. popular and mass culture are inseparable. Just as importantly for the current argument, Tarzan would also become the archetype for numerous other fantasy, science fiction, and other pulp heroes, from Buck Rogers through to Conan the Barbarian, not to mention Rocky in *Rocky Horror Picture Show*. Tarzan even went to the Earth's core, once.

Buck Rogers likewise dominated the cultural field: first created as "Anthony Rogers" in Philip Francis Nowlan's 1928 novella, *Armageddon—2419 A.D.* (published in Hugo Gernsback's SF pulp, *Amazing Stories*), Rogers went on to be the focus of a sequel by Nowlan (1929's *The Airlords of Han*)—it is these two original novellas that will be the primary focus for the analysis here. From there, Rogers was translated throughout the rest of the twentieth century into a wide variety of media—radio, film, television, and a comic strip that ran for four decades, in the last of which he was rechristened "Buck," in order, one would assume, to make sure people catch on that "Buck" was a symbol of manliness. Buck Rogers, as many commentators have noted, even transformed the English language, giving us the terms "ray gun" and "zap."

In what follows, the origins of these figures and their explicit meditations on the whiteness of hegemonic masculinity are investigated. This chapter does not offer, by any stretch, a complete genealogy of the figure of the twentieth century's "real man," but points to some of the complexities that haunt that figure from two of its most popular and pervasive twentieth-century and mass-media origins, connecting it to earlier formations of American masculinity—notably those from Hawthorne's period—that are renewed in the opening decades of the century. While the technological revolution of the twentieth century was beginning, and in the process was radically changing roles for men and women at work and at play, and while urban development, global trade, and migration were beginning to change the complexion of America and elsewhere, SF men began to look backwards (to use Bellamy's phrase) in an effort not to redefine white masculinity *per se* but to reinforce white supremacist, patriarchal hegemony. Specifically, the Romantic man—in the form of the idealistic Thoreauvian reformer returning to the woods, a type so roundly parodied by Hawthorne in *The Blithedale Romance*—faced a resurgence in the pages of SF magazines, even though those forums would seem more suited to presenting the laboratory than the leafy bower. It is for this reason that I choose to look at that quintessential re-Romanticized masculine hero, Tarzan, rather than Burroughs' more traditionally defined science fiction character, John Carter of Mars (as DeGraw does): Tarzan, in relying on traditional archetypes, himself forms a primary archetype for the manner in which the "proper" neo-Romantic man can live in the modern world.[13] To investigate the importance of this nostalgic return, I begin, then, with the masculine figure cut by Ralph Waldo Emerson.

II. COLONIAL ISOLATION

In an oft-cited passage from "The American Scholar," Ralph Waldo Emerson says of those whom he sees as fitting the category of the contemporary, degraded scholar that, "The scholar is decent, indolent, complaisant. See already the tragic consequence. The mind of this country taught to aim at low objects, eats upon itself. There is no work for any but the decorous and the complaisant."[14] A Romantic call for a new universal voice of Truth, Emerson's essay is much concerned with new definitions for Americanness and, in parts, masculinity. The mental self-cannibalism of this passage, the mind feeding upon itself, is the end result of an alienation from what Emerson calls the "Divine Soul which ... inspires all men."[15] If this self-consuming is a form of objectification by the world, then Emerson's true scholar is represented as someone who can subjectify his surroundings, consuming them in a benign form of intellectual cosmopolitanism: "The scholar is that man who must take up into himself all the ability of the time, all the contributions of the past, all the hopes of the future. He must be an university of knowledges ... in yourself slumbers the whole of Reason; it is for you to know all, it is for you to dare all."[16] The way to avoid becoming an object of consumption is to become the subject consuming, but this meal is seen as paradoxically pre-digested, and the true scholar is just waiting to recognise that he's already full. And, importantly, this recognition takes place through a relation with Nature, certainly, but also through encompassing the popular: "I embrace the common, I explore and sit at the feet of the familiar, the low ... show me the sublime presence of the highest spiritual cause lurking, as always it does lurk, in these suburbs and extremities of nature ...; there is no trifle; there is no puzzle; but one design unites and animates the farthest pinnacle and the lowest trench."[17] While he may seem here to contradict his later lament for "the mind ... taught to aim at low objects," here it is the power of the properly framed, sublime thinker that raises the lowest to the highest. Not eschewing but certainly casting a cynical eye on what we would now call "high culture," the new scholar instead sees a sublime presence in the everyday. The self-cannibalism of traditional thought thus becomes a cultural omnivorousness, intellectually digesting daily life and Nature for its spiritual sustenance.

This section begins with an admittedly basic summation of Emerson's address in order to build on the notion of omnivorous cultural consumption, to show how a cosmopolitan form of cultural consumption can and has been figured as a populist foundational support for—rather than exotic threat or progressive solution to—racist and patriarchal notions of white, and specifically Anglo-Saxon, male dominance. These connections between a popular form of cultural cosmopolitanism, race, and masculinity are perhaps best figured, at the dawning of the post-imperial, globalised age, through one of the first American mass culture icons: Tarzan of the Apes. Tarzan becomes the incarnation of what Emerson, in "Self Reliance," calls the "Saxon breast[]."[18] In many ways, Tarzan is Emerson's American Scholar.

Another of Burroughs' many novels, *The Cave Girl*, published in *All-Story* from July to September 1913, a year after *Tarzan's* appearance, can serve to introduce both Tarzan and his author's general neo-Romantic approach and its connection to Emerson's thought. The protagonist of the tale is the none-too-subtly named Waldo Emerson Smith-Jones, a "not overly courageous" man who "had been reared among surroundings of culture plus and [*sic*] ultra-intellectuality in the exclusive Back Bay home of his ancestors" and who "had been taught to look with contempt upon all that savored of muscular superiority—such things were gross, brutal, primitive. It had been a giant intellect he craved—he and a fond mother—and their wishes had been fulfilled. At twenty-one Waldo was an animated encyclopedia—and about as muscular as a real one."[19] Physically weak, overly intellectual, and overly attached to his mother, Smith-Jones is then thrust away from civilisation, an experience through which he has "forced upon him the development of attributes of self-reliance, courage, initiative, and resourcefulness that would have lain dormant within him always but for the necessity which had given birth to them."[20] Following both Emerson and the philosopher's *The Cave Girl* namesake, Tarzan is—to use Emerson's words—"that man who must take up into himself all the ability of the time, all the contributions of the past, all the hopes of the future," by romantically reconnecting with evolution's past. And because, again as for Emerson, once Tarzan recognises that "but one design unites and animates the farthest pinnacle and the lowest trench"—once he recognises his own connection to the natural world that he paradoxically evolves beyond—then there can be no threat to the power of Tarzan's "Saxon breast[]."[21] Burroughs rewrites the populist narrative of social evolution back into that of Romanticism, and in so doing brings out the pernicious notions of white supremacy that haunt them both. Simultaneously, this narrative both rejects and claims the cosmopolitan manliness of the burgeoning American empire of the twentieth century.

Burroughs' massively influential novel writes a post-imperial notion of American and international racial violence, in which cannibalism is opposed to and transformed into a modern form of economic appropriation, in turn figured as a cultural cosmopolitanism. That is, Burroughs attempts to construct a view of Anglo-Saxon dominance disconnected from contemporary European military imperialism and from the earlier forms of racial violence in the history of the Atlantic slave trade and American slavery. In so doing, Burroughs presents Anglo-Saxon dominance, Emerson's "Saxon breast[]," not as a manifest destiny, nor as the result of physical, mental, or spiritual rights conceived separately, but as a character type, a figure that embodies all of these characteristics. Of course, Burroughs was not alone in such a project, but by explicitly disconnecting the figure of Tarzan from his sociohistorical context, and by consciously building Tarzan into a mass-culture franchise (and, as one of the first of these products, helping to create that very market and the "branding" that would become so important to it), Burroughs creates a type, a Barthesian myth of Anglo-Saxon superiority that simultaneously tries to deny the repressive violence lying behind that myth. Walt Morton, rephrasing Bill Nichols' argument about images and ideology, writes, "Rampant marketing elevated the character of Tarzan to iconic status," making the character part of a symbolic exchange in which "Duplicating images pries meaning loose from a necessary link to geography, place. The signifier (Tarzan) becomes potentially free-floating, unpinned, ready for exchange within a cash nexus that determines new meaning."[22] This is not a complete freedom of signification, however, as no matter the disconnect from its literary origin, the figure of Tarzan is always circumscribed by the contexts of race, gender, and (as Morton notes) sexuality. But, the mass reproduction of Tarzan does allow the figure to serve as a space for refigurations—and reinforcements—of racial and gendered identity.[23]

But the mobility of definitions within these hegemonic identity categories is not just an effect of the mass marketing of Tarzan; it is in fact encoded into the character at his origins in Burroughs' novel, making Tarzan a prime candidate for this symbolic exchange to begin with. Cannibalism becomes the symbolic structure through which Tarzan's white masculinity gains its contradictory meanings. For Burroughs, cannibalism is a symbol of both non-white savagery and, as for Emerson, decadent civilisation, figured here in terms of European imperialism, for which Burroughs substitutes a supposedly "ethical" practice of cultural appropriation, which in turn transforms the appropriation into the figure of a cosmopolitan sophisticate.

I am by no means the first person to situate *Tarzan of the Apes* in terms of imperialism and cannibalism. Tying the novel's portrayal of cannibalism to its representation of literacy, Jeff Berglund reads the novel as highlighting "Burroughs' and his readership's potential anxieties about the eruption of foreign elements into the homogenous spheres of whiteness, manliness, and economic plenitude."[24] Likewise, Eric Cheyfitz reads in the novel a "romance of identity" in which Tarzan is granted "the 'right' to maintain the force" of "dispossessing colonial subjects and the working class."[25] Both works, significantly, discuss the role of literacy and language in the novel, focusing on the ways in which Tarzan's self-taught mastery of written English reinforces colonial ideologies that present the coloniser's language as both more advanced than and simultaneously threatened by the linguistic and racial situation of the imperial situation. As Cheyfitz argues, "The failure of dialogue, figured as a genetic inability in the other, rather than as a problem of cultural difference, is the imperial alibi for domination."[26] While Cheyfitz's argument is more nuanced in its analysis of the ambiguities of colonial discourse raised by Burroughs' representation of language and translation, for both critics the novel's engagement with a colonial history is ultimately an attempt to reinforce American and/or Western imperial dominance at a moment of perceived threat. Gail Bederman summarises this well in her foundational text, writing that "Tarzan must live the life of an animal, then a savage, in order to become a man who is both masculine and civilized."[27] Moving away from a decadent and effeminised civilisation, Tarzan, like Thoreau before him, reclaims his masculine individuality through "simplifying" his life in Nature. Burroughs continually rewrites American Romanticism in his texts, always pairing it to a notion of evolution in which white men, and white civilisation, must—as Bederman most clearly outlines—reconnect to and overpower the primitive in order to embrace fully the individualist heritage that evolution has bestowed upon them.

Such readings certainly hold true. *Tarzan of the Apes* is, throughout, a novel that reinforces the supposedly universal truth and right of Anglo-Saxon dominance and also employs the most blunt of racist depictions of black people and of black Africans in particular. Where the present reading differs, however, is in the figuration both of precisely what it is that seemingly threatens that dominance and of the location of Burroughs' solution to this "problem." Specifically, both Cheyfitz and Berglund see Tarzan as reinforcing a form of whiteness against a variety of racialized, sexualised, and classed others, following the logic of the "crisis" of hegemonic masculinity. I argue, however, that Burroughs, running parallel to Emerson, sees the biggest threat to white patriarchal dominance within itself, that its relation to the so-called savage world merely instantiates a paradoxically self-destructive spiral of self-mis-identification. Burroughs' work does posit the necessity of reinvigorating white masculinity, but does so by turning away from what are represented as decadent, European forms of imperial violence to create, instead, a whiteness that has as its foundation a cultural and racial cosmopolitanism. Rather than reinforcing what Cheyfitz calls a universalised "homogeneous America" and defend a similarly homogenised notion of whiteness,[28] *Tarzan of the Apes* argues for finding strength in the malleability of whiteness. Thus, while Berglund notes that the novel's "enunciation of whiteness as ethnicity is remarkable given that whiteness is so often, and particularly in this era, constructed as normative," and hence, according to much of so-called "whiteness studies," as invisible,[29] I would argue that Burroughs is recognising, in Wiegman's words, that "the tension between particularity and universality ... characterizes ... the changing contours of white power and privilege," that, indeed, "being particular will not divest whiteness of its universal epistemological power."[30] To expand on this, the racist logic of Burroughs' text implies that culturally or ethically "non-white" cultural practices within whiteness "itself" can reinforce, rather than challenge, white power. Like Emerson's scholar, Tarzan is "that man who must take up into himself all the ability of the time, all the contributions of the past, all the hopes of the future," and because, again as for Emerson, "but one design unites and animates the farthest pinnacle and the lowest trench,"[31] there is no threat to the power of Tarzan's "Saxon breast" except that which comes from within.

Many critics gloss the beginning of the novel in which Tarzan's parents, John and Alice Clayton, Lord and Lady Greystoke, board a ship for Africa. Importantly, John Clayton is given, by the British Crown, a secret mission to investigate "the unfair treatment of black British subjects by the officers of a friendly European power," presumably Belgium.[32] This treatment is then elaborated upon: the Europeans are luring the indigenous Africans with "glowing promises" into service to collect "rubber and ivory" but, according to the British, they are actually "held in virtual slavery" (5). The novel begins, then, by asserting black British subjects' right to protection by the Crown and by explicitly condemning the remnants of the European enslavement and systematic slaughter of indigenous Africans. While it is certainly possible to read Burroughs as positing that only "foreign" imperialism, as opposed to British and subsequently American, is problematic in this way (as Marianna Torgovnick does), all the specific references to colonialism in the novel are portrayed in this light. As Torgovnick, in an extended reading of the whole series, argues, the Tarzan novels "condemn colonialism, in unequivocal terms."[33]

This claim needs to be more nuanced, however, since among the many sources and contexts for *Tarzan of the Apes*, Western narratives of African exploration stand out.[34] The nineteenth century saw the most significant increase in the European conquest and colonial settlement of Africa, especially in the latter half of the century. By the closing decades of the nineteenth century, Belgium, England, France, and other European nations began a period of increased colonial activities throughout Africa, beginning what has been called the "Scramble for Africa." The continent was not only significant for trade and the development of settlements, but it also became a pawn in various struggles between rival European powers.

Most important to readings of *Tarzan of the Apes* was the role played by King Leopold II of Belgium (1835–1909) in the Congo. Working under the auspices of a private company that was supposedly humanitarian in its goals, Leopold hired Welsh-American explorer Henry Morton Stanley (1841–1904) to lay the groundwork to develop a privately controlled state in the Congo. Stanley had already become famous as an explorer of Africa, having found David Livingstone, who had been "lost" in Africa. From Stanley's work, Leopold II was able to found the Congo Free State. His claim to the region was recognised at the Berlin West Africa conference (1884–1885), which was held to settle various nations' colonial and economic claims to the Congo River Basin area. The conference also outlawed slave trading in the region. Later, however, Leopold's control of the rubber trade, along with the abusive treatment and mass deaths of native Africans in the area became the subject of significant political controversy. On 20 May 1903, the British House of Commons unanimously passed a motion made by Herbert Samuels that read:

> That the Government of the Congo Free State having, at its inception, guaranteed to the Powers that its native subjects should be governed with humanity, and that no trading monopoly or privilege should be permitted within its dominions, this House requests His Majesty's Government to confer with the other Powers, signatories of the Berlin General Act by virtue of which the Congo Free State exists, in order that measures may be adopted to abate the evils prevalent in that state.[35]

By 1908, Leopold lost his private control of the Congo Free State, which then became the Belgian Congo, a formal colony of Belgium.[36]

Burroughs is explicit in setting his novel within this context. His most detailed biographer, Irwin Porges, notes that the author researched Africa in the Chicago Public Library, and stories of African exploration, including those by Stanley, were immensely popular. Tarzan's father, in fact, has significant parallels to Stanley: Clayton's mission to protect "black British subjects" picks up not only on the specific political actions mentioned above, but also on controversies surrounding Stanley, who was involved with the antislavery movement but was condemned by many for his brutal attitude and actions toward native Africans, a complaint that echoes those against Leopold himself.[37] Clayton's trip, moreover, takes place in 1888, when Stanley was also in Africa—also, like Clayton was to be, on the Congo—during his famous expedition to rescue Emin Pasha, the governor of Equatoria (then a province of Egypt); Stanley details this mission in his well-known work, *In Darkest Africa* (1890). Clayton arguably also shares similarities with Livingstone and others, but the allusion to Stanley is cemented by the fact that Clayton's wife, Lady Alice, clearly takes her name from Stanley's boat, the *Lady Alice* (a ship named *Lady Alice* also appears in the second novel, *The Return of Tarzan*). While Stanley could also serve as a possible model for Tarzan himself,[38] Stanley is a closer match to the ape-man's biological father. Burroughs exploits this jumble of allusions to represent the Belgians as an imperial evil of the first order, against which Clayton stands. The similarity of Clayton to Stanley, however, also presents Clayton and his mission to "protect black British subjects" in their own ambiguous light.

Of course, none of this negates the fact that Burroughs' representation of black Africans is not just steeped in but fully constituted by racist, imperial fantasies of African cannibalism, ignorance, and savagery. Even these sickening portrayals, however, are represented as finding not just a parallel, but an origin in European colonial activities. Specifically, the Belgians use one group of Africans to hunt another, rebellious group, who had killed and eaten their earlier captors. This rebellious group is in turn attacked, and most of them killed, by the larger detachment of black soldiers in the employ of the colonisers:

> That night the black soldiers of the white man had had meat a-plenty, and this little remnant of a once powerful tribe had slunk off into the gloomy jungle toward the unknown, and freedom. But what meant freedom and the pursuit of happiness to these savage blacks meant consternation and death to many of the wild denizens of their new home. (65–66)

First intermingling imperial oppression, anticolonial rebellion, and cannibalism into one indistinguishable mix, this passage then explicitly juxtaposes the original, rebellious group's desire for freedom with that of the American Revolution, but denies them a "natural" place in their own land, turning them, in turn, into colonisers and oppressors of the natural world of which Tarzan has made himself an integral part.

The novel is thus set up in terms broadly racist and white supremacist, but seemingly not as a justification for violent colonial practices. However, this reading also has to take into account the fact that Clayton's task is never completed, that he dies without ever reaching his new post, and that his son, Tarzan, goes on to become, in his own words, "THE KILLER OF BEASTS AND MANY BLACK MEN" (102). One could read this plot trajectory as a variation of the typical romance narrative, in which the dispossessed son goes on to correct the father's misguided mistakes in life, and in the process prove himself worthy of the patrimonial estate.[39] Even within this reading, though, one must account for the father's tragic flaw; in this case, Lord Greystoke's (and hence, symbolically, the British Empire's) flaw is not the political stance of protection rather than exploitation of the black British subjects, but is instead his own cultural isolationism, his desire to maintain a Britishness that remains somehow pure within the colonies, and hence his fear that his whiteness is threatened by the colonial Other. Clayton goes to Africa to investigate the abuses of "black British subjects," but sets up a colonial imaginary in which he is isolated from his surroundings. Since the Greystokes had intended a lengthy stay, they bring with them "a great quantity and variety of stuff … so that, in addition to the many necessities they had brought, were also many luxuries" (18). The key phrase, here, for understanding Clayton's role in Burroughs' transformation of imperial whiteness, is not the "many luxuries" but, instead, the "many necessities" that the Claytons deem imperative. The fact that the Claytons see British possessions as "necessities" within a colonised Africa, even as they are going, supposedly, to critique the practices of imperialism, indicates an approach-retreat relationship to the colonial site itself, an imperial neurosis in which the Empire at once wants to protect the colonial subject while distancing itself from that subject altogether.

Even after Clayton and his wife are abandoned alone on an uninhabited part of the African coastline by the mutineers who take over their transport ship, his attempts to survive centre on recreating a British space that is physically and cognitively isolated from the landscape that surrounds it. In fact, after she is attacked by a "great bull" ape, Alice recreates the scene around her, saying "I have had an awful dream, dear. I thought we were no longer in London, but in some horrible place where great beasts attacked us," and we learn "Lady Greystoke … was never again outside the cabin, nor did she ever fully realize that she was not in England" (26, 27). Lord Greystoke is hardly less delusional, however, in his attempted denial of his surroundings:

> At first he shot much of the game from the cabin windows. … In his leisure Clayton read, often aloud to his wife, from the store of books he had brought for their new home. Among these were many for little children—picture books, primers, readers—for they had known that their little child would be old enough for such before they might hope to return to England. At other times Clayton wrote in his diary, which he had always been accustomed to keep in French, and in which he recorded the details of their strange life. This book he kept locked in a little metal box. (27–28)

Isolated physically and mentally, Clayton is defined by a series of receding spaces, from the window of his cabin (complete with "strengthened … protections" [27]), to the cloister of books, to a metal box. The encounter with colonial space is not only defined by violence, but is only undertaken when "necessary," and then only from a remove: his world within his isolated cabin is defined first by a self-referential English didacticism represented by the primers; and second by his French diary, his European intellect, which must be locked in a box within a box, translated into a language not his own in order to increase its impenetrability by the outside. Traditional forms of imperial colonialism and European cosmopolitanism are shown to exist in an inverse relationship. As one isolates oneself further from the colonial space, one becomes more cosmopolitan, and vice versa. The representation of John Clayton may at first appear to be the beginning of a critique of imperial violence, but his relationship with the colonial space is one that makes him weak: he remains as Emerson's "old scholar," isolated and relying on a European past without recognising his colonial surroundings, which in turn are seen as only a threat to an English, and British, and European whiteness that must lock itself away to be safe.

III. ME COSMOPOLITAN, YOU CANNIBAL

Opposed to this culturally isolationist colonialism stands the relationship between Clayton's son, Tarzan, and this mythologised African landscape. Raised by what Burroughs calls "anthropoid ape[s]" (24) after his parents' deaths, Tarzan's relation to the colonial space is, from the beginning, direct. As Torgovnick points out, the Tarzan novels "loathe colonialism and imperialism, and yet they valorize the ideas that made (and make) Euro-American colonialism and imperialism possible." While Torgovnick reads this as simply a reflection of the "contradictory and double" nature of American notions of "race and related issues,"[40] the character of Tarzan is precisely Burroughs' attempt to provide a racialized Anglo-Saxon ideal that supposedly transcends this conundrum. Tarzan's development and cultural appropriations are what permit him to form a "proper" relationship with the world around him, allowing him to defend his Anglo-Saxon masculinity, and to learn not to repeat what is represented as the savageness of his surrounding world.

At a pivotal moment of *Tarzan of the Apes*, the eponymous protagonist meets, kills, and prepares to eat the first human being he has ever seen, a black African named Kulonga:

> The knife with its sheath and belt caught his eye; he appropriated them. A copper anklet also took his fancy, and this he transferred to his own leg. He examined and admired the tattooing on the forehead and breast. He marveled at the sharp filed teeth. He investigated and appropriated the feathered head-dress, and then he prepared to get down to business, for Tarzan of the Apes was hungry, and here was meat; meat of the kill, which jungle ethics permitted him to eat. How may we judge him, by what standards, this ape-man with the heart and head and body of an English gentleman, and the training of a wild beast? (72)

Despite his "jungle ethics," but in keeping with the generally racist overtones of the text, Tarzan's "heart and head and body"—the holy triumvirate of sentiment, reason, and racial biology that constitutes the "ideal" ethical form of Anglo-American manhood at the turn of the century—do not allow him to physically cannibalise Kulonga. Kulonga's tribe members, conversely, are portrayed as unabashed and joyous cannibals, albeit many of the scenes of cannibalism in the novel are perpetrated on colonisers or their agents (or those who could be mistaken for such).[41]

Tarzan's innate horror at cannibalism, however, necessarily goes hand in hand with the fact that he "appropriates" Kulonga's possessions and other signs of the latter's culture. He also continues to kill black men from the village, specifically so he can claim their "various arm and leg ornaments" which he then "don[s] ... after the way he had seen them worn" (95). This passage was added to the novel after its original magazine publication, emphasising the link between cannibalism and culture. One can, for instance, distinctly see in Tarzan's actions an economic form of cultural consumption, figured through cannibalism and its denial, of the form so well critiqued by bell hooks, "wherein whatever difference the Other inhabits is eradicated, *via* exchange, by a consumer cannibalism that not only displaces the Other but denies the significance of that Other's history through a process of decontextualization."[42] But Tarzan's appropriations also function to silence the "other" in a different manner. The fact of Tarzan's cultural appropriation—when combined with the other facts that he teaches himself to read English, is taught to speak French by a French officer, is later discovered to be the rightful heir to the title of English Lord, and captures the heart of a Daisy Miller-esque American girl (and, in later novels, becomes an international gentleman spy)—demonstrates that Tarzan's ideal Anglo-Saxon manhood is constituted not just or even primarily by physical prowess, nor by a form of blunt consumer power, but instead by a form of essentialised cosmopolitan cultural access, an inborn sense of what constitutes "proper" appropriation.

Cosmopolitan desires and actions, a willingness to "become native," can therefore reinforce Anglo-Saxon patriarchal identity, rather than threaten it. In this portrayal, as in many things, Burroughs seems to be rearticulating a Romantic philosophy. As Lauren M. E. Goodlad and Julia M. Wright have argued:

> While cosmopolitanism in its ideal form is defined by a respect for other peoples and cultures, it remains yoked to the same biases which shaped the Enlightenment as a whole—Eurocentric, phallocentric, and middle-class. In the eighteenth century, the term "cosmopolitan," even as a reference to a certain "'philosophical' attitude" within "a common European civilization," cannot embrace the migrant poor, the Romany, and, until much later, women. For the term translates literally as "citizen of the world," and these groups did not have access to citizenship.[43]

The fact that Tarzan (the character and the novel) still makes violent decisions based on racist logic does not dissipate, but is instead framed within a cosmopolitan logic that makes such violence the "natural" result of a "proper" relationship to one's surroundings. Tarzan adapts to new surroundings not by altering his position, but by adopting new behaviours that still reinforce his superiority. Still willing to "kill the blacks" (240) even after moving toward "civilization"—because their skin colour makes them supposedly natural objects for Tarzan's violence—he is nonetheless willing to explore different modes of interaction. This willingness is not due to "civilization" making him question his racist assumptions, but is precisely the result of his confidence in his Anglo-Saxon superiority, a confidence that is lacking in other white men.

Tarzan's "smooth, brown skin" (209) is thus a visual metaphor for a cultural hybridity that nonetheless shores up, rather than undermines, his essential white manhood, the "heart and head and body of an English gentleman," perfecting the description of his father, who is described earlier as "a strong, virile man—mentally, morally, and physically" (6). Reversing in order "mentally" and "morally" by emphasising "heart" over "head," Tarzan can be read as correcting the hyper-rationality of Victorian whiteness, offering a re-Romanticized American definition of whiteness that asserts a moral right over all. It's not just that Tarzan's whiteness is so unassailable that it can shine through his "brown skin," it's more that he is so white he has to show it through his brownness. Tarzan is the epitome of white masculinity because it can be translated into any cultural context, across any border or boundary (unlike his father's entrenched, protected whiteness).

Burroughs' populism, and his own purported "positive personal record of intercultural/racial relations,"[44] can thus be read as reinforcing a new, populist level of racist white power based on a liberal allowance of non-whiteness, rather than an imperial violence of colonial subjection (one can think here of the British parliament's condemnation of Leopold's brutality, shored up by their own paternalist objectification of the indigenous peoples of the Congo region). Tarzan's sense of self in turn becomes a cultural mimicry that—in a partial inversion of Bhabha's reading of colonial mimicry—stabilises, rather than threatens, Tarzan's racial identity, his "Saxon breast[]," in Emerson's terms.[45] Not a "phobic myth of the undifferentiated whole white body," in Bhabha's terms,[46] Tarzan's white identity is unthreatened precisely because it can be culturally—perhaps even racially—malleable. Created at a time when the United States was engaged in a massive cultural and social debate over the influx of rural African Americans into the then largely white urban centres, as well as, in Cheyfitz's words, "when the second great wave of immigration to the United States ... was at its crest,"[47] Tarzan (the character and the book) thus uses the trope of cannibalism in order to function as an apparently racist "corrective" to progressive, liberal race relations, while simultaneously appearing to deny the most obviously violent aspects of the history of racism and imperialism (allegorized as a cannibalism Tarzan denies), a combination that has made Tarzan an especially pernicious and long-standing figure of racism in American popular culture.

IV. TECHNO-TARZAN

Tarzan is a contradictory figure of nostalgia for a masculinity lost in the decadence of civilisation, but which is nonetheless made popular through the cutting edge of multimedia popular culture. Given this contradiction between the figure and the technology that made him so popular, one might ask whether this supposedly natural masculinity could find a comfortable place *within* the culture of the scientific age of the twentieth century. Textually, after all, Tarzan continually returns to the jungle, unable to maintain his sense of self in the midst of civilisation. So, can the manly myth of Tarzan serve as anything but a nostalgic one, with little application (outside of the largely antimodern scouting and back-to-nature movements tied to Tarzan) to the contemporary world Burroughs portrayed as so decadent?[48]

While Burroughs' own John Carter may be one answer to that question (as DeGraw discusses), Buck Rogers is the very model of a modern techno-Tarzan. Building on the foundation that was, if not started, then popularised by *Tarzan of the Apes* a decade earlier, the character of Buck Rogers cements the attempt to create a re-masculinised modern man in the face of what was presented as an effeminising reliance on modern technology and international trade. Readers on occasion linked the two characters: shortly after the publication of Nowlan's first Rogers narrative in *Amazing Stories*, a reader—Carol Hodges of Miami Beach, Florida—wrote to the magazine to laud it as "one of the most entertaining stories, since I first became 'afflicted' with the Amazing Stories habit," to request a sequel and to "inquire as to the lack—regrettable to my mind—of more stories by Edgar Rice Burroughs."[49] Building on Tarzan's fixation on manhood, but retreating to and expanding on the figure of a racialized threat, Buck Rogers has, through his many incarnations, come to frame the twentieth century as a period during which white Western masculinity was placed under consistent "threat" by an effeminised, Orientalised other, an otherness that, significantly, is also represented as a characteristic of advanced technological civilisation itself. In other words, while Tarzan portrays civilisation as an emasculating force due to its lack of connection to a natural life, Buck Rogers places that narrative into a new racial dynamic, where civilisation is equated to technology which is, in turn, associated with a feminised, Orientalised other.

While details change between the various media, the overall arc of the story of Buck Rogers remains the same. In both Nowlan's original novella and in the beginning of the comic strip, the story starts with a device typical of utopian literature: Anthony Rogers falls asleep and awakens hundreds of years later. He finds himself a displaced twentieth-century man in a postapocalyptic America that is now ruled by a Chinese imperial power which, it is revealed at the end of the sequel, is actually composed of extraterrestrials. As with Tarzan, Buck Rogers holds a central position in twentieth-century America's popular imagination and is an especially iconic figure within the so-called "Yellow Peril" tradition: a recent anthology of Nowlan's work notes that he was honoured in Congress in 2002, when Curt Weldon, a Republican member of the House of Representatives, expressed his "sincere appreciation to [Nowlan] for all his contributions to American culture" (perhaps important to note here is that Weldon served on the Cox Committee in the late 1990s, which was charged with investigating transfers of U.S. nuclear weapons science technology to China).[50]

Thematically, then, Buck Rogers becomes a figure who can be slotted into different periods' incarnations of hegemonic masculinity, with the proliferation of Buck Rogers media, like that of Tarzan, allowing for a plethora of figurations of "proper" white, heterosexual manhood, along with their correlates in proper "American" technology. I focus here on the novellas and the opening year of the comic strip[51] in order to show the ways in which these works popularise a cultural narrative that takes as its foundation the idea that the technological advancement of Western civilisation breeds its own collapse through an ever-increasing disembodiment of white men: once again following a logic similar to Burroughs', Nowlan characterises technological advances as highlighting the intellectual nature of "whiteness" and the rational aspects of "manliness" to the point that white men supposedly lose a connection to their physical nature.[52]

The narrative of the "threatening" disembodiment of white masculine intellect is not new to us, of course: as I discussed in the previous chapter, Hawthorne's Aylmer, as "mad scientist," similarly portrays the interconnection of whiteness, advanced science and technology, and fragility. Likewise, Waldo Emerson Smith-Jones from Burroughs' *The Cave Girl* is the "ultra-intellectual[]" with the "fond mother" whose dormant masculinity is suppressed by this effeminising "culture plus."[53] Perhaps the best examples, though, come again from *Tarzan of the Apes*. Jane's father, Professor Archimedes Q. Porter, is the quintessential image of the "absent-minded professor," confusing a man-eating lion with an escaped zoo specimen in one of the novel's more memorable scenes. As Bederman notes of this scene, "Porter's ideology of civilized manliness is ludicrous and impotent,"[54] but it needs to be noted that this is specifically an effect of his *scientific* intellect, where the hyper-rationality of pure science is figured as the epitome of civilisation's discontents. Professor Porter's manliness is likewise called into question in a series of fiscal exchanges that echo precisely Eve Kosofsky Sedgwick's discussion of homosociality:[55] offering up Jane's hand in marriage in exchange for funding for his treasure hunt, when he cannot come through, his daughter is nearly forced to marry the evil Robert Canler. Tarzan, of course, finds Porter's treasure and saves the day, even though, at the end of the first novel, he still "loses the girl" to his cousin Clayton. Thus, Porter's manhood—as symbolised in his ability to protect and "properly" exchange his daughter—is undermined by his intellectual endeavours (even though, as Breu and Traister would point out, this "threat" does nothing to undermine the system of patriarchal exchange that is the marriage market). This critique is also made explicit in the comparison of Tarzan, in his jungle, to the "other Lord Greystoke," in London, which occurs a few times in the novel. While Tarzan "wiped his greasy fingers upon his naked thighs ... another Lord Greystoke ... sent back his chops to the club's *chef* because they were underdone, and when he had finished his repast he dipped his finger-ends into a silver bowl of scented water and dried them upon a piece of snowy damask" (70). When Tarzan kills Sabor and unleashes his "savage and triumphant pæan," at the same time "in London another Lord Greystoke was speaking to *his* kind in the House of Lords, but none trembled at the sound of his soft voice" (85).

Though tied more to social convention than intellectualism *per se*, these last examples still point to the degenerating and effeminising effects of civilisation and the necessarily masculinising effects of nature and its concomitant violence. Likewise, in Nowlan's novellas, science and its offshoots in technology come to be figured as a gendered and racial threat to a white masculinity that—due to its own hyper-rationality—is paradoxically portrayed as the source of its own undoing.[56]

Published in the August 1928 *Amazing Stories,* Nowlan's first novella, *Armageddon—2419 A.D.*, was set nearly five hundred years in the future. But the specific date in the title could be significant in itself: 2419 is, after all, a simple inversion of 1924, the year that the Johnson-Reed Immigration Act was passed (the Act is also known as The Immigration Act of 1924). This Act created a quota system for immigration to the United States based on national origins and included the "Asian Exclusion Act." While the 1924 Act is commonly read as being directed primarily at immigration from Japan and from Eastern Europe, it is also tied to a general anti-Asian racism that was earlier enshrined in law in the nineteenth-century Chinese Exclusion Act. The 1924 legislation expands that Act to curtail nearly all Asian immigration.[57] Anthony Rogers' trip through time to 2419 America offers a vision of an inverted 1924 America, a dystopian future that the 1924 Immigration Act was supposedly intended to stop. Rogers narrates the history of this future America:

> It seemed that another war had followed the First World War, in which nearly all the European nations had banded together to break the financial and industrial power of America. They succeeded in their purpose, though they were beaten, for the war was a terrific one, and left America, like themselves, gasping, bleeding and disorganized, with only the hollow shell of a victory. This opportunity had been seized by the Russian Soviets, who had made a coalition with the Chinese, to sweep over all Europe and reduce it to a state of chaos. ... But it was impossible to stave off war with the Mongolians, who by now had subjugated the Russians, and were aiming at a world empire. ... The Mongolians, with overwhelming fleets of great airships, and a science that far outstripped that of crippled America, swept in over the Pacific and Atlantic Coasts, and down from Canada, annihilating American aircraft, armies and cities with their terrific *disintegrator* rays.[58]

Myriad sociocultural fears that found their material expression in the 1924 Immigration Act find their cultural echoes in this passage. In-fighting between the non-Soviet (and presumably non-Eastern) European nations and America—what were perceived at the time as the two racially white geopolitical spaces on the globe—leaves both groups subject to invasion by the East, first Eastern Europe and then Asia, the two areas mostly targeted for exclusion by the Immigration Act.

This general engagement in the "Yellow Peril" tradition plays into the novella's larger discussion of global politics, specifically, but, because it is tied to concepts of race and "peoples," also addresses early twentieth-century notions of civilisation *per se*. In this vision, Nowlan revises Burroughs' plot, pitting the supposed decadence of modern, scientific civilisation against a neo-romantic vision of nature and self-reliance. In Nowlan's work, the decadence of civilisation is largely deflected onto the imperial power of the novel, the so-called Han Dynasty: "through these many generations," we are told, "the Hans had developed a luxury economy, and with it the perfection of gilded vice and degradation. The Americans were regarded as 'wild men of the woods'" (426). Presenting an opposition between nature and technological civilisation, and a direct correlation between "gilded vice" and "degradation," Nowlan replays the very formula popularised by Burroughs. Like Burroughs' Tarzan, the Americans in Nowlan's future are forced into a hostile wilderness, where they must refashion themselves individually and collectively. This enforced connection to nature, furthermore, following the formula's neo-Romantic structure, necessarily revitalises the Americans:

> nearly three hundred years of easily maintained security, the last century of which had been nearly sterile in scientific, social and economic progress, had softened and devitalized the Hans. It had likewise developed, beneath the protecting foliage of the forest, the growth of a vigorous new American civilization, remarkable in the mobility and flexibility of its organization, in its conquest of almost insuperable obstacles, in the development and guarding of its industrial and scientific resources, all in anticipation of that "Day of Hope" to which it had been looking forward for generations, when it would be strong enough to burst from the green chrysalis of the forests, soar into the upper air lanes and destroy the yellow incubus. (422)

Unlike Burroughs' novel, where an English lord is forced into the African jungle, rediscovering his masculine prowess within an explicitly imperial setting, Nowlan's Americans are natural products of a landscape to which they are racially attached. This is Herderian nationalism in the extreme:[59] not only connected to the land, the Americans are in fact both created and metamorphosed by it. The "ancient American centers" (422), the technological past and urban life that the Hans have taken over, are represented as holding America back from its rebirth out of the "green chrysalis" of the American landscape itself. The imperial power, meanwhile, the "Hans [*sic*] race," becomes "devitalized by its vices and luxuries, with machinery and scientific processes to satisfy its every want, with virtually no necessity of labor" (426). As with the comparisons between the Greystoke cousins in *Tarzan of the Apes*, the seeming "strength" or "weakness" of racial and national characteristics is here explicitly tied to the proximities of, respectively, nature or technology.

But there is a possible contradiction here. Nowlan does, after the fashion of Gernsbackian "scientifiction," spend much time lauding the impressive innovations that the Americans have developed in science and technology, including antigravity belts and the nearly mystical synthetic substance "Inertron," the latter of which forms "a perfect shield against the disintegrator rays" of their enemies (430). Even the editorial published on this first page of the *Amazing Stories* publication of *Armageddon—2419 A.D.* speaks to this emphasis:

> We have rarely printed a story in this magazine that for scientific interest, as well as suspense, could hold its own with this particular story. We prophecy that this story will become more valuable as the years go by. It certainly holds a number of interesting prophecies, of which no doubt, many will come true. For wealth of science, it will be hard to beat for some time to come. (422)

Likewise, when the sequel, *Airlords of Han* appeared in 1929, a similar editorial appeared, stating:

> If you have read "*Armageddon—2419 A.D.*"—and we are sure you have—you may have a slight idea what is in store for you in the present sequel. … Apparently Mr. Nowlan has developed an entirely new technique in inventing new and amazing instrumentalities, and indeed, wholly new branches of science itself, particularly science as applied to warfare. And no matter how fast a thinker and no matter how good a scientist you are, you will find that the author is always a few steps ahead of you and anticipates your own thoughts nine times out of ten.[60]

Warfare is merely an indicator of scientific progress in these brief descriptions (and in the "teaser" ads that appeared in the previous months' issues), and the stories are rendered into scientific prediction: indeed, in the second description, the act of storytelling becomes almost a meta-technology, as the author "develop[s] an entirely new technique" of invention itself. The stories seem to contradict this technological fetish, portraying the Americans as needing the landscape in order to be revitalised and protected from the technological decadence that characterises the Han empire. But, part of the Americans' vitality, as opposed to the "devitalized" nature of the World Empire, is figured precisely by burgeoning new technologies, while the Hans are described as "nearly sterile in scientific, social and economic progress" (422). But if technology is equated to civilisation, and civilisation to decadence and decay, why, then, does Nowlan place so much emphasis on the scientific and technological advances of the Americans? Why not create a Tarzan instead of a Buck Rogers?

The novella and other incarnations of Rogers do struggle with this question. The figure of Rogers himself provides the apparent solution, as is made most clear in the early installments of the original comic strip, where the future American nation/race is represented as not only conquered, but also effeminised, and specifically lacking in men. In the third strip of the series, after saving Buck when he first awakens, Wilma—Buck's love interest in all the versions of the story—asks him "Are you married?" and then explains, in the following strip, that "the Org needs more eligible bachelors." A few strips later, she wonders "if Buck really likes girls who fight" since "He says American girls weren't soldiers five hundred years ago."[61] While the original novellas are more ambiguous in their representation of women soldiers, presenting even a basis of gender equality, the comic strip elaborates on the representation of a future America that is at once on the verge of a newly energised and vigorous masculine civilisation, while simultaneously under the constant threat of becoming subservient and effeminised by the very technology that will help them gain dominance. The comic strip ties this gender portrayal into its racism since, as Patrick B. Sharp has written, the Buck of the comic strips "must repeatedly save the white woman from Mongols and half-breeds,"[62] another plot device seen in the opening dailies quoted above.

How can this technological paradox be reconciled? Rogers' character is developed in such a way that he provides a link to a primordial manhood that will maintain the proper relation between what is called the "rustic simplicity" of this new civilisation and its "laboratories and engine rooms" (429). Snatched out of time, Nowlan's Rogers is likewise snatched from the clutches of a decadent civilisation and dropped into a "vast forest" at the beginning of the novella, where he must live off of "wild game" (424, 425). This emphasis on the necessity of a connection to the wilderness—and, as we will see, the nostalgia the character embodies for a more "primitive" space and time—makes it clear: Rogers is, in fact, Tarzan in the twenty-fifth century.

A hero of the First World War (which Nowlan, like a few others, was prescient enough to call the "First" World War), Rogers remains untouched by what is represented as the decadent technological advancements of the postwar period. Moreover, the Americans of the twenty-fifth century require the connection to the past that Rogers represents in order to succeed in reclaiming the continent. After scientifically testing Rogers to make sure he is telling the truth about his origin, he has a conversation with a leader of the American forces,[63] who says: "So you fought in the First World War. Do you know, we have very little left in the way of records of the details of that war, that is, the precise conditions under which it was fought, and the tactics employed. … I think you might have a lot of ideas worth thinking over for our raid masters" (428). The necessary supplement of the need for a connection to nature is nostalgia itself, the need for a connection to the past. In order to be able to regain civilisation without its discontents, this future America needs to follow the lead of the primitive man in the proper use and exercise of that civilisation and its concomitant technologies. As Rogers narrates, "I found that my 20th Century muscles did have an advantage, in spite of lack of skill" (428). To return to the chapter's introduction, Nowlan here can be said to reframe Foucault's argument about the repressive hypothesis of sexuality, in which "Tomorrow sex will be good again" (7): in the Buck Rogers universe, men were always better in the past. Rogers becomes the image of the virile man who is untouchable by the decadence that surrounds him; his military skill is valuable precisely—if paradoxically—because he has no skill or knowledge of the military technology of the time.

This position is made clear when he is captured in *The Airlords of Han*. The enemy attempts to use its "hypnotic torture" on him, but he proves completely resistant. Being made to see a false image of Wilma, now his wife, being tortured and begging him to surrender, he realises

> subconsciously that this was not Wilma. Product of the utmost of nobility in this modern, virile, rugged American race, she would have died ... before she would have pleaded with me this way to betray my race and her honor. ... Their intelligence division also failed to pick up the fact that I was myself the product of the Twentieth Century, and not the Twenty-fifth. Had they done so, it might have made a difference. I have no doubt that some of their most subtle mental assaults missed fire because of my own Twentieth Century "denseness." Their hypnotists inflicted many horrifying nightmares on me, and made me do and say many things that I would not have done in my right senses. But even in the Twentieth Century we had learned that hypnotism cannot make a person violate his fundamental concepts of morality against his will, and steadfastly I steeled my will against them. I have since thought that I was greatly aided by my newness to this age. I have never, as a matter of fact, become entirely attuned to it. And even today I confess to a longing wish that man might travel backward as well as forward in time. (1118)

Being out of time, Rogers is both disconnected from the psychological realities of his new life and more in tune with his "fundamental concepts of morality." Moreover, the "American race," having been forced out of advanced civilisation and back into the wilderness, has recaptured a more essential "virile, rugged" nature: they are a nation of Tarzans, led by a throwback, and armed with ray guns.[64]

V. PHALECTROCENTRISM

There is still a divide between Rogers as a nostalgic image of masculinity—Rogers as Tarzan—and the desire for an America that will be relevant in the technological future—Rogers with ray guns. How, then, does Rogers' masculinity get zapped into a futurist, or future-oriented, technological America? Can Tarzan stop returning to the jungle and remain Tarzan? The general narrative of 1920s America is one in which technological advances fuel American global supremacy (the narrative that in turn fuels so much of Golden Age SF), and such technological advances lie in the supposedly unbiased realm of science. The editorial descriptions of Nowlan's novellas speak to this narrative, clearly. Just as significantly, the advertisements in *Amazing Stories* duplicate this same telos and emphasise the way in which it continually interpellates the magazine's readers and the burgeoning SF readership more generally. While there is a range of advertisements, many of them are framed through representations of the future being dominated by new technologies—from small graphics advertising guns for sale, to larger pieces for new stoves directed at women readers, to those for material promising to teach readers about the new and exciting technology of television. A selection of these advertisements can help to position the role of technology *viz.* the readership of Nowlan's work. In at least one printing, the issue of *Amazing Stories* in which *Armageddon—2419* appears begins with two full-page advertisements: one from the "University of Applied Science" in Chicago, for a book promising to train you as "a highly paid Finger Print Expert," and saying that with this skill, "Any man who can read and write, and think can make good" (384). The other, from the "Coyne Electrical School," offers courses to train you on "real live electrical machinery," claiming the possibility for earnings of "$60 to $200 a WEEK" (385). Two other ads follow the table of contents: one offering a "Startling Realization Lecture, Now Sent Entirely Free" (when you send in the "FREE REALIZATION COUPON"): this lecture, from the "American Institute of Psychology," "Explains How to Master *Your* Little Self and Do the Things *You* Want to Do" (387). The second is yet another exciting job opportunity in the field of electricity, billed as the *"WORLD'S BIGGEST, FASTEST-GROWING BUSINESS"* (388). Most of the advertisements appear at the end of the magazine, and include a mixture of smaller, inexpensive, text-based advertisements, but also larger page spreads. In this issue, these include a one-page spread that asserts that "BURIED TREASURE can still be found in CHEMISTRY" (467), while a smaller one shows a picture of a muscular man next to the promise "I Positively Guarantee to increase your arms one-half inch in size, chest one full inch, strength 25%, health, 100% in one week's time by following my instructions and using my exerciser 10 minutes mornings and at night," and all for "$1" (or so says "PROF. J. A. DRYER" from Chicago) (469). Finally, another full page, centred by a drawing of a semi-nude, seemingly injured woman, offers a subscription to the publication "Your Body," a quarterly magazine that, like *Amazing Stories*, was published by Gernsback's "Experimenter Publishing" (at this time facing bankruptcy); the ad tells the reader that this magazine is "Not a 'health magazine,' but a unique encyclopedia of practical knowledge of all things pertaining to medicine, sexology, physiology, anatomy, etc., etc." all "Handsomely printed in two colors," and promising that "It is a real encyclopedia of sex problems" (472; advertisements for "Your Body" in other issues of

Amazing Stories vary from pedagogical, domestically inflected living room scenes to the more lurid, with nude women frolicking in an Edenic riverside wilderness scene).[65]

In this material surrounding Nowlan's work, none of it uncommon in *Amazing Stories*, self-reliance, economic success, masculine prowess, and the "problems" of sexuality are paired with science, technology, and scientific authority in an inseparable cycle of progress, success, self-discovery, and sexual titillation. The readership is here positioned as largely (though not solely) male, and technology is framed as the means through which those male readers can both gain knowledge of themselves and improve their lot in life, all of which is framed within a larger narrative of the advancement of the larger society through similar means. More Emersonian than Fordist, the magazine situates the nation as being composed not of interchangeable cogs, but of socially valuable, because self-improving, individuals.

The pictures accompanying these advertisements, all showing white men (with the exception of the one white woman in the ad for "Your Body"), implicitly underscore the secondary narrative of this progress and success: the discourse of technology *per se* is shown to be inseparable from the discourses of race and gender. Beyond *Amazing Stories*, and beyond SF specifically, this period did, of course, see many examples such as these of technology's, and especially electricity's, connection to notions of men's personal power and virility: one of the more direct examples is the so-called "electric belt," the history and politics of which are wonderfully analysed by Carolyn Thomas de la Peña. As de la Peña details, the electric belt was a sex device for men, which looped around the waste and cupped a man's genitalia in "the suspensory sack," and released small charges of electricity through either a basic chemical reaction or, later, by plugging the device into an outlet. Rereading the history of the use of electrical images as design features through the advertisement history of the electric belt, de la Peña argues that "the electrified penis became a catalyst for a modern masculinity, one that could throw off inefficiencies of the nineteenth century and embrace the demands of modern intimacy, all while absorbing in the most intimate fashion the potential of a technological age."[66]

Likewise beyond such devices and advertisements, and outside of the material cultural realm, the early pulp "scientifictions" of the Gernsback era, of which Nowlan's works are prime examples, indicate a much more diffuse, and so more entangled, connection between technology and gender and race, to the point that technology and identity become mutually inclusive. In *The Airlords of Han*, Rogers, again the narrator, offers what he describes as an aside to the central narrative in order to discuss the differences between American and Han technologies. Chapters IV and V, respectively, detail "Han Electrono-Ray Science" and "American Ultronic Science" (1112; 1113). The distinctions the narrator draws are pointed ones, insofar as they echo vaguely Freudian gender paradigms. Rogers' description of his enemy's technology focuses on its "opposing circuits" and on its reliance on and creation of nothingness, or a gap, in the physical reality that surrounds it. The Han technology is based on the "broadcast [of] three distinct '*powers*' simultaneously" (1112; emphasis in original). The first component, the "starter" is described roughly in terms of 1920s telecommunications technology. It is said to be broadcast "at a frequency of about 1,000 kilocycles, had an amperage of approximately zero, but a voltage of two billion" (1112). Nonsensical in terms of actual electronics, this description of Han science, and therefore Han identity, is based around a conspicuous *lack*, around the "amperage of approximately zero" which somehow still allows a certain creative principle, in the flow of "two billion" volts. Likewise, the movement of their airships is based on passivity, with a "force exerted upward against the ship," and an energy that worked through "twin synchronizers" that "were isolated in vast spherical steel chambers with thick walls, so that nothing but air pressure would be hurled against them, and this, of course, would be self-neutralizing" (1112–13). Finally, their weaponry, a ray which could "destroy [the] polarity balance of the atom and caus[e] it to cease to exist," was able to "reduce[] matter to 'nothingness'" (1113). Characterised by lack, gaps, and mysteriously empty containers, Han technology embodies a feminine lack of vigour, an overall lack of manhood that characterises Rogers' description of their culture.

American technology, conversely, functions through complementarity. As the American scientists "progressed," Rogers states, "they developed constructive as well as destructive practice," a scientific principle that finds its material incarnation in "the great triumphs of ultron and inertron, our two wonderful synthetic elements, built up from super-balanced and sub-balanced ultronic whorls" (1113). As opposed to the supposedly "imbalanced" Han science, based solely on feminine lack, American science is represented as both "balanced" and properly virile. A matched pairing that is both destructive and constructive when necessary, composed of both "spherical shell[s]" and "a core pole" (not to mention the mysterious "*glow-spot*") (1114), American technology is placed within a heteronormative logic that emphasises the masculine, specifically in the representation of scientific discovery as a "penetration into the 'sub'-orders" (1113). In this science, size doesn't even matter, since, as Rogers tells us, "Accuracy of alignment permits beam paths no thicker than the old lead pencils I used to use in the Twentieth Century" (1114).

There is a profound distinction drawn between these two technologies, and it is one that echoes, almost to the point of comedy, sexual and gender distinctions. The fact that the comparison is set up as an aside, as an extra-diegetic, scientific exploration, is also significant. Quite markedly divorced from the action of the plot (Rogers ends the comparison, at the beginning of a new chapter, with "But to return to my narrative" [1114]), this scientific study performs what Darko Suvin has called SF's "cognitive" function, that is, its attempt to connect the unreality of the narrative to the material reality of science. Given this, the gendered descriptions of science are more than humourous archaisms of early SF, but instead become an ideological formation of the "truths" of "proper" science as opposed to the "falsities" of "improper" scientific study, again following the comments China Miéville makes in the interview discussed in the introduction.[67] And, in the end, this supposedly cognitive device plays what could be called a precognitive, ideological function: "proper" science is white, American, and male and needs to be explicitly so in order for the effeminacy and degenerative racial effects of a reliance on technology to be held at bay. In some ways, Nowlan is here replicating the transcendent power that Henry Adams, in his autobiography, famously associates with the electrical dynamo exhibit at the Chicago World's Fair; but Nowlan is perhaps attempting to recover that power for masculinity from Adams' feminised association of it with the religious power of the Virgin.[68] Writing of Adams and other canonical figures, Caleb Smith argues that "social life was being transformed by electrification and by women's increasingly visible entry into the marketplace," leading "male authorities" to "a series of reactionary moves that parried the shocks of modernity."[69] Rogers himself becomes the central image for this necessity: without a nostalgic and technologically primitive masculinity, technology will corrupt.

But Rogers is not the only figure thus employed. In *The Airlords of Han*, American supremacy in science and culture—allegorically represented as the final victory of the Americans over the Han—literally becomes about having the balls: in this case, remote-controlled exploding balls that also serve as television cameras, or eyes, which highlight the gendered ideology of the scientific identity politics at play:

> Then followed the "air balls," an unforeseen and ingenious resurrection by the Americans of an old principle of air and submarine tactics, through a modern application of the principle of remote control. ... One uneasy night ... there was an explosion near the top of a pinnacle not far from the Imperial Tower. It occurred at the 732nd level, and caused the structure above it to lean and sag, though it did not fall. Repair men who shot up the shafts a few minutes later ... reported what seemed to be a sphere of metal ... floating slowly down the shaft, as though it were some living creature making a careful examination, pausing now and then as its lens swung about like a great single eye. The moment this "eye" turned upon them, they said, the ball "rushed" down on them, crushing several to death in its vicious gyrations, and jamming the mechanism of the elevator. ... Then, said the wounded survivors, it floated back up the shaft, watchfully "eyeing" them. ... (1126)

Eastern science may be represented as an emasculating Sandman, Nowlan seems to write, but American science will respond by exploding in the Sandman's hands, causing the Eastern towers to "lean and sag."[70] Following the chapter "The Forest Men Attack," this chapter, "The Mysterious 'Air Balls,'" combines the futurism of scientific endeavour with the nostalgic portrayal of a natural, virile masculinity, once again indicated by a return to the military tactics of Buck's own time. The advance of technology, it seems, presents an ever-present threat to the "natural" order of things, as allegorised by Nowlan in the reversal of the 1924 immigration policy, in the colonisation of white, masculine America by an effeminate, Orientalised other. In order to prevent the culmination of such a threat, the futurism of technology itself must be contained by a nostalgic masculinity; this process in turn helps to project a static, monolithic image of white, male, and American superiority from the past into the always already-decadent present and ever-threatened future. In other words, the Buck Rogers story, a mobile text that comes to prominence as a multimedia work, serves as a multipronged device aimed at maintaining a monolithic cultural definition of an Anglo-Saxon and masculine America in the face of rapidly expanding media technology and a rapidly transforming American citizenry and geopolitical situation. From the phallogocentrism of Tarzan and his fascination with his father's European books, we come to a phalectrocentrism, where the masculinity of white America is both threatened and bolstered by the increasing pace of technological innovation. The speculative nature of the story of technological progress—the story of the America to come—can here be exposed as a backwards-looking antiscience, a self-perpetuating narrative of scientific and cultural progression paradoxically grounded in a necessarily static, nostalgic vision of a fully masculine, fully white America that never was.

This "solution," then, to defining a properly virile American civilisation echoes Tarzan's provincial cosmopolitanism. Where Tarzan can appropriate "other" cultures only precisely because he is, in his essence, impervious to their degenerative effects because of his connection to an essential, natural self, Buck Rogers' futurist America can employ technology without becoming decadent precisely because that technology springs from a nation of Tarzans, a nostalgic, Emersonian vision of a virile, "natural" America. Cosmopolitan consumption, for Tarzan, and the use of modern military technology, for Buck, are merely gloss, there to express and highlight their very disdain of such superfluities. These pulp icons of the early twentieth century thus point the way for white, masculine America to save itself from the threats of the new century and to project itself into the future, in an endless, fetishistic, and even narcissistic replaying of itself for itself. In Tarzan and Buck Rogers, it seems, America has two daddies. But perhaps this situation informs another possibility, one that Frank-N-Furter realised, that opens up another form of semiotic identification with these figures, a queering of SF's relation to dominance to which this book returns in its afterword.

NOTES

1. Michel Foucault, *History of Sexuality*, vol. 1, translated by Robert Hurley (1978; New York: Vintage, 1990), 7.
2. J. Jack Halberstam, *Female Masculinity* (Durham, NC: Duke University Press, 1998), 20.

3. Ed Cohen, *Talk on the Wilde Side: Toward a Genealogy of a Discourse on Male Sexualities* (New York: Routledge, 1993).
4. Christopher Breu, *Hard-Boiled Masculinities* (Minneapolis: University of Minnesota Press, 2005), 4.
5. Bryce Traister, "Academic Viagra: The Rise of American Masculinity Studies," *American Quarterly* 52, no.2 (2000): 276.
6. Arthur Schlesinger, Jr., "The Crisis of American Masculinity," *Esquire* (November 1958): 63–65.
7. I would like to thank Julia M. Wright for discussions that led to this point and Brad Congdon whose excellent in-progress work on masculinity and *Esquire* pointed me to Schlesinger's article.
8. Robyn Wiegman, "Whiteness Studies and the Paradox of Particularity," *boundary* 2, 26, no.3 (1999): 115–50.
9. Foucault, 96.
10. *Rocky Horror Picture Show*, writ. Richard O'Brien, dir. Jim Sharman (Twentieth Century Fox, 1975), DVD.
11. Erin A. Smith, *Hard-Boiled: Working-Class Readers and Pulp Magazines* (Philadelphia: Temple University Press, 2000); Bill Osgerby, "Two-Fisted Tales of Brutality and Belligerence: Masculinity and Meaning in the American 'True Adventure' Pulps of the 1950s and 1960s," in *Masculinity and the Other: Historical Perspectives*, edited by Heather Ellis and Jessica Meyer (London: Cambridge Scholars Press, 2009), 163–89.
12. See my introduction to the Oxford edition of the novel, as well as Walt Morton, "Tracking the Sign of Tarzan: Trans-Media Representation of a Pop-Culture Icon," in *You Tarzan: Masculinity, Movies and Men*, edited by Pat Kirkham and Janet Thumim (New York: St. Martin's, 1993).
13. Sharon DeGraw, *The Subject of Race in American Science Fiction* (New York: Routledge, 2007). DeGraw's study offers a tremendously useful reading of the Mars series set against the ground of Turner's frontier thesis, and I would recommend it to readers. She also attempts to present the racialism of the Mars tales as somewhat more progressive than the regressive Tarzan, though recognizing that such a progressive narrative as does exist in the tales is part of a series of contradictory political elements in Burroughs' oeuvre. On the Mars series, we would differ in degree rather than kind on our analysis, in so far as I read both Tarzan and John Carter as attempts to recuperate the supposed superiority of an antebellum white masculinity for a modern, technological age. DeGraw is right that John Carter assimilates to a degree to the explicitly social, and not just natural, settings of his new home (he marries a Martian, for example), a plot in which she perhaps correctly reads the "seeds of 'progressive' change" (52). One can read this positive vision counter-textually, planting the seeds while ploughing uphill, so to speak; such readings are valuable, as I try to show in the chapter on Hawthorne. With that said, I would point out that such a narrative of cultural assimilation can uphold, rather than challenge, white supremacy: as I discuss in the chapter on *The Matrix*, the white hero "going native" and leading his new people is in itself a pro-colonialist, racist narrative. John Carter may just be one in a long line of a particular white supremacist archetype: he may just be "Dances with Martians."
14. Ralph Waldo Emerson, "The American Scholar," in *Collected Works of Ralph Waldo Emerson*, vol. 1, edited by Alfred R. Ferguson, et al. (Harvard: Belknap P of Harvard University Press, 1971), 69.

15. Emerson, "American," 70.
16. Emerson, "American," 69.
17. Emerson, "American," 67–68.
18. Ralph Waldo Emerson, "Self-Reliance," in *Collected Works of Ralph Waldo Emerson*, vol. 2, edited by Joseph Slater, Douglas Emory Wilson et al. (Harvard: Belknap P of Harvard University Press, 1979), 41.
19. Edgar Rice Burroughs, *The Cave Girl*, *The All-Story* (July-August 1913): 622.
20. Burroughs, *The Cave Girl*, *The All-Story* (July-August 1913): 891.
21. Emerson, "Self-Reliance," 41.
22. Morton, 106.
23. To appropriate and transform Ed Cohen's discussion, referenced earlier, of a similar (but radically opposed) form of cultural characterisation, Burroughs' novel "effectively (re)produced the possibility for designating [Tarzan] as a kind of [racial] actor without explicitly referring to the specificity of his [premeditatedly racist] acts, and thereby crystallized a new constellation of [racial] meanings predicated upon 'personality' and not practices" (131). Cohen is actually discussing the homophobic newspaper reports surrounding Oscar Wilde's trials, which, in Cohen's excellent argument, inadvertently create new, non-normative sexual identities with which men could identify themselves.
24. Jeff Berglund, *Cannibal Fictions: American Explorations of Colonialism, Race, Gender, and Sexuality* (Madison: University of Wisconsin Press, 2006), 101.
25. Eric Cheyfitz, *The Poetics of Imperialism: Translation and Colonization from* The Tempest *to* Tarzan, expanded ed., (Philadelphia: University of Pennsylvania Press, 2007), 14; 21.
26. Cheyfitz, 16.
27. Gail Bederman, *Madness and Civilization: A Cultural History of Gender and Race in the United States, 1880–1917* (Chicago: University of Chicago Press, 1995), 223.
28. Cheyfitz, 4.
29. Berglund, 195 n. 3.
30. Wiegman, 117; 150.
31. Emerson, "American" 69; 68.
32. Edgar Rice Burroughs, *Tarzan of the Apes*, edited by and intro. Jason Haslam (1914; Oxford: Oxford University Press, 2010), 2. Unless otherwise noted, all subsequent references are to this edition and are cited parenthetically.
33. Marianna Torgovnick, *Gone Primitive: Savage Intellects, Modern Lives* (Chicago: University of Chicago Press, 1990), 57.
34. In what follows, I expand on the discussion in my introduction to the Oxford edition of the novel's historical context.
35. The motion as originally read was somewhat stronger in its condemnation to the Congo Free State, adding "both of the guarantees having been constantly violated." This language was removed from the final bill after an objection by A. J. Balfour regarding "the objectionable condemnation of a friendly Government." This "friendly" relationship could explain why Burroughs presents Clayton's trip as being undertaken in relative secrecy.

    Interestingly, in the discussion that followed the motion, Sir John Gorst urged the House to support it, in part by drawing a parallel between what was in the process of happening to the indigenous peoples of the Congo region and "what happened when the discovery of America took place," arguing that the Spanish, driven by "the desire for the acquisition of property," engaged in a systematic exploitation of indigenous labour, first "endeavour[ing] to induce the natives to work," them moving "to try force," until "they degenerated into a system of slavery which became so cruel that the greater part of the natives in those territories were exterminated." The examination here points to the recognised connection between imperialism, international trade, slavery, and genocide, even as the motion problematically equates the systematic abuse of native populations and unfair trade practices as potentially equal evils. ("Congo Free State," Commons Sitting of Wednesday, 20th May, 1903 [House of Commons Parliamentary Papers, 4th Ser. Vol. 122, ProQuest, British Library Electronic Database]).

36. On the particular history of colonial involvement in the Congo, and on European actions in Africa more generally, see for example, Martin Ewans, *European Atrocity, African Catastrophe: Leopold II, the Congo Free State and Its Aftermath* (London: RoutledgeCurzon, 2002).
37. For a discussion of the various controversies surrounding Stanley, including a reported use of slaves, which Stanley denied, see Driver.
38. This is the argument put forth in a note in the Penguin Classics edition of the novel (John Seelye, edited by and intro., *Tarzan of the Apes* by Edgar Rice Burroughs [London: Penguin, 1990], 279–80, n. 2:8).
39. On this motif, see Helen Cooper, *The English Romance in Time: Transforming Motifs from Geoffrey of Monmouth to the Death of Shakespeare* (Oxford: Oxford University Press, 2004).
40. Torgovnick, 62.
41. Furthering the racist logic here is the clear image, as Bederman notes, of Tarzan as "a one-man lynch mob." Bederman makes a convincing case for the "echoes" between Burroughs' descriptions of Tarzan's murders and "the narratives of Northern journalists reporting on Southern lynching" (223).
42. bell hooks, *Black Looks: Race and Representation* (Boston: South End, 1992), 31. See Hee-Jung Serenity Joo for a fascinating development of hooks' argument in relation to the subject of this book's next chapter, Schuyler's *Black No More*.
43. Lauren M. E. Goodlad and Julia M. Wright, Introduction and Keywords, in *Victorian Internationalisms*, edited by Lauren M. E. Goodlad and Julia M. Wright, spec. issue of *Romanticism and Victorianism on the Net* 48 (2007): para 6. http://www.erudit.org/revue/ravon/2007/v/n48/, accessed 18 January 2015.
44. Berglund, 10.
45. Emerson, "Self-Reliance," 41.
46. Homi Bhabha, *Location of Culture* (London: Routledge, 1994), 92.
47. Cheyfitz, 4.
48. For a quick overview of Tarzan and Scouting, see my introduction to the novel (esp. xxi-xxii).
49. *Amazing Stories* 3, no.9 (Dec. 1928): 856.
50. Lee Weinstein, Introduction, *Wings over Tomorrow: The Collected Science Fictions of Philip Francis Nowlan* (n.p.: Wildside Press, 2005), 23.
51. As Michael Tucker explains, by the end of the first year the comic strip moves beyond the setting and situation of the novellas:

    > Over the next few strips, the whole of the Mongol business is neatly swept under the rug. The great cities of Mongol colonies are, somehow, forgotten. The Mongols themselves disappear from the strip. Buck and Wilma spend most of their time (the strip ran until 1967 and had a brief afterlife as a TV program) outside of America, free or otherwise.

Tucker is correct that the strip finishes the specifically "Mongolian" plot, but the general Orientalist narrative does continue, with, as Tucker does note, even the planet Jupiter being represented "not [as] a gas giant with a crushing surface gravity, but rather a verdant jungle world with a curious resemblance to Burma or south China." (Michael Tucker, "The Dragon Lady's Well Favoured Children: The Transition from Corporatist to Individualist in Comic Strips of 1930s," *Belphegor* 4, no.1 [2004]: n.p. http://hdl.handle.net/10222/47701/, accessed 18 January 2015.

52. Nowlan thus prefigures the focus on technology and race—specifically but not solely in terms of Orientalist depictions of Eastern technological and economic threats—that would come to dominate later SF, especially in early cyberpunk. A related argument could note that there are simply no black people described in Nowlan's America, pointing to the universalizing ideology of white supremacy to be sure, but also implying the lack of a narrative need for African Americans in the narrative of white masculine victimization by the orientalised other (a narrative William Gibson would later problematize—or make even more problematic in the oft-discussed cyberpunk masterpiece, *Neuromancer* through the inclusion of the black separatist nation/space station, Zion. Some aspects of cyberpunk's relationship to race are discussed in Chapter 4, in relation to *The Matrix*).
53. Burroughs, *The Cave Girl*, *The All-Story* (July-August 1913): 622.
54. Bederman, 226.
55. See Eve Kosofsky Sedgwick, *Between Men: English Literature and Male Homosocial Desire* (New York: Columbia, 1985), 50–51.
56. In this reading, I am revising H. Bruce Franklin's quick aside to Buck Rogers in his analysis of the Vietnam War and SF, an analysis that nonetheless holds completely true: "For a simple paradigm of the American self-images that helped engineer that war, just imagine Buck Rogers–as he uses his manly skills and twenty-fifth-century technology to lead the good fight against the Mongol hordes—sporting a Green Beret" (Franklin, "The Vietnam War as American Science Fiction and Fantasy," *Science Fiction Studies* 17, no.3 [1990]: 341).
57. For an overview of the 1924 Immigration Act, including a discussion of its background and effects, see Lee A. Makela, "The Immigration Act of 1924," in *Asian American Politics: Law, Participation, and Policy*, edited by Don T. Nakanishi and James S. Lai (Oxford: Rowman and Littlefield, 2003), 51–79.
58. Philip Francis Nowlan, *Armageddon—2419 A.D.*, *Amazing Stories* 3, no.5 (August 1928): 425–26. Unless otherwise noted, subsequent quotations are from this version, and will be cited parenthetically. (For ease of citation, quotations from Nowlan's novellas are taken from their original publication in *Amazing Stories*. Reprints, both physical and online, are readily available.)
59. In his Enlightenment-era writings, Herder argues that certain innate characteristics apply to the indigenous population of certain regions; culturally, groups from nearby regions will have more similar cultures than those from further away, because of the different climate, landscape, and so on (see, e.g., Herder 38). Herder's brand of nationalism, embedded in a pseudoscientific notion of the "volk," is often connected to later Nazi ideology. (John Godfrey Herder [Johann Gottfried von Herder], *Outlines of a Philosophy of the History of Man*, translated by T. Churchill [London: Hansard, 1800]; Eighteenth-Century Collections Online, 6 January 2003; accessed 7 July 2012.)

60. Philip Francis Nowlan, *The Airlords of Han*, *Amazing Stories* 3.12 (March 1929): 1106. Unless otherwise noted, subsequent quotations are from this version and are cited parenthetically.
61. Phil Nowlan and Dick Calkins, *Buck Rogers in the 25th Century: The Complete Newspaper Dailies*, vol. 1, 1929–1930 (Neshanock, PA: Hermes Press, 2008), 18; 22.
62. Patrick B. Sharp, "From Yellow Peril to Japanese Wasteland: John Hersey's 'Hiroshima,'" *Twentieth Century Literature* 46, no.4 (2000): 437.
63. The use of the term "Boss" for the leaders of the different American "Gangs" in the novella, along with Rogers' time travel through sleep, obviously echo Mark Twain's *A Connecticut Yankee in King Arthur's Court*. In fact, *Armageddon—2419 A.D.* could be read through Twain's novel, which similarly warns against the ills of civilisation, but takes a much more nuanced approach.
64. The reinvigoration Rogers' "primitive" manliness offers to his new society is a continually recurring theme in the 1979–1981 television series, starring Gil Gerard and Erin Gray. In this series, William "Buck" Rogers offers a highly sexualized version of the character, one that—especially in the opening made-for-TV film—is directly contrasted to the effeminate and potentially queer-coded character of Dr. Elias Huer (Tim O'Connor). *Buck Rogers in the 25th Century* (aired 1979–1981, NBC: Universal, 2004), DVD.
65. See *Amazing Stories* 3, no.6 (Sept. 1928): 574. It should be noted here that the advertisements in the issue of *The All-Story* in which *Tarzan of the Apes* first appeared are much less specifically targeted and not framed through this notion of progress, due in part to its pre-war publication date and to a wider range of genres and reader expectations. Ranging from men's fashion, to tobacco, to the American Telephone and Telegraph Company, to Campbell's clam chowder, a specifically implied reader is difficult to deduce (there is even a Grape-Nuts advertisement directed at the needs of "A Business Girl"). One International Correspondence Schools full-page ad does compare the business world to Roman gladiatorial games (with the explicit message that the "Untrained Man" will be the loser in these games), but generally there is a less specific correlation between the magazine's implied consumer and the content of *Tarzan of the Apes* than there is in the more focused marketing of *Amazing Stories*.
66. Carolyn Thomas de la Peña, "Designing the Electric Body: Sexuality, Masculinity and the Electric Belt in America, 1880–1920," *Journal of Design History* 14, no.4 (2001): 279. De la Peña updates this argument in her book, *The Body Electric: How Strange Machines Built the Modern American* (New York: New York University Press, 2003). I quote the earlier article only for stylistic reasons.
67. China Miéville, "Gothic Politics: A Discussion with China Miéville," *Gothic Studies* 10, no.1 (2008): 61–70.
68. Henry Adams, *The Education of Henry Adams*, edited by Jean Gooder (London: Penguin, 1995), 360–69.
69. Caleb Smith, "Bodies Electric: Gender, Technology, and the Limits of the Human, circa 1900," *Mosaic* 41, no.2 (2008): 115.
70. I am alluding here to Freud's reading, in his essay "The Uncanny," of E. T. A. Hoffman's "The Sandman," in which the nightmare figure of the title steals children's eyes. Freud reads the story as representative of the uncanny echoes of the fear of castration following the Oedipal moment of development. Were I to offer a more specifically psychoanalytic reading of Nowlan's stories, this section

of *The Airlords of Han* could easily be read as a moment of (somewhat forced) Oedipal conflict, in which the more "primitive" or "childlike" Americans wrest symbolic power from the Hans. Here, the air-balls of the Americans, presented, as in the Sandman, as "eyes," reassert themselves against the Hans, who are in turn (and for the only time) represented through (limp) phallic imagery. (Sigmund Freud, "The Uncanny," in *Infantile Neurosis and Other Works*, Standard Edition of the Complete Psychological Works of Sigmund Freud 17, translated and edited by James Strachey, in collaboration with Anna Freud, assisted by Alix Strachey and Alan Tyson [London: Hogarth, 1955], 217–52.)

REFERENCES

Adams, Henry. *The Education of Henry Adams*. Edited by Jean Gooder. London: Penguin, 1995.

Barthes, Roland. *Mythologies*. Selected and translated by Annette Lavers. London: Jonathan Cape, 1972.

Bederman, Gail. *Madness and Civilization: A Cultural History of Gender and Race in the United States, 1880–1917*. Chicago: University of Chicago Press, 1995.

Bellamy, Edward. *Looking Backward: 2000–1887*. Edited by Alex MacDonald. Peterborough, ON: Broadview, 2003.

Berglund, Jeff. *Cannibal Fictions: American Explorations of Colonialism, Race, Gender, and Sexuality*. Madison: University of Wisconsin Press, 2006.

Bhabha, Homi. *Location of Culture*. London: Routledge, 1994.

Breu, Christopher. *Hard-Boiled Masculinities*. Minneapolis: University of Minnesota Press, 2005.

Buck Rogers in the 25th Century. NBC. Aired 1979–1981. Universal, 2004. DVD.

Burroughs, Edgar Rice. *The Cave Girl*. *The All-Story* July-August 1913: 622–903; Sept. 1913: 175–91.

———. *Tarzan of the Apes*. Edited by and intro. Jason Haslam. 1914. Oxford: Oxford University Press, 2010.

Cheyfitz, Eric. *The Poetics of Imperialism: Translation and Colonization from* The Tempest *to* Tarzan. Expanded ed. Philadelphia: University of Pennsylvania Press, 2007.

Cohen, Ed. *Talk on the Wilde Side: Toward a Genealogy of a Discourse on Male Sexualities*. New York: Routledge, 1993.

"Congo Free State." Commons Sitting of Wednesday, 20 May, 1903. House of Commons Parliamentary Papers. 4th Series Vol. 122. *ProQuest*. British Library Electronic Database.

Connell, R. W. *Masculinities*. 2nd ed. Cambridge: Polity, 2005.

Cooper, Helen. *The English Romance in Time: Transforming Motifs from Geoffrey of Monmouth to the Death of Shakespeare*. Oxford: Oxford University Press, 2004.

DeGraw, Sharon. *The Subject of Race in American Science Fiction*. London: Routledge, 2007.

de la Peña, Carolyn Thomas. *The Body Electric: How Strange Machines Built the Modern American*. New York: New York University Press, 2003.

———. "Designing the Electric Body: Sexuality, Masculinity and the Electric Belt in America, 1880–1920." *Journal of Design History* 14, no.4 (2001): 275–289.

Driver, Felix. "Henry Morton Stanley and His Critics: Geography, Exploration and Empire." *Past and Present* 133 (1991): 134–66.

Emerson, Ralph Waldo. "The American Scholar." In *Collected Works of Ralph Waldo Emerson*, vol. 1, edited by Alfred R. Ferguson, et al., 49–70. Harvard: Belknap P of Harvard University Press, 1971.

———. "Self-Reliance." In *Collected Works of Ralph Waldo Emerson*, vol. 2, edited by Joseph Slater, Douglas Emory Wilson, et al., 25–51. Harvard: Belknap P of Harvard University Press, 1979.

Ewans, Martin. *European Atrocity, African Catastrophe: Leopold II, the Congo Free State and Its Aftermath*. London: RoutledgeCurzon, 2002.

Foucault, Michel. *History of Sexuality*, vol. 1: An Introduction. Translated by Robert Hurley. 1978. New York: Vintage, 1990.

Franklin, H. Bruce. "The Vietnam War as American Science Fiction and Fantasy." *Science Fiction Studies* 17, n.3 (1990): 341–59.

Freud, Sigmund. "The Uncanny." In *Infantile Neurosis and Other Works*, 217–52. Standard Edition of the Complete Psychological Works of Sigmund Freud 17. Translated and edited by James Strachey, in collaboration with Anna Freud, assisted by Alix Strachey and Alan Tyson. London: Hogarth, 1955.

Goodlad, Lauren M. E. and Julia M. Wright. Introduction and Keywords. In *Victorian Internationalisms*, edited by Lauren M. E. Goodlad and Julia M. Wright, special issue of *Romanticism and Victorianism on the Net* 48 (2007): n.p. http://www.erudit.org/revue/ravon/2007/v/n48/. Accessed 18 January 2015.

Halberstam, J. Jack. *Female Masculinity*. Durham, NC: Duke University Press, 1998.

Hawthorne, Nathaniel. "The Birth-mark." In *Mosses from an Old Manse*, 36–56. The Centenary Edition of the Works of Nathaniel Hawthorne 10. Columbus: Ohio State University Press, 1974.

———. *The Blithedale Romance*. Edited by Richard H. Millington. New York: Norton, 2010.

Herder, John Godfrey [Johann Gottfried von Herder]. *Outlines of a Philosophy of the History of Man*. Translated by T. Churchill. London: Hansard, 1800. *Eighteenth Century Collections Online*, 6 January 2003. Accessed 18 January 2015.

Hodges, Carol. Letter. *Amazing Stories* 3, no.9 (Dec. 1928): 856.

hooks, bell. *Black Looks: Race and Representation*. Boston: South End, 1992.

Joo, Hee-Jung Serenity. "Miscegenation, Assimilation, and Consumption: Racial Passing in George Schuyler's *Black No More* and Eric Liu's *The Accidental Asian*." *MELUS* 33, no.3 (2008): 169–90.

Makela, Lee A. "The Immigration Act of 1924." In *Asian American Politics: Law, Participation, and Policy*, edited by Don T. Nakanishi and James S. Lai, 51–79. Oxford: Rowman and Littlefield, 2003.

Miéville, China. Gothic Politics: A Discussion with China Miéville." *Gothic Studies* 10, no.1 (2008): 61–70.

Morton, Walt. "Tracking the Sign of Tarzan: Trans-Media Representation of a Pop-Culture Icon." In *You Tarzan: Masculinity, Movies and Men*, edited by Pat Kirkham and Janet Thumim, 106–25. New York: St. Martin's, 1993.

[Nowlan, Phil and Dick Calkins.] *Buck Rogers in the 25th Century: The Complete Newspaper Dailies*. Vol. 1, 1929–1930. Neshanock, PA: Hermes Press, 2008.

Nowlan, Philip Francis. *Armageddon—2419 A.D. Amazing Stories* 3, no.5 (August 1928): 422–49.

———. *The Airlords of Han. Amazing Stories* 3, no.12 (March 1929): 1106–36.

Osgerby, Bill. "Two-Fisted Tales of Brutality and Belligerence: Masculinity and Meaning in the American 'True Adventure' Pulps of the 1950s and 1960s." In *Masculinity and the Other: Historical Perspectives*, edited by Heather Ellis and Jessica Meyer, 163–89. London: Cambridge Scholars Press, 2009.

Rocky Horror Picture Show. Writ. Richard O'Brien. Dir. Jim Sharman. Twentieth Century Fox, 1975. DVD.

Schlesinger, Arthur, Jr. "The Crisis of American Masculinity." *Esquire*, November 1958: 63–65.

Sedgwick, Eve Kosofsky. *Between Men: English Literature and Male Homosocial Desire*. New York: Columbia, 1985.

Seelye, John, ed. and intro. *Tarzan of the Apes* by Edgar Rice Burroughs. London: Penguin, 1990.

Sharp, Patrick B. "From Yellow Peril to Japanese Wasteland: John Hersey's 'Hiroshima.'" *Twentieth Century Literature* 46, no.4 (2000): 434–52.

Smith, Caleb. "Bodies Electric: Gender, Technology, and the Limits of the Human, circa 1900." *Mosaic* 41, no.2 (2008): 111–26.

Smith, Erin A. *Hard-Boiled: Working-Class Readers and Pulp Magazines*. Philadelphia: Temple University Press, 2000.

Stanley, Henry M. *In Darkest Africa, or the Quest Rescue and Retreat of Emin Governor of Equatoria*. London: Sampson, 1890.

Torgovnick, Marianna. *Gone Primitive: Savage Intellects, Modern Lives*. Chicago: University of Chicago Press, 1990.

Traister, Bryce. "Academic Viagra: The Rise of American Masculinity Studies." *American Quarterly* 52, no.2 (2000): 274–304.

Tucker, Michael. "The Dragon Lady's Well Favoured Children: The Transition from Corporatist to Individualist in Comic Strips of 1930s." *Belphegor* 4, no.1 (2004): n.p. http://hdl.handle.net/10222/47701/. Accessed 18 January 2015.

Twain, Mark. *A Connecticut Yankee in King Arthur's Court*. Edited by Allison R. Ensor. New York: Norton, 1982.

Weinstein, Lee. Introduction. *Wings over Tomorrow: The Collected Science Fictions of Philip Francis Nowlan*. By Philip Francis Nowlan. n.p.: Wildside Press, 2005.

Wiegman, Robyn. "Whiteness Studies and the Paradox of Particularity." *boundary 2* 26, no.3 (1999): 115–50.

Part II

Virtual Whiteness

3 The Möbius Strip of Identity and Privilege in *Black No More*

The previous two chapters focused primarily on the ways in which scientifically essentialized identities—expressed through a hegemonic white masculinity, a racist proto-feminism, and an inescapable "othering" of non-white and orientalised figures—function to shore up existing social hierarchies. In part, this is a process of creating and silencing threats to hegemonic identities, a retrenchment of dominance most obvious in the development of a violent, neo-Romantic white masculinity for the modern age in the form of Tarzan and Buck Rogers. But those threats can take on a life of their own, so to speak, or be deployed by the oppressed against the prevailing system: the scientific feminism of Mizora and the less overt critique of whiteness in the death of Wauna; Aylmer's sexual desire for the birthmark itself; and, as I imply in the conclusion to the last chapter, an erotic, and potentially queered, fixation on the male body in both the Tarzan and Buck Rogers narratives. All of these serve to introduce possible entry points into anti-hegemonic work, through the semiotic slipperiness of SF identities.

The two chapters of Part II show how George S. Schuyler's *Black No More* and the Wachowski siblings' *Matrix* series both attempt to nurture those discursive threats to whiteness (and, albeit less obviously, to masculinity), through an attack on essentialism itself, by exposing the performative, semiotic structures of race and gender, and, in this chapter, by interrogating their relationship to class. The chapters argue, however, that these works also serve to indicate that such a revolution can be co-opted, transformed into a circular reinforcement of oppression rather than fomented into a radical rupture, leading into Part III, concerning the ways in which even resistant heterotopian spaces remain vulnerable to the monologic structures of utopia.

I. THE PROBLEMS OF (STUDYING) WHITENESS

In the preface to his 1931 satiric novel, *Black No More*, Schuyler quotes an August 1930 letter from one Bela Cati that was addressed to the NAACP. The letter reads:

> Once I myself was very strongly tanned by the sun and a European rural population thought that I was a Negro, too. I did not suffer much

> but the situation was disagreeable. Since that time I have studied the problem and I am convinced that the surplus of the pigment could be removed. In case you are interested and believe that with the aid of your physicians we could carry out the necessary experiments, I am willing to send you the patent specification … and my general terms relating to this invention. … The expenses are so to say negligible.[1]

Schuyler ostensibly quotes this letter in order to show his reader part of the inspiration for *Black No More*, in which an African American doctor, Junius Crookman, channeling Hawthorne's Aylmer, perhaps, invents a machine whereby black people can be turned white in three days. Within four months, most of the black population of the United States has, in the words of the novel, "vanished … into the great mass of white citizenry" (58). By quoting this letter in his preface, though, Schuyler also ironically raises some of the central concerns of the novel. The last line Schuyler quotes, "The expenses are so to say negligible," introduces what could be called Schuyler's economics of race. By modifying the "negligible expenses" with the phrase "so to say," the letter's author implies that any expense would be negligible when compared to what he terms the "disagreeable" situation of being black. And, by introducing the idea of a patent on the whitening method, the letter also implies that a profit could be made. Economic surplus exists in a structurally inverse relationship to one's "surplus of pigment" in the logic of white supremacy here espoused. *Black No More* reconfigures each of these implications, demonstrating this intimate connection between science, American racial dynamics, and class and economic structures, where these categories are often mediated through gender difference and sexual desire. Even after the vast majority of African Americans in the novel have undergone Crookman's treatment, thus removing the supposed visual signifier upon which antiblack racism relies, that very racism, only slightly altered in its form, still acts as the basis of all of the social policies and economic forces of the country. Racism is portrayed as an ideological tool for the reproduction of the privilege of the dominant class. At the same time, however, Schuyler constructs this "anti-utopia" (as John Reilly defines the novel)[2] in such a way that this racism takes on a life of its own, beyond hegemonic economic concerns, to meet new social demands. Taking the letter's hyperbolic suggestions—and the already extant industry of skin-whitening products aimed at African Americans, and especially at women[3]—to their ironic extremes, Schuyler's novel satirises an American society in which the class system and bigoted racial and gender categories both create and are created by each other, in a seemingly endless cycle of reproduction, even as he complicates certain aspects of this position—especially in relation to gender—in his later *Black Empire* novels, to which this chapter turns in its conclusion.[4]

Black No More functions in part to highlight what Schuyler views as the ways in which race, gender, and economics function together to create America's oppressive cultural system (even as, following his growing political conservatism and general iconoclasm, it espouses his discontent with African American leaders). In order to ground my discussion of Schuyler's novel, I wish in the next few pages to trace some of the analyses of this dynamic from within—and against—the loosely configured field commonly known as "whiteness studies," specifically as it relates to the simultaneous (re)production of the privileging of whiteness and disenfranchising of blackness.[5]

David R. Roediger, in his oft-cited study of the formation of whiteness within the American working class, argues that "the working class formation and the systematic development of a sense of whiteness went hand in hand for the U.S. white working class."[6] The construction of correspondent identities for "worker" and for "white," given the temporal and geographic similarities of their construction in the so-called "founding" and "taming" of America, suggests that both function within the matrix of various dominant (and dominating) structures that serve to perpetuate the privileges of certain groups of people. In other words, the interpellation of certain individuals simultaneously as both "white" and "worker" subjects suggests that both positions function in terms of a more or less unified set of subjugating forces.

These forces, and in turn the subject positions available within them, change over time. Matthew Frye Jacobson notes that "By looking at racial categories and their fluidity over time, we glimpse the competing theories of history which inform the society and define its internal struggles."[7] In turn, understanding these competing theories can allow us to see the ways in which "power has been organized and contested on the American scene."[8] Looking at Jacobson and Roediger together, we can see race not only as a signifier of power differentials in America, but, through its association with the signifiers of class, also as one of the tools through which the dominance of certain groups is (re)produced.

Within this process, the category of whiteness holds a peculiar place. The history of the concept of whiteness is anything but untroubled; it has, at several points in its history, included and excluded various groups of people in order to defend the existing power structure. In discussing the 1790 naturalisation law (which states in part that "all free white persons ... shall be entitled to the rights of citizenship"), Jacobson writes that "inasmuch as no one was suggesting that citizenship actually be *revoked* from those who had already entered under the terms of 1790, any discussion of the total exclusion of certain groups ... tended tacitly to endorse the unifying logic of a single European race whose credentials for self-government were above reproach."[9] Richard Dyer notes the same dynamic, writing that the "shifting border and internal hierarchies of whiteness suggest that the category ... is unclear and unstable, yet this has proved its strength."[10] In other words, even though whiteness has historically been "leaky,"[11] this leakiness itself has occasionally been used to further the hegemony of the dominant society.

That the borders of whiteness are not completely static is also evidenced in the ways in which whiteness is constructed in terms of a racialized "other."

Writing of race in the colonial situation, Bhabha states that "to exist is to be called into being in relation to an otherness. ... It is a demand that reaches outward to an external object and as Jacqueline Rose writes, 'It is the relation of this demand to the place of the object it claims that becomes the basis of identification.'"[12] In other words, for (white) identity to exist, it needs to first place itself in relation to another (black) identity. While the ideological construction of whiteness and blackness (or other racialized, non-white identities, as in Nowlan's work) as opposing forces does serve "to justify white supremacy" within racist social structures,[13] it also creates a simultaneous affirmation and cancellation of any claims to the originality or self-containment of (racialized) identity. This process of identification through otherness proves especially damning to forms of identity, such as whiteness, which base their claims to privilege on notions of authenticity or inherent right.

Schuyler ironically points to this dynamic in his essay "The Negro's Greatest Gift to America," writing that blacks in America, merely by "being present ... made white people assume a superiority unknown in Europe."[14] As discussed in this book's introduction, and as will be picked up more thoroughly in the next chapter, "privileged" identities (like whiteness), as Judith Butler writes, are "perpetually at risk,"[15] and therefore engage in a performative reinforcement of themselves through a problematic reliance on an "other," less privileged identity.[16]

Forming a sense of identity against a notion of otherness, however, does serve to suppress (if not completely eradicate) a rebellion against whiteness from within its borders. This is true even when such suppression functions against a group's own interests, as is the case with the white working class. Angela Y. Davis argues that "in order to more effectively stave off resistance" to the status quo of the dominant culture's system of privilege, "the consent to racism and terror has been demagogically elicited from the white population, workers included."[17] Such consent functions ultimately not just against the victims of the elicited racism, but against the people acting on it: Schuyler points this out in his essay "Our White Folks," writing that, specifically because of its racism, the 1930s South threatened

> the standards of living in the New England Mill towns and Northern coal fields by offering cheaper labor and lower taxes,—an offer that it can make only because of the ready acceptance of low living standards by the Southern white mob out of fear that Negroes will take its poorly paid jobs. Thus the results of the stupid system are felt in sections where hardly any Negroes live at all.[18]

Thus, the (re)creation of a system of privilege based on the inclusion and exclusion of individuals from a self-policed definition of whiteness can function even in the face of biases against those who are supposedly included in the privileged group.

In the theoretical and critical literature of whiteness studies, one of the more often discussed ways in which the social efficacy of the category of whiteness has been maintained in the face of its various "leaks" is, ironically, through its erasure as a definable racial category, as was briefly mentioned in the discussion of *Tarzan of the Apes*. As Jolanta A. Drzewiecka and Kathleen Wong (Lau) point out, the invisibility of whiteness has resulted in its supposed universality.[19] By erasing itself as a race among other races, so the argument goes, whiteness seeks to move itself beyond the problematic processes of identification described above. The very existence and proliferation of whiteness may rely on its construction of blackness and other racial categories, but, if it remains hidden and unspoken, any problems in the maintenance of its boundaries will also remain hidden. In the post-Enlightenment world, where a negative embodiment is opposed to a positive metaphysical existence in an ontological hierarchy expressed in terms of race, class, and gender, to be a member of an "invisible" disembodied race is to have access to privilege.[20] As Dyer states, "There is no more powerful position than that of being 'just' human."[21]

Certainly this "generic" nature to white identity forms part of the background of Schuyler's project in *Black No More*, and his goal to a large extent is to defamiliarise whiteness in order, in Dyer's words, to make whiteness "strange" and therefore visible.[22] This dominant strain of whiteness studies is not unproblematic or universally accepted, however. Much as Traister and Breu critique masculinity studies for inadvertently working against its own radical origins, so too can the emphasis on particularising whiteness serve to turn the focus of race studies away from the voices of those groups who have been silenced by a system of white supremacy (both within the academy and without) and toward, yet again, a seemingly canonical study of white folks. More specifically, as Robyn Wiegman argues, there are problems with "rendering whiteness particular" as a political act (especially as it occurs within the disciplinary project of seeing "whiteness studies as a field"), since the contradiction between the universality and particularity of whiteness can also be seen as what "affords to white power its historical and political elasticity."[23] So, while this particularisation *does* seem to be part of Schuyler's project in the novel, he also demonstrates, as Wiegman suggests for whiteness critics themselves, "the ways that being particular will not divest whiteness of its ... epistemological power."[24] As I argue below, by no means does Schuyler naively portray the particularisation or "making strange" of whiteness as an act that is fully liberatory or revolutionary in and of itself. Instead, through a satirical representation of 1930s America, Schuyler highlights both whiteness' semiotic and performative reliance on the existence of blackness and the nonessential nature of the connection between economic privileges and whiteness. He also points to what he sees as the inseparable nature of the racial and economic systems, noting how the naturalising of an economic system based on the privilege tied to whiteness is, at the very same time, a naturalising of a material and cultural racial system based on the privilege tied to the upper class.

II. JOINING THE PARTY: RACE, GENDER, CLASS, PRIVILEGE

At the beginning of the novel, before Crookman's discovery is announced, whiteness is constructed as both a metaphor for and a determiner of social and economic privilege and is subsequently portrayed as an object of desire within the politically and economically disenfranchised world of Harlem. In the opening pages, Max Disher, the protagonist, and his sidekick, Bunny, watch a group of white people, especially a "tall, slim, titian-haired girl," enter a Harlem nightclub (20). As Max and Bunny watch, one of the white men approaches them and asks if they know where any bootleg liquor can be bought. The man then asks Max to find some for him:

> "Sure," said Max, heartily. What luck! Here was the very chance he'd been waiting for. These people might invite them over to their table. The man handed him a ten dollar bill and Max went out bareheaded to get the liquor. In ten minutes he was back. He handed the man the quart and the change. The man gave back the change and thanked him. There was no invitation to join the party. Max returned to his table and eyed the group wistfully.
>
> "Did he invite you in?" asked Bunny.
>
> "I'm back here, ain't I?" answered Max, somewhat resentfully. (21)

This scene, which introduces part of Max's motivation for turning white, emphasises the role of the economic relations between the two groups. Max is allowed to "join the party" only insofar as that joining is mitigated by an unequal and exploitative economic relationship. J. Martin Favor reads Max's "desire for whiteness" as "a symptom of the internalized racism" which also finds expression in Schuyler's stated theories on the positive benefits of miscegenation.[25] However, Max's decision to turn white later in the novel seems to fall more closely, as Jane Kuenz argues, to a focus on his desire to gain "a level and kind of economic opportunity currently unavailable to him." Kuenz goes on to argue that in *Black No More*, "wanting to be white means wanting to be a free and democratic citizen of the nation, to be included in the conceptual realm of 'America.'"[26] Max's desire for whiteness, then, falls into the general construction of white privilege discussed by critics such as Jacobson and Dyer.

That this desire should be embodied by the figure of a white woman points toward a gendered complication of discussions of race and class. Favor notes that, by naming the white woman "Helen," "Schuyler is taking aim at Homer and one of the 'foundational texts' of Western civilization; through this parody, Schuyler lays claim to and modifies yet another marker of whiteness and its supposed cultural superiority."[27] In addition to this, though, Schuyler's use of this specific form of interracial sexual desire points out that the figurations of whiteness, blackness, and privilege are reduplicated in patriarchal gender oppression. Ruth Frankenberg expands this relationship beyond the American context, arguing that "the colonial 'sexual division of labor' with respect to racism and male domination was identical" (81). Helen is, especially in the early stages of the plot, figured solely as a metaphor for the privileges Max seeks in whiteness: we are told at one point that "He had always thought of her as a refined, educated and wealthy lady" (79). This assumption (which turns out to be untrue, at least in part) speaks to the fact that Max's desire for white women is another ideologically (re)produced form of the desire for the privileges of whiteness.

That Schuyler was more than aware of the ways in which this image of white women was purely a construction, and that it served to oppress women (and men) on all sides of the colour line, is evidenced in a scene later in the novel in which a wealthy black woman, Madame Sisseretta Blandish, contemplates the terrors of becoming white: "As a white woman she would have to start all over again, and she wasn't so sure of herself. Here at least she was somebody. In the great Caucasian world she would just be another white woman, and they were becoming a drug on the market. ... She had seen too many elderly, white-haired Caucasian females scrubbing floors and toiling in sculleries not to know what being just another white woman meant" (61–62). This insight, however, and her own championing of the black community, is problematized by the fact that Blandish made her money and place in the world by operating salons that offered hair-straightening and whitening services. Robert A. Hill suggests that "The issue of beauty standards" for women, in relation to race, "was a consistent concern for Schuyler," noting, in addition to Blandish, the character of Helene Custis in his novella, *The Ethiopian Murder Mystery*.[28] Both of these characters were based on historical personages involved in the cosmetics industry—Madame C. J. Walker and Helene Curtis, respectively—underscoring Schuyler's complicated analysis of the inseparable nature of racial, gendered, sexual, and economic structures in the United States, both within and between white and black communities. However, while Schuyler does note here that the privilege associated with whiteness is internally divided along gender lines, and that gender also complicates racial divisions, especially in terms of the hegemonic construction of beauty and the desire it fuels, he still generally points toward the manner in which white privileging societies construct an "ideal" of whiteness, thus making whiteness into a gateway to economic and other social forms of privilege.

Partly due to this differential construction of gender and sexual desire in relation to whiteness and privilege, the desire for the freedom equated with male whiteness is figured as a means of constraint and exploitation (picking up on Breu's and Traister's argument that the supposed "threats" faced by dominant masculinity are, in fact, tools to further that dominance). This form of exploitation is most true at the early stages of the novel, before the possibility of actually "becoming white" exists. It is precisely the enforced desire to "join the party" that results in the exploitative situation; this desire is promulgated throughout the world of the novel, constituting more of a received notion than an individual choice. Both the desire to "join the party" and its systematic frustration become the means through which the unequal power structures surrounding race are reproduced. Schuyler's introduction of Crookman's "Black-No-More" process immediately after the nightclub scene, therefore, allows him to show what would happen if the desire for whiteness and the economic position it represents were not frustrated. The rest of the novel then explores the ways in which the racist and classist American power structure is a self-perpetuating and self-referential machine which is not based on, but rather creates, the racial and economic categories through which it is in turn defined.

Max fulfills his desire for whiteness as soon as Crookman's "sanitarium" opens. What Max perceives as the immediate implications of his transformation are made explicit:

> There would be no more expenditures for skin whiteners; no more obstacles in his path. He was free! The world was his oyster and he had the open sesame of a pork-colored skin! ... Six hours later, bathed, fed, clean-shaven, spry, blonde and jubilant, he emerged from the out-patient ward and tripped gaily down the corridor to the main entrance. He was through with coons, he resolved, from now on. He glanced in a superior manner at the long line of black and brown folk on one side of the corridor. ... It thrilled him to feel that he was now indistinguishable from nine-tenths of the people of the United States; one of the great majority. (35–36)

Max's newfound membership in the amorphous blob of American whiteness is directly related to a feeling of freedom, to doors opening almost magically and without hindrance to vast amounts of easily found wealth.[29] However, Schuyler goes on to show us that the freedom and privilege associated with whiteness are not positive things that exist in and of themselves, but rather are based on an inescapable and constantly reproduced oppression of a constructed "other." Max's jubilance is immediately followed by a feeling of superiority and a paradoxical racism.

That the supposedly positive privileges of whiteness are inescapably based on the construction of their opposite, the non-privilege of blackness, and that both can be defined in terms of economics, forms the middle part of the novel. After Max's transformation, which is mirrored in the changing of his name from Max Disher to Matthew Fisher, he moves to Atlanta and in order to make money becomes involved in a racist organisation, explicitly modeled on the KKK, called "The Knights of Nordica." When Matthew moves to Atlanta after having "passed over" (69), he encounters several whites who are violently opposed to Crookman's process:

> The attitude of these people puzzled him. Was not Black-No-More getting rid of the Negroes upon whom all of the blame was placed

> for the backwardness of the South? Then he recalled what a Negro street speaker had said one night on the corner of 138th Street and Seventh Avenue in New York: that unorganized labor meant cheap labor; that the guarantee of cheap labor was an effective means of luring new industries into the South; that so long as the ignorant white masses could be kept thinking of the menace of the Negro to Caucasian race purity and political control, they would give little thought to labor organization. It suddenly dawned upon Matthew Fisher that this Black-No-More treatment was more of a menace to white business than to white labor. And not long afterward he became aware of the money-making possibilities involved in the present situation. (64–65)

Max here realises that the creation of a racial hierarchy of social privilege is a means for the reproduction of the capitalist hierarchy that governs the American sociopolitical superstructure, as Roediger, Schocket, and others have discussed. This realisation leads to the final part of Max's transformation: this is the first instance where the protagonist is referred to solely by his "white" name, Matthew Fisher. Matthew's realisation that he too can now gain money and power from the reproduction of racist attitudes finally gives him full access to the privileges of whiteness—privileges that are characterised a few paragraphs earlier as "the hard, materialistic, grasping, inbred society of the whites" (63). Matthew's full "membership" in whiteness is predicated on his mimicry of the racist construction of blackness, in a process of identity formation very similar to that which Bhabha outlines.

Matthew's recognition of the apparent economic basis of racism, and of race itself, leads him to reproduce actively antiblack racism despite the nearly complete erasure of the visible signature of difference in skin colour. Relying on fake credentials as a white supremacist anthropologist, Matthew gains effective control of the Knights of Nordica by mimicking the forms of racist discourse.[30] This mimicry highlights, at times, the way in which Schuyler emphasises the social constructedness of race and its reliance on racism: we are told that Matthew writes racist editorials "with such blunt sincerity that sometimes he almost persuaded himself that it was all true" (106).

Ironically, Matthew relies on the existence of the Black-No-More process once again to give him access to whiteness; rather than the physical process, though, this time he uses the threat that Black-No-More constitutes against the white power structure. He informs Henry Givens, the leader of the Knights of Nordica, that "At this rate there will not be a Negro in the country in ten years, for you must remember that the rate is increasing every day as new sanitariums are opened. Don't you see that something must be done about this immediately?" (69). Antiblack racism continues not despite, but because of, the disappearance of blacks; this is only a paradox if the construction of blackness is seen as being essentially related to skin colour as opposed to economics. To bolster this position, Matthew emphasises the discourse of "blood purity"—as discussed in the first chapter of the current study—a form of racial identification that was less highlighted in the Knights' previous racist rhetoric. He then uses this discourse to reinstate the oppressive work conditions of what is referred to as "The great mass of white workers" (109). These people, the text reads, were

> afraid to organize and fight for more pay because of a deepset fear that the Negroes would take their jobs. ... They had first read of the activities of Black-No-More, Incorporated, with a feeling akin to relief but after the orators of the Knights of Nordica ... began to portray the menace confronting them, they forgot about their economic ills and began to yell for the blood of Dr. Crookman and his associates. ... Times were hard, they reasoned, because there were so many white Negroes in their midst taking their jobs and undermining their American standard of living. None of them had ever attained an American standard of living to be sure, but that fact never occurred to any of them. (109)

Matthew and his associates crush the workers' unions before they begin by making the workers turn against themselves, through the spreading of rumours about the unknown racial origin of union organisers and through the general recreation of the slowly disappearing racist hierarchies. Citing Roediger, Kuenz states that Matthew plays off a knowledge of "the construction of whiteness against blackness within the context of labor."[31] The status quo of the class system is thus perpetuated through the somewhat nonsensical continuation of white racism: "Schuyler resituates both 'blackness' and 'whiteness' in relation to an industrial and market economy increasingly willing and able to manipulate and finally obliterate any semblance of culture, tradition, and individual identity, racial or otherwise, among the people it needs to keep itself going."[32] The use of race to maintain this status quo is, as Howard J. Faulkner points out,[33] most explicitly stated in the parodic passage which lists the possible effects of the "loss" of the black population:

> Far-sighted people, North and South, even foresaw the laboring people soon forsaking both of the old parties and voting Socialist. Politicians and business men shuddered at the thought of such a tragedy and saw horrible visions of old-age pensions, eight hour laws, unemployment insurance, workingmen's compensation minimum wage legislation, abolition of child labor, dissemination of birth-control information, monthly vacations for female workers, two-month vacations for prospective mothers, both with pay, and the probable killing of individual initiative and incentive by taking the ownership of national capital out of the hands of two million people and putting it into the hands of one hundred and twenty million. (135)

The removal of racism as a tool for maintaining the economic and social hegemony is feared by the holders of power in the novel as the prelude to the complete destruction of that hegemony. As Stacy Morgan argues, *Black No More* "suggests the ironic manner in which America's racial hierarchy serves to oppress the very white masses who are so critical to its effective enactment" (349). The white workers' investment in whiteness, as Roediger and Davis see in society at large, serves only to further their own oppression at the hands of the leaders of industry. Importantly, this process is also seen as a primary step toward what is presented as a more gender-balanced workplace, in which women's rights are more respected—specifically in terms of particular forms of reproductive rights and childcare. The eradication of the racial othering on which the American labour system is based begins the unraveling of the Möbius strip of identity-based oppression that circumscribes American society.

III. RACISM'S ENDS

Despite the focus of many critics on Schuyler's definition of race as a subcategory of class structures, there are a few sections of *Black No More* in which Schuyler reverses that subordination in order to show the inseparable nature of economic and racial oppression.[34] Certain institutions and structures have as their prime motivator the desire to maintain the racial hierarchy in and of itself; and, in order to do this, an economics is constructed that is subordinated to the motivator of race. A naturalised racial hierarchy begins to move away from its ties to an economic hegemony and takes on, as it were, a life of its own. When these moments are taken into account in conjunction with the depictions of the subordination of racial constructions to economic forces, a complex portrayal of the connections between race and economics comes into relief.

The prime example of a non-economically motivated, self-perpetuated racism is the Anglo Saxon Association, run by Arthur Snobbcraft. While the men behind this racist organisation are generally of the upper class, the organisation itself is not financially oriented; money is perceived by this Association as the means to the end of racial integrity—a view of finances that is directly opposed to Matthew's and the Knights of Nordica's use and worship of money as an end in itself. The text states that Snobbcraft

> had devoted his entire life to fighting for two things: white racial integrity and Anglo-Saxon supremacy. It had been very largely a losing fight. ... Snobbcraft's pet scheme now was to get a genealogical law passed disenfranchising all people of Negro or unknown ancestry. He argued that good citizens could not be made out of such material. His organization had money but it needed popularity—numbers. (153–54)

The financial status of the Anglo Saxon Association is only given importance in relation to the goal of reinforcing and expanding the existing hierarchies of racial prejudice. The configuration of whiteness here also points to the ways in which a naturalised racial discourse can disrupt the economic hegemony rather than support it, since for Snobbcraft whiteness is itself split into an ontological hierarchy. Despite the fact that Snobbcraft's organisation joins forces with the Knights of Nordica, their joint status is tenuous at best. We are told that Snobbcraft's willingness to work with them in no way negates his view of the distinction between the Anglo-Saxons and the rest of the so-called whites: Snobbcraft "had no love for the Knights of Nordica which, he held, contained just the sort of people he wanted to legislate into impotency, social, economic and physical, [but] he believed he could use them to gain his point" (154). Rather than opening up the borders of whiteness to deal with threats from "outside," Snobbcraft's use of the Knights is similar in function to the white group's exploitative use of Max to buy bootleg liquor at the beginning of the novel. But the mirrored reflection also holds true: representing older forms of racial divisions and hegemonic power, the Anglo Saxon Association, in its anachronism, gestures to the ambiguity of racial categories and to the possibility for social change.

The alignment between the Anglo Saxon Association and the Knights of Nordica near the end of the text becomes a satiric synecdoche for what I see as Schuyler's complex vision of the American social structure. *Black No More* can be read as complicating interpretations of Schuyler's vision of racism as being merely one result of economic oppression, as Kuenz does, or readings of Schuyler and his texts as examples of a diehard if somewhat paradoxical assimilationist viewpoint, as some of his earlier critics do, and, indeed, as he often portrayed himself.[35] The portrayal of the embattled codependency of the Knights of Nordica and the Anglo Saxon Association, the former using racism as a means of gaining money, the latter using money as a means of perpetuating racism, leads to an understanding of the apparently unending and inseparable Möbius strip of economic and racial oppression. Each may alter the superficial form of the other, but the substance remains; they are two interconnected nodes in a matrix of social ills.

Such a reading is supported by the dual ending of *Black No More*. On one hand, the genealogical project that Snobbcraft finances ends up revealing that most of the supposedly white characters, including Snobbcraft himself, have at least one black person in their ancestry, thus making these characters black according to their own definitions and therefore removing them from the privileges of whiteness. In addition, a study conducted near the end of the novel shows that Crookman's whitening process actually makes people whiter than the so-called average Caucasian, as measured by the arbitrary semiotics of race. The result of this revelation is the apparent reversal of the racial power dynamic:

> To a society that had been taught to venerate whiteness for over three hundred years, this announcement was rather staggering. What was the world coming to, if the blacks were whiter than the whites? Many

> people in the upper class began to look askance at their very pale complexions. If it were true that extreme whiteness was evidence of the possession of Negro blood, of having once been a member of a pariah class, then surely it were well not to be so white! ... The new Caucasians began to grow self-conscious and resent the curious gazes bestowed upon their lily-white countenances in all public places. (219–20)

As Benjamin S. Lawson writes of this point in Schuyler's novel, the apparent impossibility of using "self-conscious contrast ... as a way to identify the self and assert superiority" means that "Race must be recreated."[36] The relations between visual signifiers and the systems of oppression have reversed, but the system of oppression remains. Again we can return to Tarzan's "brown skin," which serves to reinforce his whiteness rather than undermine it (though in Tarzan's case, this seeming disjunction between visible signifier and racial signified is erased by his absolute confidence in his own identity, whereas here we see more what Butler would call the dominant culture's "*panicked* imitation of its own naturalized idealization").[37]

On the other hand, this reversal, which again situates race as a tool for the furthering of economic hierarchies, is complicated by the fate of Snobbcraft and his genealogist, Dr. Samuel Buggerie. Finding themselves to be genealogically black according to their own formation of the one-drop rule, the two racists (who, with Givens, are leading the Democratic Party) attempt to fly out of the country as they are being hunted down. Their plane breaks down and drops them within a stereotypically presented backwoods white southern town. In a stunning feat of logistical foolishness, they do themselves up in blackface to escape notice, reasoning that since "real niggers are scarce now ... nobody would think of bothering a couple of them, even in Mississippi. They'd probably be a curiosity" (201). In other words, a pair of white-looking black men, who will be lynched if anyone recognises them, "mask" themselves as black men in order to escape racism, relying on a twisted principle of supply and demand: the fewer "real" blacks there are, the more they will be worth. (When this vision of race and economics is compared to the paradox of the Knights of Nordica's reproduction of racism *because* of the "disappearance" of blacks, one can see how the Anglo Saxon Association's and the Knights of Nordica's views of the relationship between race and economics are diametrically opposed, even though both fall within an equally objectifying capitalist logic of supply and demand—one sees the scarcity of black people as increasing their value, while the other sees it as increasing their threat.)

Snobbcraft and Buggerie, however, fail to take into account the ways in which a naturalised racism (which they helped to construct) can function outside of economic principles: they are roasted alive when they are discovered.[38] The power structure of the town in which this happens, represented by the figure of Reverend Alex McPhule, is focused completely on the elimination of blacks and the perpetuation of the most violent forms of racism. When Crookman's process seems to eliminate the need for this perpetuation, the town and Reverend McPhule's religious authority begin to fall apart. However, the murder of Snobbcraft and Buggerie reinforces the racist foundations of the community:

> When the roasting was over and the embers had cooled, the more adventurous members of Rev. McPhule's flock rushed to the stake and groped in the two bodies for skeletal souvenirs such as forefingers, toes and teeth. Proudly their pastor looked on. This was the crowning of a life's ambition. Tomorrow his name would be in every newspaper in the United States. (218)

The violence of McPhule's and the town's racism functions not simply as a means of gaining power, but as the end result of that power—here the power structure is once again centred on racism, even while elsewhere the recreation of an economics-based power structure is flourishing. While McPhule does steal some money from Snobbcraft's pocket, this is presented as an afterthought, merely a finishing touch on the real "reward" of perpetuating a violent racist hegemony. While race may not be presented as an essential category in the body of the novel, McPhule's town is used as an example of how, due to its naturalisation, it can still function as such. Pointing to his recognition of such a naturalisation of racism, Schuyler wrote, in reaction to the Scottsboro case, that "anybody who is at all familiar with the Southern psychology knows that no class issues are involved save of the most remote and inconsequential kind. It is a race issue pure and simple."[39]

Through the pairing of these scenes, then, Schuyler's satire shows that, in America, racism and economic oppression cannot exist without each other: they each presuppose the other's existence. Instead, racial and economic oppression create a mutually fulfilling and self-perpetuating social dynamic, just as the earlier scenes focusing on women's relative positions placed gender within the same cycle. Thus, Schuyler seems to say that an attack on only one of these subjects—whiteness, for example—cannot succeed on its own. Even though the forms may change, without a multipronged attack—including not only race and class, but gender issues as well—the various discourses of bigotry will tend to recreate each other. After all, "Buggerie" functions within a clearly homophobic logic to point to the weakness or impotence of whiteness. This name, in conjunction with Schuyler's depictions of gender, whiteness, and beauty, shows the ways in which gender, sexuality, race, and economics are defined in terms of each other within the novel.[40] The circular nature of these oppressions is emphasised by a capitalised line inserted near the end of the text, which seems to function as an authoritative comment on the society satirised by the book: after McPhule's success with Snobbcraft and Buggerie, the text simply states "AND SO ON

AND SO ON" (218). Oppression, at the end of the novel, may be visited upon whites, but at the end of the day, Schuyler seems to be saying, it's still the same old song, forcing Dr. Crookman, in the very last line of the novel, to "smile[] wearily" (222).

IV. NEW POSITIONS?

An earlier version of this chapter ended with the section above. But left out of that conclusion are the new positions achieved by individuals within this admittedly circular vision of identity and oppression. That is to say, while the conclusion that we are left with "the same old song" on a macrostructural level is true, still the world of *Black No More* has changed, at least for Max, Helen, and their family. Exploiting that semiotic slipperiness of race and thereby highlighting its performative nature—both of which are allowed by the SF novum of Crookman's process—Max is able to build the quintessentially happy, nuclear family. And, this family is one that is completely content with its own complicated blackness: since Crookman's process actually leaves "black" people visibly whiter than natural-born "white" people, the privileged people of this brave new world are now dying their skin brown or tanning, in order to prove their natural "right" to privilege. This is, clearly, a satirical gesture to the unchanging need of humans to hierarchise amongst themselves and is part of the circular logic indicated by "AND SO ON AND SO ON." But still, one is left at the end of the novel with a world that privileges blackness, one in which Max and Helen's children are privileged precisely because they are of mixed race. One can see in here Schuyler's admittedly utopian vision of the possibilities of a racially mixed America.[41] But, the novel is also thus opening the possibility of a positive space for the (white) race traitor, a space that is inherently tied to gender and sexual desire.

But, given Schuyler's recognition, through his depiction of Blandish, of the gender inequities within and between racial categories, the fact that it is interracial heterosexual desire that leads to this new world is problematic: the salvation for America, Schuyler seems to suggest, lies in the stereotypical vision of black men's desire for white women. Certainly Schuyler's own vision of the social possibilities for racial intermarriage is well known, but the apparent passivity of the women here troubles this vision. Does the novel simply silence its own latent feminist critique?

Perhaps. But, elsewhere Schuyler does offer at the least a complication of this position, in his serially published "Black Internationale" novellas, written under the pseudonym Samuel I. Brooks, and republished under his real name as *Black Empire* in 1991. In these novellas, Dr. Henry Belsidus first creates an underground network of other African Americans, designed to build funds for his master plan: to free the continent of Africa from white rule and unite it under his own. That plot—and its fruition—takes place in the first novella, *The Black Internationale: Story of Black Genius Against the World*. In the second—*Black Empire: An Imaginative Story of a Great New Civilization in Modern Africa*—the majority of global political power is placed in Belsidus' unified Africa; following a world war, Africa becomes the global superpower, to the point where, "The glory that was once Egypt's and Ethiopia's and Benin's and Timbuctoo's and Songhoy's and Morocco's shall again make Africa first in the family of nations."[42]

Much can be said of these combined works, including the ways in which their plots present a reclaiming of Africa from the material forces of imperialism and colonialism. They also play with, only to deny, the cultural imperialism of mythical representations of Africa manifested by such works as *Tarzan of the Apes* (the second novella includes representations of African cannibals who nearly eat members of Belsidus' party—including the narrator—because they mistake them for French colonisers). As I conclude this chapter and gesture toward the next, however, I want to focus on one particular figure: Martha Gaskin, a white woman who loves Dr. Belsidus, who stands by his side throughout both works, and who helps him succeed in his quest for global domination. Her support goes so far that she leads the mission to execute fifteen thousand white Europeans.

Gaskin is positioned prominently at the end of both novellas. At the end of *Black Internationale*, she is seen by the narrator, Carl Slater, while she "look[s] longingly at [Belsidus]. She realized she would never possess this black man for whom she had risked so much, and I felt sorry for her."[43] At the end of *Black Empire*, this time in its concluding lines, the narrator again spies her in a crowd, and sees "her blonde hair looking odd among those Negroes. She was twisting her tiny handkerchief in her hands, while a pair of tears coursed unnoticed down her cheeks."[44] This is a fraught scene, one that complicates the implications of DeGraw's assertion that Belsidus and Gaskin "finally reside together in Africa."[45] Instead, the pairing of these concluding scenes, as editors Robert A. Hill and R. Kent Rasmussen argue, can "suggest that Belsidus' relationship with Gaskin will never be emotionally consummated. Martha Gaskin is permitted to sacrifice everything in order to serve Belsidus, but as a symbol of the white race, she is punished by being denied a full relationship with him," pointing to Schuyler's "profound criticism of the oppressiveness of race" and of racial divisions.[46] In this reading, the representation of Gaskin is the inverse of *Mizora*'s representation of racist eugenics: here, stereotypically racialized gender plots (the myth of the black man's use of the passive white woman) are used to challenge dominant racist narratives concerning the political and military ability of African Americans.

Gaskin's tears can be read against Max's and Helen's smiles, with the utopian planning of Belsidus seen as overly segregated compared to *Black No More*'s satirical refusal of utopian solutions, where Max/Matthew, Helen, and their family choose instead a materialised happiness in the moment. But, no matter how one reads Gaskin's tears (especially those at the end of *Black Empire*, which are *not* tied explicitly to her love for Belsidus), still she can be read—perhaps against the grain—to offer a new entry point into white involvement in black liberation struggles, one that is not figured within what Spivak identifies as the colonialist logic of "white men saving brown women from brown men,"[47] which we will see reenacted to a point in *The Matrix*, or even a more generalised logic of "white people saving brown people." Instead, there is another possibility here, in which white people work for black people who are saving black people. Importantly, and working somewhat against Hill's and Rasmussen's argument, it is not a "full relationship" that Gaskin is denied at the end of *Black Internationale*, but the ability to "possess" a "black man"—it is a specifically racialized dominance that is denied her in the relationship. Moreover, one cannot simply position Gaskin within a passive or domestic gendered role, given her leadership in the action that slaughters white technicians and others. Perhaps, then, we can read Gaskin as an attempt—if not a fully realised one—to escape racial and gender codes that serve to reinforce the hegemonic, very material power of capital that we see at play in *Black No More*. At the very least, Gaskin exposes the fissures in hegemonic identity opened up by the recognition of the performative and semiotic nature of its supposedly grounded foundations. It is to these fissures—and the difficulty of exploiting them within the material frameworks of popular culture, specifically—that I turn in the next chapter's analysis of *The Matrix* and its attempt to encode a digital race revolution.

NOTES

1. George S. Schuyler, *Black No More: Being an Account of the Strange and Wonderful Workings of Science in the Land of the Free, A. D. 1933–1940* (1931, Boston: Northeastern University Press, 1989), 14; ellipses are Schuyler's. Unless otherwise noted, subsequent quotations are from this edition and will be cited parenthetically.
2. John M. Reilly, "The Black Anti-Utopia," *Black American Literature Forum* 12 (Fall 1978): 107–09. Reilly, writing in 1978, uses the term "anti-utopia" somewhat broadly, writing that "the anti-utopia may be as comprehensive as the utopia, providing a detailed portrayal of the whole range of human social life; but the conservative motive of anti-utopia colors the representation with a tone of ridicule" (107). I would agree that the novel is an anti-utopia, but follow Lyman Tower Sargent's later and more specific definition of the term, in which it is used, in contradistinction to "dystopia," "to describe those works that use the Utopian form to attack either Utopias in general or a specific Utopia. (Some of the numerous works using Bellamy's future Boston to attack Bellamy are anti-utopias without being dystopias)" (Sargent, "The Three Faces of Utopianism Revisited," *Utopian Studies* 5, no.1 [1994]: 8).
3. In his article "A Negro Looks at Negroes," Schuyler himself deals with the skin-whitening and hair-straightening industry and what it says about the cultural and economic emphasis placed on being "paler of pigment and straighter of hair" both within and outside of the African American communities of his day (Schuyler, "A Negro Looks at Negroes," *Debunker and the American Parade* [Oct. 1930]: 28).

4. In focusing on the relations between race and economics in Schuyler's work, and on whiteness and privilege in particular, I am both building on a body of critical material and differing significantly from DeGraw's study of Schuyler in her book on race and SF (Sharon DeGraw, *The Subject of Race in American Science Fiction*, New York: Routledge, 2007). DeGraw situates the majority of her analysis primarily as a response to Jeffrey Tucker's positioning of Schuyler in relation to African American politics; thus, she does not deal with economics except in passing, nor with those critical readings of *Black No More* and Schuyler's other work that demonstrate his tight imbrication of race and class (including work by Jane Kuenz and an earlier version of the current argument).
5. Wiegman, discussed below, provides a much more detailed and in-depth critical overview of the whiteness studies and its relation to race studies and the academy (Robyn Wiegman, "Whiteness Studies and the Paradox of Particularity," *boundary* 2 26, no.3 [1999]: 115–50).
6. David R. Roediger, *The Wages of Whiteness: Race and the Making of the American Working Class* (New York: Verso, 1991), 8.
7. Matthew Frye Jacobson, *Whiteness of a Different Color: European Immigrants and the Alchemy of Race* (Cambridge: Harvard University Press, 1998), 6.
8. Jacobson, 9.
9. Jacobson, 74.
10. Richard Dyer, *White* (New York: Routledge, 1997), 19–20.
11. Philip C. Wander, Judith N. Martin, and Thomas K. Nakayama, "Whiteness and Beyond: Sociohistorical Foundations of Whiteness and Contemporary Challenges," in *Whiteness: The Communication of Social Identity*, edited by Thomas K. Nakayama and Judith N. Martin (London: Sage, 1999), 15.
12. Homi Bhabha, *Location of Culture* (London: Routledge, 1994), 44.
13. Michael Eric Dyson, "Giving Whiteness a Black Eye," interview with Ronald E. Chennault, in *White Reign: Deploying Whiteness in America*, edited by Joe L. Kincheloe, Shirley R. Steinberg, Nelson M. Rodriguez, and Ronald E. Chennault (New York: St. Martin's, 1998), 302.
14. Schuyler, qtd. in George Hutchinson, *The Harlem Renaissance in Black and White* (Cambridge: Belknap-Harvard University Press, 1995), 292–93.
15. Judith Butler, "Imitation and Gender Insubordination," in *Inside/Out*, edited by Diana Fuss (New York: Routledge, 1991), 23.
16. For specific discussions of whiteness' reliance on blackness in American literature and culture, also see Ralph Ellison, "What America Would Be Like Without Blacks," in *Black on White: Black Writers on What It Means to Be White*, edited by David R. Roediger (New York: Schocken Books, 1998), 160–67; and Toni Morrison, *Playing in the Dark: Whiteness and the Literary Imagination* (New York: Vintage, 1990)—the latter is taken up at several points in the current work.
17. Angela Y. Davis, "Political Prisoners, Prisons, and Black Liberation" (1971), in *The Angela Y. Davis Reader*, edited by Joy James (Oxford: Blackwell, 1998), 50.
18. George S. Schuyler, "Our White Folks," in *Black on White: Black Writers on What It Means to Be White*, edited by David R. Roediger (New York: Schocken Books, 1998), 77–78. Eric Schocket also defines the reasoning behind the white worker's self-destructive consent to racism, arguing, "Their racial identity does not redouble their class identity (contrary to what some maintain) but evades it, becoming a blank screen for the projection of those American fantasies of

uplift" ("'Discovering Some New Race': Rebecca Harding Davis's 'Life in the Iron Mills' and the Literary Emergence of Working-Class Whiteness," *PMLA* 115, no.1 [2000]: 57). Also see Roediger, *Wages*).

19. Jolanta A. Drzewiecka and Kathleen Wong (Lau), "The Dynamic Construction of White Ethnicity in the Context of Transnational Cultural Formations," in *Whiteness: The Communication of Social Identity*, edited by Thomas K. Nakayama and Judith N. Martin (London: Sage, 1999), 198 ff. For discussions of ways in which attempts are made to make whiteness discursively "invisible" within and by the dominant culture, see, for example: Dyer; Valerie Babb, *Whiteness Visible: The Meaning of Whiteness in American Literature and Culture* (New York: New York University Press, 1998); Dreama Moon, "White Enculturation and Bourgeois Ideology: The Discursive Production of 'Good (White) Girls,'" in *Whiteness: The Communication of Social Identity*, edited by Thomas K. Nakayama and Judith N. Martin (London: Sage, 1999), 177–97; and Monica Beatriz deMello Patterson, "America's Racial Unconscious: The Invisibility of Whiteness," in *White Reign: Deploying Whiteness in America*, edited by Joe L. Kincheloe, Shirley R. Steinberg, Nelson M. Rodriguez, and Ronald E. Chennault (New York: St. Martin's, 1998), 103–21.
20. For an elaboration of the relationship between embodiment and identity, see Sidonie Smith, *Subjectivity, Identity, and the Body: Women's Autobiographical Practices in the Twentieth Century* (Bloomington: Indiana University Press, 1993) and the discussion of her work in this book's introduction.
21. Dyer, 2.
22. Dyer, 10.
23. Wiegman, 149–50.
24. Wiegman, 150.
25. J. Martin Favor, *Authentic Blackness: The Folk in the New Negro Renaissance* (Durham: Duke University Press, 1999), 131.
26. Jane Kuenz, "American Racial Discourse, 1900–1930: Schuyler's *Black No More*," *Novel* 30, no.2 (1997): 185. Elaine K. Ginsberg makes explicit the general relation between passing (for white) and the desire for economic enfranchisement, writing that "the cultural logic of passing suggests that passing is usually motivated by a desire to shed the identity of an oppressed group and gain access to social and economic opportunities," although she goes on to note that "the rationale for passing may be more or less complex or ambiguous and motivated by other kinds of perceived rewards" (Elaine K. Ginsberg, "The Politics of Passing," in *Passing and the Fictions of Identity*, edited by Elaine K. Ginsberg [Durham: Duke University Press, 1996], 3).
27. Favor, 130.
28. Robert A. Hill, in George S. Schuyler *Ethiopian Stories*, compiled and edited by Robert A. Hill (Boston: Northeastern University Press, 1994), 43 n. 34.
29. Julia M. Wright pointed out—when I delivered an earlier version of this paper—that the use of the phrase "open sesame" in relation to the benefits of whiteness could foreshadow Matthew's engagement in racial discourse, by participating in an Orientalist rhetoric.
30. For a discussion of the relation between *Black No More* and the pseudoscientific discussions of race (which Matthew parodies), see Stacy Morgan, "'The Strange and Wonderful Workings of Science': Race Science and Essentialism in George Schuyler's *Black No More*," *CLA Journal* 42, no.3 (1999): 331–52. Jeffrey A.

Tucker also discusses Schuyler's work in relation to science, critiquing what he sees as Schuyler's attraction "to a narrowly defined scientific ideal" and an "overinvest[ment] in the notion of scientific objectivity," an argument against which DeGraw places her chapter on the novel (Jeffrey A. Tucker, "'Can Science Succeed Where the Civil War Failed': George S. Schuyler and Race," in *Race Consciousness: African-American Studies for the New Century*, edited by Judith Jackson Fossett and Jeffrey A. Tucker [New York: New York University Press, 1997], 136–52).

31. Kuenz, 184.
32. Kuenz, 171.
33. Howard J. Faulkner, "A Vanishing Race," *CLA Journal* 37, no.3 (1994): 274–92.
34. The shifting dynamic in the understanding of race and class can be seen as part of the larger dynamics of Schuyler's life and career: he moved, as Henry Louis Gates, Jr. points out, between left and right political poles and in his relations to the understanding of race. Gates suggests that these shifts constituted "not a simple drift from left to right but a complicated, painful journey filled with the sort of 'double-consciousness' that continues to raise disturbing questions about what racism does to people in America" ("A Fragmented Man: George Schuyler and the Claims of Race," review of *Black Empire* by George S. Schuyler [Samuel I. Brooks], *New York Times Book Review* [20 Sept. 1992]: 42). While I am not suggesting that Schuyler's portrayal of economics and race in *Black No More* constitutes such a marked version of double consciousness, but rather function together within a larger matrix, Gates' reading can shed light on *Black No More*'s position in Schuyler's career.
35. For discussions of Schuyler, assimilation, and his critics, see: Ann Rayson, "George Schuyler: Paradox Among the 'Assimilationist' Writers," *Black American Literature Forum* 12 (1978): 102–06; and Michael W. Peplow, *George S. Schuyler* (Boston: Twayne, 1980).
36. Benjamin S. Lawson, "George Schuyler and the Fate of Early African-American Science Fiction," in *Impossibility Fictions: Alternativity—Extrapolation—Speculation*, edited by Derek Littlewood and Peter Stockwell (Amsterdam: Rodopi, 1996), 94.
37. Butler, 23.
38. In an earlier version of this chapter, I stated that this scene was "decidedly unsatiric[]," but William W. Cook and James Tatum critique this statement, writing that "it is precisely the workings of hatred in both the author of the satire and the events within it that raise it to the kind of savagery familiar in Juvenal and Swift" (*African American Writers and the Classical Tradition* [Chicago: University of Chicago Press, 2010], 407 n. 25). This criticism is well taken, and I would now more closely follow Oscar R. Williams, who notes more subtly that "Of all the ironies in *Black No More*, the Buggerie and Snobbcraft lynching is the most disturbing" (Oscar R. Williams, *George S. Schuyler: Portrait of a Black Conservative* [Knoxville: University of Tennessee Press, 2007], 53). Indeed, I agree with DeGraw that Samuel R. Delany describes it best: "Though the term did not exist, here the 'humor' becomes so 'black' as to take on elements of inchoate American horror" (Samuel R. Delany, "Racism and Science Fiction," *New York Review of Science Fiction* 120 [1998], Rpt. *nyrsf.com*: n.d. n.p.; DeGraw, 78).
39. Quoted in Rayson, 105; also see Kuenz, 172.

40. As Roediger states about the efficacy of destabilizing whiteness, "a critique of whiteness is *both* the precondition and the result of *both* class and antiracist struggles" ("White Workers, New Democrats, and Affirmative Action," in *The House that Race Built: Black Americans, U.S. Terrain*, edited by Wahneema Lubiano [New York: Pantheon, 1997], 60); however, perhaps framing it as "a" rather than "the" precondition would also open up other trajectories, including those that challenge the centrality of "whiteness" in "whiteness studies."
41. As espoused, for example, in his early essay, "Racial Intermarriage in the United States." See Williams, 67; 154.
42. George S. Schuyler, *Black Empire*, edited by Robert A. Hill and R. Kent Rasmussen (Boston: Northeastern University Press, 1991), 258.
43. Schuyler, *Black Empire*, 142.
44. Schuyler, *Black* Empire, 258.
45. DeGraw, 80.
46. Robert A. Hill and R. Kent Rasmussen, "Afterword," in Schuyler, *Black Empire*, 283.
47. Gayatri Chakravorty Spivak, *A Critique of Postcolonial Reason: Toward a History of the Vanishing Present* (Cambridge, MA: Harvard University Press, 1999), 284.

REFERENCES

Babb, Valerie. *Whiteness Visible: The Meaning of Whiteness in American Literature and Culture*. New York: New York University Press, 1998.

Bhabha, Homi. *Location of Culture*. London: Routledge, 1994.

Breu, Christopher. *Hard-Boiled Masculinities*. Minneapolis: University of Minnesota Press, 2005.

Burroughs, Edgar Rice. *Tarzan of the Apes*. Edited and introduction by Jason Haslam. 1914. Oxford: Oxford University Press, 2010.

Butler, Judith. "Imitation and Gender Insubordination." In *Inside/Out*, edited by Diana Fuss, 13–31. New York: Routledge, 1991.

Cook, William W. and James Tatum. *African American Writers and the Classical Tradition*. Chicago: University of Chicago Press, 2010.

Davis, Angela Y. "Political Prisoners, Prisons, and Black Liberation." 1971. In *The Angela Y. Davis Reader*, edited by Joy James, 39–60. Oxford: Blackwell, 1998.

DeGraw, Sharon. *The Subject of Race in American Science Fiction*. London: Routledge, 2007.

Delany, Samuel R. "Racism and Science Fiction." *New York Review of Science Fiction* 120 (1998). Rpt. *nyrsf.com*: n.d. N.p. Web. 19 Jan. 2014.

Drzewiecka, Jolanta A. and Kathleen Wong (Lau). "The Dynamic Construction of White Ethnicity in the Context of Transnational Cultural Formations." In *Whiteness: The Communication of Social Identity*, edited by Thomas K. Nakayama and Judith N. Martin, 198–216. London: Sage, 1999.

Dyer, Richard. *White*. New York: Routledge, 1997.

Dyson, Michael Eric. "Giving Whiteness a Black Eye." Interview with Ronald E. Chennault. In *White Reign: Deploying Whiteness in America*. Edited by Joe L. Kincheloe, Shirley R. Steinberg, Nelson M. Rodriguez, and Ronald E. Chennault, 299–328. New York: St. Martin's, 1998.

Ellison, Ralph. "What America Would Be Like Without Blacks." In *Black on White: Black Writers on What It Means to Be White*, edited by David R. Roediger, 160–67. New York: Schocken Books, 1998.

Faulkner, Howard J. "A Vanishing Race." *CLA Journal* 37, no.3 (1994): 274–92.

Favor, J. Martin. *Authentic Blackness: The Folk in the New Negro Renaissance*. Durham: Duke University Press, 1999.

Frankenberg, Ruth. *White Women, Race Matters: The Social Construction of Whiteness*. Minneapolis: University of Minnesota Press, 1993.

Gates, Henry Louis, Jr. "A Fragmented Man: George Schuyler and the Claims of Race." Rev. of *Black Empire*, by George S. Schuyler [Samuel I. Brooks]. *New York Times Book Review* 20 Sept. 1992: 42.

Ginsberg, Elaine K. "The Politics of Passing." Introduction. In *Passing and the Fictions of Identity*, edited by Elaine K. Ginsberg, 1–18. Durham: Duke University Press, 1996.

Hutchinson, George. *The Harlem Renaissance in Black and White*. Cambridge: Belknap-Harvard University Press, 1995.

Jacobson, Matthew Frye. *Whiteness of a Different Color: European Immigrants and the Alchemy of Race*. Cambridge: Harvard University Press, 1998.

Kuenz, Jane. "American Racial Discourse, 1900–1930: Schuyler's *Black No More*." *Novel* 30, no.2 (1997): 170–92.

Lawson, Benjamin S. "George Schuyler and the Fate of Early African-American Science Fiction." In *Impossibility Fictions: Alternativity—Extrapolation—Speculation*, edited by Derek Littlewood and Peter Stockwell, 87–105. Amsterdam: Rodopi, 1996.

Moon, Dreama. "White Enculturation and Bourgeois Ideology: The Discursive Production of 'Good (White) Girls.'" In *Whiteness: The Communication of Social Identity*, edited by Thomas K. Nakayama and Judith N. Martin, 177–97. London: Sage, 1999.

Morgan, Stacy. "'The Strange and Wonderful Workings of Science': Race Science and Essentialism in George Schuyler's *Black No More*." *CLA Journal* 42, no.3 (1999): 331–52.

Morrison, Toni. *Playing in the Dark: Whiteness and the Literary Imagination*. New York: Vintage, 1990.

Patterson, Monica Beatriz deMello. "America's Racial Unconscious: The Invisibility of Whiteness." In *White Reign: Deploying Whiteness in America*, edited by Joe L. Kincheloe, Shirley R. Steinberg, Nelson M. Rodriguez, and Ronald E. Chennault, 103–21. New York: St. Martin's, 1998.

Peplow, Michael W. *George S. Schuyler*. Boston: Twayne, 1980.

Rayson, Ann. "George Schuyler: Paradox Among the 'Assimilationist' Writers." *Black American Literature Forum* 12 (1978): 102–06.

Reilly, John M. "The Black Anti-Utopia." *Black American Literature Forum* 12 (Fall 1978): 107–09.

Roediger, David R, ed. *Black on White: Black Writers on What It Means to Be White*. New York: Schocken Books, 1998.

———. *The Wages of Whiteness: Race and the Making of the American Working Class*. New York: Verso, 1991.

———. "White Workers, New Democrats, and Affirmative Action." In *The House that Race Built: Black Americans, U.S. Terrain*, edited by Wahneema Lubiano, 48–65. New York: Pantheon, 1997.

Sargent, Lyman Tower. "The Three Faces of Utopianism Revisited." *Utopian Studies* 5, no.1 (1994): 1–37.

Schocket, Eric. "'Discovering Some New Race': Rebecca Harding Davis's 'Life in the Iron Mills' and the Literary Emergence of Working-Class Whiteness." *PMLA* 115, no.1 (2000): 46–59.

Schuyler, George. *Black Empire*. Edited by Robert A. Hill and R. Kent Rasmussen. Foreword by John A. Williams. Boston: Northeastern University Press, 1991.

———. *Black No More: Being an Account of the Strange and Wonderful Workings of Science in the Land of the Free, A.D. 1933–1940*. 1931. Boston: Northeastern University Press, 1989.

———. *Ethiopian Stories*. Compiled and Edited by Robert A. Hill. Boston: Northeastern University Press, 1994.

———. "A Negro Looks at Negroes." *Debunker and the American Parade* (Oct. 1930): 27–38.

———. "Our White Folks." In *Black on White: Black Writers on What It Means to Be White*, edited by David R. Roediger, 71–84. New York: Schocken Books, 1998.

Smith, Sidonie. *Subjectivity, Identity, and the Body: Women's Autobiographical Practices in the Twentieth Century*. Bloomington: Indiana University Press, 1993.

Spivak, Gayatri Chakravorty. *A Critique of Postcolonial Reason: Toward a History of the Vanishing Present*. Cambridge, MA: Harvard University Press, 1999.

Traister, Bryce. "Academic Viagra: The Rise of American Masculinity Studies." *American Quarterly* 52, no.2 (2000): 274–304.

Tucker, Jeffrey A. "'Can Science Succeed Where the Civil War Failed': George S. Schuyler and Race." In *Race Consciousness: African-American Studies for the New Century*, edited by Judith Jackson Fossett and Jeffrey A. Tucker, 136–52. New York: New York University Press, 1997.

Wander, Philip C., Judith N. Martin, and Thomas K. Nakayama. "Whiteness and Beyond: Sociohistorical Foundations of Whiteness and Contemporary Challenges." In *Whiteness: The Communication of Social Identity*, edited by Thomas K. Nakayama and Judith N. Martin, 13–26. London: Sage, 1999.

Wiegman, Robyn. "Whiteness Studies and the Paradox of Particularity." *boundary 2* 26, no.3 (1999): 115–50.

Williams, Oscar R. *George S. Schuyler: Portrait of a Black Conservative*. Knoxville: University of Tennessee Press, 2007.

4 Coded Discourse

Romancing the (Electronic) Shadow in *the Matrix*

Criticism on the Wachowski siblings' science fiction film, *The Matrix* (1999), has generally followed along the lines of early criticism on the cyberpunk fiction of the late 1980s. This isn't really surprising, since critics and fans of both the film and the subgenre have portrayed *The Matrix* as the first successful filmic translation of the imagery of cyberpunk, which is usually seen as being founded by, and epitomised in, William Gibson's 1984 novel *Neuromancer*. As P. Chad Barnett forcefully puts it, "the corpse-cold body of cyberpunk has been revived by a film that has brought the true feel of that notorious word to the screen for the first time."[1] Going beyond the superficial use of a computer-generated realm of existence in such earlier films as *Tron* (1982), *Lawnmower Man* (1992), and *The Thirteenth Floor* (1999), *The Matrix*, as the argument goes, captures the full flavour of cyberpunk, including not only the notion of a complete mental projection into a computerised net, but also the "retro-future" feel of the genre, where space-age computer technology coexists with grime, filth, and perhaps most importantly, an all-encompassing urban decay, characterised by Gibson as "The Sprawl."[2] Cyberpunk's imagery, meanwhile, is often said to coexist with the textual creation of a new form of postmodern identity, a cybernetic, posthuman ontology in which, to quote Barnett again, "a host of technologies ... place *real* human forms at risk of extinction," primarily because "the flesh is burdensome wetware, exchanges are all symbolic in an electronic land of signs, and reality is virtual at best."[3] David Lavery notes in his essay on *The Matrix* and virtual reality that "Convinced that 'physical reality is tragic in that it's mandatory,' virtual realists are ready to break with that seemingly irrevocable precedent."[4] Further, cyberpunk and its progeny have, it's been argued, helped with this split, creating, or at least aiming for "a new 'mode' of being," a "truly abstract space of imprecise possibilities," brought about through the genre's representation of "technological and posthuman indeterminacy."[5] *The Matrix*, then, within this critical framework, is supposedly the cinematic refinement of this posthuman identity, the indeterminacy of which is shown narratively in the film's reliance on the classic science fiction plot of the alternate world (in which the main characters realise that the world around them is somehow fake, and they must break through the appearances in order to discover and inhabit reality).[6]

But, does the film actually present an image of this supposedly freeing and utopian realm of the posthuman? Is there an ontological critique fueling the Wachowskis' use of such much-discussed (and oft-parodied) visuals as "bullet time" (which seems to slow time to the point that a bullet's path can be clearly seen), their use of 360° of still-picture cameras arranged in minutely timed sequence?[7] The images created with these techniques—including the blurred multiplication of characters' bodies as they move more quickly than should be possible, and Neo's (Keanu Reeves) ability, in both the first and final films, to move beyond his own body, "infecting" the repressive program of Agent Smith (Hugo Weaving)—may seem to imply visually a form of de-individuated subjectivity that finds its reflection in the film's portrayal of communal resistance cells of rebellious humans. Despite, or perhaps because of, these heroic effects, the question remains, though: does *The Matrix* truly offer a radical critique of enlightenment subjectivity, or does it simply reproduce dominant biases, specifically surrounding gender and race? Perhaps the "posthuman indeterminacy" of the film and the genre is really only window dressing for the reproduction of dominant ideological identity constructs, an argument perhaps supported best by Joshua Moss' online review, "Breaking the Cyberpunk Curse," in which he writes that *The Matrix* "has mythic structure. Dream meditations on the values of life. A poetic Christ-like resurrection at the climax. Not to mention hot chicks in tight leather."[8]

Such arguments about the reproduction of the dominant culture's ideological framework have been made about cyberpunk in general, and Gibson's *Neuromancer* trilogy in particular. Sharon Stockton argues that the classic cyberpunk hero is someone who "is removed entirely from problems of influence and given the status of prime mover, of pure subject in a world of pure object, of phallic projection into a feminized matrix that approximates the universe."[9] Nicola Nixon further states that the "corporate collectives" against which Gibson's heroes fight are invariably figured as a generally orientalist, usually Japanese, threat. Arguing, in effect, that Gibson's works—however unwittingly—reproduce the yellow-peril narratives of Nowlan's Buck Rogers, she writes of Gibson's cyberspace "cowboys" that "It seems telling that the American icon of the cowboy, realized so strongly in Reaganite cowboyism, the quintessence of the maverick reactionary, should form the central heroic iconography in cyberpunk."[10] Ross Farnell opens a similar discussion, writing of the first two books in Gibson's "post-cyberpunk," nanotechnology trilogy that, "Beneath an aesthetics of difference hides a subterranean narrative of conservative sexuality and gender, old 'norms' in new digital clothes," a reading Farnell doubles through an analysis of race in Gibson's work.[11] Thus, there are two basic readings of cyberpunk that could lend themselves to *The Matrix*. In one, as Farnell goes on to argue, an idealised heterotopia is constructed. Using the term more to mean a "utopia of difference" than in Foucault's more radical sense (as discussed later in this book), Farnell sees this heterotopia as a space that stands as a "solution"—however "open-ended"—to conservative narratives;[12] indeed, at one point Barnett reads *The Matrix* "As a heterotopian construct."[13] In the other reading, the genre reproduces the discourses of white male supremacy, as Stockton and Nixon see in Gibson's first trilogy. I want to argue, though, that while *The Matrix* is problematic in precisely the ways Stockton and Nixon suggest, simply seeing the film as such a reproduction of dominance would miss out on some of the nuances that *are* created by its explicit meditations on the nature of subjectivity and of ideology "itself." *The Matrix* can be read as a text that allows both of these readings, using a disturbed and disturbing set of plots and images surrounding gender and race that can be seen to point to the performative nature not just of those "coarse axes" of identity discussed by Sedgwick (gender, race, sexuality) but also of the assertion of normative power—dominance itself becomes a performative structure. This is not to say that the exercise of power has no material effect, any more than saying gender and race are performative denies the lived realities people experience due to them. Instead, identifying the assertion of *natural* right and power as performative allows one to analyse the mythologies of power, in Barthes' sense, that are at play in and around these other social categories. This reading may allow the film, and perhaps cyberpunk in general, to be used as an entry point into—but certainly not an ultimate depiction of—a critique of the exclusionary nature of enlightenment subjectivity. Slavoj Žižek gestures toward this in his essay on *The Matrix* when he writes that "Cyberspace was supposed to bring us all together in a Global Village; however ... instead of the Global Village, the big Other, we get the multitude of 'small others,' of tribal particular identifications at our choice."[14] While Žižek might deny the revolutionary efficacy of such identifications, and despite his lack of elaboration on the racial implications of this statement, such an argument can be made through a specific analysis of the film's allusions to and images of African Americans and African American discursive traditions, all of which seem to point to an explicit critique of American racism and white power, only to be undercut by the main plot concerning Neo. However, certain gender constructions call this dominant plot into question, especially as figured through the rearticulation of the racist film tradition of the mammy figure in the character, "The Oracle" (played by Gloria Foster in the first two films, and Mary Alice in *Revolutions*). Moving from the previous chapter's study of Schuyler's analysis of the early decades of the twentieth century, we now leap ahead to the closing decades, but both works expose the virtual nature of "race" as a foundation of social structures; where Schuyler's work recognises that such an exposure of race's semiotic structures is not, in itself, a means to undermine those structures, *The Matrix* and its sequels seem to forget this lesson, subordinating their potentially radical critique to the material demands of Hollywood film—something that happens even more glaringly in the Wachowskis' adaptation of *Cloud Atlas*, to which I will turn at the end of this chapter.[15]

I. VIRTUAL RACE WAR

The Matrix's central plot concerns a human rebellion against the Artificial Intelligence (AI) that has taken over the earth and uses human beings as its power source. The AI keeps its human "batteries" docile by creating the artificial, cyber-realm of the Matrix, or what we know as the real world of the late 1990s. A handful of critics have analysed the fact that this rebellion is, to a degree, raced as an African American rebellion against a white power structure.[16] In addition to what I would argue is the racially specific casting of Laurence Fishburne as Morpheus, the "father" to the family of rebels that comes to include Neo, and in addition to the racialized domestic setting of the Oracle's apartment, the film as a whole relies on what is, in America and elsewhere, a racially charged narrative: the emancipation of a population of people held as slaves. In the scene in which Neo first meets Morpheus, the latter attempts to describe the Matrix. Morpheus says, "It is the world that has been pulled over your eyes, to blind you to the truth," to which Neo responds, "What truth?" Morpheus answers, "That you are a slave, Neo. Like everyone else, you were born into bondage."[17] That this line is spoken by an African American only adds to *The Matrix*'s appropriation of the trope of slavery as a means through which to define the quest for freedom. As Toni Morrison has written in the section of *Playing in the Dark* from which my chapter's title is taken, the "Africanist narrative (that is, the story of a black person, the experience of being bound and/or rejected)" is often used in (white) American literature, and I would add film, "as a means of meditation—both safe and risky—on one's own humanity," providing "opportunities to contemplate limitation, suffering, rebellion, and to speculate on fate and destiny."[18] Morrison's discussion is almost lifted into the same scene of *The Matrix*, when Morpheus and Neo first meet:

> MORPHEUS: You have the look of a man who accepts what he sees, because he is expecting to wake up. Ironically, this is not far from the truth. Do you believe in fate, Neo?
> NEO: No.
> MORPHEUS: Why not?
> NEO: Because I don't like the idea that I'm not in control of my life.
> MORPHEUS: I know exactly how you feel.

Žižek, when quoting this same passage, finds it necessary to point out that Morpheus is "the African-American leader of the resistance group," but does not explain why this is significant.[19] The casting of Fishburne as Morpheus, especially when the screenplay introduces him only as a "DARK FIGURE," serves to highlight the Africanist narrative, to use Morrison's term, that is present in the film. In this reading, Neo's assertion of free will in the face of an overly deterministic, subjugating structure is placed in relief by and gains its moral and ethical force from the words of the black character, who "know[s] exactly" what such an assertion means.

However, Morpheus' race may seem to make this not an African-*ist* narrative, but in fact a narrative of African American resistance. That is, Morpheus' story may be his own, not Neo's, allowing for a metaphorical identification of the Matrix AI with contemporary ideological structures of white power, and Morpheus' resistance cell with a contemporary black rebellion against that structure. This reading is especially supported by the fact that the AI's repressive apparatuses are embodied as white policemen or agents. Indeed, in *The Matrix Reloaded*, the figure who presents itself to Neo as the "Architect" of the Matrix itself (Helmut Bakaitis), the apparent wizard behind the machine and authority behind the law, is also white (and, being dressed in white and sitting in a white room, is figuratively thc "whitest" character of the films, duplicating the visually white space of the blank "construct" that Morpheus uses to explain the Matrix to Neo, in a pair of scenes that echo nothing so much as the funeral procession in *Mizora*).[20] Moreover, the security cameras that observe Neo's interrogation in the first film are shown in *Reloaded* to be part of the literally panoptic wall of screens in the Architect's room. The Architect embodies the panopticon, becoming the all-seeing eye that observes and imprisons, attempting to ideologically and physically control all of humanity.

As my reference to the panopticon suggests, this identification of the Matrix and authority, and especially law enforcement, is in the first film explicitly used to critique the institutional racism of American policing.[21] Morpheus battles with the agent known by the nearly pseudonymous name of the dominant culture—"Smith." The only dialogue they exchange during the fight happens near the beginning, with Smith introducing himself:

> SMITH: The great Morpheus. We meet at last.
> MORPHEUS: And you are?
> MORPHE: "Smith." Agent Smith.
> MORPHEUS: You all look the same to me.

This dialogue is followed by one of the more brutal fight scenes in the film, in which Agent Smith seriously injures Morpheus, leaving him broken and bloody. The fight does not end there, however; instead, leaving Morpheus on the floor, Smith walks out of the bathroom in which the battle takes place and says to a group of uniformed policemen, "Take him." Immediately upon hearing this command, the group of police rush into the room and kick and beat the fallen Morpheus. The action and visuals in this scene directly allude to George Holliday's infamous videotape of the LAPD's savage beating of Rodney King, a similarity Douglas A. Cunningham notes in both versions of his essay:[22] while the King video is shot from a distance and at a slight angle, and *The Matrix* scene is shot from directly above, both "scenes" show a black man lying on the ground, occasionally in a foetal position, surrounded by police who, with extraordinary force, are beating him with batons. The racially charged humour of a black man telling a white cop "you all look the same to me," when combined with the obvious visual allusion to the King videotape, would certainly seem to point to a reading of this film as a story of a black rebellion against the white power structure.

This reading seems valid given the host of other allusions to the history of African American resistance: Morpheus, during an interrogation by Agent Smith following the beating, is chained to the chair in what looks somewhat like a cinematic replica of the infamous courtroom sketch of Black Panther Bobby Seale gagged and chained during the Chicago 7 trial—an allusion strengthened by the fact that the cyber-city created by the Matrix uses Chicago's street names[23]; earlier, when Morpheus is teaching Neo how to fight in the Matrix, bending the computer-based rules of the simulation, Morpheus performs quite a stunning Ali Shuffle before continuing to beat Neo—anyone who catches that shuffle and the explicit reference to Muhammad Ali therefore has access to another allusion to African American resistance (this boxing reference is expanded by the appearance, in *Reloaded*, of African American boxer Roy Jones, Jr.).

Moving beyond these brief allusions and beyond the character of Morpheus, the "last human city" left on the planet in the film is called Zion, a biblical allusion that serves not only to reference Israel, but also more generally the Promised Land in Judeo-Christian tradition; more significantly for this argument, Zion was used in both ante- and postbellum African American Christian theology as a term connected to freedom (as evidenced by the African Methodist Episcopal Zion Church, which "grew out of the merciless enslavement of our African forefathers," and has included such famous people in the history of black resistance as Frederick Douglass and Sojourner Truth).[24] Zion also figures large in Rastafari, as the African promised land (as Grisso, in his online analysis of *The Matrix*, points out). This connection is even present within the narrow cyberpunk tradition: Zion is the name of the separatist, space-dwelling, black Rastafarian group in Gibson's *Neuromancer*. When the audience finally gets to see Zion in *Reloaded*, the city is multiracial, and many—if not most—of the positions of power are held by people who are visibly non-white. Cementing the explicit use of Zion as a figure of African American resistance and freedom (especially, but not solely, for an academic audience) is the cameo in both *Reloaded* and *Revolutions* by Cornel West, playing "Counsellor West" on the city's ruling council. West's real-life position within African American studies, and the self-naming of his character, point to the films' explicit engagement with African American history and resistance.

Further to this connection, several online reactions and reviews, and later academic criticism, note the racial characterisation of Zion in one other particular way, writing—often without further comment—that Morpheus' speech in *Reloaded* to the city's population is reminiscent of Martin Luther King, Jr.'s "I Have a Dream" speech. While the comparisons drawn in these reactions are largely undetailed, seeming to pick up more on the emotive and visual relations between the two speeches, there are in fact some echoes of content.

Most prominently, Morpheus' speech repeats the phrase "one hundred years," a repetition which also occurs early in King's speech. Whereas King's emphasis, however, is on the continuing oppression of African Americans despite the signing of the Emancipation Proclamation "one hundred years" earlier, Morpheus' only point is that, after "one hundred years," the inhabitants of Zion "are still here!" Both speeches highlight the oppression of the black (or, in *Reloaded*, largely black) populace, but King's is focused on a future dream of freedom from this oppression, while Morpheus focuses on the past and largely on the maintenance of the status quo of Zion's position, a possible retrenchment to which I will return later in this chapter.

Before we see West or Zion, however, in the first film there is the rebel ship itself, and the Oracle's apartment within the Matrix, which I will deal with in more detail below. Both of these settings, like Zion in *Reloaded* and *Revolutions*, are figured as mostly black, but at the very least multiracial spaces that stand opposed to *all* of the city scenes wherein Neo is being introduced to the Matrix. These latter spaces are, visibly anyway, largely or completely white, as are all of the cops and agents in the Matrix's "employ." So, up to a point, this film is one that depicts a specifically African American rebellion against a silencing dominant culture that literally builds itself using the bodies of those under its control. In other words, this film could be read as an extended allegory for a black resistance to contemporary social structures of white power, and, as Sanchez and Boyd read it, as a multiracial engagement with critical race studies itself and with larger African American resistance struggles.

But this reading is only available to a point. In many ways, *The Matrix* is, as King and Leonard point out,[25] a science fiction version of Hollywood's interracial buddy flick, perhaps best seen in the *48 Hrs.* and *Lethal Weapon* series, and parodied—again to a point—by the *Rush Hour* films. Indeed, some of Robyn Wiegman's statements about the role of race in *Lethal Weapon* could be simply mapped onto *The Matrix*:

> *Lethal Weapon* revamps race and gender relations in the contemporary moment by figuring the white man as both victim of the social order and its rejuvenated hero. ... [Mel Gibson's character] Riggs is shown [at the beginning of the film] lying in bed smoking a cigarette, his mobile home strewn with debris. A man on the edge of breakdown ... Riggs is lost, the squalor of his environment indicative of his alienation. ... Here, in a reversal of paternalistic ideology, it is the white man who ... can be restored to life only through the aid of the black "father"—the figure responsible, in the film's resolution, for drawing the alienated white man back into the folds of sanity and the bourgeois family.[26]

Wiegman's description of the opening of *Lethal Weapon* echoes exactly the introduction of Neo in *The Matrix*. Neo is shown asleep in front of his computer in his unkempt, single-room apartment, only to be awakened by messages on his computer. Then there is a knock on Neo's door, and he engages in a shady software deal with a cybergoth named Choi:

> NEO: You get caught using that …
> CHOI: Yeah, I know, this never happened. You don't exist.
> NEO: Right.
> CHOI: Something wrong, man? 'Cause you look a little whiter than usual.

The scene as a whole, then, as in Wiegman's reading of *Lethal Weapon*, shows the white character, in the "squalor of his environment," which seems "indicative of his alienation." Indeed, one of the first images of Neo in this scene (and in the movie), shot from above, shows him literally encircled by the detritus of the technological world. Grimy computer equipment and other forms of mess surround him, taking up more than half of the screen and extending beyond three sides of the shot.[27] The cramped nature of the image in his apartment is heightened by a slow rotation, indicating that Neo, before his actual and figurative awakenings, is completely delimited and subjugated by his social surroundings. In this version of the trope, the subjection is explicitly tied to his looking "whiter than usual." At this point in the first film, Neo is also beginning to be "restored to life" by Morpheus, described later by the character Tank (Marcus Chong) as a "father," again echoing Wiegman's description. Father-figure Morpheus is not the hero of this film; the "whiter than usual" son, Neo, is.[28] The pairing of these two characters, generically inscribed in the buddy movie, brings us back to Morrison's construction of white American literature as a romancing of the shadow, as a racist appropriation of an Africanist narrative in order to further the self-worth of the white hero.

Additionally, Neo's heroic quest is one that is based on suppositions that have implications in terms of race. Specifically, Neo's status as the chosen one, as the saviour predicted by the Oracle, is founded on his ability to completely control the hyper-rational, disembodied realm of the Matrix. As Stockton's article demonstrates, the realm of cyberspace is figured ontologically as a space of dominance, what she refers to as the space "of pure subject in a world of pure object."[29] The Matrix, like cyberspace, is a site of mental disembodiment, the Cartesian cogito almost completely severed from the body. Historically, unfettered access to this traditional humanist notion of the individual has been represented as being limited to the privileged members of the dominant culture. As discussed in this study's introduction, Sidonie Smith writes that this Enlightenment identity is characterised by disembodiment and rationality, and therefore contains a "hierarchy" that delimits who is and who is not considered part of the supposedly universal human, as in biased scientific and other epistemologies that constructed women and people of colour as inherently "irrational."[30] In other words, the hyper-rationality of the Cartesian duality that Neo enacts is in many ways the same one enacted by Aylmer's experiments and performed to varying degrees by Tarzan and Anthony "Buck" Rogers: it is a rationality based on conventions and practices of othering. These conventions specifically get played out, in the film, in racialized terms that recreate the contemporary privileged positioning of white men, despite the coded (sub)narrative of black rebellion. Thus, just after Neo is informed that "the Matrix has you"—that is, when he first becomes cognizant of his existence as a disembodied mental projection—he is said to be "even whiter than usual."

On the surface, there may seem to be a problem with this reading. After all, Neo is fighting for humanity's freedom, for the end of the Matrix's control, and therefore, apparently, for the reembodiment of the population. He seems to be fighting against the hyperextended demonic parody of the Cartesian duality in which people in the Matrix exist purely mentally while being unaware of the very physical violations perpetrated on their bodies in rows upon rows of human farms. In *Reloaded*, in fact, a glorification of human physicality is figured through the paired scenes of Neo and Trinity (Carrie-Anne Moss) having sex and a prewar gathering in Zion. While Trinity and Neo consummate their relationship, the rest of Zion's citizens participate in an orgiastic, rave-cum-religious festival of dance, the camera providing in both cases very close shots of sections of sweaty bodies in constant contact with each other.[31] Isn't Neo therefore, in all of the films—but as laid out emphatically in the first—fighting against the disembodied, transcendent, purely rational, "universal" subject that Smith discusses, and working toward a reintegration of the previously marginalized, embodied subjects?

The answer to this question is complex and ambiguous. Yes, Neo seems to be fighting for this reembodiment rather than his own transcendent mastery, but he is doing it through his thorough control of and complete existence as the hyper-rational subject. This is centrally the cyber-version of the interracial buddy flick, a digital *Dances with Wolves* or a cyber-Tarzan swinging through an electronic and urban jungle in which the non-white and/or female characters must wait for the white male hero to save the day. And, in *The Matrix*, the salvation is achieved through the final realisation of the racially charged, Enlightenment ontology that Sidonie Smith discusses. This racialization is especially apparent in the scene in which Neo saves Morpheus from the interrogation of Agent Smith. After shooting all of the agents present in the room with a very large machine gun (which he holds just above his groin in an obvious assertion of his phallic power), Neo looks at Morpheus and says, very quietly, "Get up." This phrase is repeated a few times in the film, generally when people are trying to make their own projected bodies move while in the Matrix, functioning almost as if it were a software command. In this scene, it is only when Neo executes this command that Morpheus is able to break his chains and get out of the room. But even then Morpheus doesn't make it to safety by himself; Neo has to jump out of the helicopter and catch him in midair.

II. THE GENDERED BODY ELECTRIC

As in *Black No More*, however, the introduction of a gendered narrative complicates the racialized plot in the film, pointing toward the primarily performative, nonessential nature of the heroic identity that Neo realises. First, both his romantic relationship with Trinity and her position in terms of what is supposedly "his" destiny problematize his existence as "pure subject," as the transcendent individual who acts through his will and his will alone. There are several scenes in which Trinity rescues or otherwise controls Neo, but two of them are especially significant. The first occurs immediately before Neo rescues Morpheus. Trinity and Neo are on the roof of a building engaged in a gun battle with an agent, in probably the most famous—and most often spoofed—scene of the film. The agent shoots at Neo, who dodges all of the bullets, only getting grazed a few times. Neo moves as fast as the agents themselves, something no one has done before. Indeed, the portrayal of the speed of his movement mimics Neo's burgeoning transcendence beyond the physical: showing Neo maintaining a posture that defies gravity and anatomy, this effect represents, in keeping with the logic of the plot, a traditional form of hegemonic masculinity, showing Neo's ability to transcend the body through his mental control.

Despite this depiction of his transcendent mastery, however, the other thing no one has done before is win a battle with one of the agents, and everybody thinks that Neo, the One, can do this. But, in this scene, it is Trinity who shoots the agent, after managing to get beside him without being noticed. It is Trinity who saves the day by using the phallic power, represented again by the gun, which Neo constantly tries to assert. The implication that everyone was so busy looking at Neo that no one saw her sneak up functions almost allegorically for the resistant gendered reading of the film in which Trinity is the One (in an obvious religious allusion). In fact, Trinity's ability to manipulate the Matrix in the same way that Neo does explicitly confuses gender paradigms. Based on the same bigoted epistemology discussed before, women are also othered through embodiment.[32] In her second scene in the film, Trinity introduces herself to Neo in a bar:

> NEO: Who are you?
> TRINITY: My name is Trinity.
> NEO: Trinity. *The* Trinity? That cracked the IRS d-base?
> TRINITY: That was a long time ago.
> NEO: Jesus.
> TRINITY: What.
> NEO: I just thought, um … you were a guy.
> TRINITY: Most guys do.

Trinity's control of cyberspace, her ability to inhabit Stockton's realm of "pure object" as a "pure subject," disrupts gender assumptions, as is also shown when she defeats armed policeman in the opening scene of the film. Trinity thus calls into question the gender paradigms associated with the Cartesian notion of self that supposedly supports Neo's identity as the male hero.[33]

This gender reversal becomes especially evident in another scene in which Trinity saves Neo. Near the end of the film after Neo has apparently been killed by the agents, as Barnett briefly mentions,[34] Trinity engages in a parodic mimicry of Prince Charming awakening sleeping beauty: telling Neo's seemingly dead body that she loves him, she then awakens him with a kiss. After he comes back to life, Trinity executes the same control command that Neo uses on Morpheus, telling him to "Get up," which he does, and then, of course, saves the day. But this explicit gender reversal, and its repetition of the earlier scene with Morpheus, points to the ways in which Neo's identity, his pure subjectivity, is performatively enabled by the gendered, embodied figure which the dominant ontology would deny by defining it as "other." Here, we can once again return to Butler, who argues that the supposed dominance of heterosexuality "is perpetually at risk, that is, that it 'knows' its own possibility of becoming undone,"[35] and so is in a constant process of being compared to various "other" sexualities without which it would cease to be understandable as a category. In the classic deconstructive move of Butler's argument, an essentialized, "dominant" identity always presupposes the very others it would erase or deny, thus denying its own "essential" or "originary" status.

III. THE ANGEL IN THE MACHINE

The viewer would seem to be left, then, with a film that, on the one hand, problematically enacts what Morrison discusses as the appropriation of the Africanist narrative in an attempt to support the dominance of whiteness, while, on the other hand, critiques the gendered implications of that dominant discourse of identity, much as *Mizora* does.[36] In *Reloaded*, this relationship is phrased succinctly in a dialogue between Trinity and Neo: speaking of the citizens of Zion, the rebels, Trinity tells Neo, "they need you," to which he replies, "I need *you*." The character of the Oracle ties these two narratives together, though, and finally offers a comment on the performativity of identity writ large. The figure of the Oracle, as Hester-Williams briefly notes, is very much cast as a representation of the racist and sexist stereotype of the mammy, most famously portrayed by Hattie McDaniel in *Gone with the Wind* (1939). This stereotype was perpetuated through both proslavery and abolitionist works in the nineteenth century, and introduced into film, as Lisa M. Anderson discusses, most famously in *Gone with the Wind*, but also in *Birth of a Nation* (1915), *Imitation of Life* (1959), and even in 1980s television in Nell Carter's character on *Gimme a Break*. Anderson defines the mammy figure as

> the symbol of black motherhood as perceived by whites. In the mythic construction, the black woman "mammy" is the caretaker of the

> whites' homes and children first, and her own second. Her primary duties are to the whites for whom she works. ... In essence, then, the mammy is a black woman who focusses her time, love, devotion, and attention on whites, particularly her "adopted" white family, rather than on her own black family.[37]

Certainly the Oracle fulfills this part of the stereotype, looking after the various children—most of them white—who are sent to her for testing to see if they are "the One." She also fulfills the more physical attributes of the stereotype, who, as Anderson describes, is "typified visually" in part by her place in the kitchen, "her apron, and her large size, as well as her racial markers."[38] Also, the Oracle fills the role of "comic relief," to a point, as do traditional depictions of the character-type.[39] On this level, then, the Oracle seems to serve the same stereotypical purpose as Morpheus' character: she is there to provide support for the white hero.[40]

But, because of her place in the resistance and all of the films' constantly doubled sense of representation created by the figuring of the Matrix itself, the Oracle appears to be more of a redeployment, conscious or otherwise, of the mammy stereotypes, and, as with Trinity, her support of Neo in effect shows his lack of power. The Oracle expands on the bigoted stereotypes of the mammy, especially as portrayed in *Gone with the Wind*. Anderson notes that, in that film, Mammy is "the all-knowing and interfering (with good intentions) guardian of the family."[41] Bogle likewise writes that, in *Gone with the Wind*, Mammy is the "all-seeing, all-hearing, all-knowing commentator and observer."[42] Extending the stereotypical character's powerful position in the centre of the house, the Oracle literally becomes an "all-knowing" and interfering character, as her title suggests. In fact, in the original script as it appears on several online sites, the Oracle's apartment is described as "a part of Zion's mainframe" that is "hidden inside the Matrix so that we can access it." One could read this line, in conjunction with the use of the mammy stereotype, as a form of ironic mimicry—as the rebellious others signifyin' on dominant sexist and racist discourse, hiding the rebellion against the white matrix until it is too late.[43]

However, *The Matrix* still seems to be left with the problem that it is Neo, the One, who saves the day. But the Oracle is the figure through whom the problematic raced narrative of Neo and Morpheus and the gendered critique offered by Trinity's character become joined. Only through the Oracle's interference with Neo is he able to become "the One." As Morpheus says to Neo near the end of the film, "She told you exactly what you needed to hear." The Oracle also explicitly makes fun of Neo's assertion that "he doesn't believe in all that fate crap," ironically suggesting that his identity is in fact a determined one, not the self-contained individual of Enlightenment ontology. The Oracle points out that Neo's supposedly dominant gendered *and* raced identity is performative, in Butler's sense. His dominance in general is not essential to his nature; it cannot in fact exist without those through whom he expresses dominance. Neo needs the multiplicity of the Oracle, Trinity, and Morpheus in order to be the One (and the names of the latter two reflect multiplicity "itself").[44]

But, at the end of the first film, Neo *has* finally assumed the mantle of the "One," the "superman" (a reference made explicitly in *Reloaded*), and in order to do this, he, and the film, must repress the exposure of the non-essential and therefore tenuous "nature" of his heroic identity. And this is why, at the end of *The Matrix*, we do not see Neo ultimately freeing everyone from the bondage of the Matrix, and why we also don't see any of the characters who supported and maintained his identity throughout the film. Neo calls the mainframe Matrix intelligence on a phone line, and says:

> I know you're out there. I can feel you now. I know that you're afraid. You're afraid of us. You're afraid of change. I don't know the future. I didn't come here to tell you how this is going to end. I came here to tell you how it's going to begin. I'm going to hang up this phone, and then I'm going to show these people what you don't want them to see. I'm going to show them a world without you. A world without rules and controls, without borders or boundaries, a world where anything is possible. Where we go from there is a choice I leave to you.

Neo then leaves the public phone, and flies into the air, fulfilling the supernatural saviour role of the traditional comic book superhero. There are more sinister implications to Neo's speech, however. Neo cannot function outside of the dominant ontological matrix and still be the self-contained singular hero—the One without the Other—because the performative nature of this identity has been exposed. In order to maintain his own dominant position, as well as maintain the generic heroic ending and make the first film hold together, Neo must instead offer a continual existence inside the Matrix.

So, directly opposing Rebekah Simpkins' assertion that "By removing the control, Neo sets the prisoners free," the first film ends with those controls still in place.[45] At the end of *The Matrix*, after all, Neo does not awaken everyone to "the real," but instead exploits the continued functioning of the Matrix, leaving the illusion intact so that he can fly. As Žižek writes, "all these 'miracles' are possible only if we remain WITHIN the VR sustained by the Matrix ...: our 'real' status is still that of the slaves of the Matrix."[46] The words "system failure" may flash on the Matrix's "screens," but the system still continues to work. Neo's attack in effect supports the continued existence of the exploitative structure itself, which is why he leaves the final "choice" to this dominant structure.

Indeed, as we learn in *Reloaded* and *Revolutions*, this act of reproduction (or "revolutions" in the circular sense) could actually be one of Neo's *intended* roles. The "free will" that the Oracle, in her role as a program for the Matrix, injected into the ideological system in order to make it function properly occasionally introduces anomalies in the system, of which Neo, and the "ones" who came before him, are the culmination; fail safes are therefore set into the system in order to ensure that Neo keeps the program running. And, at the end of the trilogy, when the Matrix itself is overtaken by the viral Agent Smith in a virtual coup over the control of the governing AI, Neo does in fact restore the program's "balance" (a continual theme in the final film). Destroying Smith by sacrificing himself, Neo does not eradicate the Matrix, but instead allows the program to evolve into a new stability (a "Neo"-conservative protection of the system, perhaps). This may mean "peace" for the human inhabitants of Zion, but it most assuredly does not mean freedom. If Morpheus is correct when he states, in the first film, that "as long as the Matrix exists, the human race will never be free," then the Architect's promise to the Oracle at the end of *Revolutions*, to free those who "want out," rings hollow. Indeed, the Architect and the Oracle may not even be talking about freeing the humans, but instead about freeing such independent programs as the girl, Sati (Tanveer Atwal). This suspicion seems especially true given the Architect's question in the same sequence, asked in a sinister tone, "Just how long do you think this peace is going to last?" The Oracle's response, "As long as it can," is met by the Architect with only a scoffing laugh.

The central narrative conflict of the two sequels thus concerns Neo's ambiguous position as either rebel *or* exploited and programmed dupe who is doomed to repeat, in unending revolutions, his *support* for the system. Neo's ultimate, Christlike sacrifice may not free humans at all, beyond "saving" the largely decimated Zion. Instead, the salvation he offers appears to serve the governing AI itself, saving it from the infestation of Smiths. Neo destroys Smith's upstart insurgency, but leaves the ruling machine class fully in control. Even if that class has opened up to admit such newer, "useless" programs as Sati, who is capable of, or even symbolises the type of self-sacrificing love that Neo also embodies, the fact of the matter remains that the Matrix is *still* running at the end of the trilogy, and the final scene, while so visibly multiracial as to resemble a Benetton advertisement, focuses solely on the machine world and independent programs, with no humans to be seen. The oppressed underclass of remaining humans, the slaves, are at best tangentially mentioned, and perhaps not at all. In this reading, Morpheus' joy over the "end of the war" is a new form of contentment with the dominant power, rather than a victory over it. The war is over, but Zion does not win.[47] Even Trinity's gender challenges are replaced by banal repetitions of Hollywood sexism: Neo must penetrate her in *Reloaded* to save her after she's shot, and in *Revolutions* she becomes the stereotypically "self-less" woman, sacrificing herself for Neo. Neo may in turn sacrifice himself, but Trinity's death is represented as being committed solely because of her romantic love of Neo, while Neo's death serves to save the world.

This generic sexism, combined with an oblique orientalism, can also be seen in the character of Sati, from the sequels, whose very name represents this self-sacrificial love: "Sati" is the term for the controversial Hindu practice in which the widow would immolate herself on her husband's pyre. Even though this particular character lives, her parents must sacrifice themselves to the dominant AI in order to ensure her survival. This storyline, when combined with the use of the term "sati" to represent a character who helps introduce the emotion of love to the machine world, is problematic at best, as it reproduces the association and idealisation of self-sacrifice with the passive—and, in this instance, childlike—female character.

The entire trilogy thus largely repeats the overall trajectory of the first film. In both the first and (reportedly) final installments, Neo destroys the repressive apparatus of Smith, demonstrating a mastery over the larger computer system itself, and purportedly "saves" Zion by ushering in a new world order. This plot, moreover, echoes directly a racialized rebellion in which an oppressive, racist social structure is replaced by a new harmonious multiracial order. This movement in turn highlights the performativity of the dominant AI, which seems to need the very rebellion it represses in order to maintain its functions.[48] But, this apparently positive allegory of racial transformation and of the nonessential nature of dominance is again undercut, since it takes place only in the context of ultimately maintaining the matrix that controls the rules of the game. In fact, at the very end of *Revolutions*, the Architect promises freedom for some, but validates his word only by saying, with a smile, "What do you think I am? Human?" Freedom can ultimately only be granted at the behest of the dominant class, it seems, and only that class can legitimate the grant.

This approach-retreat relationship to the radical questioning of race, gender, and the oppressive social hierarchies in which they are implicated is made even clearer in the Wachowskis' cinematic return to SF, in the 2012 adaptation of David Mitchell's 2004 novel, *Cloud Atlas*. While the transformation of Mitchell's six "nested" storylines, set in different periods, into a series of quick-cut scene juxtapositions between the timelines is an interesting attempt to transform the complicated textual narrative into an equally complicated cinematic one, the film generates continuity between the storylines in part by employing the same actors to portray different roles in the different timelines. Raising similar questions of identity as the Matrix films, *Cloud Atlas* uses both intricate and sometimes rather transparent make-up and costuming to transform actors' sexes, races, ages, body types, and so on. Simultaneously, the film explores problems of sexual identity, various forms of exploitation, and resistance. In addition to being highlighted by the actors' transformations, these themes are represented through changes to language and culture that take place as the decades and centuries pass in the film.

The easy argument to make about the film's casting is that it attempts to represent a transcendent humanity that exceeds the particularities of historically situated identity, with "true love" winning through in the end. But to make that argument is to ignore the ways in which the particular characters played by a single actor are varied in motivation, morality, and eventual outcome. Instead, like the closing scene of *Revolutions*, the film seems to insist on recognising the role of difference as such, following Butler's performative theory to its endpoint to note that while identities are fluid and not fixed, constructed and not natural, still it is the psycho-semiotic interplay between them (rather than a decontextualized transcendence) from which pleasure arises.

However, in its play with racial identity, especially, the film seems to forget its *own* material context, specifically the very particular role of cinema in the development and distribution of certain forms of racism. The film features mostly (though not solely) white actors in the main roles, which leads to several of those actors having to don a form of "yellowface," a form of racial cross-dressing that has a long—and unmitigatedly racist—history in Hollywood film (one of the most often cited—because one of the most egregious—examples being Mickey Rooney's role in *Breakfast at Tiffany's*). This use of yellowface, and the relative dearth of Asian actors in lead roles (with the exception of Doona Bae), led to a public critique of the film by the Media Action Network for Asian Americans and to several condemnations of the film, even as it could be read as attempting to challenge racial typing.[49] The film's attempted racial play, seemingly indicating the mutability of race and its lack of essential characteristics, unlike Schuyler's satirical vision, founders on the rocks of the material practices of white supremacy, in which white actors are seen to be "universal" enough to adapt to other races. The performative critique of race as an ideological semiotic structure, which is allowed by the film's non-realist plots and non-mimetic structure, is thus undermined by the actual racist practices of film history that the directors employ. As with making "whiteness" particular as a political strategy, highlighting the mutability of race can in fact reproduce the very white supremacy the strategy supposedly attacks, if the material conditions of the critique itself are not taken into account.

In *The Matrix*, this division between theoretical model and material practice, and this movement of an explicitly racially charged social critique followed by its silencing, is echoed in the music played during the closing credits: the first song, Rage Against the Machine's "Wake Up," deals with the assassinations of Martin Luther King, Jr. and Malcolm X, with the repeated lines "He turned the power to the have-nots / And then came the shot," only to be followed by Marilyn Manson's "Rock is Dead," the chorus of which ends with "So fuck all your protests and put them to bed."[50] Rage Against the Machine's specifically radical, specifically racial social message is transformed into Manson's amorphously rebellious, largely apolitical statement about the media and shock-rock. Likewise, *The Matrix*'s and the entire trilogy's radical subnarratives may highlight the problematic nature of Neo's and the AI's power, but neither Hollywood nor its revivification (or vivisection) of cyberpunk want to allow these politicised narratives to break through their own encoding.

If the "purely" semiotic and SF attempts to re-encode race as presented in Schuyler's and the Wachowskis' narratives find themselves unable to articulate a space beyond the racist matrixes with which they began, could a material attempt to construct physical spaces—reworkings of utopia, in other words—prove more successful? The next part of this study takes us back into the 1960s—with a chapter mapping Frank Herbert's somewhat New Wave experiment in *The Santaroga Barrier* and revisiting Gibson, in his post-cyberpunk, nanotech series, moving into the concluding chapter, analysing Octavia Butler's response to utopias in her Patternmaster series. Combining the utopian elements of the texts in Part I and the performative analyses of Part II, these works attempt to take advantage of the satirical elements of Schuyler, the hopeful free-play of *The Matrix*, and the material concerns of *Mizora*, all in order to give voice to Aminadab's laughter, his ultimate judgement on Aylmer's—and Tarzan's, and Buck's, and Neo's—assertion of dominance.

NOTES

1. P. Chad Barnett, "Reviving Cyberpunk: (Re)Constructing the Subject and Mapping Cyberspace in the Wachowski Brothers' Film *The Matrix*," *Extrapolation* 41, no.4 (2000): 360.
2. Gibson's first trilogy of novels, *Neuromancer* (1984), *Count Zero* (1986), and *Mona Lisa Overdrive* (1988), are often referred to as the "Sprawl Trilogy." In these novels, the Sprawl is what remains of the Atlantic seaboard and surrounding areas (it is also referred to as BAMA, the Boston-Atlanta Metropolitan Axis). Barnett compares *The Matrix* to a list of alternate-reality films which he reads as "manifestations and symptoms of postmodern culture" (Barnett 2000, 362), while Lavery contrasts *The Matrix* to many of the same films I list, seeing those films' "use of virtual reality" as "for the most part … forgettable." In this same passage, Lavery also mentions one other explicitly cyberpunk film, *Johnny Mnemonic* (1995), also starring Keanu Reeves, the screenplay of which was written by Gibson, based on his own short story (David Lavery, "From Cinespace to Cyberspace: Zionists and Agents, Realists and Gamers in *The Matrix* and *eXistenZ*," *Journal of Popular Film and Television* 28, no.4 (2001): 156 n. 6).
3. Barnett, 360; 361.
4. Lavery, 152.
5. Ross Farnell, "Posthuman Topologies: William Gibson's 'Architexture' in *Virtual Light* and *Idoru*," *Science Fiction Studies* 25, no.3 (1998): 472; 475.
6. The alternate reality plot is perhaps best exemplified by the works of Philip K. Dick, who has become almost synonymous with such storylines. See, for example, his novels *Eye in the Sky* (1957) and *The Man in the High Castle* (1962).
7. For a discussion of the different technical aspects of *The Matrix*, see Angela Ndalianis, "The Frenzy of the Visible: Spectacle and Motion in the Era of the Digital," *Senses of Cinema* 3 (Feb. 2000), http://sensesofcinema.com/2000/feature-articles/matrix-2/, accessed 18 January 2015.
8. Joshua Moss, "Breaking the Cyberpunk Curse." 18 May 2000. SPACE.com, accessed 31 March 2002.
9. Sharon Stockton, "'The Self-Regained': Cyberpunk's Retreat to the Imperium," *Contemporary Literature* 36, no.4 (1995): 589.

10. Nicola Nixon, "Cyberpunk: Preparing the Ground for Revolution or Keeping the Boys Satisfied?" *Science Fiction Studies* 19, no.2 (1992): 224–25. On this point, it should be noted that the Matrix films also include references to Hollywood Westerns, especially in the "showdown" scenes between Neo and Agent Smith: the standard tumbleweed is replaced with old newspapers blowing across the screen, an allusion Ndalianis also notes.
11. Farnell, 471. I elaborate on this discussion in Chapter 5 below. For other discussions of the connections between cyberspace, cyberpunk, identity politics, and related issues, see, for example: Karen, Cadora, "Feminist Cyberpunk," *Science-Fiction Studies* 22, no.3 (1995): 357–72; Neil Easterbrook, "The Arc of Our Destruction: Reversal and Erasure in Cyberpunk," *Science-Fiction Studies* 19, no.3 (1992): 378–94; Veronica Hollinger, "Cybernetic Deconstructions: Cyberpunk and Postmodernism," *Mosaic* 23, no.2 (1990): 29–44; and Claire Sponsler, "Beyond the Ruins: The Geopolitics of Urban Decay and Cybernetic Play," *Science-Fiction Studies* 20, no.2 (1993): 251–65. Both Samuel R. Delany ("Zelazny/Varley/Gibson—and Quality," in *Shorter Views: Queer Thoughts and the Politics of the Paraliterary* [Hanover: Wesleyan University Press, 1999], 271–91) and Rob Latham ("Cyberpunk=Gibson=*Neuromancer*," Review of *Fiction 2000: Cyberpunk and the Future of Narrative*, *Science-Fiction Studies* 20, no.2 [1993]: 266–72) discuss problems in early cyberpunk criticism, especially its emphasis on *Neuromancer* and subsequent near-erasure of other writers (especially, but not only, women writers).
12. Farnell, 475.
13. Barnett, 366.
14. Slavoj Žižek, "The Matrix, or The Two Sides of Perversion," *lacan.com*, 28 October 1999, http://www.lacan.com/zizek-matrix.htm, accessed 18 January 2015. Žižek's essay is an online version of a paper delivered at the symposium, "Inside the Matrix." Parenthetical citations to this essay refer to paragraph numbers.
15. While the Wachowski siblings did conceive of the Matrix story as a trilogy, the first film is obviously set apart as a standalone piece (perhaps a move necessary before funding was secured for the sequels). The latter two movies, conversely, were shot simultaneously and consist of one heavily integrated storyline, leading the studio to release them only six months apart. In simple terms, the first film lays the groundwork for this second storyline but does not end with "to be concluded," as *Reloaded* does. Additionally, a pre-history to the speculative world of the Matrix is offered in several of the short animated films of *Animatrix*, while the video game *Enter the Matrix* offers another storyline that ties into the trilogy. Because *The Matrix* does stand alone, however, the argument presented here will focus centrally on that first film. But *The Matrix* obviously sets up the discursive map for its sequels; given this fact, I will draw on details from the other material when necessary to elucidate my argument.
16. Around a dozen analytical articles explicitly focusing on race in relation to the series have appeared, including those listed in the bibliography by Aimee Bahng, Melba Joyce Boyd, Douglas Cunningham, Peter X Feng, Theresa Geller, Kim Hester-Williams, C. Richard King and David J. Leonard (both "Is Neo White" and "Racing"), Lisa Nakamura, Leilani Nishime, Jane Park, Tani Dianca Sanchez, and Claudia Springer (frustratingly, many of these articles—including an earlier version of this chapter—were published within a few years of each other, so due to the time-lag of academic publishing don't take into account each other's arguments).

These works can be roughly—though not precisely—placed into a few categories: they can be condemnatory, critiquing the films' perceived racism (Feng, King and Leonard, Bahng, though she analyses fanfiction authors' exploitation of the films' self-contradictions); laudatory, praising the films' perceived progressive aspects (Boyd, Cunningham [2003], Sanchez, and Geller, who focuses on gender in the first film, but through it reads an interesting "queering" of racial expectations); or as a more complex—or confused—negotiation (Cunningham [2009], Hester-Williams, Nishime, Park—albeit these authors often conclude by falling on one side or the other). Likewise, the essays can focus on the role of whiteness and/or blackness (e.g., Boyd, Hester-Williams, Sanchez), or on multiraciality, with the last often taking as a starting point Keanu Reeves' own "ambiguous" or multiracial identity (e.g., Feng, Nishime, Park). Joanne Morra and Marquard Smith also deal briefly with Morpheus' blackness as part of a larger psychoanalytic reading of the film's portrayal of desire.

Outside of the traditional academic sphere, and especially following the release of the sequels and the first sight of Zion's population in *Reloaded*, several reviews and audience responses published online have mentioned the visible presence of black people in the films, if not the role of race in terms of the plot(s). Most of these discussions and reactions have been positive, focusing, as Simon Woolley puts it in his *Operation Black Vote* review, on the ways that the film's casting demonstrates how "the boundaries of racial stereotypes can be effectively challenged without always using an overtly racial theme" (Simon Woolley, "*Matrix Reloaded*: Race Matters," *Operation Black Vote*, 19 Dec. 2005, http://www.obv.org.uk/news-blogs/matrix-reloaded-race-matters, accessed 18 January 2015). Esther Iverem, film critic for SeeingBlack.com writes in her review, "The Matrix Reloaded: A Fierce and Nappy Future," that "In this vision of the future, Black folks have survived and they are fierce and in the leadership," arguing that the rave scene in *Reloaded* "is filled with lots of beautiful, post-apocalyptic Black folks who are rendered with spirit and humanity, not as stereotypes. Think of the cover of Marvin Gaye's 'I Want You' transported light years to funky science fiction." ("*The Matrix Reloaded*: A Fierce and Nappy Future," *SeeingBlack.com*, 9 May 2003, http://www.seeingblack.com/2003/x051403/matrix_daddydaycare.shtml, accessed 18 January 2015). Similarly, Andrew O'Hehir, in his Salon.com review, refers to "the crunchy, liberated, polysexual and anti-racist society of Zion" ("A Future Worth Fighting For," *Salon.com*, 15 May 2013, http://www.salon.com/2003/05/15/matrix_reloaded, accessed 18 January 2015). Some audience reactions do see the film's racial politics as more conservative, however: Grisso, writing for *Africans Unbound Magazine* on TheAfrican.Com, asks, "Isn't the savior figure [of *The Matrix*] again white, and perhaps calculated, like the false white depictions of Jesus, not to liberate but to further enslave? Isn't it again the Moor who teaches him and raises him up, only in the end to kneel before him and bow to his supposed divinity[?]" (Grisso, "The Key to The Matrix," *Africans Unbound Magazine*, *TheAfrican.Com*, accessed 9 October 2014, http://theafrican.com/Magazine/matrix.htm, accessed 18 January 2015). Grisso's article is accompanied by a link to discussions he's had with readers about their responses to the film, and to his article, which nicely show the range of reactions to race in the film.

17. All quotations, unless otherwise noted, are my own transcriptions from the films. The purported original script and various transcriptions of the first movie are available on several web sites, and the screenplay is available on the DVD-ROM portion of the DVD release of the film. There are also numerous fansites

dedicated to *The Matrix*, many of which contain excellent resources. Matrix-Fans.net contains a wealth of information.

18. Toni Morrison, *Playing in the Dark: Whiteness and the Literary Imagination* (New York: Vintage, 1990), 53.
19. Žižek, 24.
20. The "colour coding" of other characters in *Reloaded* builds on this depiction of the Architect. Specifically, the "Twins" occupy an interesting liminal space in terms of colour. These two ghostly characters are "hench-programs," if you will, for one of the rogue programs in the film. These rogues, including the Oracle, form a central part of the plot of *Reloaded* and *Revolutions*; they are previously powerful Matrix AI programs who are deemed no longer necessary by the Matrix, and have chosen "exile" over erasure by the system. Thus, they occupy the position of—and act very much as—what Althusser would call "the former ruling classes," who challenge the new dominant ideology because they "are able to retain strong positions" in the power structure (Louis Althusser, "Ideology and Ideological State Apparatuses [Notes Towards an Investigation]," in *Lenin and Philosophy and Other Essays*, translated by Ben Brewster [1971, New York: Monthly Review Press, 2001], 99). The most obvious example of this is the program called "The Merovingian" (Lambert Wilson), his title referring to the deposed French royal line who, in various conspiracy mythoi, are said to hold still the power of the Holy Grail. Thus, the Merovingian, the Oracle, the Keymaker (Randall Duk Kim), the Trainman (Bruce Spence), and others serve varying interests for and against the dominant structure. The Twins, occupying this liminal space working for the Merovingian, are covered in white makeup, and have powdered white dreadlocks and black lips, functioning as an odd form of "whiteface" (given the fact that the actors, Neil and Adrian Rayment, are white). Further, the Trainman, introduced in *Revolutions*, furthers the Africanist narrative of the film in that he runs an "underground railroad," which is used to transport rogue programs from the central core of the Matrix.
21. For discussions of racism in the U.S. police force and criminal justice system, see, for example, Davis, and Hawkins and Thomas.
22. Douglas A. Cunningham, "Stalling Zion: Hegemony through Racial Conflict in The Matrix," *Rhizomes* 7 (2003): par. 20–22, http://rhizomes.net/issue7/cunning.htm, accessed 18 January 2015; "Stalling Zion: Hegemony, Whiteness, and Racial Discourse in The Matrix Phenomenon," in *At Home and Abroad: Historicizing Twentieth-century Whiteness in Literature and Performance*, edited by La Vinia Delois Jennings (Knoxville: University of Tennessee Press, 2009), 265–6.
23. *Gagged and Chained* is the title of an album with an interview with Bobby Seale and a re-enactment of the trial. That the Wachowskis are from Chicago does not, I think, negate the allusion, as it simply makes it more likely that they would know of the Chicago 7 trials. In fact, the purported original script, available on several online sites, explicitly has the film set in Chicago.
24. Quoted from the A. M. E. Zion Church's homepage, http://www.amez.org, accessed 18 January 2015. Melba Boyd also notes the implications of the use of Zion in relation to African American cultural history ("The African American Presence and the Resolution of Race in *The Matrix* Trilogy," *Black Renaissance/Renaissance Noire* 5.3 [2004]: 132).
25. C. Richard King and David J. Leonard, "Is Neo White? Reading Race, Watching the Trilogy," in *Jacking in to the* Matrix *Franchise*, edited by Matthew Kapell and William G. Doty (New York: Continuum, 2004), 41–42.

26. Robyn Wiegman, "Black Bodies/American Commodities: Gender, Race and the Bourgeois Ideal in Contemporary Film," in *Unspeakable Images: Ethnicity and the American Cinema*, edited by Lester D. Friedman (Urbana: University of Illinois Press, 1991), 321–22.
27. The angle of the shot and the way in which Neo is encircled are both echoed by the later image of Morpheus encircled by the police officers. The scenes could offer paired but differing images of subjection, with the ideological containment of the malcontent white—and white-collar—worker being compared to the physically repressive, violent containment of the black activist. The form of enclosure in Neo's apartment is later echoed by the stereotypical "cubicle farm" where Neo, as the properly interpellated worker "Thomas Anderson," is employed. At several points, the cubicle's walls frame the shot, creating a sense of constriction and claustrophobia that is heightened by the fact that Reeves must crouch to remain inside the frame.
28. In several discussions of the films, critics note that Reeves himself is multiracial, having, as Peter X Feng writes, "an English mother and a Chinese-Hawaiian father." Feng goes on to note that "While Reeves reportedly describes himself as white, Asian American spectators frequently label Reeves as Asian Pacific passing as white" (Peter X Feng, "False and Double Consciousness: Race, Virtual Reality and the Assimilation of Hong Kong Action Cinema in the Matrix," in *Aliens R Us: The Other in Science Fiction Cinema*, edited by Ziauddin Sardar and Sean Cubitt [London: Pluto, 2002], 155). On this point, also see: LeiLani Nishime, "*The Matrix* Trilogy, Keanu Reeves, and Multiraciality at the End of Time," in *Mixed Race Hollywood*, edited by Mary Beltrán and Camilla Fojas (New York: New York University Press, 2008), 290–312; and Jane Park, "Virtual Race: The Racially Ambiguous Action Hero in *The Matrix* and *Pitch Black*," in *Mixed Race Hollywood*, edited by Mary Beltrán and Camilla Fojas (New York: New York University Press, 2008), 182–202. These nuanced readings often engage with the global nature of the contemporary film industry, and the relationships of racial coding, audience readings, and globalization in ways not fully engaged here.

    While I am convinced by these readings, I do not fully agree that, diegetically, the films' representations of Neo are as racially ambiguous as some of the authors would contend. In this scene, Neo is obviously coded as white—the sarcastic emphasis on being "whiter *than usual*" implies that he's really very white to begin with. While Park reads Neo as an example of Richard Dyer's "dark white man" (191) and Nishime reads Neo's border-crossing as an indication of his (encoded) multiraciality, neither deals with this scene. That said, like Nishime, I can see some value in reading Neo in this way, if only to highlight the way in which the performativity of racial and other forms of identification cannot, ultimately, struggle through the films' larger hegemonic debts. Given this scene, however, the current paper will read Reeves' character, Neo, as white, as do some other critics (e.g., Hester-Williams, King and Leonard). (The inverse of this relationship between an "Asian Pacific actor passing as white" and white actors in yellowface occurs in the Wachowskis' adaptation of *Cloud Atlas*, discussed below.)
29. Stockton, 589.
30. Sidonie Smith, *Subjectivity, Identity, and the Body: Women's Autobiographical Practices in the Twentieth Century* (Bloomington: Indiana University Press, 1993), 9–10.

31. In *Revolutions*, this pseudo-religious celebration of the body is demonically parodied in the Merovingian's "bar," where the dance floor is equally crowed. Rather than an ecstatic celebration of life through the glorification of the "natural" human body, this dance is populated by largely docile individuals wearing—and often covered head to toe by—rubber and metal BDSM gear. The body here is not celebrated, but locked away and punished.
32. For discussions of the ways in which women's ontology is tied to the body, see, for example, Sidonie Smith and Susan Bordo (*Unbearable Weight: Feminism, Western Culture, and the Body* [Berkeley: University of California Press, 1993]), as well as Chapter 1 of this study.
33. This revision of gender expectations continues in *Reloaded* and *Revolutions* mostly through the character Niobe (Jada Pinkett Smith). Niobe is set up as the consummate pilot—evoking such comments as "Oh damn, woman, you can drive"—thus assuming the traditionally hegemonic- and hyper-masculine role of the "flyboy," as constructed in, to take two of the best examples, *Top Gun* (1986) and *Only Angels Have Wings* (1939).
34. Barnett, 364.
35. Judith Butler, "Imitation and Gender Insubordination," in *Inside/Out*, edited by Diana Fuss (New York: Routledge, 1991), 23.
36. *Reloaded* offers the same problem, but somewhat reversed—the war between the humans and the machine is figured much less ambiguously as a multicultural and multiracial, but primarily black, resistance to the white power structure, while Neo exercises much more traditionally patriarchal, comic-book heroics to save Trinity's life. These heroics culminate in a traditional rendering of the Sleeping Beauty myth (as opposed to its reversal in the first film). As I will discuss later, Neo penetrates Trinity's body with his hand, using his hyper-rational control of the Matrix, in order to bring her back to life. In *Revolutions*, meanwhile, Trinity fulfills the role of the woman who sacrifices herself because of love for "her man."
37. Lisa M. Anderson, *Mammies No More: The Changing Image of Black Women on Stage and Screen* (Lanham: Rowman and Littlefield, 1997), 10.
38. Anderson, 10.
39. Anderson, 39. For a detailed, historicized discussion of the figure of the mammy in relation to other black stereotypes in American film, see Donald Bogle, *Toms, Coons, Mulattoes, Mammies, and Bucks: An Interpretive History of Blacks in American Films*, 3rd ed. (New York: Continuum, 1994).
40. *Reloaded* and *Revolutions* subtly juxtapose this image of the mammy to a less stereotypical portrayal of black motherhood in the character of Cas, played by Gina Torres, although her scenes are relatively short. Torres herself has a fairly long history of playing strong characters in science fiction and fantasy television, including roles on *Hercules: The Legendary Journeys* (1995–1999), *Cleopatra 2525* (2000–2001), and the Joss Whedon television vehicle, *Firefly* (2002), and its cinematic sequel, *Serenity* (2005).
41. Anderson, 17.
42. Bogle, 88.
43. This dual positioning of the Oracle would seem to be expanded when, in *Reloaded* and *Revolutions*, the viewer learns that she is in fact a rogue program, functioning simultaneously within and outside, for and against, the Matrix. See Gates' classic discussion of signifyin' in *The Signifying Monkey*.

44. Neo's need for the "other(s)" and the performative nature of his dominance are also expanded in the two sequels, in which Neo's position between Zion and the Matrix is much more complex: Neo's very being could be used to serve the Architect, an apparently powerful representative of the Matrix, even as he thinks he is rebelling. As to the names, "Morpheus" may not reflect multiplicity in its allusion to the Greek god of dreams, but in the world of science fiction film, the first syllable of his name immediately brings to mind the ability to "morph" or change shape. This abbreviation for metamorphosis gained popularity with the film *Terminator 2* (1991).
45. Rebekah Simpkins, "Visualizing Jean Baudrillard's *Simulacra and Simulation* through *The Matrix*," *Notes on Contemporary Literature* 30, no.4 (2000): 9.
46. Žižek, 28.
47. Another reading could be done here, perhaps, focusing on an allegory for the Middle East, resulting in the now traditional call for a "two-state solution" for peace in "Zion." Indeed, an international perspective does begin to be offered in *Reloaded*, when the Architect's view screens are filled with footage of international conflicts, including images from World War II, the Vietnam War, and the conflicts in the Middle East. Such an internationalist allegory, however, does not work for the first film, with its references specifically to African American resistance. This shift from a focus on (national) racial oppression to international politics could be said to be offered in the *Animatrix*, in which the beginning of the war between human and machine is blamed on the humans, who would not let the machines live in peace. Two pieces from *Animatrix*, "Second Renaissance" Parts I and II, detail the humans' enslavement of conscious machines, and further explain the machines' fight for rights in terms of American racial politics (including reference to a "Million Machine March"). These two animated shorts—written by the Wachowskis and directed by Mahiro Maeda—then go on to describe the first robot nation as being set up in the wake of a pogrom against the robots, and place this "new nation" in the Middle East. The new country is called 01, or "Zero One," which when said aloud obviously echoes "Zion." A performative relationship of dominance, in which supposedly "natural" binaries of control and resistance are constantly flipped, can again be read here: humans see themselves as superior to labouring machines, only to be later reduced to an inferior "labour" force as batteries. Again, though, this information is not contained in the largely separate first film, which does set up the oppression and resistance in terms of American racial politics, with the AI serving as the oppressive white power structure. This disparity between the first film and the subsequent works is especially highlighted by Morpheus' claim in *The Matrix* that "we don't know who struck first"; this doesn't mesh with the *Animatrix* shorts, which show the entire history as being contained in Zion's mainframe, which Morpheus could access. The first film does present in many ways, then, a separate vision of the Matrix "universe." See *The Animatrix*, prod. Lana and Andy Wachowski (Warner Bros, 2003), DVD.
48. The idea that the AI and Zion need each other, in an endless cycle or revolution (mimicking the prehistory offered in the *Animatrix*), is emphasized by the visuals in *Revolutions* of the attack on Zion. The egg-like outer sphere of the city is penetrated by the Sentinels—attack robots that look like squid when seen up-close, but seem more like sperm when seen in a cluster from a distance. In fact, the scene in *Revolutions* in which the multitude of sentinels breaks into

Zion *closely* resembles (as Julia M. Wright pointed out to me after we saw the film) William Blake's engraving of the "Circle of the Lustful" in Dante's *Divine Comedy* (William Blake, *The Complete Graphic Works of William Blake*, edited by David Bindman [London: Thames and Hudson, 1986], fig. 647). An imagistic sexual tie between Zion and the Matrix AI could also be read in the fight between Neo and Smith in *Revolutions* which, in its nearly balletic form, is reminiscent more of the consummating dance scenes in Hollywood musicals than of a fight to the death (the "fight scene as sex scene" motif is taken to an extreme in the opening to the animated short "Final Flight of the Osiris" from *Animatrix*, where two characters slowly strip each other during a sword fight. The story was also written by the Wachowskis and is set after *The Matrix* and before *Reloaded*). These visuals can thus be interpreted as reinforcing the relationship between the (dominant) AI and the (subjugated) Zion as a mutually necessary reinforcement of, rather than attack against, the other.

49. "MANAA Asserts Offensive Use of Yellowface Make-up and Exclusion of Asian Actors in the Film 'Cloud Atlas,'" *Eyes and Ears: The Newsletter of the Media Action Network for Asian Americans,* 3 April 2013, http://newsletter.manaa.org/2013/04/manaa-asserts-offensive-yellowface-make-up-and-exclusion-of-asian-actors-in-cloud-atlas/, accessed 18 January 2015. I would like to thank Christine Yao for pointing me to these discussions.
50. Rage Against the Machine, "Wake Up," *Rage Against the Machine* (Sony, 1992), CD; Marilyn Manson, "Rock is Dead," *Mechanical Animals* (Nothing/Intersope, 1998), CD.

REFERENCES

Althusser, Louis. "Ideology and Ideological State Apparatuses (Notes Towards an Investigation)." In *Lenin and Philosophy and Other Essays*, translated by Ben Brewster, 85–126. 1971. New York: Monthly Review Press, 2001.

Anderson, Lisa M. *Mammies No More: The Changing Image of Black Women on Stage and Screen*. Lanham: Rowman and Littlefield, 1997.

The Animatrix. Prod. Lana and Andy Wachowski. Warner Bros., 2003. DVD.

Bahng, Aimee. "Queering *The Matrix*: Hacking the Digital Divide and Slashing into the Future." In The Matrix *in Theory*, edited by Myriam Diocaretz and Stefan Herbrechter, 167–92. Amsterdam: Rodopi, 2006.

Barnett, P. Chad. "Reviving Cyberpunk: (Re)Constructing the Subject and Mapping Cyberspace in the Wachowski Brothers' Film *The Matrix*." *Extrapolation* 41, no.4 (2000): 359–74.

Blake, William. *The Complete Graphic Works of William Blake*. Edited by David Bindman. London: Thames and Hudson, 1986.

Bogle, Donald. *Toms, Coons, Mulattoes, Mammies, and Bucks: An Interpretive History of Blacks in American Films*. 3rd ed. New York: Continuum, 1994.

Bordo, Susan. *Unbearable Weight: Feminism, Western Culture, and the Body*. Berkeley: University of California Press, 1993.

Boyd, Melba Joyce. "The African American Presence and the Resolution of Race in *The Matrix* Trilogy." *Black Renaissance/Renaissance Noire* 5, no.3 (2004): 129–43.

Butler, Judith. "Imitation and Gender Insubordination." In *Inside/Out*, edited by Diana Fuss, 13–31. New York: Routledge, 1991.
Cadora, Karen. "Feminist Cyberpunk." *Science Fiction Studies* 22, no.3 (1995): 357–72.
Cloud Atlas. Directed by the Wachowskis and Tom Tykwer. Warner Bros., 2012. Blu-ray.
Cunningham, Douglas A. "Stalling Zion: Hegemony through Racial Conflict in *The Matrix*." *Rhizomes* 7 (2003): n.p. http://rhizomes.net/issue7/cunning.htm. Accessed 18 January 2015.
———. "Stalling Zion: Hegemony, Whiteness, and Racial Discourse in *The Matrix* Phenomenon." *At Home and Abroad: Historicizing Twentieth-century Whiteness in Literature and Performance*. Edited by La Vinia Delois Jennings, 255–83. Knoxville: University of Tennessee Press, 2009.
Davis, Angela Y. "Racialized Punishment and Prison Abolition." In *The Angela Y. Davis Reader*, edited by Joy James, 96–107. Oxford: Blackwell, 1998.
Delany, Samuel R. "Zelazny/Varley/Gibson—and Quality." In *Shorter Views: Queer Thoughts and the Politics of the Paraliterary*, 271–91. Hanover: Wesleyan University Press, 1999.
Dick, Philip K. *Eye in the Sky*. 1957. New York: Vintage, 2003.
———. *The Man in the High Castle*. 1962. New York: Vintage, 1992.
Easterbrook, Neil. "The Arc of Our Destruction: Reversal and Erasure in Cyberpunk." *Science Fiction Studies* 19, no.3 (1992): 378–94.
Farnell, Ross. "Posthuman Topologies: William Gibson's 'Architexture' in *Virtual Light* and *Idoru*." *Science Fiction Studies* 25, no.3 (1998): 459–80.
Feng, Peter X. "False and Double Consciousness: Race, Virtual Reality and the Assimilation of Hong Kong Action Cinema in the Matrix." *Aliens R Us: The Other in Science Fiction Cinema*. Edited by Ziauddin Sardar and Sean Cubitt, 149–63. London: Pluto, 2002.
Gates, Henry Louis, Jr. *The Signifying Monkey: A Theory of African-American Literary Criticism*. Oxford: Oxford University Press, 1988.
Geller, Theresa L. "Queering Hollywood's Tough Chick: The Subversions of Sex, Race, and Nation in *The Long Kiss Goodnight* and *The Matrix*." *Frontiers: A Journal of Women Studies* 25, no.3 (2004): 8–34.
Gibson, William. *Count Zero*. New York: Arbor House, 1986.
———. *Mona Lisa Overdrive*. New York: Bantam, 1988.
———. *Neuromancer*. New York: Ace, 1984.
Grisso. "The Key to *The Matrix*." *Africans Unbound Magazine*. n.d. Accessed October 11 2014. http://theafrican.com/Magazine/matrix.htm/.
Hawkins, Homer and Richard Thomas. "White Policing of Black Populations: A History of Race and Social Control in America." In *Out of Order? Policing Black People*. Edited by Ellis Cashmore and Eugene McLaughlin, 65–86. New York: Routledge, 1991.
Hester-Williams, Kim D. "Neoslaves: Slavery, Freedom, and African American Apotheosis in *Candyman*, *The Matrix* and *The Green Mile*." *Genders* 40 (2004). http://www.genders.org/g40/g40_williams.html/. Accessed 19 January 2014.
Hollinger, Veronica. "Cybernetic Deconstructions: Cyberpunk and Postmodernism." *Mosaic* 23, no.2 (1990): 29–44.
Iverem, Esther. "The Matrix Reloaded: A Fierce and Nappy Future." *SeeingBlack.com*. 9 May 2003. http://www.seeingblack.com/2003/x051403/matrix_daddy-daycare.shtml/. Accessed 18 January 2015.

King, C. Richard and David J. Leonard. "Is Neo White? Reading Race, Watching the Trilogy." In *Jacking in to the* Matrix *Franchise*. Edited by Matthew Kapell and William G. Doty, 32–47. New York: Continuum, 2004.

———. "Racing the Matrix: Variations on White Supremacy in Responses to the Film Trilogy." *Cultural Studies <=> Critical Methodologies* 6 (2006): 354–69.

King, Martin Luther, Jr. "I Have a Dream." In *A Testament of Hope: The Essential Writings of Martin Luther King Jr.* Edited by James Melvin Washington, 217–20. San Francisco: Harper and Row, 1986.

Lane, Mary E. Bradley. *Mizora: A Prophecy*. Edited by Jean Pfaelzer. New York: Syracuse University Press, 2000.

Latham, Rob. "Cyberpunk=Gibson=*Neuromancer*." Review of *Fiction 2000: Cyberpunk and the Future of Narrative*. Edited by George Slusser and Tom Shippey. *Science-Fiction Studies* 20, no.2 (1993): 266–72.

Lavery, David. "From Cinespace to Cyberspace: Zionists and Agents, Realists and Gamers in *The Matrix* and *eXistenZ*." *Journal of Popular Film and Television* 28, no.4 (2001): 150–57.

"MANAA Asserts Offensive Use of Yellowface Make-up and Exclusion of Asian Actors in the Film 'Cloud Atlas.'" *Eyes and Ears: The Newsletter of the Media Action Network for Asian Americans,* 3 April 2013, http://newsletter.manaa.org/2013/04/manaa-asserts-offensive-yellowface-make-up-and-exclusion-of-asian-actors-in-cloud-atlas/. Accessed 18 January 2015.

Marilyn Manson. "Rock is Dead." *Mechanical Animals*. Nothing/Intersope, 1998. CD.

The Matrix. Written and directed by the Wachowskis. Warner Bros., 1999. DVD.

The Matrix Reloaded. Written and directed by the Wachowskis. Warner Bros., 2003. DVD.

The Matrix Revolutions. Written and directed by the Wachowskis. Warner Bros., 2003. DVD.

Morra, Joanne and Marquard Smith. "*The Matrix*: Morpheus in Exile." *West Coast Line* 35.2 (2001): 20–38.

Morrison, Toni. *Playing in the Dark: Whiteness and the Literary Imagination*. New York: Vintage, 1990.

Moss, Joshua. "Breaking the Cyberpunk Curse." *SPACE.com*. 18 May 2000. Accessed 31 March 2002. http://www.space.com/sciencefiction/movies/matrix_cyberpunk_000518.html/.

Nakamura, Lisa. "The Multiplication of Difference in Post-Millennial Cyberpunk Film: The Visual Culture of Race in *The Matrix* Trilogy." In The Matrix *Trilogy: Cyberpunk Reloaded*. Edited by Stacy Gillis, 126–37. London: Wallflower, 2005.

Ndalianis, Angela. "The Frenzy of the Visible: Spectacle and Motion in the Era of the Digital." *Senses of Cinema* 3. Feb. 2000. http://sensesofcinema.com/2000/feature-articles/matrix-2/. Accessed 19 January 2015.

Nishime, LeiLani. "*The Matrix* Trilogy, Keanu Reeves, and Multiraciality at the End of Time." In *Mixed Race Hollywood*. Edited by Mary Beltrán and Camilla Fojas, 290–312. New York: New York University Press, 2008.

Nixon, Nicola. "Cyberpunk: Preparing the Ground for Revolution or Keeping the Boys Satisfied?" *Science Fiction Studies* 19, no.2 (1992): 219–35.

O'Hehir, Andrew. "A Future Worth Fighting For." *Salon.com*. 15 May 2003. http://www.salon.com/2003/05/15/matrix_reloaded/. Accessed 18 January 2015.

Park, Jane. "Virtual Race: The Racially Ambiguous Action Hero in The Matrix and Pitch Black." In *Mixed Race Hollywood*. Edited by Mary Beltrán and Camilla Fojas, 182–202. New York: New York University Press, 2008.

Rage Against the Machine. "Wake Up." *Rage Against the Machine*. Sony, 1992. CD.

Sanchez, Tani Dianca. "Neo-Abolitionists, Colorblind Epistemologies and Black Politics: The Matrix Trilogy." In *The Persistence of Whiteness: Race and Contemporary Hollywood Cinema*. Edited by Daniel Bernardi, 102–24. London: Routledge, 2008.

Schuyler, George. *Black No More: Being an Account of the Strange and Wonderful Workings of Science in the Land of the Free, A.D. 1933–1940*. 1931. Boston: Northeastern University Press, 1989.

Simpkins, Rebekah. "Visualizing Jean Baudrillard's *Simulacra and Simulation* through *The Matrix*." *Notes on Contemporary Literature* 30, no.4 (2000): 6–9.

Smith, Sidonie. *Subjectivity, Identity, and the Body: Women's Autobiographical Practices in the Twentieth Century*. Bloomington: Indiana University Press, 1993.

Sponsler, Claire. "Beyond the Ruins: The Geopolitics of Urban Decay and Cybernetic Play." *Science Fiction Studies* 20, no.2 (1993): 251–65.

Springer, Claudia. "Playing It Cool in *The Matrix*." In *The Matrix Trilogy: Cyberpunk Reloaded*. Edited by Stacy Gillis, 89–100. London: Wallflower, 2005.

Stockton, Sharon. "'The Self-Regained': Cyberpunk's Retreat to the Imperium." *Contemporary Literature* 36, no.4 (1995): 588–612.

Wiegman, Robyn. "Black Bodies/American Commodities: Gender, Race and the Bourgeois Ideal in Contemporary Film." In *Unspeakable Images: Ethnicity and the American Cinema*. Edited by Lester D. Friedman, 308–28. Urbana: University of Illinois Press, 1991.

Woolley, Simon. "*Matrix Reloaded*: Race Matters." *Operation Black Vote*. 19 Dec. 2005. http://www.obv.org.uk/news-blogs/matrix-reloaded-race-matters/. Accessed 18 January 2015.

Žižek, Slavoj. "The Matrix, or The Two Sides of Perversion." 28 October 1999. http://www.lacan.com/zizek-matrix.htm. Accessed 18 January 2015.

Part III

Muting Utopia

5 Bridging Divides in *The Santaroga Barrier* and *All Tomorrow's Parties*

Part II demonstrated the significance of recognising race and gender as imbricated performative structures, within a general understanding of the material effects of the "virtual" matrix of ideological identity structures. Part III builds on this conclusion to show how such a recognition can result in re-formations of the utopian elements of American SF. Analysing lesser studied works of three well-known contemporary SF authors—Frank Herbert, William Gibson, and Octavia Butler—Part III argues that these texts offer complicated visions of the space and politics lying behind contemporary utopian visions of race and gender in America. The current chapter moves from Herbert's cautionary tale of the facility of utopian thinking to imperial and white-supremacist practices in *The Santaroga Barrier* to Gibson's slightly more hopeful, if ultimately frustrated, vision of a heterotopian reality in his nanotech trilogy (which in turn rewrites Samuel R. Delany's heterotopian bridge in his Nevèrÿon series). This chapter thus points to the never-ending inversions of utopian thought, and so to the difficulty of effectively critiquing from within the hegemonic structures of sexism and racism in the United States. From there, the final chapter takes this complexity to its zenith in Octavia E. Butler's *Patternmaster* series. Unlike the earlier conservative or utopian thinking of a Hawthorne or Lane, but building on the satiric vision of Schuyler, all of these works—written during or after the various civil rights struggles of the 1960s and 1970s—point to the unending work of the social and semiotic shifts required in any sustained critique of racial and gendered hierarchies. Unlike *The Matrix*, however, these works imply that such shifts can be radical, if ultimately unpredictable. Where Herbert explicitly critiques the dangers of allowing an unchecked, Hawthorne-like conservatism—based on paradoxically transcendental foundations—to structure social policy, Gibson and Butler explore the possibilities inherent in a more grounded, but therefore always shifting, social framework. All three works, meanwhile, code the relations of hegemony and resistance through figures of silence, people who seemingly stand outside of the semiotic constraints of verbal discourse, especially as that is figured within hegemonic social structures. Bringing us full circle to Aminadab's oddly significant but impenetrable laughter at the end of "The Birth-mark," these silent characters may seem to signify the lack of voice afforded to the raced or gendered other of the dominant class, but may ultimately offer the expanded semiotic possibilities that Delany sees in SF, translating them into a social commentary.

I. THE STAKES OF THE WHITE PICKET FENCE

Herbert's 1968 novel, *The Santaroga Barrier*, uses the SF staple of a collective or hive identity somewhat traditionally, in order to comment on issues of individuality and autonomy, on the one hand, and social well-being and progress on the other. Such SF collectivities, as Peter Brigg has argued in his analysis of Herbert's use of the trope, allow one in turn to draw an "obvious parallel between fictional considerations of the collective mind and the ongoing problems in the United States and other democracies."[1] Herbert's novel, however, figures these "ongoing problems" specifically in terms of race. It does so in order to comment on race relations late in the civil rights era and to point toward larger national issues, specifically surrounding isolationism and imperialism. *The Santaroga Barrier* sets up a community based on a collective mind that is, at first, explicitly isolationist in an attempt to protect itself from invasion or destruction by outside forces, forces that are in turn figured as economically exploitative, trying to turn Santaroga's citizens into what the new business parlance calls "human capital." But, the novel portrays this protective isolationist stance as turning into its own exploitative force, a metaphorically imperial power, because the self-definition of the collective demands—as its foundation and its fetish—a demonised, racialized other against which the collective is placed in relief. In "evolving"—with all of the racialized history of that word, from Galton to Lane to Burroughs and beyond—from a protective isolationism to a preemptive strike force, this particular American collective follows the humanist myth, trying to become a collectively rational figure which then defines who is and who is not a member of the human family. The novel posits a community of Aylmers (or perhaps of Hawthornes) who have combined those transcendental beliefs with a version of existential philosophy and a flavouring of B. F. Skinner's behaviouralism, updating American "individualism" into a collective terror. Positioning this analysis within a commentary on the racist real estate practices that would be a focus of the 1968 Civil Rights Act, the novel thus serves as a warning against an unreflexive participation in a collective process of identification and its reliance on a hierarchized othering, especially as that collective process is undertaken under the ideological guise of American individualism.

Herbert's novel takes place in the fictional Californian town of Santaroga, which has become a bane on state and national businesses because the Santarogans refuse to participate to a meaningful degree in any non-Santarogan economics.[2] Even when they do need to rely on outside business, for instance to ship in oil for the local service station, they do so on nontraditional terms, shopping as independent buyers rather than going through the major companies, in order to ensure the best price. But, by and large, Santaroga is an isolationist community whose main objective, as the

Santarogan refrain would have it, is to "take care of our own."[3] On the surface, then, the "Barrier" of the novel's title is the economic and cultural barrier that isolates Santaroga from the rest of the nation, a barrier set against, as William F. Touponce writes, "all outsiders who want to exploit the valley commercially."[4] The barrier is figured physically in the first paragraph of the novel, in a direct allusion to More's *Utopia*, by the "crescent-shaped turn-off" in the mountains that frame the valley, which, in another allusion, help to make the valley almost like "an island sheltered from storms" (1).[5]

The "Barrier" also takes two other forms, however, as a mental and cultural barrier that separates the inhabitants of this seeming utopia from outsiders. Mentally, the inhabitants are linked in a largely unconscious collectivity that is created by eating a local mushroom-like drug called Jaspers which, as a few critics have noted, takes its name from the existentialist philosopher/psychologist Karl Jaspers.[6] The main character of the novel as well, Gilbert Dasein, takes his last name from Jaspers' use of the word *Dasein* to denote the most basic, mundane, being of the world—being as object; Jaspers' use of the term *Dasein* is thus much different from, and should not be confused with, that of his erstwhile colleague, Heidegger, who uses it to signify a much more invested existence.[7] As William Earle writes, for Jaspers, *Dasein* "is simply an empirical existent ... something which lives in space and time, a thing among other things."[8] But, Jaspers pairs his *Dasein* to a term he appropriates from Kierkegaard, *Existenz* (a word also referenced in SF, as the title for David Cronenberg's film about collective identities). Jaspers' *Existenz* is usually defined roughly as a more metaphysical, transcendent, authentic existence. As Jaspers writes, "without Existenz everything seems empty, hollowed out, without ground, fake, because everything has turned into endless masks, mere possibilities, or mere empirical existence."[9] This is, moreover, a primarily individualist transcendence: "I am Existenz only as I know Transcendence as the power through which I genuinely am myself," he writes.[10] But, this individualist existentialist life is, for Jaspers, nonetheless ultimately universalist, or at least gestures toward a universalising community. Human communication ties together each transcendental, individual, *Existenzen* through Reason: "reason is again present in order to bring Existenzen separated by an abyss of absolute distance together into communication."[11] *Existenz*, then, could be read as a form of faith in a transcendence that exists in a tension with the everyday world:

> there is rest nowhere in temporal existence. Rather there is always movement issuing forth from the ultimate substantial ground—movement in the tension between the individual and the universal, between the actual and the total range of the possible, between the unquestionable immediacy of existential faith and the infinite movement of reason.[12]

Existenz is an existence at once universal and individual, one that, when tied to Reason, can serve as a cure to the modernist malaise which is epitomised by Eliot's "Hollow Men" and their "shape without form," or the likeness between our lives and "a patient etherised" in "Prufrock."[13]

Relying on Jaspers' notion of the individual's ability to transcend the world of the merely experiential, while at the same time to bind with other transcendental individuals through the power of Reason, Herbert represents the drug Jaspers as both enabling a more enlightened consciousness in the individual and also heightening the unconscious connection between members of the community:[14] basically, Santaroga, because of the drug, becomes a collective of philosopher kings all set on identical goals. Indeed, the drug fuels this unconscious collectivity to the point where each and every member functions as one organism to protect the community against "outside" threats. In some ways, then, Jaspers and Santaroga fulfill the New England transcendentalists' dream of a rugged individualism that is nonetheless tied to the universal "higher laws" (to quote a chapter title from Thoreau's *Walden*), a connection that explains why a state senator in the novel refers to the Santarogans as "a last outpost of American individualism. They're Yankees, Down Easters living in California" (4–5). The economic barrier, then, the community's isolationism, protects this transcendentalist *Existenz* culture from encroachments by the merely *dasein* outside world, which would "equate[]" Jaspers "with LSD, with narcotics" and thus wipe the community "out of existence" (98).[15]

Herbert thus picks up on the contemporary discourse of drug and youth counterculture in order to portray Santaroga as a community that, like the hippy ideal, denies and moves beyond consumer culture. In fact, early in the novel, Dasein—a university professor hired to make a market survey of Santaroga, and to investigate its isolationist ways—sees indications that Santaroga is a community that does fall largely in line with the resistance movements of the counterculture. For example, when Dasein reads the local paper for the first time:

> The left-hand column carried an international news summary whose brevity and language startled Dasein. It was composed of paragraph items, one item per story.
>
> Item: "Those nuts are still killing each other in Southeast Asia."
>
> It slowly dawned on Dasein that this was the Vietnam news. …
>
> Item: "The Geneva disarmament talks are disarming nobody except the arrogant and the complacent. We recall that the envoys were still talking the last time the bombs began to fall."
>
> Item: "The United States Government is still expanding that big hidey hole under the mountain down by Denver. Wonder how many military bigshots, government officials and their families have tickets into there for when the blowup comes?" …
>
> Dasein lowered the paper, stared at it without seeing it. The damned thing was subversive! Was it written by a pack of Communists? Was that the secret of Santaroga? (49–50)

While a red scare novel would fit in with certain cold war representations of collective identity—as in such cold war SF films as *Invasion of the Body Snatchers* (1956) and, arguably, *Village of the Damned* (1960)—Herbert quickly goes onto show that the Santarogans are not communists, nor are they a hippy-like commune. In fact, Dr. Piaget, the patriarch of the community (named after cognitive psychologist Jean Piaget),[16] goes so far as to say that Santarogans are not like "the unwashed, sandaled users of LSD" (155).

By appropriating this discourse, though, Herbert can show the Santarogans as a community of resistance, who are fighting against the homogenising, hegemonic forces of the surrounding society. To Dr. Piaget, and Santarogans in general, the "outside" world is an "insane" place, where people are doomed to "eat themselves up" (184) because, unlike the enlightened Santarogans, the outside world of late-stage capitalism cannot live for the future well-being of the entire group, a problem symbolised and perpetuated, in their eyes, by the television. Win Burdeaux, a Santarogan whose characterisation I discuss in more detail below, says to Dasein:

> "The whole world of the permanent expediency out there, that whole world is TV. … The outside works on the temporary expedient, Doctor Gil. You must know that. And the temporary always turns into the permanent, somehow. The temporary tax, the necessary *little* war, the temporary brutality that will cease as soon as certain conditions end … the government agency created for the permanent *interim* …" (176)

Furthermore, the shock and awe created by this "permanent interim" are filtered for the "outside" American populace through the TV, leading to the realisation that people have "never had anything real. [Life] was all illusion … delusion" (176). The Santarogans, conversely, are able to see through these simulacra. Their isolationist stance is geared to protect them from the companies and market forces that would see them only as units of economic growth rather than seeing them as functioning humans. As Dr. Piaget states, "Outside, they value whatever can be measured, counted or tabulated. Here, we go by different standards" (154). Being "anti-*outside*," as Piaget describes Santaroga, isolating themselves physically, mentally, and economically, is an attempt to protect Santarogans from interpellation by the "outside" ideologies.

Santaroga thus becomes an entire community seemingly based on Thoreauvian transcendental ideals: this may not be utopia; it may be Walden Pond. Tim O'Reilly notes that Herbert wrote *Santaroga* "In deliberate imitation of [B. F.] Skinner's *Walden Two*," a relation that is clear in the ways in which the Santarogans continually speak in behaviourist-inflected psychologized speech, and in the fact that the town's educational system echoes that in Skinner's utopia.[17] Still, one can also see direct echoes of Thoreau here: for example, both Piaget and Thoreau deny being "antigovernment," in Piaget's words (184), or one of the "no-government men" in Thoreau's,[18] while both still function as isolationists who deny much of the government's and the market's power over them. Given the extended use of Karl Jaspers, the Neoplatonic, Romantic ideals of Thoreau are set into even greater relief since, as O'Reilly notes, Herbert himself once stated that "While I imagine he would have denied it, Jaspers was Platonic."[19] In some ways, following in the footsteps of Hawthorne, though to different ends, Herbert critiques the Neoplatonic transcendence of Thoreau, the great American isolationist utopian.[20]

But Piaget's statement, quoted above, ends with an affirmation of Santaroga's "different standards." The question then becomes, what standards does Santaroga inculcate beyond its simple resistance to the outside? If they are not the "unwashed, sandaled" counterculture, and they are not "antigovernment," espousing the liberatory rhetoric of the day, then what is it they do espouse? An answer to these questions lies in the several descriptions of Santaroga as an image of the past. On Dasein's arrival at the town's hotel, the reader is told that "It was a scene Dasein was to think of many times later as his first clue to the real nature of Santaroga. The effect was that of holding time securely in a bygone age" (7). Later, he thinks that the hotel had "an aura of the Nineteenth Century. [He] half expected to see a maid in ruffled cap ... or a portly banker type with tight vest and high collar, an expanse of gold chain at the waist" (19). In other words, as Dasein realises later in the novel, "The Santarogans were conservatives ... unchanging" (155). What the novel presents is an image not of a radical or revolutionary community, but of one attempting to hold onto the values of an idealised American past, where the rugged individual is paradoxically the collective norm of the country, where each citizen acts on his or her own conscience, but each conscience obeys the same transcendental higher law. This is a town that denies the semiotic fluctuation and instability that I argue is inherent in SF, instead attempting to rigidly codify a never-changing stability of both signification and, concomitantly, social order.

II. "LOCAL COLOR": CONSERVING (WHITE) UTOPIA

Herbert's critique of this seemingly countercultural utopia is precisely aimed at its conservatism. In necessarily rendering life static, the utopian vision must deny the instability of signification and that permits for change and development itself. In making this argument, I am aware that I am (or Herbert is) falling into what Kenneth M. Roemer calls that category of "muckrakers (or 'stuckrakers') preoccupied with exposing elements in literary utopias that tend toward changeless states."[21] Still, I trust that he would agree that I make this statement within my larger claim that SF texts can crack open the stagnancy of conservatism through their own reflective and reflexive semiotics, hence Herbert's ability to critique SF utopias within his decidedly SF text, pointing precisely to what Roemer calls "the contradictions in utopian narratives between their revolutionary, or at least evolutionary, claims and their sometimes dull portraits of stagnant societies."[22] Indeed, this portion of the current book aims to show how certain authors try to negotiate those contradictions.

Utopias, Herbert is arguing, *all* fall into what Karl Mannheim has deemed the oxymoronic utopia of the conservative mentality.[23] Mannheim asserts that a true utopian idea is "incongruous with the state of reality in which it appears,"[24] since utopias are necessarily critical of the status quo: one hardly needs to long for a more perfect world if one is perfectly content with this one, after all. In this way, the "utopian mentality," to use Mannheim's term, is precisely characteristic of the "cognitive estrangement" that Suvin sees in SF, even as it participates politically in the transformative nature of SF semiotics that I trace in the introduction.

Because of this fact, Mannheim states that the "Conservative mentality as such has no utopia," and so "Only the counter-attack of opposing classes and their tendency to break through the limits of the existing order causes the conservative mentality to question the basis of its own dominance, and necessarily brings about ... a counter-utopia which serves as a means of self-orientation and defense."[25] Whereas liberal or other progressive utopias are thus governed by a certain futurity, the conservative mentality is oriented toward the past, Mannheim states, in a form of nostalgia. In the conservative "utopia" (actually figured precisely as the current topos), "the past is experienced as virtually present,"[26] since every aspect of the past had to exist in order to lead to the perfection that is the status quo.

Hence Santaroga's "time out of joint" feel, its reproduction of antebellum America in the heart of its town. Of course, as with all fetishized objects of nostalgia, this "utopian" ideal of the American past never existed in the first place. Just as the "aura of the Nineteenth Century" should bring with it not just romanticized memories of maids and robber barons, but of the class exploitations lying behind those images, and just as it should of course recall slavery, the construct of the Romantic individual of the transcendentalists carries its own historical baggage. As Sidonie Smith writes, this Neoplatonic Romantic individual is the foundation of a democratic subject which "can claim equal access to the universally human";[27] in other words, this is the foundation for a collectively organised group of individuals, but it is one, as Smith goes on to detail, that is based on a hierarchy of othering, as discussed earlier in this book. This hierarchical exclusion is explicitly at play in Santaroga where, as Piaget succinctly states of the difference between Santarogans and others, "We are men. ... They are not" (154).

The problems of this othering practice and its link to Santaroga's conservation of an American past are pointed out in the novel through race, and through the figure of blackness in particular. The central black character is Win Burdeaux, a Santarogan who, like Dasein, came from the "outside." Burdeaux is portrayed as a subaltern native informant for Dasein, both serving Dasein and connecting him to Santaroga (this position is one I complicate, below). But, beyond this characterisation, he also becomes the central racial referent of the novel, highlighting for the reader the biases and bigotries inherent in Santaroga's collective. This referencing begins with a connection between Burdeaux and Santaroga's "timelessness." On their first meeting, Dasein says to Burdeaux:

> "I note you're the only Negro waiter here," Dasein said. "Isn't that kind of type casting?"
> "You asking if I'm their *show* Negro, sir?" The waiter's voice was suddenly wary.
> "I was wondering if Santaroga had any integration problems."
> "Must be thirty, forty colored families in the valley, sir. We don't rightly emphasize the distinction of skin color here." The voice was hard, curt.
> "I didn't mean to offend you," Dasein said.
> "You didn't offend me." A smile touched the corners of his mouth, was gone. "I must admit a Negro waiter is a kind of institutional accent. Place like this ..." He glanced around the solid, paneled room. "... must've had plenty of Negro waiters here in its day. Kind of like local color having me on the job." Again, that flashing smile. (11)

While Santaroga is integrated, Burdeaux' role as the "show Negro" *is* emphasised at the end of this dialogue. Also, Burdeaux' assertion that "the distinction of skin color" isn't emphasised in Santaroga is itself belied a little later in the novel, when he tells Dasein that his daughter, Willa, is marrying the white son of a "native" Santarogan. Burdeaux says:

> "George, Cal's daddy, came over and put his arm across my shoulder. 'Well there, Win, you old nigger bastard,' he said, 'we better have us a good drink and talk together because our kids are going to make us related.' That was it, Mr. Dasein. He didn't mean a thing calling me nigger. It was just like ... like the way we call a pale blond fellow here Whitey. It was like saying my skin's black for identification the way you might come into a room and ask for Al Marden and I'd say: 'He's that red-headed fellow over there. ...' As he was saying it I knew that's all he meant. It just came over me. It was being accepted for what I am. It was the friendliest thing George could do and that's why he did it. ... You know, when I told Annie about that afterward, I cried. I was so happy I cried." (16)

Burdeaux' rationalisations of George Nis' use of that particular racist expletive are belied by the story itself: unlike the "Whitey" example, which is nominalized with a capital, this is not a nickname, and George Nis himself implicitly points out this distinction by referring to Burdeaux by name first, and tagging "bastard" onto the end of the sentence. The same point can be made in response to Burdeaux' example of pointing someone out: George already knew who he was. But, these logical problems with the story, which

Dasein seems to ponder as he tries "to follow the train of Burdeaux' meaning" (16), are subsumed by the emotive effect of the incident. Burdeaux cries because he is "so happy" to be referred to in racist terms.

What Burdeaux comes to represent in the novel is the embodiment of the "proper" assimilation of outsiders into Santarogan society. Burdeaux becomes the example that Dasein is supposed to follow. But, by using a subservient black figure to represent this ideal assimilation, and by setting that figure within "an aura of the Nineteenth Century," Herbert demonstrates that the only type of difference that Santaroga will tolerate is one that is completely subservient to the paternalistic power structure. This relationship is made most clear in a passage near the end of the novel when, during a discussion with Dasein, Burdeaux repeats George Nis' use of the racist expletive, this time negatively internalised by Burdeaux himself:

> "Burdeaux scowled, then: "Sir, when I first came here, I was an ignorant *nigger*. Now, I'm an educated Negro ... *and* a Santarogan. I no longer have the delusions which I ..."
>
> "So you *did* try to fight it!" [Dasein says]
>
> "Yes ... I fought it. But I soon learned how foolish that was." (174)

Here, the racist expletive, despite Burdeaux' earlier defence of its use, is identified as a purely negative term, a negativity reinforced by the use of italics. Burdeaux' assimilation allows him to transform into "an educated Negro" but, as we saw in the earlier passage, that's *not* how George Nis sees him.

Burdeaux is thus defined, even in his own words, as the "properly" assimilated other, and this figure, when combined with the problems with the transcendentalist figure, help to turn the novel into a discussion of assimilation and segregation. In the years leading up to the book's publication, at the height of the civil rights movement, these very issues were of course at the forefront of American politics and debate, culminating in the year of the book's publication with the passage of the Civil Rights Act of 1968, outlawing discriminatory real estate and housing practices.[28] Herbert's use of these themes is not unintentional, either, as the debate over housing in Santaroga is explicitly tied to national discussions of housing practices, and these are in turn connected to race: Dasein does not complete his market survey of Santaroga, and when he doesn't contact the chair of his department, Chami Selador, for several days, Selador comes to Santaroga looking for him. This visit occurs immediately after Dasein takes a huge dose of pure Jaspers, which finally makes him become "properly" assimilated into Santaroga. Selador obviously doesn't know this fact, and so attempts to get information—preferably regarding a potential violation of housing laws—on Santaroga from Dasein. In his first mention of Dasein's earlier research on the valley, Selador says "The real estate board ... is interested that no one but Santarogans can buy property in the valley. It may be they've violated antidiscriminatory legislation" (227). Dasein denies this accusation and, after a longer discussion, Selador asks Dasein "Have you gone native?" Then we are given Dasein's internal response:

> The question, coming from the darkly eastern face, couched in that Oxford accent, struck Dasein as supremely amusing. Selador, of all people! To ask such a question. Laughter bubbled from Dasein. Selador misinterpreted the response. "Well," he said, "I should hope you hadn't." "Humanity ought to be the first order of interest for humans," Dasein said. (229)

While Dasein's philosophical, humanist response seems to take the sting out of his mockery of what is presented as Selador's own history of assimilation, we need to remember that for the Santarogans, as the character Piaget states, people on the outside are not human (154). What Herbert presents in this passage is a non-white outsider accusing Santaroga of disobeying anti-discrimination laws. While this accusation may not be technically true, given Burdeaux' estimation of the number of black families in the valley, it is true in a larger sense, since, as Burdeaux himself illustrates, only those who properly fit into the nostalgic "aura of the Nineteenth Century" become truly "Santarogan." Dasein's response that "humans ought to be the first order for humans" likewise may be read to repeat a superficial call for "color blindness" that effectively supports the dominant white majority.[29] This is a community based on an overly romantic, racist vision of race relations in the century before the civil rights movement, but Herbert goes on to highlight the sinister nature of this nostalgic view: when this vision is called into question by the "improperly" assimilated Selador, Dasein kills him in what is presented as, in the context of the rest of the novel, an unconscious, Jaspers-fuelled desire to protect what is now his community.

Even if one was tempted to question the racial elements of Santaroga's segregation from the rest of society, based on the black characters who do live there, the novel emphasises that racist discourse lies at the base of the community's practices. At the inquest into Selador's death, the state official who comes to investigate, Mr. Garrity, is described by the newly assimilated Dasein in racial terms: "*What was that look in Garrity's eyes?* Dasein asked himself. A black savage in Africa might have peered that way into a white man's shiny city. Strange ... angry ... frustrated man" (238), a quotation that should be paired with Piaget's earlier assertion that "We're not savages here" (63). Santaroga explicitly becomes the white city that is inaccessible to the "black savage." Its isolationism is based on a bigotry that, if not racist in the most visible sense, is still racist in its motivation. From Thoreauvian isolation, then, we come to Tarzan's cabin: the protected white space in the midst of a "black" and "savage" "Africa."

Indeed, the fear of an unrestrained, unassimilated blackness is what fuels the protective nature of the town's collective unconscious. When Dasein thinks at one point of destroying Jaspers altogether, an unconscious fear grips him, feeling like "a monster rising out of a black lake" (217). Earlier, as he tries to escape from the town, "Dasein sensed a looming black shape, anonymous, terrifying" (115). The unconscious fear of blackness arises every time Dasein threatens the security of Santaroga, forcing him to rethink his plan: this is what Toni Morrison sees in American literature as a "terror" of "darkness, with all the connotative value it awakened."[30] If Lane's Mizora is characterised by an indistinguishable whiteness during the funeral scene, Herbert's Santaroga brings into relief the black other against which that unchanging whiteness defines itself. In Herbert's novel, the collective unconscious of the isolated town is fixated on this terror of an unrestrained blackness that appears whenever there is an "outside" threat.

Herbert concludes the novel by showing the conjoined impetus of this segregationist, isolationist policy: the equal and opposite reaction of intervention. In order to protect themselves from such "savages" as Garrity, the reader learns, "Santaroga was preparing itself to reach out" into "the wide-wide world" (239). Upon this realisation, Dasein thinks, "*The only good defense is a good offense*" (239). Dasein himself is a stage of this operation, "*That's why I was chosen*," he thinks just before this, "*And Burdeaux … and the others … whoever they are*" (239). And this "choosing" of connections to the outside points to another aspect of Santaroga's isolationism, one that places it even more firmly in the past, and connects it to the larger argument of this study. While gender lurks even further in the background of Santaroga's (and the novel's) social imagination, it too is tied to the nostalgic isolationism of the town. The town's "aura of the Nineteenth Century" also invokes, after all, "a maid in ruffled cap, apron with a bow at the back, long skirt and black stockings, sensible shoes" (19). If Dasein's investigation is his ostensible reason for being there, his primary motivation for going is Jenny Sorge: "It wasn't the munificent sum those chain stores were paying the university for this study, nor the generous salary provided for himself. He had come because this was where Jenny lived," "lovely, nubile Jenny" (3; 2). And, whenever he attempts to go against the Jaspers-fuelled will of the community, it might be the "dark shape" that threatens him (paired with Selador represented as a threat), but it is Jenny who serves to bring him back into the fold, Jenny who will "protect" him (110). Deciding to get married at the end, Jenny can be read as the final image of Santaroga's conservative utopia: less a conscious subject than an objectified prize of an out-of-time marriage market, used to lure Dasein to the town to begin with. The paternalism of the town is thus connected not only to a racist discourse, but to a sexist one, as well. Santaroga is Aylmer's lab, but one whose experiments are about to break free.

The closing pages of the novel can demonstrate quite deftly that stringent segregationist or isolationist policies, based as they are on feelings of xenophobia and superiority, are inextricably linked, rather than opposed to, expansionist, even imperialist desires.[31] Ultimately, then, this imperial desire, combined with the racial and patriarchal imagination of this supposed utopia, explains why Burdeaux, and not Jenny, is the perfect "native informant": not because he "knows where Dasein is coming from," so to speak, but because he models the proper interface between inside and outside, where the latter is always subservient to the former. The "native informant" is a staple of the utopian tradition, the figure who explains the society to the ignorant interloper from "our" mundane world; Burdeaux' race and position in the town, however, also tie him to the more colonial implications of the term, in relation to relative power and agency. As Gayatri Chakravorty Spivak writes, contemporary "native informants" "attempt to make their own history as they act ... a part they have not chosen, in a script that has as its task to keep them silent and invisible" (85). Burdeaux as scripted informant thus becomes the lens through which Dasein's perspective of the world as outsider is finally inverted: far from being on the margin, Santaroga's perception is of itself as metropole, and the outside as colonial periphery designed for domination.

But *The Santaroga Barrier* ends with some hope for the world outside, if not for the "hero" Dasein. At key points in the novel, there are indications that some people have an adverse reaction to the Jaspers. Rather than reach the seemingly heightened state of awareness of the other townspeople, these people become "oddly dull-eyed, slow in their actions" (37) and are relegated to menial labour on the factory line in the town's cheese cooperative. More than just drones in the co-op's "hive," "guarding, gathering food" (33), these figures become indentured servants or slaves for the town, with their "legs ... held in stocks" at their workstations (37). When Dasein refers to them as "zombies" and demands to know "*What*" they are, he is told that "they're useful members of the community," but who, in Dasein's words, are "ruined" by Jaspers (96). If the collective unconscious of the town expresses a fear of a blackness barely kept at bay, these workers become the material condition of the town's maintenance of its whiteness, with the factory in which they are kept "loom[ing] whitely behind its fence" (33). These figures thus become reflections of the town itself: presuming they are more free than those "outside," and hence more "human," the town is actually a repressive force, maintaining an underclass of workers, still considered part of the collective "us" of hegemonic whiteness, even as they cannot participate in the full economic privilege of the dominant white class (thus fulfilling the role of the white worker as discussed by David R. Roediger and outlined in my discussion of Schuyler's *Black No More*).

But, importantly, the town's very need for these othered-but-still-us workers also exposes the fractures and hierarchies in this supposedly communal society—fractures equally highlighted and repressed by the figures of Win Burdeaux and Jenny Sorge. In Mannheim's terms, this conservative "utopia" rejects any radical notion of "inner freedom" for all (the goal of the liberal humanist utopian impulse) in favour of "'objective freedom,' to which the former must adjust itself" (239). It is the sinister command that others "*must* adjust" to this vision, in the attempt to stabilise what the conservative Santarogans see as the "objective" truth of the world, that Herbert critiques. After ingesting a massive amount of pure Jaspers, Dasein briefly feels like "a moth in a glass cage, a frantic thing fluttering against his barriers" (240). This "fluttery feeling behind [the] eyes," we learn earlier in the novel (124), is an indication that Dasein's Jaspers immersion is failing, that he is becoming, in his words, "a zombie" (135), incapable of thought. As the person who has taken more Jaspers at once than anyone before (223), Dasein comes to embody the gated community, even as he is figured as its protection against the outside world. Dasein *is* Santaroga and both its threat *and* its failure to maintain what is referred to in the very first paragraph of the novel as its "white barrier fence" (1). As Dasein feels "fluttery" behind the eyes after ingesting the potion, one can almost imagine Aminadab laughing in the background.

III. BRIDGING UTOPIA'S DIVIDES

If Herbert's novel points to the sinister aspects of a utopian desire, arguing that the borders of utopia, the dividing line between "us" and "them," presents an always already xenophobic and potentially imperialist drive, then the books of William Gibson's nanotech trilogy—also called the Bridge trilogy—and specifically the final novel, *All Tomorrow's Parties*, similarly attempt but ultimately fail to find a more open, permeable space within which the silenced figure can give voice to the laughter of Aminadab. Gibson underscores the difficulty of creating that space: the silenced figure becomes the paradoxically shifting center of an always redefined heterotopia, a space demarcated by its radical difference from hegemonic or normative social structures.

As I noted in the discussion of *The Matrix*, some critics deal with the political ramifications of Gibson's earlier cyberpunk works in terms of their problematic relationship to contemporary America's gendered and raced social structures. Important for this chapter specifically is Farnell's argument, which states of the first two books in Gibson's "post-cyberpunk," nanotechnology trilogy that, "Beneath an aesthetics of difference hides a subterranean narrative of conservative sexuality and gender, old 'norms' in new digital clothes."[32] Farnell goes on to laud what he sees as Gibson's attempt to address this problem through the creation of a "truly abstract space of imprecise possibilities," brought about through the trilogy's "technological and posthuman indeterminacy."[33] For Farnell, this indeterminacy is created through a postmodern utopia that works against the grain of Gibson's otherwise "conservative and frequently predictable narrative closures."[34] Likewise, Graham Murphy, quoting Cory Doctorow, sees in Gibson's second trilogy "both agency and … a glorification of 'possibility,'" indicating "Gibson's larger faith in the interstitial."[35] I argue, conversely, that the series does not ultimately construct, as Farnell sees, an idealised "heterotopia" that stands as a "solution" to such conservative narratives as the Santarogan vision or the white supremacy that grounds Mizora's feminism, nor does it simply fall into a reproduction of the discourses of white male supremacy, as Sharon Stockton and Nicola Nixon see in Gibson's first trilogy.[36] Instead, the nanotech series points to the difficulties of maintaining the "permanent revolution," or the emphasis on the "interstitial" that heterotopia demands, even as, like *The Matrix* and *Black No More*, it highlights the panicked and performative nature of hegemonic claims to an "essential" or natural social order based on hierarchical domination. Gibson's trilogy can thus be read not as a predictive and generalised idealisation of "a new 'mode' of being,"[37] but as a depiction, if not a critique, of the processes involved in contemporary structures of racial and gendered dominance. These novels place such structures firmly within the "postmodern" contemporary and not merely as "conservative" archaisms, as Herbert's novel presents them. In other words, where *Mizora* reproduces the politics of white supremacy to support its more progressive feminist politics, and where Herbert critiques such political moves through his depiction of Santaroga, Gibson highlights the ways in which even the postmodern heterotopia can be co-opted by hegemonic systems of othering. Prefiguring *The Matrix*, the nanotech series still goes beyond its later descendent (and its earlier cyberpunk inspirations) by placing the figure of final control not in a central AI that figures a hegemonic control, but in a silenced, racialized character who figures the contingent and always shifting grounds of identity. In this series, in other words, we see the beginning of a recuperation of Aminadab and of Herbert's zombies, a recuperation that we will see expanded (and again recursively complicated) in the next chapter on Octavia Butler.

The nanotech trilogy, consisting of the novels *Virtual Light*, *Idoru*, and *All Tomorrow's Parties*, follows two central and intertwined plot lines. First is a narrative that focuses on Cody Harwood, who, for all intents and purposes, is the richest man in the world, but who remains behind the scenes, functioning through the cover of several shadow companies (Harwood is thus an early version of Hubertus Bigend from Gibson's recent series of books, beginning with *Pattern Recognition*, often referred to as the Blue Ant trilogy, after Bigend's corporation, but which could be called the "End of History" series). In *Virtual Light*, Harwood is attempting to control the redevelopment of San Francisco after a massive earthquake, which leaves a significant percentage of the city's population homeless and living on the San Francisco-Oakland Bay Bridge. These events take place within the context of a Balkanization of America, in which California has split into two states, America's central government has become a completely ineffective and superficial figurehead, and the only real power, as in most of Gibson's work, resides in large multinational corporations. Of all of these, Harwood's corporate empire is poised to become the dominant one. Harwood's plan, in *Virtual Light*, for cementing this power is to rebuild the fractured San Francisco though a series of shadow companies, using a recently developed architectural nanotechnology which literally grows new buildings. Knowing the entire plan of this new city, Harwood arranges to buy all of the significant property on which the city will be rebuilt, and thus effectively to purchase the entirety of San Francisco—and from there, presumably, the world, as any traditional megalomaniac sci-fi villain would. This plot is foiled in the first novel, but Harwood continues his attempts to "retain viability" in a new nanotech-driven world order.[38] Harwood says, in *All Tomorrow's Parties*, that "If the world is to be reborn, I wish to be reborn in it, as something akin to what I am today" (175). Harwood is an allegorical figure of the negotiations of Gramscian hegemonic power, which may experience slight shifts in composition or emphasis with the advent of new forces of production, but which still manages to maintain the relations of power of the status quo.[39]

Running parallel to this narrative, especially in the latter two novels, is one in which an artificial intelligence "embodied" as a hologram, known as an idoru, attempts to fulfill a Pinocchio wish of becoming a "real" person by using the exact same nanotechnology to embody herself that Harwood would use to cement his dominant position in the power structure. Tying these two narratives together are the two typically flawed, Gibsonian heroes: Rydell, a generally unemployed cop/rent-a-cop from Tennessee; and Chevette, a sometimes bike messenger who lives on the Bridge. Through the course of the three novels, Rydell and Chevette help the idoru fulfill her wish for embodiment, in the process of which they foil all of Harwood's plans to be in control of the new nanotech world.

These combined plots reproduce a narrative thread common in Gibson's cyberpunk works, one that is both complicated and replicated in *The Matrix*, in which a white, individualised, masculine hero is pitted against a collective, Orientalised, and feminised enemy. Certainly the nanotech trilogy, like *The Matrix*, fits into this general framework. Rydell, the ostensible hero, makes his whiteness "embarrassingly obvious," to use Stockton's words (594), throughout both *Virtual Light* and *All Tomorrow's Parties*, the books that frame the trilogy. Rydell constantly comments on the racial "makeup" of non-white characters, using race as his primary identifier while maintaining a conspicuous silence about whiteness itself, in a classic ideological reproduction of the dominance of whiteness—as discussed in my reading of *Black No More*—in which it "defines" itself as the one "race" that doesn't need identification. Rydell acts out his police-trained background with constant and consistent acts of racial profiling, even while denying that he does so. Indeed, race is Rydell's main identity signifier: it is central for him even when he recognises the shifting nature of its application; and, his racialized vision is consistently tied to the perception of gender. Near the beginning of *All Tomorrow's Parties*, Rydell is working as a rent-a-cop at a convenience store known as the Lucky Dragon. As the store's security, Rydell has to do a "curb check" to tell the prostitutes and homeless people to move away from the store:

> There was a Japanese girl standing out there with a seriously amazing amount of legs running down from an even more amazingly small amount of shorts. Well, sort of Japanese. Rydell found it hard to make distinctions like that in LA. Durius said hybrid vigor was the order of the day, and Rydell guessed he was right. This girl with all the legs, she was nearly as tall as Rydell, and he didn't think Japanese people usually were. But then maybe she'd grown up here, and her family before her, and the local food had made them taller. ... But, no, he decided, getting closer, the thing was, she wasn't actually a girl. Funny how you got that. Usually it wasn't anything too obvious. It was like he really wanted to buy into everything she was doing to *be* a girl, but some subliminal message he got from her bone structure just wouldn't let him. (10)

Even though Rydell sees racial identities as being problematic, his first identification of a person is based on apparent race, and when that fails him due to a recognition of the problems with simplistic determinations of biological "race," gender becomes an ultimate bodily signifier, tied not just to gender performance but to "bone structure," a biological essentialism that allows him to abandon what to him is the dangerous train of thought on the arbitrariness of race.

Thus, Rydell's position as the central protagonist of Gibson's complex series of plots mimics the privileging of white masculinity of the "cowboyism" that Nixon and Stockton see as the central motif of the cyberpunk series. Unlike their readings of that earlier trilogy, however, the nanotech books explicitly figure the evil multinational as being a product of Western economic imperialism.[40] This shift would seem to have profound effects on the figuring of Rydell's (unconscious) racial and gender agenda.

Part of Harwood's plan for the maintenance of his economic dominance is a reintegration of the Bridge inhabitants into mainstream society, especially in terms of economic exchange. As it exists throughout the entire trilogy, the Bridge is a self-sufficient and self-governing squatter's domain that avoids authoritarian or centralist forms of economic or government control. Added to this, the Bridge is figured as a completely multiracial, multi-linguistic, and generally multiplicitous society. This multiplicity is the reason that Farnell pictures the Bridge as Gibson's creation of a heterotopia, a "counterculture ... where the structure and its inhabitants form a 'singularity,' ... a multi-racial heterogeneity of lawless coexistence" (464). Indeed, the random construction of shelters on the Bridge and the "difference" that itself characterises the inhabitants strike Rydell in *Virtual Light* as a positive force:

> This place had just *grown*, it looked like, one thing patched onto the next, until the whole span was wrapped in this formless mass of *stuff*,

> and no two pieces of it matched. There was a different material anywhere you looked, almost none of it being used for what it had originally been intended for. ... He found himself grinning at it all, and at the people, none of them paying him the least attention, cannibalistic or otherwise. They looked to be as mixed a bunch as their building materials: all ages, races, colors. ...[41]

Rydell "grins" at the bridge populace, gaining an undefined pleasure from what he sees as the Bridge's mixture, despite having been previously told by employees of Harwood, following a vaguely Tarzan-like racism, that the Bridge was full of "cannibals."[42] The threat that the Bridge poses to the Harwood's dominance and Western economic hegemony is thus tied, in Rydell's mind at least, to its racial makeup. More a *bricolage*-vigour than a "hybrid" one, the Bridge epitomises Gibson's approach to what he views as "the Street's" reappropriation and redeployment of the dominant culture.[43]

The physical structure of the Bridge is inspired by Hak Nam, or the Kowloon Walled City, in Hong Kong, which was dismantled in 1993: in the trilogy, "Hak Nam" is also the name for a hacker web site.[44] Beyond this direct reference, however, Gibson's Bridge also clearly reworks another famous heterotopian bridge for the history of SF: the Bridge of Lost Desire in Samuel R. Delany's Nevèrÿon series of novels and stories, discussed briefly in the introduction to this study. Delany's fantasy series pivots around a Bridge which is the centre of both licit and illicit trade, and the focus of the works' negotiations of what is perceived as a predominantly sexualised set of social and linguistic power exchanges; the last volume published in the series, *Return to Nevèrÿon*, was originally published under the title *The Bridge of Lost Desire*, emphasising the bridge's centrality to the series. Even more closely, however, Gibson's Bridge echoes Delany's autonomous zone in *Trouble on Triton: An Ambiguous Heterotopia*. Lawless zones set up on each of the already generally open societies of moon-colonies, the "unlicensed zone," or "u-l" is presented as "fulfill[ing] a complex range of functions in the cities' psychological, political, and economic ecology."[45] Not as chaotic as many would fear (as Harwood's employees do, fearing the cannibalism on the Bridge), these sites become less "relief valves" that serve to maintain the functioning of the larger society (as with Neo in the sequels to *The Matrix*), than mirrors against which the dominant society can judge its own development (or lack thereof).[46] Important to the very concept of Delany's heterotopian spaces, as made clear by the subtitle of *Trouble on Triton*, is their unceasing and uncomfortable ambiguity, the inability to pin down any specific political relation to the hegemonic system of which they are a part, and yet there is also a profound recognition that they are, in fact, deeply interrelated to that system, even as they highlight the otherwise unconscious assumptions of the hegemonic structures that surround them.

In this way, the heterotopia Delany is creating, on which Gibson relies, functions much more along the lines of Foucault's original definition of the term than Farnell's appropriation of it, where it implicitly reads as a utopia based on difference—Farnell does cite Foucault, but in positioning the heterotopia of the Bridge as "the last place of resistance to all-pervasive consumer consumption and privatization," the heterotopia's role is reduced merely to inversion. For Foucault, this inversion is only one of the functions of the heterotopia, since unlike the "non place" of the utopia, heterotopias are "real places—places that do exist and that are formed in the very founding of society—which are something like counter-sites, a kind of effectively enacted utopia in which the real sites, all the other real sites that can be found within the culture, are simultaneously *represented, contested, and inverted*."[47] As with my definition of SF in the introduction, heterotopias are not reducible to the "mundane" reality of the societies they exist within, but instead reconfigure that reality, rendering a space from which we can view that mundanity as a fiction that can be interpreted. Foucault even uses the mirror, as I do, to explain this function, writing that the mirror "makes this place that I occupy at the moment when I look at myself in the glass at once absolutely real, connected with all the space that surrounds it, and absolutely unreal, since in order to be perceived it has to pass through this virtual point which is over there."[48] The heterotopia—be it Santaroga, Gibson's or Delany's bridges, autonomous zones within cities, mirrors, or SF itself—rearranges the discursive and material relations of society in ways that can be resistant or not, but which nonetheless twist and alter the structural relations that maintain society as it is, presenting them in a new, virtual light. Heterotopias, like SF, constitute a "redistribution of the sensible," to use Jacques Rancière's terms.[49]

The Bridge figures prominently in the series, and the plots of the two framing novels specifically focus on Rydell's and Chevette's use of the Bridge and its inhabitants in order to foil Harwood's megalomaniacal plans. A significant part of these plans, then, is to crush the potential for resistance that the Bridge contains and represents. Discussing his placement of a Lucky Dragon store at the entrance to the Bridge, Harwood says:

> our studies indicated that positioning it there would encourage walk-on tourism, and that is a crucial aspect of normalization. ... There is an ongoing initiative to bring the bridge community back into the fold, as it were. But the issue is sensitive. ... Autonomous zones do offer a certain insulation from the monoculture, but they seem not to lend themselves to recommodification, not in the same way. We don't know why exactly. (*All Tomorrow's Parties*, 174–75)

Harwood's project, then, is to recommodify those places and people that escape the economic monoculture of the West that he represents. Therefore, Rydell's and Chevette's attempt to thwart this plan would seem to place them on the side of "autonomous zones," and, subsequently, on the side of heterogeneity.

Indeed, in *All Tomorrow's Parties* these heterotopian spaces are revisited, at first seemingly rendered as less ambiguous spaces of counter-hegemonic resistance. Chevette thinks to herself at one point that the Bridge "is a world within the world, and, if there be such places between the things of the world, places built in the gaps, then surely there are things there, and places between them, and things in those places too" (80–81). Gibson here seems to be directly mapping Foucauldian identity politics onto this future heterotopia (a parallel made somewhat stronger by Gibson's metaphoric use of the panopticon in one chapter's title). This is a space again of Foucault's "plurality of resistances, each of them a special case,"[50] that is, a space of "places built in the gaps" that can resist determination by dominant ideological apparatuses.

The Bridge's and Rydell's economic positioning, however, does in fact lead to another development in the text that belies the positive nature of heterogeneity. Throughout the text, Rydell is slotted into a stereotypical version of white trash, known in the series as "meshbacks" because of their baseball caps. Most of his close acquaintances and friends are also so positioned. His rent-a-cop partner and best friend, Sublett (his name itself positioning him as existing outside of an ownership class), lives in an insulated trailer park community that literally worships television (a neat inversion of Santaroga's disdainful vision of television and the world it represents). In order to be allowed into the compound, Rydell and Chevette have to masquerade as members of the fictional Christian sect "Aryan Nazarene," stating that "We wouldn't want to even come *in* there, say you got … *any* kind of race-mixing. Race-traitors all *over*, these days."[51] This racist diatribe goes on for another half-page, after which they are presumed righteous enough to be let into the trailer park. The positioning of these poor whites as equally disenfranchised as the Bridge populace, but as being radically opposed to the heterogeneous nature of the Bridge, is mimicked in *All Tomorrow's Parties* by another of Rydell's acquaintances, Buell—a country western singer. Buell's lyrical genius is said to come from an attempt to cement a white "ethnic" past and identity. Rydell's and Chevette's anti-imperial, heterogeneous championing is thus betrayed by its support from exclusionary and violent racist practices.

The complex movements from the apparent lauding of a multiracial heterotopia to the seemingly unavoidable and, as it is portrayed, pragmatic usage of white supremacist isolationism ultimately betrays an instability in racial identities. Buell's promoter says that his singing is "a 'roots' thing. Buell wants to take it back, back there past Waylon and Willie, to some kinda dark 'primal kinda heartland.' Kinda. Thing" (140–41). This music, as Chevette's friend Tessa describes it, is aimed specifically at "a disenfranchised, mostly white proletariat … barely hanging on in post-post-industrial America" (140). However, Buell's supposed white "rooted" ethnicity is in fact supported by and highlighted by a "dark … primal presence," a colouring of essence best described, again, in terms of Morrison's "Africanist presence," the "dark past" that she notes as being described as a "blank darkness" "through which historical, moral, metaphysical, and social fears, problems and dichotomies could be articulated."[52] Like the dark presence that characterises Santaroga's collective unconscious and protects their town from outsiders, Buell's, and the trilogy's, emphasis on whiteness could not exist without the "dark primal presence" that literally renders the white promoter speechless, unable to further articulate Buell's connection to "the disenfranchised, mostly white proletariat," leaving her trailing off into a meaningless jumble, "Kinda. Thing." The isolation of the trailer park's residents and their refusal to identify with the Bridge inhabitants clearly perform an ideological function, working to maintain the relations of production and power, the social divisions necessary for the functioning of hegemony, even as others are working to "bridge" those divides.

The trailer park thus serves as the heterotopia, in Foucault's sense, to the Bridge, even as both serve a similar role to the dominant society. These continual inversions—this *mise en abyme* of SF reflections on itself—serve to demonstrate the complexities and ultimately impossibilities of containing heterotopia as a form of resistance. Despite Gibson's seemingly less ambiguous take than Delany's, we come to the same difficulty of articulating resistance as such—because to do so would mean, like Santaroga, to "reach out" to the wider world with one's message of absolute, utopian truth.

This depiction of the racialization of the heterotopia, with all of its political ramifications, combined with a similar analysis of gender, is replayed in the trilogy's other central plot line concerning the idoru. The idoru, like the Bridge, is seen by Rydell as an embodiment of heterogeneity, and what he refers to earlier as "hybrid vigour." The first time Rydell sees the idoru, in *All Tomorrow's Parties*, he thinks that "she had to be one of Durius' examples of hybrid vigor, but saying which races and been mixed was beyond him" (152–53). As a hologram, paradoxically embodying the "post-human," the idoru also seemingly exists post-race, although Rydell still strives to use his central form of identification. His attempt to foil Harwood becomes entangled in a plot to help the idoru to become literally embodied through the use of nanotechnology—this goal is accomplished at the end of the last novel, although she is the one who guides Rydell in how to accomplish it. Rydell's traditional space as the white male hero saving the day, then, is in fact enabled by the "post-race," post-feminine heterotopic ideal.

But is it? Even more than Neo (though perhaps less than Buck), Rydell is still the stereotypical white male romantic hero who saves the day and gets the girl, the Bridge community does become more incorporated into the larger society at the end, although not according to Harwood's plan, and the idoru's quest to become "real" is precisely a quest to abandon her resistant identity to become identified as an embodied feminine subject, an embodiment through which women have historically been marginalised. And, indeed, after her multiple embodiment as a series of physical, nanotech beings, the idoru vanishes from the storyline altogether, becoming the "selfless" figure of marginalised feminine embodiment. Given these textual facts, then, clearly the "ideal" nature of the heterotopia that Farnell lauds ceases to be viable. But does what I, echoing Delany, have been referring to as the ambiguity of the heterotopian space also fail? Is it finally commodified back into the hegemonic relations of the dominant capitalist, white, and male hegemony?

IV. THE SOUND OF SILENCE

The beginnings of an answer to these questions can be found in the character of Silencio, a Latino youth who only appears in the final novel of the trilogy. As his name suggests, Silencio remains almost completely nonverbal throughout the novel—speaking only facts and details about specific watches—until a postscript shows him several years after the conclusion of the central plots. Silencio fills the role that the nearly all-powerful artificial intelligence entities fill in the cyberpunk series. In those novels, as Terence Whalen argues, Gibson's creation of "the matrix"—which the *Matrix* films, while relying on, would later visualise so differently from Gibson's more abstract virtual space—"is structurally meaningless to any individual consciousness, which is why Gibson must invent corporate and artificially intelligent subjects that can thrive in the rich fields of data."[53] Constructing *artificial* beings who understand the totality of the social structures based around this flow of information allows Gibson to posit a sense of unity to his Romantic quest narratives, while still being able to portray a *fragmented* human world that the hero must strive to overcome. In *All Tomorrow's Parties*, though, this all-encompassing knowledge of the web is positioned in Silencio, who seems to have a form of autism and can both navigate and encompass the entire matrix through his fascination with antique watches: Silencio does not communicate through the full range of spoken language, but only in the intricacies of watch-collectors' facts; people slowly recognise that he has an uncanny ability to search the web for antique watches, and because of this manages to get into sites and databases that the best computer hacker cannot enter. In order to finally beat Harwood's plans for world domination, Rydell and his friends code Harwood into the web as a watch, and tell Silencio to look for it. He finds the watch, Harwood is exposed, and his plans are foiled.

The text describes Silencio's vision of the matrix as he searches for Harwood: "But very far away, he feels it, the watch. He knows it, and it is there still, but only this distance, these gray fields of light. Gone again. No. There is the system: the system of all watches. Similarities. Differences. The words. A coding. Nothing is lost within the system" (254). Silencio embodies the semiotic potentials of SF language itself: the "coding" here serving multiple purposes as both the "code" of the semiotic structure of language *and* the binary code that composes the matrix, but also the *encoding* of power in the range of racial, gendered, and other identities that exist on the

Bridge and elsewhere in the novel, including Silencio's own (un)silenced othering. Encompassing both "similarities" and "differences," this silent, explicitly racially marginalised character (161) is solely responsible for the "happy ending" of the traditional romance plot. The fact that the trilogy ends with a chapter dedicated to and entitled "Silencio," and also, for the first time, gives him the ability to converse more widely (to a point), can point us to an understanding of how the Romantic narrative of white male success and privilege is ultimately only possible through the use of a silenced and othered figure. As Morrison writes, the notions of freedom and the power of the individual that are figured in romance narratives are "highlighted" and "inevitably yoked" to questions of race.[54] More significantly, however, the conclusion to both the series and *All Tomorrow's Parties* may indicate that it is those voices silenced by the dominant narrative that are, in fact, most important. Denying the "happily-ever-after" moment for Rydell, the conclusion of the trilogy with Silencio and his speech points to a realisation that the borders of dominance are not completely static, and that difference is not so easily contained as the physical space of the Bridge may make it seem. Silencio articulates Aminadab's final laugh. Silencio's silence in the main body of the narrative can, in this case, be read as the final incommensurability of heterotopian (and SF) resistance, insofar as they cannot be rendered into the simple signified within the realm of hegemonic (and realist) representation.

Reading Silencio as a figure of radical—and necessarily endless—resistance to hegemonic control is likewise encoded into the object of his obsession: mechanical watches. In the lead-up to the novel's publication, Gibson published a piece in *Wired* magazine concerning his own obsession with mechanical and antique watches—and the fact that this obsession led the famously un-wired Gibson onto the Internet. In so doing, the author implicitly articulates an aspect of Silencio's function in the novel:

> vintage mechanical watches are among the very finest fossils of the pre-digital age. Each one is a miniature world unto itself, a tiny functioning mechanism, a congeries of minute and mysterious moving parts. Moving parts! And consequently these watches are, in a sense, alive. They have heartbeats. They seem to respond, Tamagotchi-like, to "love," in the form, usually, of the expensive ministrations of specialist technicians. Like ancient steam-tractors or Vincent motorcycles, they can be painstakingly restored from virtually any stage of ruin.[55]

Watches present a Benjaminian "aura" of authenticity, but paradoxically at a remove. If for Benjamin, authenticity is negated by mechanical reproduction, for Gibson it is negated by the "clean" digital—the mechanics that seem to work behind the scenes, never to be seen. Here, authenticity and aura are created precisely by, not a pre-modern, but a pre-postmodern notion of construction, a mechanical—indeed physical—culture *per se*: watches simulate love like the Tamagotchi digital pets, through physical rather than virtual interaction. His description of eBay, where he buys his watches, similarly echoes this: fully a part of the digital world of late-stage capitalism and globalism, still eBay offers the functions of the "Kapali Carsi, the grand bazaar" in Istanbul. A paradoxical symptom of and respite from the amorphous Borgesian assault of the "postmodern," eBay makes Gibson "glad we still have a place for things to change hands. Even here, in this territory the map became."[56]

Silencio's quest for the map of all watches—the map that is the territory of the digital age—may seem on the surface as a simple search for authenticity, and his silence a form of transcendence that we see Santaroga extol in its *Existenz*. Figuring silence or authenticity as a form of radical opposition is, however, an obviously politically suspect position to take, especially when it is represented as the (necessary) silence of the racially marginalised. Recognising this problem, perhaps, Gibson's afterward offers an older Silencio a final act of vocalization, in which he performs the role of an unending correction to the entropy of the (post)modern world. Now the owner of a watch repair shop, he is depicted with a young boy—a Silencio of the next generation—who brings a found watch to him for repair. Silencio uses an automated repair "bed" to fix the watch, and he and the boy

> watch as [the watch] rises smoothly on edge, as if of its own accord, and then seems to sink, impossibly, as if through the shallow bed and the glass beneath. ...
>
> Silencio looks at the watch on his wrist, a military Jaeger-LeCoultre, RAAF. "Nine minutes," he said. "There's coffee."
>
> ... Within the bed, the rusted disk of the watch is being read and disassembled. Molecules are moving. In nine minutes it will rise again, bright and perfect as the day it first left its factory in Switzerland.
>
> "I want to watch," the boy says.
>
> Silencio understands. He goes to get the coffee. (277)

This concluding scene of the novel replays Silencio's introduction, in his own first trip to the watch shop, down to the Jaeger-LeCoultre and the coffee. Here, the Bridge builds its fractal community, repeating itself with minor differences, in order to develop a community that would otherwise be silenced. Indeed, in the nearly mystical automatic repair bed, we see an image of such a community, repairing itself. Playing on the metonymic nature of SF language, the boy may not want to "watch" as in visually observe the repair of the timepiece: he may in fact want to "watch," where the object of the timepiece itself is transformed into a verb. The boy wants to "watch" himself, to become the intricate, authentic, endlessly repairable object, just as the timepiece is. Silencio understands this desire to *be* the watch.

In Silencio, then, we see the beginnings of the promise of SF to disrupt the semiotic and hence ideological systems of domination at play in the mundane world. In his piece on mechanical watches, Gibson writes that "They're pointless in a peculiarly needful way; they're comforting precisely because they require tending" ("My Obsession"). So too is the local community in the global age: here, in the heterotopian space—a space necessarily deemed "useless" and uncommodifiable by the dominant culture—new voices can be found, and the intricate daily work of (re)building a sense of identity and community can be foregrounded. This is the frustrated promise of Max and Neo, but—perhaps—here realised.

I write "perhaps" because one can still read against this grain, in which one lauds the heterotopian again as simply a new, if endlessly revised, form of utopia. This final moment also removes the "aura"—the resistance—that Silencio represents. He doesn't fix the watch, after all, nor can he or the child even see that happen. It takes place within another nanotechnological box which seems to take over his role as repairman. Highlighting the inherent hint of the obsolete within the Deist concept of god-as-watchmaker, Silencio may speak, but he can do so precisely because he is part of the semiotics of his time, resistant no more. Against what is, admittedly, even my own desire to, like Wilde, find release in aesthetic pointlessness, this scene is simply a repetition of the earlier one, and Silencio's voice still circles around the "pointless" watch which is fixed by technology he doesn't control. Rather than reading this as Gibson's "street" reappropriating technology, we can read this to mean that Silencio—like the Bridge, like Neo, like Max, like Dasein—is now part of the system (of economics, of race, of gender, of language), albeit a slightly changed system. This ending, in other words, can also be read to foreshadow that of *The Matrix* series: while concluding with Silencio's voice rather than an Architect's demonstrates Gibson's attempt to push beyond the constrictions that *The Matrix* series falls back into—to give power back to the Street—still we are not left with a fully "new world" that SF promises, and its resistance seems played out. Silencio's radical opposition must be folded back into mundane, repetitious verbal acts. He is, in other words, "humanised": in a certain liberal humanist logic, this is of course a positive thing but, as we have seen, historically the concept of the "human" has been used in far from universalizing ways, and instead has been riven with particularization, hierarchies, and exclusion. Silencio's "humanisation" here—as opposed to his humanity—must be read in so-called scare quotes, as a function of the dominant culture rather than a rejection of it. His final vocalisation is an ironic echo of the idoru's humanisation and her subsequent narrative (re)marginalisation.

But if even the sounding of silence cannot figure a fully resistant SF language, then is such even possible? If the heterotopian space of the Bridge is, as in Foucault's definition, a site like SF itself, that—in Rancière's words—can redistribute the sensible, then what does it mean that such a redistribution is an unsustainable act, that it always risks the possibility of becoming mundanely *sensible*? In the next chapter, I turn to Octavia Butler's *Patternmaster* series, one of the most engaged theorisations of resistance—be it in the form of utopia or heterotopia, and again figured through the paired subjectivities of race and gender. Analysing both preexisting and newly formed social patterns, Butler's series asks intricate questions concerning the ways in which such patterns and their disruptions feed into each other, in an attempt to articulate whether even resistant patterns must ultimately be absorbed by the dominant system of relations, or reform into their own hegemonic—and hence exclusionary—systems. Butler, in other words, analyses both the pattern that Herbert presents and Gibson's attempt to escape it. Following that discussion, however, I move to a conclusion that offers some vision of a radical alterity that relies on Silencio's effective if obsessive fascination with watches, the "useless" melding of the aesthetic and the mechanical (another way, one could say, of defining SF).

NOTES

1. Peter Brigg, "Frank Herbert: On Getting Our Heads Together," Mosaic 13, no.3–4 (1980): 193.
2. Santaroga is seemingly based on Santa Rosa, with the Jaspers "cheese cooperative" being "based upon ... the Marin French Cheese Company in Petaluma, near Santa Rosa" (Brian Herbert, *Dreamer of Dune: The Biography of Frank Herbert* [New York: Tor, 2003], 218). Santa Rosa, coincidentally, has a somewhat storied history of being the SF location of choice for hive-mind takeovers: it is also the possible basis of the town of Santa Mira in the novel and film *Invasion of the Body Snatchers* (novel 1954; film 1956).
3. Frank Herbert, *The Santaroga Barrier* (1968. New York: Tor, 2002), 157. Unless otherwise noted, subsequent quotations will be from this edition and will be cited parenthetically.
4. William F. Touponce, *Frank Herbert* (Boston: Twayne, 1988), 110.
5. In More's work, Utopia is "crescent-shaped" and "sheltered from the wind" (Thomas More, *Utopia*, edited by George M. Logan and Robert M. Adams, translated by Robert M. Adams, rev. ed. [Cambridge: Cambridge University Press, 2002], 41).
6. See Brigg; Tim O'Reilly, *Frank Herbert*, (n.p.: Frederick Ungar Publishing, 1981), http://www.oreilly.com/tim/herbert/, accessed 19 January 2015; and Leon Stover, "Is Jaspers Beer Good for You?" *Extrapolation* 17 (1976): 160–67.
7. The friendship between Heidegger and Jaspers and their influence on existentialism is complex and made even more complicated by Heidegger's ties to the Nazis. Heidegger was a member of the Nazi party, but the degree to which he was an active adherent or passive dupe is the subject of debate. Jaspers denounced Heidegger severely for his Nazi affiliation, basically accusing Heidegger during the denazification process of being unable to move his thought beyond his own petty concerns and being "extraordinarily uncritical." At one point, citing Max Weber, Jasper referred to Heidegger as being among the "children who grab hold of the wheel of history [and] are crushed" (Jaspers, "Letter" 148; 149). In other words, Jaspers saw Heidegger as being unable to see beyond the "dasein" day-to-day world: at the least, as Jaspers would see it, this was a fairly disastrous state for a philosopher.

8. Karl Jaspers, *Reason and Existenz: Five Lectures*, translated by William Earle (n.p.: Noonday Press, 1955), 11.
9. Jaspers, *Reason*, 63.
10. Jaspers, *Reason*, 61.
11. Jaspers, *Reason*, 66.
12. Jaspers, *Reason*, 68–69.
13. T. S. Eliot, *Collected Poems 1909–1962* (1963. New York: Harcourt, 1991), 79; 3.
14. Clearly the drug Jaspers and its effects echo Herbert's most famous novel, *Dune*, and its use of spice. Both drugs serve to heighten consciousness in a manner that echoes some of the more idealistic descriptions of hallucinogens, from Aldous Huxley forward. *Dune* adds to this the ability for some to use spice as a means to foresee the future, but also uses this device to warn against the problems of an overly rigid or structured view of human potential. The hero of *Dune*, Paul Muad'Dib, views the future largely as an unchangeable path, which leads to a massive, murderous "jihad." His son, Leto, especially as portrayed in the fourth novel of the series, *God Emperor of Dune*, forces humanity into a more chaotic, unrestrained, and ultimately unpredictable universe, one even he can't control, in an effort to maintain human survival. As we will see in *Santaroga*, monologic utopian visions are here shown to be both stultifying and ultimately violently imperialist in their effects. In both works, individuals or groups mistake their limited, dasein vision as a transcendent, universal one.
15. The discussions of psychology as a tool of the dominant culture pairs Herbert's novel clearly to that other anti-utopia, Aldous Huxley's *Brave New World*, but perhaps even more clearly to a contemporary work: Ken Kesey's *One Flew Over the Cuckoo's Nest*, which likewise presents a community kept separate from the larger society, in part by an enforced use of drugs. Kesey's novel more explicitly points to the deadening effects of such separation, which Herbert gestures to at the end. But the drug references also tie Herbert's work to Kesey's (as a possible critique of the latter), given that Kesey was one of the early subjects of the CIA's LSD experiments, and he then went on to form the collective, hallucinogen-fuelled group, "The Merry Pranksters," which itself grew directly out of the remnants of the Beat Generation.
16. Jean Piaget is best known for his theories of children's cognitive and social development. In relation to Herbert's novel, the most significant aspect of Piaget's work may be his emphasis on combining the structures and methodologies of "sociology [and] genetic psychology" (Jean Piaget, *The Moral Judgment of the Child*, translated by Marjorie Gabain [1932. Oxon: Routledge, 2002], 325). Using both disciplines, Piaget aimed to understand not only the "moral development of the child" (the title of one of his best known works) from inborn, instinctual drives, but also the social development of cooperation and justice, values which he understood as "empirical"—rather than more amorphously spiritual—and which could be scientifically analyzed (and hence improved).
17. O'Reilly, 6; quotations from O'Reilly's text are taken from the online version, and parenthetical references are to chapter number. Skinner's novel presents a utopian community based on his theories that human behaviour could be shaped and improved through a systematic process of positive reinforcement, which would thus remove what he saw as the socially conditioned problems of jealousy, competition, and so on. Insofar as the community of Santaroga embodies this technique, but, as we will see, transforms its more negative tendencies into

an unconscious form of violence directed at non-community members, Herbert is clearly critiquing Skinner. Several actual communities attempted to enact Skinner's model, to varying levels of success: for a discussion of such communities, see Hilke Kuhlmann, *Living* Walden Two: *B. F. Skinner's Behaviourist Utopia and Experimental Communities* (Urbana: University of Illinois Press, 2005).

18. Henry David Thoreau, "Resistance to Civil Government," in *Reform Papers, edited by Wendell Glick* (Princeton: Princeton University Press, 1973), 64.
19. Herbert, qtd. in O'Reilly, 6.
20. In addition to Hawthorne's "The Birth-mark," one should think here of his analysis of the utopian community of Brook Farm, in his novel *The Blithedale Romance:* like Dasein, the narrator of that novel sees himself as an outsider, the ironic observer, of the community. Unlike Herbert's novel, Hawthorne portrays the collapse of the community, but still presents its ideals nostalgically, a division one can see in the conclusion to "The Birth-mark," as well.
21. Kenneth M. Roemer, *Utopian Audiences: How Readers Locate Nowhere* (Amherst: University of Massachusetts Press, 2003), 117.
22. Roemer, 118.
23. Mannheim, widely known as the originator of the "sociology of knowledge," wrote *Ideology and Utopia*, originally published in Germany in 1929. It explores the problems of the rising of fascism, but also offers analyses of the utopian thought of religious millenarians, liberal humanists, socialists, and conservatives.
24. Karl Mannheim, *Ideology and Utopia: An Introduction to the Sociology of Knowledge*, translated by Louis Wirth and Edward Shils (1936. San Diego: Harvest, 2001), 192.
25. Mannheim, 230.
26. Mannheim, 230.
27. Sidonie Smith, *Subjectivity, Identity, and the Body: Women's Autobiographical Practices in the Twentieth Century* (Bloomington: Indiana University Press, 1993), 9.
28. Signed into law by Lyndon Johnson, the Fair Housing Act made it illegal "To refuse to sell or rent after the making of a bona fide offer, or to refuse to negotiate for the sale or rental of, or otherwise make unavailable or deny, a dwelling to any person because of race, color, religion, sex, familial status, or national origin" (Fair Housing Act. Sec. 800. 42 U.S.C. 3601 et seq., *United States Department of Justice*, U.S. Dept. of Justice, accessed 9 October 2014, http://www.justice.gov/crt/about/hce/title8.php).
29. Leslie G. Carr's *"Color-Blind" Racism* (London: Sage, 1997), for example, explores the functions of "color blindness" as a "new White nationalist ideology" (140).
30. Toni Morrison, *Playing in the Dark: Whiteness and the Literary Imagination* (New York: Vintage, 1990), 37.
31. In this representation of supposedly static utopianism as a force of imperial "conquest," Herbert's critique looks forward, at least in part, to Harvey L. Gable Jr.'s critique of Skinner's *Walden 2*, in which he states that the novel's:

> machinery metaphor also hints at conquest. In *Walden Two* ..., the political machinery that regulates and subdues nature must be imposed from above. Robert Geiser makes the point that behavior modification is a technology,

> and for it to function effectively the subject must be drawn within the environment of that technology. … Skinner knows that realization of his vision depends on the creation of self-regulating creatures whose idea of fulfillment has been changed not only in work but in leisure—or, more accurately, whose idea of work and leisure have been subsumed into the larger work of the community. Like all Utopians, the residents of Walden Two spend their "leisure" hours almost exclusively in educational pursuits. "In Walden Two," [the character] Frazier brags, "education goes on forever." Why so? Because (human) nature, while theoretically nonexistent, continues to push back against the forces of regulation that occupy its territory; it must be constantly subdued by ongoing "reeducation" (Harvey L. Gable, Jr., "*Walden Two*, Postmodern Utopia, and the Problems of Power, Choice, and the Rule of Law," *Texas Studies in Literature and Language* 41.1 [1999]: 3).

As the sarcastic aside to the "theoretically nonexistent" human nature may indicate, however, Gable is centrally interested in critiquing what he sees as an academic lauding of "postmodernism" (here conflated with a vaguely poststructuralist notion of identity) in favour of a reassertion of the need for "tradition," which he argues is "nonideological," a pure form of knowledge "worked out dialectically in the play between man and nature, an impersonal consensus which, like a literary canon, is ultimately democratic" (11): beyond what is, arguably, the demonstrable historical falsity of that last statement, we can also hear in this passage an oddly Santarogan sentiment, in the desire to see "tradition" as purely removed from the ideological backgrounds of its formation.

32. Ross Farnell, "Posthuman Topologies: William Gibson's 'Architexture' in *Virtual Light* and *Idoru*," *Science Fiction Studies* 25, no.3 (1998): 471.
33. Farnell, 475.
34. Farnell, 475.
35. Graham Murphy, "Post/Humanity and the Interstitial: A Glorification of Possibility in Gibson's Bridge Sequence," *Science Fiction Studies* 30, no.1 (2003): 86; 81. James H. Thrall makes a similar argument about the Bridge community in the series functioning in a nearly utopian manner, seeing in it even some of the nostalgic elements of *The Santaroga Barrier*, writing that "Gibson's vision trades almost nostalgically in memories of tangible hearth and home. There is a marked absence of white picket fences surrounding neat lawns on the bridge, but even so it is, in some ways, very small-town" (James H. Thrall, "Love, Loss, and Utopian Community on William Gibson's Bridge," Foundation 91 [2004]: 98). However, while he notes the shifting role of race and racism in Gibson's texts, they are not seen as complicating this vision at all.
36. Nicola Nixon, "Cyberpunk: Preparing the Ground for Revolution or Keeping the Boys Satisfied?" *Science Fiction Studies* 19, no.2 (1992): 224–25; Sharon Stockton, "'The Self-Regained': Cyberpunk's Retreat to the Imperium," *Contemporary Literature* 36, no.4 (1995): 588–612.
37. Farnell, 472.
38. William Gibson, *All Tomorrow's Parties* (New York: Ace, 2000), 175. Unless otherwise noted, all subsequent quotations will be from this edition and will be cited parenthetically.
39. Raymond Williams' classic definition of Gramsci's (admittedly amorphous) notion of hegemony describes well the various social strata into which Harwood wants to

inject his control: "Hegemony is ... not only the articulate upper level of 'ideology,' nor are its forms of control ordinarily seen as 'manipulation' or 'indoctrination'"; instead, "hegemony" is constituted of "a whole body of practices and expectations, over the whole of living" (*Marxism and Literature* [Oxford: Oxford University Press, 1977], 110). Harwood could, further, be a figure of what Connell calls "hegemonic masculinity," here embodying the racial and classed dynamics of patriarchal capitalism (R. W. Connell, *Masculinities*, 2nd ed [Cambridge: Polity, 2005]).

40. This causal relationship can also be seen, to a point, in Gibson's earlier works, but the later novels make it clearer.
41. William Gibson, *Virtual Light* (New York: Bantam, 1994), 194.
42. Gibson, *Virtual*, 194.
43. Gibson's approach here echoes Dick Hebdige's analysis of punks' subcultural redeployment of the dominant culture, one that allows for a certain, though limited, agency. See Dick Hebdige, *Subculture: The Meaning of Style* (London: Routledge, 1981).
44. See Seo-Young Chu for an analysis of the way in which Gibson uses the metaphor of the urban space to construct his vision of "cyberspace-as-Internet" (138–9).
45. Samuel R. Delany, *Trouble on Triton: An Ambiguous Heterotopia*, foreword by Kathy Acker (Hanover, NH: Wesleyan University Press, 1996), 8.
46. Delany's most extended meditation on this sort of space is in his opus, *Dhalgren*, set in a post-catastrophe, isolated city called Bellona, which exists in the geographic centre of the United States. See my paper on *Dhalgren* and Gibson's *Pattern Recognition* for a more thorough discussion.
47. Michel Foucault, "Of Other Spaces," *Diacritics* 16, no.1 (1986): 24; emphasis added.
48. Foucault, "Of Other," 24.
49. Jacques Rancière, *The Politics of Aesthetics: The Distribution of the Sensible*, translated by Gabriel Rockhill (New York: Continuum, 2004), 45.
50. Michel Foucault, *History of Sexuality*, vol. 1, translated by Robert Hurley (1978, New York: Vintage, 1990), 96.
51. Gibson, *Virtual*, 298.
52. Morrison, 38; 37.
53. Terence Whalen, "The Future of a Commodity: Notes Toward a Critique of Cyberpunk and the Information Age," *Science Fiction Studies* 19, no.1 (1992): 85–86.
54. Morrison, 38.
55. William, Gibson, "My Obsession," *Wired* 7, no.1 (Jan. 1999), http://archive.wired.com/wired/archive/7.01/ebay.html, accessed 19 January 2015.
56. Gibson, "My Obsession."

REFERENCES

Brigg, Peter. "Frank Herbert: On Getting Our Heads Together." *Mosaic* 13, no.3–4 (1980): 193–202.

Carr, Leslie G. *"Color-Blind" Racism*. London: Sage, 1997.

Chu, Seo-Young. *Do Metaphors Dream of Literal Sheep: A Science-Fictional Theory of Representation*. Cambridge, MA: Harvard University Press, 2010.

Delany, Samuel R. *The Bridge of Lost Desire*. New York: Arbor House, 1987. Revised and reprinted as *Return to Nevèrÿon*. Hanover, NH: Wesleyan University Press, 1994.

———. *Trouble on Triton: An Ambiguous Heterotopia*. Foreword by Kathy Acker. Hanover, NH: Wesleyan University Press, 1996.

Eliot, T. S. *Collected Poems 1909–1962*. 1963. New York: Harcourt, 1991.

Fair Housing Act. Sec. 800. 42 U.S.C. 3601 et seq. *United States Department of Justice*. U.S. Dept. of Justice. n.d., accessed 9 October 2014, http://www.justice.gov/crt/about/hce/title8.php/.

Farnell, Ross. "Posthuman Topologies: William Gibson's 'Architexture' in *Virtual Light* and *Idoru*." *Science Fiction Studies* 25, no.3 (1998): 459–80.

Foucault, Michel. *History of Sexuality*, vol. 1: An Introduction. Translated by Robert Hurley. 1978. New York: Vintage, 1990.

———. "Of Other Spaces." *Diacritics* 16, no.1 (1986): 22–27.

Gable, Harvey L., Jr. "*Walden Two*, Postmodern Utopia, and the Problems of Power, Choice, and the Rule of Law." *Texas Studies in Literature and Language* 41, no.1 (1999): 1–15.

Gibson, William. *All Tomorrow's Parties*. New York: Ace, 2000.

———. *Idoru*. New York: Berkley, 1997.

———. "My Obsession," *Wired* 7, no.1 (Jan. 1999), http://archive.wired.com/wired/archive/7.01/ebay.html/. Accessed 19 January 2015.

———. *Neuromancer*. New York: Ace, 1984.

———. *Virtual Light*. New York: Bantam, 1994.

Haslam, Jason. "Memory's Guilted Cage: Delany's *Dhalgren* and Gibson's *Pattern Recognition*." *ESC* 32, no.1 (2006): 77–104.

Hawthorne, Nathaniel. "The Birth-mark." In *Mosses from an Old Manse*, 36–56. The Centenary Edition of the Works of Nathaniel Hawthorne 10. Columbus: Ohio State University Press, 1974.

———. *The Blithedale Romance*. Edited by Richard H. Millington. New York: Norton, 2010.

Hebdige, Dick. *Subculture: The Meaning of Style*. London: Routledge, 1981.

Herbert, Brian. *Dreamer of Dune: The Biography of Frank Herbert*. New York: Tor, 2003.

Herbert, Frank. *Dune*. 1965. New York: Berkley, 1977.

———. *God Emperor of Dune*. 1981. New York: Berkley, 1983.

———. *The Santaroga Barrier*. 1968. New York: Tor, 2002.

Huxley, Aldous. *Brave New World* and *Brave New World Revisited*. New York: HarperPerennial, 2004.

Invasion of the Body Snatchers. Dir. Don Siegel. 1956. Olive Films, 2012. Blu-ray.

Jaspers, Karl. "Letter to the Freiburg University Denazification Committee, December 22, 1945." In *The Heidegger Controversy: A Critical Reader*. Edited by Richard Wolin, 144–51. Cambridge, MA: MIT Press, 1993.

———. *Reason and Existenz: Five Lectures*. Translated by William Earle. N.p.: Noonday Press, 1955.

Kesey, Ken. *One Flew Over the Cuckoo's Nest*. 1962. London: Penguin, 2002.

Kuhlmann, Hilke. *Living* Walden Two*: B. F. Skinner's Behaviourist Utopia and Experimental Communities*. Urbana: University of Illinois Press, 2005.

Mannheim, Karl. *Ideology and Utopia: An Introduction to the Sociology of Knowledge*. Translated by Louis Wirth and Edward Shils. 1936. San Diego: Harvest, 2001.

More, Thomas. *Utopia*. Edited by George M. Logan and Robert M. Adams. Translated by Robert M. Adams. Rev. edited by Cambridge: Cambridge University Press, 2002.

Morrison, Toni. *Playing in the Dark: Whiteness and the Literary Imagination*. New York: Vintage, 1990.

Murphy, Graham. "Post/Humanity and the Interstitial: A Glorification of Possibility in Gibson's Bridge Sequence." *Science Fiction Studies* 30, no.1 (2003): 72–90.

Nixon, Nicola. "Cyberpunk: Preparing the Ground for Revolution or Keeping the Boys Satisfied?" *Science Fiction Studies* 19, no.2 (1992): 219–35.

O'Reilly, Tim. *Frank Herbert*. N.p.: Frederick Ungar Publishing, 1981, http://www.oreilly.com/tim/herbert/. Accessed 19 January 2015.

Piaget, Jean. *The Moral Judgment of the Child*. Translated by Marjorie Gabain. 1932. Oxon: Routledge, 2002.

Rancière, Jacques. *The Politics of Aesthetics: The Distribution of the Sensible*. Translated by Gabriel Rockhill. New York: Continuum, 2004.

Roediger, David. *The Wages of Whiteness: Race and the Making of the American Working Class*. New York: Verso, 1991.

Roemer, Kenneth M. *Utopian Audiences: How Readers Locate Nowhere*. Amherst: University of Massachusetts Press, 2003.

Skinner, B. F. *Walden Two*. 1948. Indianapolis: Hackett, 2005.

Smith, Sidonie. *Subjectivity, Identity, and the Body: Women's Autobiographical Practices in the Twentieth Century*. Bloomington: Indiana University Press, 1993.

Stockton, Sharon. "'The Self-Regained': Cyberpunk's Retreat to the Imperium." *Contemporary Literature* 36, no.4 (1995): 588–612.

Stover, Leon E. "Is Jaspers Beer Good For You?" *Extrapolation* 17 (1976): 160–67.

Thoreau, Henry David. "Resistance to Civil Government." In *Reform Papers*. Edited by Wendell Glick, 63–90. Writings of Henry D. Thoreau. Princeton: Princeton University Press, 1973.

———. *Walden*. Edited by J. Lyndon Shanley. Writings of Henry D. Thoreau. Princeton: Princeton University Press, 1971.

Thrall, James H. "Love, Loss, and Utopian Community on William Gibson's Bridge." *Foundation* 91 (2004): 97–115.

Touponce, William F. *Frank Herbert*. Boston: Twayne, 1988.

Village of the Damned. Dir. Wolf Rilla. 1960. *Village of the Damned/Children of the Damned*. Warner, 2004. DVD.

Whalen, Terence. "The Future of a Commodity: Notes Toward a Critique of Cyberpunk and the Information Age." *Science Fiction Studies* 19, no.1 (1992): 75–88.

Williams, Raymond. *Marxism and Literature*. Oxford: Oxford University Press, 1977.

6 Octavia Butler's Exceptional Minds, Collective Identities, and The Moynihan Report

Given the tie that we have seen already between the spatial and racial politics of the utopian tradition and the practices of the nation from the nineteenth century forward, it should not be surprising to see contemporary SF writers exploiting that same tradition in order to critique the ease with which U.S. national and larger Western politics slides into utopian, pseudo-eugenicist practices.[1] As *Mizora* and other works demonstrate, many early utopias are figured as solutions to what can generically be called the "race" and "gender" problems of the West. Lane's text and Charlotte Perkins Gilman's *Herland*, for example, project separatist feminist societies that are also racist, that have bred out or violently "eliminated" non-white men and women. There have been, of course, disturbing and very much extant echoes of these fictional non-places throughout U.S. history, most obviously, in the postbellum period, in the histories of segregation and lynching, up to the present-day segregation of gated communities, surrounded by preserves of labour.[2] More specifically, there have been continued attempts to further eugenicist practices as a part of national or state policy: June Dwyer, for example, traces "the role that the burgeoning eugenics movement in the United States played in the production of [immigration] laws."[3]

Octavia E. Butler, in her early and critically underdiscussed Patternist series, and especially in the second novel, *Mind of My Mind*, updates this genre by creating a genealogy of power and knowledge in which earlier conceptions of race and nation meet a contemporary globalised consumer economy. In the series, race, gender, class, and other identity categories, in their various manifestations, become part of a human network of power relations, but it is a network in which the humans are designed to be continually consumed. Moreover, just as Herbert's novel can be read as thematizing a reactionary response to the 1968 Civil Rights Act, *Mind of My Mind* specifically addresses the role of the African American community within the nation in terms that respond precisely to the infamous 1965 Moynihan Report.[4] Revising current critical consensus on the Patternist series, I will argue here that, in *Mind of My Mind* and the series in general, even a post-Foucauldian understanding of the networked dynamics of power is shown to be vulnerable to the utopia, the no-space, the "final frontier," the glaring void of the "city upon a hill."

The few critics who have focused on this series tend to see, in the pattern itself, a progressive, poststructuralist, and/or mobile notion of power; to quote Hazel Carby, "the pattern is a fictional device for theorizing the construction of social relations, communal solidarities, and loyalties. It is only within the parameters of the pattern, for example, that a multi-racial, inter-racial, and multi-ethnic community is represented."[5] While Carby does recognise that these social relations are "fraught with struggles over power and control," she, as most of the few critics of these novels do, shunts the blunter aspects of "control" to the side to celebrate the complex networking of power relations that Butler creates.[6] Possibly the first analysis of the representation of power in the Patternist series, by Janice Bogstad, does deal more explicitly with the issue of directly repressive control, stating that *Patternmaster*, specifically, "exposes us to the ultimate result of putting absolute power in the hands of a few individuals,"[7] but likewise notes that the later text, *Survivor*, "is more about the establishment of a power equilibrium."[8] My aim here is not to read against such analyses, but rather to add to them a discussion of the layer of complexity that is created by Butler's willingness to explore the limit cases of "power and control," where negotiation ends and absolute subjugation begins. Following a brief overview of the series, I will argue that *Mind of My Mind* exposes the way in which such limit cases are encoded even in arguably liberal, progressive assumptions lying behind such political exercises as the Moynihan Report. Through her pattern, Butler's series, and in particular *Mind of My Mind*, deftly portrays the ways in which attempts to create an even seemingly progressive utopian society, one beyond race, gender, and class oppressions, end up replicating those structures due to the absolutist underpinnings of utopian and exceptionalist politics.[9]

I. PATTERN FORMATION

The Patternist series consists of five novels, including Butler's first published novel, *Patternmaster*, from 1976. Ending with *Clay's Ark*, published in 1984, this series was not published as a traditional, chronological series. The first novel is actually set the furthest into the future, while the second, *Mind of My Mind*, is set in modern-day America. The fourth, *Wild Seed*, is set roughly from the sixteenth or seventeenth century through to the eighteenth (and thus is set, importantly, during the rise and solidification of the Atlantic slave trade). The other two novels are set between these periods, and include one, *Survivor*, which Butler refused to have republished during her lifetime: she described the novel in an interview, stating, "Some humans go up to another world, and immediately begin mating with the aliens and having children with them. I think of it as my *Star Trek* novel."[10] The only other long work Butler wrote during this span was her most well-known and analysed text, *Kindred*, which some have read as part of the Patternist cycle, though Butler herself did not,[11] a fact that makes the general lack of scholarly interest in this series odd. This critical gap is all the more problematic because the Patternist series is her most extensive related series of works, and it sets up many of the formal and thematic elements of her later material (religious communities, breeding and eugenics programs, physical and mental mutation). Through these elements, furthermore, the series offers in many ways her most complex analysis of power, a topic that, as many critics have noted, would be addressed again and again in her work.

Wild Seed and *Mind of My Mind* give a rough history of the "Patternist world," up to the present day, a history which is then continued chronologically into a speculative future in *Clay's Ark*, *Survivor*, and the original *Patternmaster*. The storylines follow the results of a centuries-long breeding experiment started by a character named Doro, a mutant who has vampiric qualities: he is able to mentally leap from one body to another, taking complete control of the new body and erasing the identity of its original inhabitant. Doro "takes people," as it is described, both as a form of sustenance and for pleasure, but is seemingly immortal because of it. A Nubian born at some point during the height of ancient Egypt, Doro's original body died sometime before what is described as an Egyptian imperial raid. As he transports his consciousness through countless bodies, Doro begins to realise that some people "taste" better than others, and realises that such morsels are in fact telepaths, or latent telepaths, and so he begins his breeding program in order to "farm" these people, and along the way forms communities which he also protects from the outside world. His program eventually results in the creation of Mary, the central protagonist of *Mind of My Mind* and mother of a new "Patternist" group of telepaths. Mary is described as a more complete Doro, what he would have become if he "hadn't died that first time—died before [he] was fully formed."[12] Rather than switch bodies, and "kill" telepaths as she takes them, instead Mary's mind becomes the central node in a vast "pattern" of telepaths, all of them linked through her. Before this, telepaths were socially incompatible and could not live too close to each other, but the pattern both forces them together and adds to their individual mental stability. Mary calls telepaths from around the country and also helps to bring more "latents" through their transition to become complete members of what she starts to call "a Patternist society" (150). As we see Doro thinking, Mary "was some sort of mental queen bee, gathering her workers to her instead of giving birth to them" (149).

Mind of My Mind begins with Doro visiting Mary and her mother Rina, to check up on his stock, so to speak. Rina, we are told in the opening line of the novel,

> had become a prostitute. … Sometime during [Doro's] eighteen-month absence, she had moved from the house he had bought her—an expensive house in a good neighbourhood. And though he had made arrangements with a Forsyth bank for her to receive a liberal monthly allowance, she still needed the men. And the liquor. He was

> not surprised. By the time he knocked at her door, the main thing he wanted to do was see whether his daughter was all right. ... The child was asleep, her breathing softly even. Doro turned on a light and looked at her more closely. She was three years old now, small and thin, not especially healthy-looking. Her nose was running. (1–2)

Doro then discovers that Rina has been allowing her clients to beat Mary. This opening section of the novel, focalised through Doro, thus repeats dominant portrayals of a crime- and disease-ridden ghetto, populated by a seemingly permanent underclass that, despite "a *liberal* monthly allowance," continually sinks into abjection. Written in the years following the controversy sparked by the 1965 Moynihan Report, this representation of urban American poverty bears a special resonance.[13] Indeed, Doro repeats the most controversial of Moynihan's claims by blaming Rina's situation on his own absence. The most often lambasted section of Moynihan's Report is that which seems to blame the dominance of black women within family structures for the poverty among urban African American families, a "symptom of liberal insensitivities," as James Berger writes, that overshadowed the Report's "endorsement of major investments in employment, housing, and health-care programs."[14] One of the more logically challenged portions of the Moynihan Report reads:

> In essence, the Negro community has been forced into a matriarchal structure which, because it is to [sic] out of line with the rest of the American society, seriously retards the progress of the group as a whole, and imposes a crushing burden on the Negro male and, in consequence, on a great many Negro women as well.
>
> There is, presumably, no special reason why a society in which males are dominant in family relationships is to be preferred to a matriarchal arrangement. However, it is clearly a disadvantage for a minority group to be operating on one principle, while the great majority of the population, and the one with the most advantages to begin with, is operating on another. This is the present situation of the Negro. Ours is a society which presumes male leadership in private and public affairs. The arrangements of society facilitate such leadership and reward it. A subculture, such as that of the Negro American, in which this is not the *pattern*, is placed at a distinct disadvantage.[15]

Just as being a single mother, for Moynihan, places a "crushing burden" on absentee fathers first, and the mothers only secondarily and less consistently, Doro too feels the "burden" of his lack of connection to his wife and child—or, more properly, wives and children. Starting with the second sentence of the novel, the reader is told, "Doro had left her alone for eighteen months. Too long. For the sake of the daughter she had borne him, he should have visited more often" (1). Doro's absence, represented here as the absence of male sexuality and dominance in the household ("the daughter she had borne *him*"), lies at the heart of Rina's self-destructive and abusive behaviour. Even though Doro provides financially for her, his absence alone is, in his mind, enough to make her abandon her "expensive house in a good neighborhood."

Indeed, the larger representation of contemporary America in the novel seems, at first, to follow this and others of the more problematic assertions in the Moynihan Report. While the foundations of Doro's new "society" are portrayed as coming from the underclasses, and as being rife with drug and alcohol abuse, violence, and poverty, Doro's burgeoning "subculture" (to echo the Moynihan Report) does have more "stable" telepaths living throughout the country. While there are some variations in their economic background, race, and gender, all of these figures exercise power through traditional social apparatuses—including business, family, politics, and religion—and the larger portion of them explicitly support patriarchal and/or racist social structures.[16] Moreover, the most powerful telepath among Doro's "family" explicitly follows Moynihan's portrayal of patriarchal, white households as being the most socially and economically "successful." For Moynihan, whereas (as one section heading puts it) "The Breakdown of the Negro Family Has Led to a Startling Increase in Welfare Dependency," conversely "The white family has achieved a high degree of stability and is maintaining that stability."[17] More specifically, the Moynihan Report reads, under the heading "The Failure of Youth," in the chapter, "The Tangle of Pathology":

> The white family, despite many variants, remains a powerful agency not only for transmitting property from one generation to the next, but also for transmitting no less valuable contracts with the world of education and work. In an earlier age, the Carpenters, Wainwrights, Weavers, Mercers, Farmers, Smiths acquired their names as well as their trades from their fathers and grandfathers. Children today still learn the *patterns* of work from their fathers even though they may no longer go into the same jobs.
>
> White children without fathers at least perceive all about them the *pattern* of men working.
>
> Negro children without fathers flounder—and fail.[18]

(The last two sentences, isolated and offset as paragraphs of their own, are, admittedly, followed by the sentence "Not always, to be sure," though that modification is closely followed by a sentence beginning, "But.") In these passages, white families are defined not only in terms of their patrilineal heritage, but also by their roles as producers within jobs that form the economic base and foundation of civilisation (carpenters, farmers, smiths, and so on). The logic of Moynihan's argument is blunt: in properly functioning societies, fathers transmit culturally and socially productive models of behaviour to their children, and this model of social generation is, for Moynihan, a "whites only"—or "to be sure," a "whites mostly"—club. More significantly, though, Moynihan presents this familial and social structure as a rigid model, yes, but one that can expand its scope: "Children today still learn the *patterns* of work from their fathers even though they may no longer go into the same jobs." Moynihan's white family is successful and evolving; his black family is a floundering, failing, one.

Butler's novel seems at first to follow this portrayal of the successful, patriarchal, and white family—perhaps I should write, instead, "successful *because* patriarchal and white family"—in contradistinction to the floundering and failing underclass in the novel. Doro's most stable telepath is Karl, the most powerful of the group that Doro calls his "actives," a term which could be read as being tied not just to agency, but also to productivity. The novel is told through the perspectives of all of these actives, along with Mary, Doro, and Emma (another immortal character), each being given separate sections throughout the text. Each section is largely focalised through a separate central "active," though Mary is the only character who narrates in the first person.[19]

We see Karl and his surroundings first as focalised through Doro, in a description that should be paired to that of Rina's broken down house (one given in the first lines of Doro's opening section, the other in the opening passages of his second):

> Actives were nearly always troublesome, Doro thought as he drove his car down Karl Larkin's long driveway. He already knew that Karl was not in his house, that he was somewhere in the back yard, probably in the pool. … Karl was in the pool. Doro could see him across a parklike expanse of grass and trees. Before Doro could reach him, though, the gardener, who had been mowing the lawn, drove up to Doro on his riding mower. (28–29)

Karl's "parklike expanse" of a mansion, sequestered behind enough land to need a "long driveway," and its various material amenities, obviously stands opposed to Rina and Mary's surroundings, highlighting his relative social standing and success. This passage occurs, additionally, just as Doro arranges for Karl and Mary to be married. Karl is supposed to help Mary through what Doro calls her "transition" into a full "active," something which occurs in adolescence. Significantly, Karl's success is quite explicitly tied to his control over his subordinates, and over a woman (and, over time, women) who occupies the role of common-law wife before Mary appears:

> Karl owned his servants more thoroughly than even Doro usually owned people. Karl owned their minds. They were just ordinary people who had answered an ad in the Los Angeles *Times*. Karl did no entertaining—was almost a hermit except for the succession of women whom he lured in and kept until they bored him. The servants existed

> more to look after the house and grounds than to look after Karl himself. Still, he had chosen them less for their professional competence than for the fact that they had few if any living relatives. Few people to be pacified if he accidentally got too rough with them. He would not have hurt them deliberately. He had conditioned them, programmed them carefully to do their work and obey him in every way. He had programmed them to be content with their jobs. He even paid them well. But his power made him dangerous to ordinary people—especially to those who worked near him every day. In an instant of uncontrolled anger, he could have killed them all. (29)

Karl's success is evidenced not just by his material wealth, but by his complete, allegorically ideological control over others (a control that can turn to violence in a moment because "power [is] dangerous to ordinary people" who cannot exercise any power of their own). Setting the (potential for) violence aside for a moment, the description of Karl demonstrates, as in the Moynihan Report, that social and cultural success begins and ends with the supposedly necessary, sovereign male figure, embodied by Karl, but ultimately "disembodied" as a concept through the figure of Doro.[20]

In fact, the novel seems even to go beyond the Moynihan Report in terms of its support for the necessity of dominant institutions for the stability of society—other actives, both men and women, white (predominantly) but also black, exploit arenas ranging from evangelical church meetings, small-town politics, and, again, even more aggressive forms of sexism and racism to maintain what they see as stable communities around them. The novel thus seems, at first, to run the gamut of ideological apparatuses in order to naturalise the status quo represented or constructed in the Moynihan Report and elsewhere.[21] Even Mary seems to recognise this stability; she thinks that once she has married Karl and passed transition (and is thus safely ensconced within a patriarchal white household), "Then maybe for a change I'd be one of the owners instead of one of the owned" (42). Thus, marriage, adulthood, activity, whiteness, a patriarchal family structure, and ideological and repressive subjection of others all tie in together to create what will become a stable and productive social structure: this is, in many ways, the same conservative "utopia" designed in that other gated community, Santaroga.

II. DEGRADING PATTERNS

Unsurprisingly, though, Butler creates this oppressive stability only to critique it, explicitly undermining the notion that it is the integrally intermingled patriarchal whiteness of the dominant culture that creates a social stability. As evidenced by Karl's potential for and history of violence, Butler implies in *Mind of My Mind*—but highlights in *Wild Seed*—the fact that this stability only exists because of the history of explicit, violent oppression, including the history of slavery. Thus, Butler foregrounds racial and sexual oppression as ever-present and continually reproduced causes of the apparent stability of the white family. The Moynihan Report does similarly discuss slavery as a particular cause of the economic racial inequality in America, but effectively constructs it as a secondary cause, leading to the "real" problem of the black matriarchy; all of these problems, in turn, can only be solved by the white power structure. Seemingly combating and reversing this perspective, Butler's novels instead focus on the fact that Doro—the disembodied idea of the sovereign and therefore endlessly mobile subject—strives to maintain a certain inequality as part of his attempt to create what is continually referred to as his "empire." Mary states:

> Doro wanted an empire. He didn't call it that, but that was what he meant. Maybe I was just one more tool he was using to get it. He needed tools, because an empire of ordinary people wasn't quite what he had in mind. That, to him, would be like an ordinary person making himself emperor over a lot of cattle. Doro thought a lot of himself, all right. But he didn't think much of the families of half-crazy latents he had scattered across the country. They were just his breeders—if they were lucky. He didn't want an empire of them either. (*Mind* 86)

Doro is thus set up as the ultimate sovereign subject, lord over not just "ordinary" people, but over the subjects who are themselves exceptional, who in turn rule (supposedly ethically) many of the ordinary subjects in their lives, thus making this empire—like Santaroga or Buck Rogers' "gangs"—a stand-in for an exceptionalist America. Indeed, Karl's house, and specifically his "fantastic library," is described on one occasion in terms that resonate with imperial behaviour, since "Most of the floor was covered by the biggest oriental rug [Mary] had ever seen" (35). The definition of Doro's empire of empires is detailed in a conversation with Mary. He says that he began his breeding project when he realised that certain people's minds "tasted best" when he took them (90). Mary replies to this statement, saying:

> "But we're not still just food, are we?"
>
> [Doro replies:] "Some of my latents are. But my actives and potential actives are part of another project. They have been for some time."
>
> "What project?"
>
> "To build a people, a race."
>
> So that was it. I thought about it for a moment. "A race for you to be part of?" I asked. "Or a race for you to own?"
>
> He smiled. "That's a good question. [... T]o get an active, I have to bring together people of two different latent families–people who repel each other so strongly that I have to take one of them to bring them together. That means all the actives of each generation are my children. So maybe the answer is ... a little of both." (90–91)

Doro is an ideal consumer who is both part of a "race," "nation," or "empire" (those terms being as confused and intertwined for Doro as they were for Burroughs) and its predator. This depiction of Doro highlights the ways in which a hyper-extended consumerism and an exceptionalist definition of nation both necessarily bring with them a permanent underclass—without which the empire would collapse—both feeding and being destroyed by those in the dominant position, and who themselves also work to maintain and expand the people/nation/empire itself. The history of racism that lurks in the background of the Moynihan Report is here revealed. The economic and other oppressions of the African American population are not indirect results of an amorphous history of externally applied oppression that leads to an internal communal "pathology," which in turn can be "corrected" only by the dominant culture, as Moynihan would have it, but is rather a direct and continuous requirement of the continued stability of white, upper-class dominance. Butler thus exposes the liberal evasions of the Moynihan Report and the logic that undergirds it.

III. PATTERN REFLECTIONS

But, *Mind of My Mind* and the other Patternist novels go beyond this simple critique. The Moynihan Report, as the quotations I've used suggest, emphasises what it sees as a pathological "pattern" (a word used almost two dozen times in the Report) within black communities. The passage above, however, also highlights Doro's—the ultimate consumer's and ruler's—absolute reliance on reproducing the "latency" and abjection of an underclass in order to "activate" his own racial, national, and imperial goals. Butler, however, shows that the white and patriarchal social pattern, *because* it relies on the maintenance of certain other patterns, is itself pathological.[22] And, because of its reliance on its necessary abjected other, this dominant pattern can actually be overtaken or rewritten into a dominant black matriarchal society.

After Mary goes through transition—which she can only do with the help of Karl—it becomes obvious that she is different from all of Doro's previous "actives." Mary's mind reaches out and takes hold of all of the other actives, rendering them incapacitated for a brief time and then forcing them physically to go to her, no matter where they are when it happens. Mary reflects on the occurrence:

> I couldn't have said what I was doing. I knew Karl was still with me. His mental voice was still reaching me. I didn't mean to grab him the way I did. I didn't realize until afterward that I had done it. And even then, it seemed a perfectly natural thing to do. It was what I had done to the others. Others, yes. Five of them. They seemed to be far away from me, perhaps scattered around the country. Actives like Karl, like me. …

> Their thoughts told me what they were, but I became aware of them—"saw" them—as bright points of light, like stars. They formed a shifting pattern of light and color. I had brought them together somehow. Now I was holding them together—and they didn't want to be held. (54)

Mary becomes the centre of this new social pattern, a union of violently disparate people who had never before been brought together, including a leader of a religious community, who siphons strength from her congregation even as she psychokinetically heals them; a virulently racist white woman who does not like being a telepath, but especially does not like being vulnerable to the thoughts of black people, what she calls "*that* alienness" (80); a man who completely mentally controls the inhabitants of a small town, recreating a feudal relationship complete with an ongoing and constantly enacted *droit de seigneur*; and two other, less violent individuals. They all initially resist Mary's control, which she seemingly cannot break herself, but soon they begin to recognise benefits. All of them gain more control over their abilities, and latents, who otherwise could not go through transition and were doomed to miserable lives of near insanity, are brought through and also achieve a mastery of their abilities.

Much like Delany or Gibson's heterotopias, which present groups that exist in multiple relations with the dominant culture—not simply dominated nor resistant—this new social pattern, or, in Mary's words, "Patternist society" (150), could be read alongside of Judith Butler's argument that "agency begins where sovereignty wanes. The one who acts (who is not the same as the sovereign subject) acts precisely to the extent that he or she is constituted as an actor and, hence, operating within a linguistic field of enabling constraints from the outset."[23] The constrained subject seems to become in itself (so to speak) a fundamentally freeing concept. Elaborating on a Lacanian sense of the self as split subject, Judith Butler writes that "The rift in the subject is paradoxically its capacity to move beyond itself, a movement that does not return to where it always was, identity as movement in the promising sense."[24] The new Patternists seem to lose their absolute, individualist sovereignty, but at the same time gain new forms of power and authority within a communal structure. Doro watches one of the new Patternists, Seth, who had "accepted Mary's authority as, years before, he had accepted Doro's. Now he watched to see how she handled it. He seemed surprised when, days later, she gave him charge of her cousin Jamie, but he accepted the responsibility. After that, he seemed to relax a little" (144–5). Personal responsibility and self-negation work together in a seemingly ethical fashion. As Mary says to Karl near the end of the novel, invoking the gothic to describe the horror of Doro's imperial sovereignty, "I'm not the vampire [Doro] is. I give in return for my taking. … God, I've got ethics all of a sudden." Karl replies, "You've had them for some time, now, whether you were willing to admit to them or not" (206). Mary, in turn, at the centre of the network, appears to her Patternist subjects as less a sovereign than a purely representative leader, who holds authority solely due to the fact that she *must*, constantly, "draw on" the "experiences" of others in order to exist (144). This community, led by a black matriarch, becomes a group based on an exchange of power across a network, where each subject seems to be fully aware of the benefits and losses, the checks and balances, of that network. The very communal "pattern" damned by Moynihan—what he calls "The matriarchal pattern of so many Negro families [which] reinforces itself over the generations" (Chapter 4)—is represented as a success. Indeed, this success is arguably shown through the Patternists' use of the traditional discourse and structures of U.S. society. The original group of actives Mary pulls in form the "First Family," and they then become a town, complete with a Patternist school, a form of Patternist policing, control of the local government, and so on, mounting a silent and silencing coup after which the Patternists control all of the ideological and repressive apparatuses of their community. And, at the end of the novel, when Doro attempts to kill Mary because the two of them have become, in her words, "competitors" (192), the entire community lends its mental strength to Mary, allowing her to encapsulate Doro's identity within the pattern and kill him. Doro, thinking that power still functions in a top-down fashion, thinks he is simply "delegating authority to [Mary]" (95), that "final authority still rested" with him (187), and so he cannot properly negotiate the system of agential exchanges that the pattern represents.

IV. MUTED PATTERN

Despite this reliance on traditional discursive constructions of nation as the pattern is formed, the novel seems to suggest that this community has finally found a more ethical form of power distribution, a recognition of the complex interactions of power within a multiracial, gender equitable social system, echoing the intersectional politics of postmodern and poststructuralist feminist, queer, and anti-racist politics. Like Donna Haraway's cyborg feminists, the Patternists exercise a networked power, in which no one position seems to take control.[25] The Patternists seem to recognise that power does come from beneath (the latents and actives, such as Rina, who represent the underclass of traditional America), and that difference should be lauded and embraced rather than silenced and shunned. Indeed, as mentioned above, this is how many critics read the portrayal of power here and elsewhere in Butler's oeuvre.[26] Meanwhile, the supposedly "pathological" matriarchy of the Moynihan Report becomes the central device for social success.

However, in keeping with many of Butler's other works—which very rarely offer an easy (or at ease) reversal or even flattening of an oppressive binary—in order to maintain this reading of a utopic, postmodern community of power-in-play for *Mind of My Mind*, one must ignore the oppression that lies at its foundation: the exploitation of the "mutes," the normal humans mentally conditioned and controlled by the Patternists, just as Karl earlier controls his servants. At that earlier point, Mary recognises that these people are nothing more than the stereotypical "silent, contented slaves" who "worked, or ... sat in their quarters watching television and waiting for the master's voice" (39). After she begins to build her own version of "empire" (138), after she accepts her "proprietary ... feelings toward" the other Patternists (55), she also silently adjusts her distaste with the enslaving of the "mutes." A discussion between Doro and Emma, another immortal, also born in Africa, and the only character who manages to remain outside of the Patternist society,[27] highlights this new oppressive relationship. Doro tells her that the Patternists have

> "completely taken over the best section of town. They did it quietly, but still Mary thought it safest for them to control key mutes in city hall, in the police department, in—"
>
> [Emma exclaims] "Mutes!"
>
> He looked annoyed, probably with himself. "It's a convenient term. People without telepathic voices. Ordinary people."
>
> "I know what it means, Doro. I knew the first time I heard Mary use it. It means niggers! ... I tell you, you're out of control, Doro. You're not one of them. You're not a telepath. And if you don't think they look down on us non-telepaths, us niggers, the whole rest of humanity, you're not paying attention." (155)

Just as the revolutionary democracy that was the American republic managed to ignore the ontological paradox and material brutality of slavery at its foundation, so too must this seemingly exceptional utopian group ignore its exploitation of the mutes. Lewis Call focuses on this passage as well, noting the "non-consensual" slavery that mutes are subject to, but instead of dealing with the normal "mute" of the average human being, he instead focuses on Doro, the non-telepathic but still sovereign imperial figure. Thus, following the traditional critical line, Call argues that the Patternist series "reappropriate[s] slavery, and transform[s] it from an ethical abomination into something beautiful," comparing it to the erotic forms of BDSM in Delany's Nevèrÿon works.[28] Peter Sands likewise states that critics have noted "the ironic reversals of slavery and eugenics ... in the *Patternist* series," though he notes in passing that the "normals" are "doomed to slavery."[29] In fact, the clear inversion of "mute"—from an epithetical shortening of "mutant" to a slur about "normal" people—indicates just such an inversion. When reading the text as actually being about the silenced voices of the normal "mutes," however, these "ironic reversals" invert and become old-fashioned duplications; as Bogstad writes, "non-psionics are essentially slaves with no escape alternative."[30] From an equitable because constantly shifting and self-aware network of power relations, the pattern becomes a perfected global consumer culture, complete with the economic and other oppressions implied thereby. Mary may not be a simple gothic "vampire" to her Patternists, but as a group they have revivified the material horror of American slavery, lashing their power to the mutes' exploitation. The Patternist "First Family" thus replicates on another body the very inequities they suffered at the hands of the actual "First Families" of the U.S. political structure.

This futurist utopia, then, is reined in by its own history no less than are the Mizorans, Tarzan, or the Santarogans. Its complex power structure is limited by the metaphors its members use to describe it, both those of empire and of traditional America, and by the material actions used to create and maintain it: slavery, combined as always with mental or ideological conditioning. And, indeed, Butler has stated that *Mind of My Mind* is "about slavery."[31] The novel, and the series, becomes a warning that any form of utopianism in politics, no matter its motivation, will end in the replication of traditional biases, especially as those politics are used to bolster an unchecked consumerism in the dominant culture. Butler thus could be exploiting what Delany argues about SF, and indeed about all "narrative fiction," that perhaps it cannot

> propose the *radically* successful metaphor. At best, what both modes can do is break up, analyze, and dialogize the conservative, the historically sedimented, letting the fragments argue with one another, letting each display its own obsolescence, suggesting (not stating) where still another retains the possibility of vivid, radical development. But responding to those suggestions is, of course, the job of the radical reader. (The 'radical metaphor' is, after all, only an interpretation of preextant words.)[32]

The slippery semiotics of SF—metafictionally represented in the pattern—revert to reproductions of the status quo. Butler remains, then, among those unique SF writers who use the genre reflexively to comment on this conservative sediment, this repetitive radicalism, always forcing the reader, as Elyce Rae Helford argues of "Bloodchild," into an "uncomfortable, compromised" critical position (271). Placing imperial, racist, and seemingly progressive structures into dialogue within an SF frame, Butler can completely undercut the biased assumptions of the Moynihan Report, while also pointing to the racial, economic, and sexual disparities of solutions that rely centrally on increasing the consumer abilities of the economic underclasses. As Katrine Dalsgård argues of Toni Morrison's *Paradise*, Butler's "deconstruction of … exceptionalism" likewise "figures as a warning that the mechanisms of violence and marginalization are also at work in counter-discursive national historical narratives" (246). Expanding on the logic of Herbert's novel, and exposing the politics of Lane's, *Mind of My Mind* argues that all utopian solutions, even those that seem progressively self-aware, need their exceptions, that such final solutions always place someone at the bottom of the food pyramid, that transforming a ghetto into a gated community, like transforming a patriarchy into a matriarchy, is just moving places within the pattern.

Just as in the ending to the *Twilight Zone* episode analysed in the introduction, Butler is pointing to the ways in which even the most radical possibilities for transformation can slip back to the mundane. But what of those SF predictions of the coming of something new? What of the possibilities it promises? The concluding afterword to this book returns to these questions and attempts to answer them through the figure of the robot and its encoding of what Lee Edelman has called the radical alterity of the death drive.

NOTES

1. In addition to Octavia E. Butler's works, see, to take just a few of the many examples, Derrick Bell's famous "Space Traders," in which African Americans are traded to aliens, in a mimicry of the slave trade, and the 1997 film, *Gattaca*.
2. Laura Salvini details Butler's own reworking, in *Parable of the Sower*, of gated communities ("'Our Wall': Octavia E. Butler's *Parable of the Sower* and T. Coraghessan Boyle's The *Tortilla Curtain*," in *America Today: Highways and Labyrinths*, edited by Gigliola Nocera, proceedings of the XV biennial Conference Siracusa, November 4–7, 1999 [Siracusa, Italy: Grafià, 2003], 264–72).
3. June Dwyer, "Disease, Deformity, and Defiance: Writing the Language of Immigration Law and the Eugenics Movement on the Immigrant Body," *MELUS* 28, no.1 (2003): 106.
4. The Moynihan Report is more properly titled, *The Negro Family: The Case for National Action*.
5. Hazel V. Carby, "Figuring the Future in Los(t) Angeles," *Comparative American Studies* 1, no.1 (2003): 27.
6. Carby, 27.
7. Carby, 28.
8. Carby, 29; also qtd. in Sandra Y. Govan, "Connections, Links, and Extended Networks: Patterns in Octavia Butler's Science Fiction," *Black American Literature Forum*, 18, no.2 (1984): 83. Bogstad also interviewed Butler for the same issue of *Janus* in which this short article appears and asked the author about the issue of "the heavy-handed control that is so much a part of" the early Patternist books, including *Mind of My Mind*: Butler responds: "what I really wanted to do was just take some people who were fairly ordinary and see what they did with [great power], and I really didn't see them being that gentle. I mean, they're not evil, they're just people" (Octavia E. Butler, "Butler Interviewed," Interview by Janice Bogstad, *Janus* 4, no.4 [1978/79]: 31). Sharon DeGraw very briefly touches on the Patternist series in the conclusion to her book, primarily as an indication of the ways in which contemporary SF authors are beginning to attend to "the body as a site of racial exploration," focusing on Doro's choice generally to present himself to Mary in a black host body as a "form of psychic essentialism ... with racial and sexual connotations" (*The Subject of Race in American Science Fiction* [London: Routledge, 2007], 177; 178). It is those connotations that, I argue, are precisely the primary focus of the series, and which form the kernel of Butler's complex analysis of power and the social structures of the late twentieth-century United States.

9. In this reading, I am following recent appraisals of American exceptionalism and its relation to utopian thought. Specifically, I am drawing on Katrine Dalsgård, who writes:

   > Among literary historians, however, there is fairly general consensus about the definition offered by Thomas B. Byers in his 1997 article "A City upon a Hill: American Literature and the Ideology of Exceptionalism": "American exceptionalism … is the claim that America is … unique, one of a (superior) kind—and generally that that kind carries with it a unique moral value and responsibility." From this perspective, American exceptionalism resounds the story of the small group of Puritan pilgrims who fled from persecution in England in the early seventeenth century in order to establish an exemplary Christian community—"a city upon a hill," as it was termed by their leader, John Winthrop—in the new world. ("The One All-Black Town Worth the Pain: [African] American Exceptionalism, Historical Narration, and the Critique of Nationhood in Toni Morrison's *Paradise*," *African American Review* 35, no.2 [2001]: 234.)

   This definition of exceptionalism, Dalsgård writes, continues "a general European desire for a *utopian* 'place that was not Europe but rather its opposite'—a desire that had preoccupied the European imagination even before the American continent was discovered" (234; emphasis added). The "unique … (superior) kind" of human that the Patternists represent, combined with their supposedly ethical subjugation of others can thus be read as an allegory for the strain of American thought that views the nation through a utopian, exceptionalist lens.
10. Octavia E. Butler, "Octavia E. Butler Plants an Earthseed," interview by Therese Littleton, *Amazon.com*, accessed October 12, 2014, http://www.amazon.com/gp/feature.html?ie=UTF8&docId=11664.
11. Govan, 87.
12. Octavia E. Butler, *Mind of My Mind* (1977. New York: Warner, 1994), 157. Unless otherwise noted, subsequent quotations will be from this edition and will be cited parenthetically.
13. While Rina and Mary, along with many other of Doro's latents are African American, it should be pointed out that Mary herself notes that they, along with the population of the inner city, are multiracial, which is why I tend to use the term "underclasses" throughout, to indicate the economic but also multiplicitous (including racial and gendered) social biases at work.
14. James Berger, "Ghosts of Liberalism: Morrison's *Beloved* and the *Moynihan Report*," *PMLA* 111, no.3 (1996): 412.
15. Office of Policy Planning and Research, United States Department of Labor, *The Negro Family: The Case for National Action* [The Moynihan Report], March 1965, Chapter IV, http://www.dol.gov/dol/aboutdol/history/webid-meynihan.htm (*sic*), accessed 20 January 2015; emphasis added.
16. As my wording suggests, there are exceptions to this general statement, but even in their exceptionality they still point to an exercise of unchecked power. The major exceptions are Rachel and Ada. Rachel is a black woman who works as a successful "travelling faith healer" (68); but even Rachel needs a male figure to work with and through—Eli, her "Cousin, business manager, lover, slave" (71)—thus at least publicly eschewing her own matriarchal role. Her healing

is also, to a certain degree, exploitative, in that she vampirically draws strength from her congregation. Ada, meanwhile, is herself abused by her husband, and yet we learn on her introduction that she had been using her mental powers to "force [him] to stay with her" (80), in complex reproduction of power and trauma. Seth Dana, meanwhile, may seem isolated and relatively kind, but even he decides to "fix" a woman for his brother, Clay (65).

17. Office, Chapter II.
18. Office, Chapter IV; emphasis added.
19. The original draft of *Mind of My Mind* was told completely from Mary's perspective, but Butler changed this after losing the manuscript (Butler, "Butler Interviewed," 31).
20. Doro's ability to retain a coherent sense of self despite his constant switching of bodies, his identity's essential disembodiment, can be read as a figuration of Enlightenment subjectivity itself, which Sidonie Smith reads as configured as a "discrete core, abstracted from society" and which "escapes all forms of embodiment" (*Subjectivity, Identity, and the Body: Women's Autobiographical Practices in the Twentieth Century* [Bloomington: Indiana University Press, 1993], 6). Significantly for the present argument, and as discussed in the introduction, Smith argues that this Enlightenment ontology contains an "implicit ... hierarchy wherein what is and is not," and who is and is not, "appropriate, at any given juncture, to the universal subject gets staked out" (Smith, 9–10).
21. On ideological and repressive apparatuses, see Louis Althusser, "Ideology and Ideological State Apparatuses (Notes Towards an Investigation)," in *Lenin and Philosophy and Other Essays*, trans. Ben Brewster (1971. New York: Monthly Review Press, 2001), 85–126.
22. The Moynihan Report does not actually define what it means by "pathology" in any specific sense, despite the centrality of the word itself to the report (especially in the metaphorical phrase, "tangle of pathology" which is the title of, and appears throughout, Chapter IV). The report seems to use pathology as an uncomplicated opposition to "social health" (which in turn seems to mean "normal" or, more accurately, "dominant" family structures).
23. Judith Butler, *Excitable Speech: A Politics of the Performative* (New York: Routledge, 1997), 16.
24. Judith Butler, "Collected and Fractured: Response to *Identities*," in *Identities*, edited by Kwame Anthony Appiah and Henry Louis Gates, Jr. (Chicago: University of Chicago Press, 1995), 447.
25. Donna Haraway, *Simians, Cyborgs, and Women: The Reinvention of Nature* (New York: Routledge, 1991).
26. In addition to the specific readings of the Patternist series by Call and Sands cited below, see Carby. Similarly, Frances Bonner writes of both the Patternist and Xenogenesis series that "Difference is not just a given that is accepted, it is something which is intensified, enhanced and valued, even if not unequivocally" ("Difference and Desire, Slavery and Seduction: Octavia Butler's *Xenogenesis*," *Foundation* 48 [1990]: 55), while Cathy Peppers references Butler's emphasis on "xenophilia in place of xenophobia" ("Dialogic Origins and Alien Identities in Butler's *Xenogenesis*," *Science Fiction Studies* 22, no.1 [1995]: 60). Jim Miller insists in reading the "world full of violence, degradation, and hate" in *Parable of the Sower* and "much of Butler's other work" as "the aporetic ideal of reciprocity" which presents "the face of hope in our post-utopian moment"

("Post-Apocalyptic Hoping: Octavia Butler's Dystopian/Utopian Vision," *Science Fiction Studies* 25, no.2 [1998]: 357–58).

27. Emma, also known as Anyanwu, is also the central figure, with Doro, of *Wild Seed*. Doro originally finds her in Africa and takes her to North America aboard a slave ship.
28. Lewis Call, "Structures of Desire: Erotic Power in the Speculative Fiction of Octavia Butler and Samuel Delany," *Rethinking History* 9, no.2/3 (2005): 285.
29. Peter Sands, "Octavia Butler's Chiastic Cannibalistics," *Utopian Studies* 14, no.1 (2003): 10, 5.
30. Bogstad, 28.
31. Stephen W. Potts, "'We Keep Playing the Same Record': A Conversation with Octavia E. Butler," *Science Fiction Studies* 23, no.3 (1996): 332.
32. Samuel R. Delany, *Flight from Nevèrÿon* (1985. Hanover: Wesleyan University Press, 1994), 348.

REFERENCES

Althusser, Louis. 2001. "Ideology and Ideological State Apparatuses (Notes Towards an Investigation)." In *Lenin and Philosophy and Other Essays*, translated by Ben Brewster, 85–126. New York: Monthly Review Press, 1971.

Bell, Derrick. "The Space Traders." In *Dark Matter: A Century of Speculative Fiction from the African Diaspora*, edited by Sheree R. Thomas, 326–55. New York: Time Warner, 2000.

Berger, James. "Ghosts of Liberalism: Morrison's *Beloved* and the *Moynihan Report*." *PMLA* 111, no.3 (1996): 408–20.

Bogstad, Janice. "Octavia E. Butler and Power Relationships." *Janus* 4, no.4 (1978/79): 28–29.

Bonner, Frances. "Difference and Desire, Slavery and Seduction: Octavia Butler's *Xenogenesis*." *Foundation* 48 (1990): 50–62.

Butler, Judith. "Collected and Fractured: Response to *Identities*." In *Identities*, edited by Kwame Anthony Appiah and Henry Louis Gates, Jr., 439–47. Chicago: University of Chicago Press, 1995.

———. *Excitable Speech: A Politics of the Performative*. New York: Routledge, 1997.

Butler, Octavia E. "Butler Interviewed." Interview by Janice Bogstad. *Janus* 4, no.4 (1978/1979): 29–31.

———. *Clay's Ark*. 1984. New York: Warner, 1996.

———. *Mind of My Mind*. 1977. New York: Warner, 1994.

———. "Octavia E. Butler Plants an Earthseed." Interview by Therese Littleton. *Amazon.com*, accessed October 12, 2014. http://www.amazon.com/gp/feature.html?ie=UTF8&docId=11664.

———. *Patternmaster*. 1976. New York: Warner, 1995.

———. "'Radio Imagination': Octavia Butler on the Poetics of Narrative Embodiment." Interview by Marilyn Mehaffy and AnaLouise Keating. *MELUS* 26, no.1 (2001): 45–76.

———. *Survivor*. New York: Doubleday, 1978.

———. *Wild Seed*. 1980. New York: Warner, 1999.

Call, Lewis. "Structures of Desire: Erotic Power in the Speculative Fiction of Octavia Butler and Samuel Delany." *Rethinking History* 9, no.2/3 (2005): 275–96.

Carby, Hazel V. "Figuring the Future in Los(t) Angeles." *Comparative American Studies* 1, no.1 (2003): 19–34.

Dalsgård, Katrine. "The One All-Black Town Worth the Pain: (African) American Exceptionalism, Historical Narration, and the Critique of Nationhood in Toni Morrison's *Paradise*." *African American Review* 35, no.2 (2001): 233–48.

DeGraw, Sharon. *The Subject of Race in American Science Fiction*. London: Routledge, 2007.

Delany, Samuel R. *Flight from Nevèrÿon*. 1985, Hanover: Wesleyan University Press, 1994.

Dwyer, June. "Disease, Deformity, and Defiance: Writing the Language of Immigration Law and the Eugenics Movement on the Immigrant Body." *MELUS* 28, no.1 (2003): 105–21.

Gattaca. Written and dir. Andrew Niccol. Columbia, 1997. DVD.

Gilman, Charlotte Perkins. *Herland and Related Writings*. Edited by Beth Sutton-Ramspeck. Peterborough, ON: Broadview, 2012.

Govan, Sandra Y. "Connections, Links, and Extended Networks: Patterns in Octavia Butler's Science Fiction." *Black American Literature Forum*, 18, no.2 (1984): 82–87.

Haraway, Donna. *Simians, Cyborgs, and Women: The Reinvention of Nature*. New York: Routledge, 1991.

Helford, Elyce Rae. "'Would You Really Rather Die than Bear My Young?': The Construction of Gender, Race, and Species in Octavia E. Butler's 'Bloodchild.'" *African American Review* 28, no.2 (1994): 259–71.

Lane, Mary E. Bradley. *Mizora: A Prophecy*. Edited by Jean Pfaelzer. New York: Syracuse University Press, 2000.

Miller, Jim. "Post-Apocalyptic Hoping: Octavia Butler's Dystopian/Utopian Vision." *Science Fiction Studies* 25, no.2 (1998): 336–60.

Office of Policy Planning and Research, United States Department of Labor. *The Negro Family: The Case for National Action* [The Moynihan Report]. March 1965, http://www.dol.gov/dol/aboutdol/history/webid-meynihan.htm, accessed 20 January 2015.

Peppers, Cathy. "Dialogic Origins and Alien Identities in Butler's *Xenogenesis*." *Science Fiction Studies* 22, no.1 (1995): 47–62.

Potts, Stephen W. "'We Keep Playing the Same Record': A Conversation with Octavia E. Butler." *Science Fiction Studies* 23, no.3 (1996): 331–38.

Salvini, Laura. "'Our Wall': Octavia E. Butler's *Parable of the Sower* and T. Coraghessan Boyle's *The Tortilla Curtain*." In *America Today: Highways and Labyrinths*, edited by Gigliola Nocera, 264–72. Proceedings of the XV Biennial Conference Siracusa, November 4–7, 1999. Siracusa, Italy: Grafià, 2003.

Sands, Peter. "Octavia Butler's Chiastic Cannibalistics." *Utopian Studies* 14, no.1 (2003): 1–14.

Smith, Sidonie. *Subjectivity, Identity, and the Body: Women's Autobiographical Practices in the Twentieth Century*. Bloomington: Indiana University Press, 1993.

Afterword

The Robot's Howl: SF as Death Drive

The overall argument that this book has made is that the analysis of race and gender in American SF can offer a way of reading the resistant and generative social possibilities of SF, and, in that argument's mirror image, that SF can offer new ways of analysing the intersections of gender, race, and other identity structures in American culture. The semiotic instability and plurality of SF, I argued in the introduction, give SF the linguistic and material capabilities that "mundane" fiction (or the "mundane" reading thereof, at least) lacks for the incisive analysis of social and cultural biases. All of the chapters have endeavoured to demonstrate the tremendous possibilities SF offers for such pointed political critiques.

And yet I, for one, am left feeling somewhat disappointed. The promise that SF makes to its readers, at least in its most amazing garb, is to offer us "new worlds." If, as I argue in the introduction, SF is a queering of realism, then as José Esteban Muñoz writes of intersectional and multiracial queerness, SF should allow us to "dream and enact new and better pleasures, other ways of being in the world, and ultimately, new worlds."[1] But what my theoretical introduction and each of the chapters here has exposed is that SF not only fails to offer new worlds and seems unable to present what Delany calls the "*radically* successful metaphor,"[2] but in fact can reproduce the most grotesque parts of our own world, as in "The Birth-mark" or *Mizora*, swinging with Tarzan or zapping with Buck. Other SF, as my definition of the term suggests it must, offers cutting and brilliant critiques of aspects of its contemporary social system, but much of what has been read here—and, I would argue, all of the best SF—has a difficult time positing "new" or at least "better" worlds; even the utopian forms studied here end up circling the reproduction of what Delany refers to as "the world that *is*, alas, the case."[3] While Muñoz's argument would lay the blame on the "abstract" nature of SF utopias, even his hopeful work hedges its claims, writing that the state of being enacted by "the anticipatory illumination of art" is "knowable ... as a utopian feeling," but only "*to some extent*."[4] The self-reflexive, self-analytical mode that constitutes some of the most socially astute SF necessarily refuses the possibility of a stable or final ground, hence the anti-utopian message of Butler's piece. Perhaps Malcolm Reynolds, the hero of Joss Whedon's very genre-aware 2005 film, *Serenity* (a sequel to his TV series *Firefly*, and a canny reworking of the interrelated rewritings of *The Tempest* in *Brave New World* and *Forbidden Planet*) puts it best: political attempts to make new worlds, no matter how self-aware, will eventually "swing back to the belief that they can make people … better." Reynolds, speaking as an avatar of SF itself, responds to this belief, asserting, "And I do not hold to that. So no more runnin'. I aim to misbehave."[5] The goal of providing "new worlds" may seem laudable, as does the notion of "better people," but the problem comes from the subject (whether individual, collective, or institutional) who decides that he, she, they, or it has the right *to make* people better, according the rubric set by that dominant, deciding subject. So SF, with its incommensurable semiotic slipperiness, injects itself into the system as outlaw, with an "aim to misbehave." (As I mention in the introduction, though, an aim doesn't always hit its target, a problem perhaps signalled in *Serenity* and its television progenitor through their imagining of a future unification of China and America, even as both are largely devoid of Asian actors.)

But still, my introduction—and specifically its epigraphs—also suggests that SF can offer us new figures with which we can reshape our own identities: whether we want to be Dorothy Gale or Frank-N-Furter, "SF provides us," I write, "with the theoretical fuel not only to 'dream it,' but also to 'be it,' whatever we can imagine that 'it' to be." Like Mr. Universe in *Serenity*, who surrounds himself with screens depicting the endless play of media, SF recognises that "you can't stop the signal": the endless semiotic play of culture seems to allow for the endless possibility to be surprised by new forms of identification, by the pleasure that Judith Butler finds in difference itself. Even at the moment of death, Mr. Universe is surprised by the endless cycles of identities and their enactment: "Mal, guy killed me with a *sword*. How weird is *that*?"

Ultimately, however, as Dorothy and Frank both learn, we have to go home sometime. The identifications SF allows us, the fantastic space of possibilities it creates, *are* necessarily at odds with the material world—just as Mannheim states of the utopian idea *per se*. In the end, the "new world" SF offers us is one of resistance—to our world, ourselves, and even self-reflexively within and toward SF itself. *Rocky Horror*'s identification of Tarzan's and Buck's (and Charles Atlas' and Flash Gordon's) ideal male bodies as queer erotic objects—a practice repeated in the material history of muscle magazines—is a case in point of such a creative, and pleasurable, resistance.

There is another model for such a creative impulse being founded in "negativity," and it lies in Freud's concept of the death drive, specifically as reworked by Lee Edelman in his queer polemic, *No Future*. Though Muñoz critiques Edelman's argument as one that should, to a degree, be eschewed for a more hopeful focus on an intersectional queer future, I see in it the explosive, destructive energy that is nonetheless necessary for SF and queer critiques to reach escape velocity, to leave what Delany defines as the gravitational pull of one world and enter into the free-fall realm between worlds, that space of semiotic contestation, chaos, and freedom between worldviews that is necessary in turn to even begin to imagine another mode of being.[6] From there, one's destination is always an "anticipatory illumination,"[7] but one needs that explosion first, and then continued explosions to adjust and change course. This gravity-breaking energy permits one to leave behind the normative world both Muñoz and Edelman critique in order to play in an open field in a way that might lead, in Edelman's words, to "something I want to call 'better.'" This is not Malcolm Reynold's fear of being made "better" by the dominant culture; this more vague, more semiotically and socially unconstrained "better" "promises ... absolutely nothing," and so denies the forceful closure of the ideal.[8] In other words, this discursive space should not be mistaken for a Kantian transcendence; as with free fall in a microgravity environment, this relative lack of semiotic constraint is not beyond "gravity"—materiality and ideology—as such, but is created by the competing and complementary forces of various ideological masses: one could see it as a spatial metaphor for the linguistic theory outlined by Bakhtin, where the opposed monologic and heteroglot forces present in any discourse lead to the dialogic nature of language.[9] By way of an open-ended conclusion, then, this afterword explores the energy inherent in the act of reading SF as literature's and America's death drive, by looking to foundational visions of America *as* SF, starting outside the nation's borders with Fritz Lang's 1927 film *Metropolis*, and ending in the 1950s outside traditional definitions of SF, with Allen Ginsberg's poems, "Howl" and "America," by way of Ralph Ellison's novel, *Invisible Man*. All of these works portray the alterity offered by SF by presenting one of its most iconic figures: the killer robot.

I. FRITZ LANG'S AMERICA

This afterword begins where the introduction started: from the outside looking in, but this time rather than *Rocky Horror*'s queering vision of American SF, we turn to the vision of German filmmaker, Fritz Lang. His *Metropolis* stands as the largest spectacle, and most expensive production, of the silent-film era. A science fiction dystopia that comments on the increasing divisions—financial, social, and cultural—between capital and labour, the film is superficially influenced by Marx, though perhaps more directly by H. G. Wells' *The Time Machine*, in its presentation of a world above—literally at the top of giant skyscrapers—populated by a pampered, decadent, and seemingly physically and culturally evolved upper class, and a degenerate, dirty, permanent underclass who maintain the functioning of the technologically advanced society solely for its use by their "betters." In this portrayal, Lang was explicitly presenting his vision of the pre-depression United States: Lang once stated that "*Metropolis* ... was born from my first sight of the skyscrapers of New York in October 1924. ... I thought that it was the crossroads of multiple and confused human forces, blinded and knocking into one another, in an irresistible desire for exploitation, and living in perpetual anxiety."[10] The film makes its thesis explicit, both at the beginning and in its triumphant, comic conclusion, with title cards that read "The Mediator between the head and hands must be the heart!," where the head is clearly associated with the overly rational capitalist, the hand with the enforced physicality of labour, and the heart with the sentiment that is missing from both.[11] A liberal rather than radical argument, the film thus follows along the traditional SF line, made famous in *Frankenstein*, that sentiment must always temper the extremes of human nature, be they the coldness of rationality or the heat of the physical self. Lang's film likewise calls for a utopian unity of labour and capital through the generative function of sentiment.

But, in Lang's film, proper sentiment is rendered only as a sexually (re)productive force following the heteronormative paradigm that Lee Edelman has described as "reproductive futurism." For Lang, economic production only becomes a problem when technology separates it from an organic *re*production. If technology is put in the service of a society focused on a patriarchal, heteronormative reproduction, then capital and labour can synthesise and be directed at the only truly human goal: the production of sons. The only good tech, in Fritz Lang's America, is a sexually reproductive tech. Against what we can call his reproductive technology, Lang pits two central images of a destructive technology: the so-called "man-machine" Maria, and the demonic, man-eating factory, Moloch. In different ways, these machines become queer machines which release a jouissance, a sexual energy geared not at reproduction, but at a pleasure-full, revolutionary destruction of their own foundations in the capitalist machinery of the state. Reading *Metropolis* both through Edelman and through Allen Ginsberg's appropriation of Lang's Moloch, these technologies can be seen to point to the unstable queer death drive of technology itself, where technology always sits on the cusp of reproductive futurism and ecstatic decadence, between Eros and the death drive. In turn, this comment on futurist technology, on the novum, can be turned to SF itself: rather than rationally extrapolating—(re)producing—a new world from the foundations of the present, SF destabilises the epistemological and ontological bases of "our world," fracturing our standard, comfortably "cognitive" assumptions into the shattered mirror of multiple perspectives.

Debuted in Germany in 1927, the film depicts the city of Metropolis as controlled by Joh Fredersen, who manages the machinery that keeps the futuristic city powered. He has a son, Freder, who, like all of the sons of the rich, spends his day at play in a constructed garden of Eden at the top of the city's skyscrapers. Meanwhile, at ground level and below are the workers, who literally work themselves to death in factories that deliver power to the city. Unbeknownst to Joh Fredersen, the workers are beginning to assemble in protest, led by the beautiful Maria who preaches that they change the system through love, rather than violence. Seeing Maria one day when she leads a group of children to the garden of the rich, Freder immediately, of course, falls in love, and follows her into the bowels of the city, where he witnesses the workers' lives for the first time. He has a vision that the central machinery is actually the demon Moloch, devouring the city's inhabitants as sacrifices to its own demonic power. He switches places with a worker and supports Maria's peaceful rebellion. Meanwhile, in the city above, his father learns of the rebellion and goes for advice to the mad scientist Rotwang. Rotwang has created a shape-shifting robot in the form of Joh's dead wife and Freder's mother, Hel, who Rotwang also loved. Joh uses this robot, in the guise of Maria, to take over the workers' rebellion and turn it violent, so that he has an excuse to crush the rebellion. Long story short, the violent rebellion threatens to destroy the city, drowning all of its children, but Freder and the real Maria save both the day and the children, while the false robotic Maria is burned at the stake, and then Freder and Maria bring the workers and the owners together in a final scene, with Freder, and his and Maria's love, fulfilling the prophesied role as the heart that mediates the hand and the head.[12]

Depending on how one reads the allegory, the film can be read to present what Mannheim would deem a typical liberal utopian narrative, with the contradictions inherent in the division of labour giving way not to revolution (which is presented as serving the interest of capital) but to love. But this love is figured in two particular ways: it is, first, the heteronormative love between Freder and Maria and, second, through them, the love for children, which demands that children be protected because they are the embodiment of the future. As Edelman has argued, this "reproductive futurism" presents a logic wherein the idea of the Child becomes the fetishistic figure of the future itself: in this logic, without a future, society has no structuring principle, and therefore descends into chaos and meaninglessness. The protection of the Child, as the extant talisman of this always threatened future, must therefore be of paramount importance, and anyone or anything that may be a threat to the Child is therefore an irreducible alterity, an ontological threat to the basis of civilisation itself. As Edelman convincingly argues, this threat is often presented as a queer one, and so queerness becomes inextricably associated with this destructive alterity.

Edelman reads this logic in part through P. D. James' SF novel *Children of Men*, but one can see it at play clearly in *Metropolis*. While the film opens with the famous scene of workers marching mechanically into and out of the underground factories during a shift change, it is, importantly, juxtaposed to a scene portraying the sons of the rich gallivanting with women who, no less mechanically, are taught to perform to attract the men's desires. Freder chases one of these women around a fountain in a seemingly playful manner, only to be awoken from his utopic, patriarchal and capitalist fantasy by the appearance of Maria at the entry to the garden, surrounded by Dickensianly filthy street urchins. As she implores both the children and the sons of the rich to recognise each other as "brothers," Freder grabs his heart (a clearly symbolic gesture repeated throughout the film by both Freder and Maria), and the smile disappears from his face.

The obvious reading here, that Freder is moved to an awakening by the sentiment embodied in the innocent Maria, has been consistently savaged as either naive, or more sinisterly as laying the cinematic groundwork for the form of propaganda that would be employed in the next decades by Goebbels and the Nazi party, as Andreas Huyssen has noted.[13] More recent critics, specifically Huyssen and Stephen Jenkins before him, read *Metropolis* in terms of its gendered representations. What Huyssen does not pay attention to in this scene, much as Freder does not (something Jenkins notes),[14] is the role of the children:[15] the almost always silent, suffering children that only appear in a few key scenes of the movie. Maria's pathos and Freder's sentimental awakening, both later directed at the workers, are framed by their desire to protect and nurture the innocent children.

Opposed to what is, following Edelman's analysis exactly, the heteronormative futurism of this protection of the children, the film presents various "perverse" loves, all of which revolve around the "machine-man," the robotic Maria. Created by Rotwang in honour of Hel, the machine-man, like Victor Frankenstein's creature, is a constructed human life that denies both a heterosexual origin and an innocent childhood. This figure goes beyond Frankenstein's monster, however, and echoes more closely the neologistic "robots" of Karel Čapek's 1920 play *R. U. R.*: as in Čapek's work, the robots are the creation of a group of men who fixate their shared sexual desire onto the figure of one woman.[16] In this case, Hel's mechanistic doppelganger becomes the locus for a homosociality that denies the importance of the future by fixating its sexual energies on a dead past. The literal translation of the German Maschinenmensch into the English "machine-*man*" in the English versions of the film (rather than the equally correct "machine-human") is thus an *apropos* decision. This is a machine-woman, but she is literally the embodiment of men's homosocial anxieties and desires, figured within the homophobic logic of reproductive futurism as the destructive force of the death drive: the creation of the robotic Hel becomes the ultimate if paradoxical heterosexist portrayal of queer desire as sterile and necrophiliac. Freud's notion of the homosexual desire that provides the psychological basis of the formation of civilisation is thus presented,[17] following a neo-Romantic vision, as an always extant, if hidden, threat: as society becomes more and more technologically advanced and so removed from Nature and its biological reproduction, libidinally charged homosocial ego modelling becomes the queer death drive. After all, Freud says of the death drive that its "task ... is to lead organic life back into the inanimate state."[18] The destructive and inorganic robot becomes a figure that combines the paradoxically animated energies of this drive toward the inanimate.

After the machine-man is transformed at Joh's request into a demonic double of Maria, this sexually charged death drive takes on ecstatic proportions and leads directly to the near sacrifice of the city's children. Robot Maria causes chaos in exactly the way that Joh Fredersen wants, eroticising the rebellion by objectifying her own body, and turning the workers' unleashed libidinal energy against the state, such that Joh has his excuse to crush the workers. But she also subverts Joh's plan by turning this same process against the sons of the rich. Just as she does for the workers in her speeches, she turns herself into the eroticised object of the male gaze in highly stylised, orientalist strip teases for the rich, but in doing so becomes anything but passive. Instead, she manipulates and directs those libidinal energies into male-on-male violence, thereby exposing the violent sexual tensions underlying the seemingly innocent sexual play in the garden scene, and, just as the death drive does, exposing the discontents in this seemingly peaceful, functional civilisation. Men become caricatures of lust and begin exercising their phallic power—not sexually, over the objectified women of the garden, and not even in a capitalist sublimation, over the workers, but through direct phallic violence against each other, killing themselves and each other first with swords and then with guns. Robot Maria thus becomes a locus not simply of the "whore" of the angel-whore dichotomy, as Huyssen notes, but also a locus for a queer death drive, in which the absolute ecstasy of unfettered libidinal drives becomes a violent penetration of male-on-male violence which brings society itself to its knees.

These paired violences lead to the near death of all of the innocent children in town. As the workers' revolutionary zeal reaches its zenith, they all abandon their homes, rush into the center of the city, and smash the "heart" machine, leading to the failure of the city's mechanical infrastructure. As the workers dance in a sinister mockery of a children's play circle, the city begins to flood. In the centre square of the workers' residences, first one child, then another, then what seems to be hundreds and thousands of children run panicking through the street as the water rises. The human Maria realises what is happening and runs to the central square where there's an alarm. As countless children reach for her, begging to be saved, she sounds the alarm, drawing both the rest of the city's children and Freder to her. Against the radical opposition of the queer death drive embodied in technology, the film pits the formation of a future-oriented society as family: as Jenkins writes, "The figures ... who are associated with 'excess,'" notably including "the robot Maria" are all "removed" at the end of the film.[19] And so son is reunited with father, children with parents, labour and capital learn to work together, and all are united in the figure of the happy heterosexual couple, longing, one can just tell, to sing out from the silent screen, "The sun'll come out tomorrow!"[20]

But there's a problem for this straight logic: this hetero-utopia is made possible only through the existence of the queer possibilities of technology that are silenced in the name *of* that future: just as Neo at the end of *The Matrix* doesn't actually destroy the enslaving computers, labour and capital in the film join hands to keep the city's technologies running. Even beyond diegesis and into the material context, this is a blockbuster film, the largest of its time, employing cutting-edge technology and, as with so many later creature features of B-films, is advertised by the sexualised figure of the robot. Again, this portrayal follows the pattern of Edelman's argument: the very thing that keeps this radical alterity alive "is the futurism desperate to negate it."[21] The presentation of technology becomes even more paradoxical, as it is both the central threat and the central salvation for the supposedly innocent future. We can connect this to Edelman's Child: he states that the phrase "A family is created,"

> like Freud's "a child is being beaten" ... strategically elides the agency by which this end is achieved. No fucking could ever effect such creation: all sensory experience, all pleasure of the flesh, must be borne away from this fantasy offuturity secured, eternity's plan fulfilled, as "a new generation is carried forward." Paradoxically, the child of a two-parent family thus proves that its parents *don't* fuck and on its tiny shoulders it carries the burden of maintaining the fantasy of a time to come in which meaning, at last made present to itself, no longer depends on the fantasy of its *attainment* in time to come.[22]

Likewise, modern technology "proves" that capitalism itself isn't exploitative and carries on its ceramic, metal, and digitised shoulders the burden of maintaining the fantasy of a division of labour that isn't divided and isn't really labour after all: many of us turn to the screens on our phones, and their image of a shiny, clean, interconnected future, and laud the revolution (digital or otherwise) somehow inherent in them, even as we ignore the discovery of child labour in the smartphone supply chain.[23] If the death drive of technology is embodied in Moloch and robot Maria, it is salvaged for the capitalist future in a state innocent of itself, through the image of the heterosexual couple, Freder and Maria, tugging together on the technological phallus of the city's klaxon, as they save the children and end the unproductive sexual desire arising from the city's repressed underbelly.

II. THE JOYS OF KILLER ROBOTS

For Edelman, however, the critique of reproductive futurism and its construction of the queer as its radical other, as death, is only step one. Step two is to proclaim the queer death drive, to be a harbinger of its spirit of alterity and to deny the necessity of the future. And, in fact, reproductive futurism does this already: in order to proclaim the innocence of the Child and the future it contains, its other must be constantly asserted and then beaten back. Edelman coins the term "sinthomosexuals"—a combination of the Lacanian "sinthome," or symptom, and "homosexual"—to represent this "impossible, inhuman" force that lies behind such futurist platitudes as "no child left behind." "Sinthomosexuals" embody and announce the "haunting, destructive excess bound up with [reproductive futurism's] pious sentimentality," the "insistent Real always surging in its blood" that it attempts to deny in its Imaginary future.[24]

What better figure, then, of the sinthomosexual than the synthetic creations of Maria and Moloch, both destroyed by and yet necessary for the creation of the innocent future presented as beginning at the end of

Metropolis. We can already see the start of such an ecstatic release on the pages of Donna Haraway's "A Cyborg Manifesto," but even in the endlessly complex, integrated irony of that essay, and certainly in several of its later enthusiasts, this excess is reined in by the necessary futurity of its own project.[25] Can the negativity embodied in these technological figures ever break through the rhetoric of futurity that both creates and denies them? Can SF's "new worlds" ever escape the gravitational pull of their own cultures?

Well, as Steven Bruhm has recently and deftly shown, the Child, while undeniably figured across the political spectrum in the ways Edelman describes, still has also been represented in ways that challenge both the status quo and its always immanent future: the monstrous child, the possessed child, the murderous child—in short, the gothic child—all offer cultural alternatives to the innocent Child, and in so doing help us to get over the future. As Bruhm recently stated, "Edelman's child is always sentimental, never gothic. And while such a stabilizing move is ultimately necessary for his profoundly destabilizing argument, … gothicists know better: the children [gothicists] habitually encounter are as likely to sterilize, poison, or explosively decimate the future as they are to ensure it."[26] Well, SF also knows better. Technology is always bifurcated: while the homosocial and even queer figure of the robot in *Metropolis* is diegetically silenced by the power of "natural" reproductive futurism, still the synthetic image transcends its diegesis.

And this is where Allen Ginsberg's appropriation of Lang's Moloch and his transformation of the sacrificed, sentimental child enters the picture. In both "Howl" and "America," Ginsberg unleashes the SF, technoqueer narrative that *Metropolis*' futurism both creates and suppresses. Part 2 of "Howl" famously invokes a vision of Moloch deeply influenced by Lang's portrayal of Freder's hallucinatory vision. As in Lang's film, the Moloch of Ginsberg's poem stands in for the exploitative technologies of capitalism itself. In a passage that Ginsberg says was directly influenced by *Metropolis*,[27] the speaker exclaims:

> Moloch whose mind is pure machinery! Moloch whose blood is running money! …
> Moloch whose factories dream and choke in the fog! Moloch whose smokestacks and antennae crown the cities! …
> Moloch! Moloch! Robot apartments![28]

The allegorical landscape of Lang's city is here rendered explicit and material, with Ginsberg's breath-length lines sounding not so much like a jazz saxophonist (the usual description of the style), but instead like the gears in *Metropolis*' machinery, or the marching steps of its workers.[29]

Moreover, seeming to demonstrate Edelman's argument that reproductive futurism dominates all sides of the political spectrum, Ginsberg uses Moloch because of its mythological association with child sacrifice.

Capitalist and technological production, as in the film, is presented in the poem as the lethal opposite of "natural" reproduction, leading to the death of children, in this case to the sacrifice of the vibrancy of the Beat Generation: "the best minds of [a] generation" are "destroyed by madness," but that madness is brought on by "Moloch! Solitude! Filth! Ugliness! Ashcans and unobtainable dollars!" all of which culminate in "Children screaming under the stairways!"[30]

As much as Ginsberg's poem, read in this light, repeats the neo-Romantic allegory of Lang's film, with the innocents of the Beat Generation standing in for the Child of the reproductive future, still there is an attempt in the poem, as in Edelman's book fifty years later, to recognise the necessity of queer alterity and to uncover within technological futurism its sinthomosexual double. After all, while the Beat Generation is described as innocent, and at the end of Part I is represented through the Christian salvation ethos that characterises reproductive futurism, still these figures are not quite the innocent Child of political rhetoric. These figures are also the queer Child, both sexually and following Edelman's configuration of the opposition of the death drive. These sacrificed children use their "cock and endless balls" to directly oppose the heteronormative future, "the one eyed shrew of the heterosexual dollar the one eyed shrew that winks out of the womb."[31] Likewise, their deaths may seem recuperative, but only insofar as those deaths are also meaningless and chased inexorably, as in Ginsberg's portrayal of Bill Cannastra, who died climbing out of a subway while it was moving. If anything, "Howl" is a heroic catalogue of the visible symptoms of the unconscious death drive.

In conjunction with the appropriation of Lang's Moloch, this cataloguing of the endless resistance presented by the queer death drive seems to render Ginsberg's poem hopelessly conflicted in the way Edelman presents reproductive futurism as always conflicted: it denies the death drive embodied in capitalist machinery and modern technology even as it arguably celebrates the queer death drive of the Beat Generation. This tension reaches the surface when the speaker states that it is "Moloch in whom I sit lonely! Moloch in whom I dream angels! Crazy in Moloch! Cocksucker in Moloch! Lacklove and manless in Moloch!"[32] Moloch is both the force that destroys and the figure against which his visions—his creativity and poetry itself—are possible. The terrors of capitalist futurism lead to the speaker being "lacklove and manless" but also provides the pleasure of becoming the "Cocksucker in Moloch." It is this tension that leads to the ecstasy and jouissance of the "Footnote to Howl!" in which the speaker, entrenched in the ecstasy of the utter lack of (re)production in America, can find everything "Holy!" in its present, rather than future, moment.

So where does this leave us? Ginsberg is clearly struggling to reach the radical alterity of Edelman's *No Future*, which is more clearly grasped in something like Burroughs' *Wild Boys* or his other SF grotesques, even as he retains a vestige of the neo-Romanticism that characterises such other beat writers as Kerouac or John Clellon Holmes.[33] Where Edelman sees reproductive futurists as inadvertently creating and maintaining the category of the sinthomosexual, here, perhaps, Ginsberg is moving in the opposite direction.[34]

But, in conclusion, what about robots? What about the technology that is necessary for capitalism's future—its reproduction of itself—even as it is derided by (some) reproductive futurists as sterile and threatening: as queer? In other words, what about SF? Reading Lang through Ginsberg allows us to see that, ultimately, futurist technology, and speculative fictions, are the queer death drive of materialism and materiality themselves. SF is the figure that Ginsberg's poem tries to transform the Beat Generation into: perhaps "Howl" should start "I have seen the best robots of my generation rendered obsolete ..."

It is this vision that Ginsberg more clearly presents at the end of the poem "America." This poem ironically lists both the various complexities of being a queer socialist in 1950s America and the contradictions of the nation's self. Pointing, as I did through the epigraphs to this book in my introduction, to the ways in which we identify ourselves through the figures of popular culture, the speaker states:

> I'm addressing you.
> Are you going to let our emotional life be run by Time Magazine?
> I'm obsessed by Time Magazine. ...
> It's always telling me about responsibility. Businessmen are serious. Movie producers are serious. Everybody's serious but me.
> It occurs to me that I am America.
> I am talking to myself again.[35]

The "you" of the addressee and the "I" of the speaker are united in being defined as "America" as that is, in turn, defined by *Time*. In this case, though, that identification is out of joint, as the speaker feels alienated by the unreflexivity—the seriousness—of that America.

And this "serious" America is defined explicitly in terms of its ignorance and biases:

> America it's them bad Russians.
> Them Russians them Russians and them Chinamen. And them Russians.
> The Russia wants to eat us alive. The Russia's power mad. She wants to take our cars from out our garages.
> Her wants to grab Chicago. Her needs a Red Reader's Digest. Her wants our auto plants in Siberia. Him big bureaucracy running our fillingstations.
> That no good. Ugh. Him makes Indians learn read. Him need big black niggers.
> Hah. Her make us all work sixteen hours a day. Help.

> America this is quite serious.
> America this is the impression I get from looking in the television set.
> America is this correct?[36]

The dominant class of America maintains hegemonic control through popular culture's reflection and circular perpetuation of the citizenry's ignorance and racism, with various others positioned as threats against which the "serious" America must defend itself. This is Anthony "Buck" Rogers' America all over again, and the worship of television critiqued by Gibson and Herbert.

Continuing from the last passage, however, the poem ends with a contradictory image of technological production:

> I'd better get right down to the job.
> It's true I don't want to join the Army or turn lathes in precision parts factories, I'm nearsighted and psychopathic anyway.
> America I'm putting my queer shoulder to the wheel.[37]

While the Moloch-like factories produce the tools of America's death drive, and the speaker turns away from it, still he doesn't turn away from technological production altogether. Instead, recognising that this death drive is the motor of society, he turns it to expose it. Putting his "queer shoulder" to the motor of state, he is not furthering the production of the weapons of American empire, but instead exposing the necessary hypocrisy of a reproductive futurism that is always already governed by an ecstatic death drive it continues to suppress. Just as Freud's civilisation is, through the Oedipal, founded on a homosocial desire, the neo-Romantic endings of *Metropolis* and Part I of "Howl," as well as the technological fetish of modern capitalism, are only possible through the endless creation and abjection of the queer machine.

Another possible example of such a robotic alterity, one tied even more directly to the focus of this book, appears in Ralph Ellison's *Invisible Man*. Near the end of that SF novel, after the narrator has gone both literally and figuratively underground, he has a vision in which he is castrated by the spectres of the various white men in his life, and his "two bloody blobs" are "cast ... over the bridge."[38] But as he sees the world through his pain, he turns to the men and says "there hang not only my generations wasting upon the water ... But your sun ... And your moon ... your universe."[39] The narrator recognizes that vicious and violent racism and its concomitant gender and sexual fetishes both fuel and destroy the ideological and material machinery of America. And at the moment of that recognition, a robot comes into being: "high above me now the bridge seemed to move off to where I could not see, striding like a robot, an iron man, whose iron legs clanged doomfully as it moved."[40] The history of slavery and objectification, of an enforced alterity, turns on its society now as a destructive force, and though the narrator exclaims that they "must stop" this force, it is only upon its release that he "awoke in the blackness." As the violence of othering necessarily turns its radical disruption back on the society that maintains it, a new awakening of blackness may become possible. And it is at that point that the narrator realizes that his "world has become one of infinite possibilities."[41]

In the logic of reproductive futurism, what is recognized as "human"—what is "visible man"—can only be defined as that which reproduces itself and fetishizes that created "other," be it in innocence which the individuated subject has always already lost, or in the racialized, gendered, classed, or otherwise marginalised and abjected figures that hegemony must constantly invoke and silence.[42] The unstable position of technology and the SF portrayal of the future itself, as always existing between reproduction and destruction, therefore has the ability to rend us from this practice, if only in the moment of incarnating the abject critique. Robots, in this reading, are not the totalising sign of productivity itself (in which the robot is both the signifier of a larger production cycle and the zenith of that production, its ultimate signified); instead, robots, like Ginsberg at the wheel, like Ellison's bridge, and like revolution itself, become the ultimate counter-production. Torn from reproductive futurism, what SF's "new worlds" truly offer us is the destruction of the supposedly "human" utopian future that would deny a place for those who don't meet its narrow identity categories: Ginsberg's poems ecstatically identify—and identify with—the "outside" of Santaroga, the borders and graves of Mizora, with Buck and Tarzan's victims, with the satiric ambiguity of Max Disher and the overly serious "whoa" of Neo, with Silencio and his fellow mutes, with the laughter of Aminadab.

If, as I write in the introduction, SF can be read as the queering of realism, then it is as the dominant culture's death drive that it does so: SF provides the speculative challenge to our primary definitions of reality, the first step necessary in the creation of fiction as such, even as its movement away from reality is a move away from the understandable, an anti-telos that denies the finality of meaning altogether. If SF is the limit case of reality, the limit case of SF is the truly alien, that which exists beyond the range of the conceivable: SF figures the death of culture. If, as Sidonie Smith points out, certain dominant definitions of the human follow hierarchical othering structures, then the ecstasy of the SF novum—Aminadab's laughter, that fantastic unreality—lies precisely in its ability to deny altogether the need for the static definition of mundane humanity, of the citizens of utopia and their directed futurity. In other words, we must deny the terror of that mundane humanity which reproduces the present as the future and embrace instead the ecstasy of undirected possibility that the semiotic chaos of SF offers. If to be human is to be consistently mundane, then we must embark on the robot's perpetual, fantastic mission to kill all humans.

NOTES

1. José Esteban Muñoz, *Cruising Utopia: The Then and There of Queer Futurity* (New York: New York University Press, 2009), 1.
2. Samuel R. Delany, *Flight from Nevèrÿon* (1985. Hanover: Wesleyan University Press, 1994), 348.

3. Samuel R. Delany, "Science Fiction and 'Literature'—or, The Conscience of the King," in *Starboard Wine: More Notes on the Language of Science Fiction*, rev. ed. (Middletown, CT: Wesleyan University Press, 2012), 81.
4. Muñoz, 3; emphasis added.
5. *Serenity*, writ. and dir. Joss Whedon (Universal, 2005), Blu-ray.
6. Samuel R. Delany, *The American Shore: Meditations of a Tale of Science Fiction by Thomas M. Disch—"Angouleme,"* (1978. Middletown, CT: Wesleyan University Press, 2014), 160.
7. Muñoz, 3.
8. Lee Edelman, *No Future: Queer Theory and the Death Drive* (Durham, NC: Duke University Press, 2004), 5. In this reading, then, Muñoz' anticipatory feeling and Edelman's better actually meet in a free-floating middle ground, rather than oppose each other.
9. See M. M. Bakhtin, *Discourse in the Novel*, in *The Dialogic Imagination: Four Essays*, by M. M. Bakhtin, edited by Michael Holquist, translated by Caryl Emerson and Michael Holquist (Austin: U of Austin P, 1981), esp. 269–72.
10. Fritz Lang, *Fritz Lang: Interviews*, edited by Barry Keith Grant (Jackson: University Press of Mississippi, 2003), 68.
11. *Metropolis [The Complete Metropolis]*, dir. Fritz Lang, screenplay by Thea von Harbou (1927, Kino, 2010), Blu-ray.
12. The film's 1927 opening night is the only known time that the entirety of Lang's final cut was shown. When the masters were shipped to the United States, the two-and-a-half hour film was cut and re-edited into an approximately ninety-minute version and was likely shown at a higher frame-rate than that in which it was originally shot. So, for decades, the film was confused if not incomprehensible, although it still achieved a significant cult following. Attempts in the past few decades were made to try to bring the film closer to the original, but there were large sections that were simply missing. Bits and pieces were found here and there, but in 2008 a 16mm copy, likely of the original or at least nearly complete film was found in Argentina. The missing, very low-quality footage was remastered and combined with recent high-quality footage, and the result—a likely complete, largely excellent copy of the film—was released to Blu-ray and DVD in 2011 (the film's history is detailed on that release, facts from which I have summarized here).
13. Andreas Huyssen, "The Vamp and the Machine: Fritz Lang's *Metropolis*," in *Perspectives on German Cinema*, edited by Terri Ginsberg and Kirsten Moana Thompson (New York: G. K. Hall, 1996), 624–40. This essay reproduces an excerpt from Huyssen's book, *After the Great Divide: Modernism, Mass Culture, Postmodernism* (Bloomington: Indiana University Press, 1986).
14. Stephen Jenkins, "Lang: Fear and Desire," in *Fritz Lang: The Image and the Look*, edited by Stephen Jenkins (London: British Film Institute, 1981), 83.
15. Jenkins' reading is convincing, especially in his analysis of Maria as a threat to the patriarchal order that is subsequently silenced by a restructuring of that order in the figures of Joh, Freder, and the Foreman at the end of the film.
16. Karel Čapek, *R. U. R.*, translated by Claudia Novack (London: Penguin, 2004). In addition to being the source of the now multi-language word "robot," Čapek's play also presents us with the first robot rebellion, one which sets out to "kill all humans." In his play, the robots—decidedly meaty, if still artificial, creatures—are used for all labour, turning human life into one of ease. The robots, however, in a clearly pro-labour allegory, overthrow their human oppressors, killing all

but one human, who is needed to help them unlock the secret of reproduction. At the end, however, this proves unnecessary, as the robots discover love, then sex, then reproduction, leading the final living human to utter a paean to the glories of nature in the play's somewhat unsatisfying neo-Romantic conclusion.

17. See Sigmund Freud, "On Narcissism: An Introduction," in *On the History of the Psycho-Analytic Movement Papers on Metapsychology and Other Works*, Standard Edition of the Complete Psychological Works of Sigmund Freud, vol. 14, translated and edited by James Strachey, in collaboration with Anna Freud, assisted by Alix Strachey and Alan Tyson (London: Hogarth, 1957), esp. 96; 101–02.
18. Sigmund Freud, *The Ego and the Id*, Standard Edition of the Complete Psychological Works of Sigmund Freud 19, translated and edited by James Strachey, in collaboration with Anna Freud, assisted by Alix Strachey and Alan Tyson (London: Hogarth, 1961), 40.
19. Jenkins, 87.
20. *Annie*, dir. John Huston (1982, Sony, 2012), Blu-ray.
21. Lee Edelman, *No Future: Queer Theory and the Death Drive* (Durham: Duke University Press, 2004), 66.
22. Edelman, 41.
23. My comments here refer to a number of specific stories about labour practices in the technology industry (see, for example, Juliette Garside, "Child labour uncovered in Apple's supply chain," *The Guardian* 25 January 2013, http://www.theguardian.com/technology/2013/jan/25/apple-child-labour-supply; and Se Young Lee, "Samsung Elec to pass fewer orders to China supplier in child labour response," *Reuters* 5 August 2014, http://www.reuters.com/article/2014/08/05/us-samsung-elec-labour-china-idUSKBN0G508120140805), as well as to the (Western) reports of the importance of social media to the so-called Arab Spring, reports that were complicated by the protestors and revolutionaries on the ground (see my and Joel Faflak's introduction to *The Public Intellectual and the Culture of Hope* for some discussion of this [Toronto: University of Toronto Press, 2013], 3–28). All of these stories recall Ursula K. Le Guin's analysis of such relations in "The Ones Who Walk Away from Omelas," in *The Wind's Twelve Quarters* (New York: Harper, 1975), 275–84.
24. Edelman, 153–54.
25. Donna Haraway, *Simians, Cyborgs, and Women: The Reinvention of Nature* (New York: Routledge, 1991).
26. Steven Bruhm, "The Global Village of the Damned," paper presented at International Gothic Association Biennial Conference (University of Heidelberg, Heidelberg, Germany), 4 August 2010. I'd like to thank Steven Bruhm again for allowing me to quote from this paper. See also Bruhm's earlier essay, "Nightmare on Sesame Street," in which he argues that "The sexual child, the Gothic child, is not the fallen child; rather, it is the open fault-line on the landscape of our fantasies, fantasies that must endow our (inner) children with a sexuality we need to constitute ourselves yet to destroy in our 'children'" ("Nightmare on Sesame Street: or, the Self-Possessed Child," *Gothic Studies* 8, no.2 [2006]: 110–11).
27. Ginsberg notes the influence of Lang in his annotations to "Howl." See Allen Ginsberg, *Howl: Original draft*, edited by Barry Miles (New York: Harper, 1986), 139; 140.
28. Allen Ginsberg, "Howl," in *Collected Poems: 1947–1997* (New York: Harper, 2006), 139.

29. Ginsberg likewise notes that another line describing Moloch as a "Cannibal dynamo" references "the opening industrial-heartbeat sound track of Fritz Lang's terrific film *M* (1931); also his *Last Will of Dr. Mabuse* (1933)" (Ginsberg, *Howl: Original draft*, 140).
30. Ginsberg, "Howl," in *Collected Poems*, 134; 139.
31. Ginsberg, "Howl," in *Collected Poems*, 134; 136.
32. Ginsberg, "Howl," in *Collected Poems*, 139.
33. In a decidedly less-than-celebratory statement, Kerouac still senses the possibilities of SF in relation to the death drive, writing in his "Essentials of Spontaneous Prose" that "Modern bizarre structures (science fiction, etc.) arise from language being dead, 'different' themes give illusion of 'new' life" (Jack Kerouac, "Essentials of Spontaneous Prose," in *The Portable Beat Reader*, edited by Ann Charters [London: Penguin, 1992]. 58). See my essay on Kerouac for a discussion of his neo-Romanticism and representations of race (Jason Haslam, "'It was my dream that screwed up': The Relativity of Transcendence in On the Road," *Canadian Review of American Studies* 39, no.4 [2009]: 443–64).
34. This tension is reflected in Mark Doty's analysis of the poem, in which he says both that *Howl* presents "decidedly not a middle-class position toward the erotic" and that the poem is rendered "acceptable" in part because "Eros has been spiritualized in the West ever since the Song of Songs" ("Human Seraphim: 'Howl,' Sex, and Holiness," in *The Poem that Changed America: "Howl" Fifty Years Later*, edited by Jason Shinder [New York: Farrar, 2006], 17). The growing acceptance of *Howl* as a "great American poem" moves us from the excess of Thanatos, to the acceptability of Eros, and through to the glorification of biblical—one is tempted to say missionary—sex.
35. Allen Ginsberg, "America," in *Collected Poems: 1947–1997* (New York: Harper, 2006), 155.
36. Ginsberg, "America," in *Collected Poems*, 155–56.
37. Ginsberg, "America," in *Collected Poems*, 156.
38. Ralph Ellison, *Invisible Man* (1952; reprint, New York: Vintage 1995), 569.
39. Ellison, 570.
40. Ellison, 570.
41. Ellison, 576. For another reading of Ellison's robot and its relation to the novel's conclusion, from within an SF framework, see Lisa Yaszek's *The Self Wired: Technology and Subjectivity in Contemporary Narrative* (London: Routledge, 2002). In this more humanist interpretation, the "dystopic" robot stands apart from the narrator's more "hopeful" vision of the "future" (31). See also Scott Selisker, "'Simply by Reacting?': The Sociology of Race and *Invisible Man's* Automata." *American Literature* 83, no. 3 (2011).
42. Edelman makes a similar point about the category of the "human" and sinthomosexuals relation to it (153).

WORKS CITED

Bakhtin, M. M. *Discourse in the Novel.* In *The Dialogic Imagination: Four Essays*, by M. M. Bakhtin, edited by Michael Holquist, translated by Caryl Emerson and Michael Holquist, 259–422. Austin: University of Texas Press, 1981.

Bruhm, Steven. "The Global Village of the Damned." Paper presented at the International Gothic Association Biennial Conference: Gothic Limits/Gothic Ltd. University of Heidelberg: Heidelberg, Germany. 4 August 2010.

———. "Nightmare on Sesame Street: or, the Self-Possessed Child." *Gothic Studies* 8, no.2 (2006): 98–210.

Čapek, Karel. *R. U. R.* Translated by Claudia Novack. London: Penguin, 2004.

Delany, Samuel R. *The American Shore: Meditations of a Tale of Science Fiction by Thomas M. Disch—"Angouleme."* 1978. Introduction by Matthew Cheney. Middletown, CT: Wesleyan University Press, 2014.

———. *Flight from Nevèrÿon.* 1985, Hanover: Wesleyan University Press, 1994.

———. "Science Fiction and 'Literature'–or The Conscience of the King." In *Starboard Wine: More Notes on the Language of Science Fiction*, revised edition, 61–81. Middletown, CT: Wesleyan University Press, 2012.

Doty, Mark. "Human Seraphim: 'Howl,' Sex, and Holiness." In *The Poem that Changed America: "Howl" Fifty Years Later*, edited by Jason Shinder, 11–18. New York: Farrar, 2006.

Edelman, Lee. *No Future: Queer Theory and the Death Drive*. Durham, NC: Duke University Press, 2004.

Ellison, Ralph. *Invisible Man.* 1952. Reprint, New York: Vintage, 1995.

Faflak, Joel, and Jason Haslam. Introduction. In *The Public Intellectual and the Culture of Hope*. Edited by Joel Faflak and Jason Haslam, 3–28. Toronto: University of Toronto Press, 2013.

Freud, Sigmund. *The Ego and the Id.* Standard Edition of the Complete Psychological Works of Sigmund Freud 19. Translated and edited by James Strachey, in collaboration with Anna Freud, assisted by Alix Strachey and Alan Tyson. London: Hogarth, 1961.

———. "On Narcissism: An Introduction." In *On the History of the Psycho-Analytic Movement Papers on Metapsychology and Other Works*, 73–102. Standard Edition of the Complete Psychological Works of Sigmund Freud 14. Translated and edited by James Strachey, in collaboration with Anna Freud, assisted by Alix Strachey and Alan Tyson. London: Hogarth, 1957.

Garside, Juliette. "Child labour uncovered in Apple's supply chain." *The Guardian* 25 January 2013, http://www.theguardian.com/technology/2013/jan/25/apple-child-labour-supply.

Ginsberg, Allen. *Collected Poems: 1947–1997*. New York: Harper, 2006.

———. *Howl: Original draft facsimile, transcript, and variant versions, fully annotated by author, with contemporaneous correspondence, account of first public reading, legal skirmishes, precursor texts, and bibliography*. Edited by Barry Miles. New York: Harper, 1986.

Haraway, Donna. *Simians, Cyborgs, and Women: The Reinvention of Nature*. New York: Routledge, 1991.

Haslam, Jason. "'It was my dream that screwed up': The Relativity of Transcendence in On the Road." *Canadian Review of American Studies* 39, no.4 (2009): 443–64.

Huyssen, Andreas. "The Vamp and the Machine: Fritz Lang's *Metropolis*." In *Perspectives on German Cinema*, edited by Terri Ginsberg and Kirsten Moana Thompson, 624–40. New York: G. K. Hall, 1996.

Jenkins, Stephen. "Lang: Fear and Desire." In *Fritz Lang: The Image and the Look*, edited by Stephen Jenkins, 38–124. London: British Film Institute, 1981.

Kerouac, Jack. "Essentials of Spontaneous Prose." In *The Portable Beat Reader*, edited by Ann Charters, 57–58. London: Penguin, 1992.

Lang, Fritz. *Fritz Lang: Interviews*. Edited by Barry Keith Grant. Jackson: University Press of Mississippi, 2003.

Lee, Se Young. "Samsung Elec to pass fewer orders to China supplier in child labour response." *Reuters*, 5 August 2014, http://www.reuters.com/article/2014/08/05/us-samsung-elec-labour-china-idUSKBN0G508120140805.

LeGuin, Ursula K. "The Ones Who Walk Away from Omelas." In *The Wind's Twelve Quarters*, 275–84. New York: Harper, 1975.

Metropolis [*The Complete Metropolis*]. Dir. Fritz Lang. Screenplay by Thea von Harbou. 1927. Kino, 2010. Blu-ray.

Muñoz, José Esteban. *Cruising Utopia: The Then and There of Queer Futurity*. New York: New York University Press, 2009.

Selisker, Scott. "'Simply by Reacting?': The Sociology of Race and *Invisible Man*'s Automata." *American Literature* 83, no. 3 (2011): 571–96.

Serenity. Written and directed by Joss Whedon. Universal, 2005. Blu-ray.

Yaszek, Lisa. *The Self Wired: Technology and Subjectivity in Contemporary Narrative*. London: Routledge, 2002.

Index

For Product Safety Concerns and Information please contact our EU representative GPSR@taylorandfrancis.com
Taylor & Francis Verlag GmbH, Kaufingerstraße 24, 80331 München, Germany

www.ingramcontent.com/pod-product-compliance
Lightning Source LLC
Chambersburg PA
CBHW071518110726
47908CB00003B/876

* 9 7 8 1 1 3 8 5 4 7 7 7 3 *